The Garrett, P.I., Series by Glen Cook

GILDED LATTEN BONES

A GARRETT, P.I., NOVEL

GLEN COOK

A ROC BOOK

ROC
Published by New American Library, a division of
Penguin Group (USA) Inc., 375 Hudson Street,
New York, New York 10014, USA
Penguin Group (Canada), 90 Eglinton Avenue East, Suite 700, Toronto,
Ontario M4P 2Y3, Canada (a division of Pearson Penguin Canada Inc.)
Penguin Books Ltd., 80 Strand, London WC2R 0RL, England
Penguin Ireland, 25 St. Stephen's Green, Dublin 2,
Ireland (a division of Penguin Books Ltd.)
Penguin Group (Australia), 250 Camberwell Road, Camberwell, Victoria 3124,
Australia (a division of Pearson Australia Group Pty. Ltd.)
Penguin Books India Pvt. Ltd., 11 Community Centre, Panchsheel Park,
New Delhi - 110 017, India
Penguin Group (NZ), 67 Apollo Drive, Rosedale, North Shore 0632,
New Zealand (a division of Pearson New Zealand Ltd.)
Penguin Books (South Africa) (Pty.) Ltd., 24 Sturdee Avenue,
Rosebank, Johannesburg 2196, South Africa

Penguin Books Ltd., Registered Offices:
80 Strand, London WC2R 0RL, England

First published by Roc, an imprint of New American Library,
a division of Penguin Group (USA) Inc.

First Printing, November 2010
10 9 8 7 6 5 4 3 2 1

Copyright © Glen Cook, 2010
All rights reserved

ROC REGISTERED TRADEMARK — MARCA REGISTRADA

Printed in the United States of America

1

For a long time it always started with a beautiful woman at the door, sometimes in the middle of the night. That had ended. Good things do. I wasn't in that racket anymore. There was only one beautiful woman for me. She was on my side of the door already.

Tinnie Tate. Tinnie had wreaked all sorts of changes in my life.

Tinnie had the word out: Garrett, that most marvelous specimen of former Marine, was no longer one of TunFaire's serious players, however you cared to define that term. Mama Garrett's boy was now devoutly monogamous. He reserved his vast professional acumen for the benefit of the Weider brewing empire and, more importantly, for that of the Amalgamated Manufacturing Combine. The man hadn't hit the mean streets in a rat's age. Which was pleasing to many and unpopular with a much smaller crowd.

Bottom-feeders and parasites really liked the new Garrett. He was out of their lives. The reverse was true for workmen at the breweries and Amalgamated. Garrett had this habit of turning up just when some underpaid and underappreciated genius was about to enhance his income by reassigning ownership of company property.

My wondrous new life.

2

It did begin with a beautiful woman in the middle of the night—a stunning redhead bereft of any perspective other than her own. She gouged me in the ribs with a specially sharpened fingernail. "Wake up, Malsquando."

"Again? What? Are you trying to set a new record?"

"We'll work on that tomorrow night. We have another problem, now. There's somebody downstairs."

We lived in two-story quarters we had carved out of a little-used part of the Amalgamated Manufactory Annex. Something rattled down below, followed by a vague, exasperated curse.

I was awake now, my head filling with subjects I might offer for discussion once we got out of whatever this was. Like maybe the fact that this situation could not have come up had we made our nest at my house.

I was like liquid getting out of bed. Silently flowing. Not even a gurgle. I armed myself with an oaken head knocker that no amount of fussing or whining had compelled me to divorce.

Just in time.

The bedroom door opened with a faint creak. I was behind it, wound up. The villain entering carried a damped-down lantern. That cast just enough light for someone whose night vision had fully adapted. It revealed Tinnie lying there mostly uncovered and wearing nothing, apparently asleep. An impressive sight, I've got to admit.

Lucky me, I'd seen it enough not to be distracted. Much.

"There's something wrong here, Butch." The whisperer

leaned in just far enough to offer the back of his mostly bald head.

I seized the day, whacked that mole. Down he went. I spun around the edge of the door—to stare down the length of twelve pounds of razor-edged steel. I couldn't imagine anybody having forged a sword that big. The eyes behind that monster did not belong to somebody in a merciful mood, nor even somebody truly sane.

Tinnie uncovered the goods, arrogantly showing off how lucky Garrett was. The eyes that knew no mercy did recognize those marvels when they saw them.

Clang! That blade brushed aside. *Thump!* A solid whack to the temple. Half a minute to make sure the villains didn't come back on us. Then, "Trollop."

"How's your health, big boy?" She had some clothes on, now. She had become the promise, not the literal truth.

"I had him."

"Sure, you did. Just a little insurance."

"Something to tell the grandkids about."

"Garrett. What the hell is going on? Are you into something? You promised. What are you into?"

"Nothing. When would I have the chance?" That was one of the costs of our monogamy. I had no life that didn't include Tinnie, nor should I want one as she interpreted monogamy.

Tinnie is a natural-born redhead, long on emotion and not so long on reason. Yet she did recall that our arrangement had not left me time to get involved in the sort of adventures I used to enjoy. "I'm not sure I believe you, but I'll go out on a limb and take your word."

"Bless you. I just had a marvelous idea. How about, instead of you sparking arguments by letting your imagination run wild, we ask our guests what brings them here?"

Tinnie grunted.

She can be reasonable. It just doesn't happen all that often.

3

Neither nocturnal adventurer wanted to share. Neither said a word. Tinnie set limits to how vigorously I could ask questions. She wouldn't let me get loud or messy.

She could be stubborn about stuff like that. This time she insisted on drafting a night-shift nephew to run to down the Al-Khar to collect a squad of TunFaire's self-proclaimed finest.

They responded to the Tate name.

If the boy had used mine, the tin whistles might have taken weeks. The Tates have friends in that community of people who think law and order are good for commerce. They have the kind of money that rears up on its hind legs and howls for immediate attention. The red tops nearly beat themselves to the AMC Annex, where Tinnie had us keeping house.

That was her idea of a compromise. She did not want to live in my house. I was dead set against being pulled in and converted into another drone in the Tate family hive.

"This would not have happened on Macunado Street," I observed. "They wouldn't have gotten through the door. Unless Old Bones wanted to play with them. And we'd know what it was all about already."

They say women change once they get their talons in and locked. I wouldn't presume to enter an opinion. But I am willing to admit that spending time at my place, even with the Dead Man wide awake, had been no problem for Tinnie back when we were just real good friends.

She ignored me. She was working herself up to make a deal with the minions of the law. She ignored our captives, too.

Those two would have a tale to tell their grandkids. If they got lucky, a miracle would happen, lightning would strike, and they would evade the labor gang that was their certain fate at the moment.

A tin whistle named Scithe led the red tops. Scithe was a little too appreciative of a certain redhead. Not a friend, by any means. Most lawmen don't even trust each other. But he was decent and reasonable, outside his weakness for ginger.

Scithe said, "I don't understand, Miss Tate. You're still associating with this known antisocial type."

"He's like a wart. Hard to get rid of. And he does have entertainment value. For now, though, I'd be ever so grateful if you could take these two men somewhere and ask them why they interrupted my rest."

Scithe made an unhappy noise. He considered the villains. They, only now, were getting a grasp on the bleakness of their prospects.

They hadn't struck me as drunk. Maybe they smoked something before they got what seemed like a good idea at the time.

They had to be brothers. The older one muttered, "We're screwed." The only thing either had said yet. They hadn't tried to talk their way out, using ridiculous logic and excuses, which is what these morons usually do.

"Not necessarily true, my friend," Scithe said. "As a Civil Guard officer, I'm permitted a certain amount of discretion. You could walk away from this with nothing but your bruises. If you're the stubborn sort, though, it's a safe bet you'll spend time in the Bledsoe, healing up so you can put in a few years helping reclaim the Little Dismal Swamp."

"Shit," the younger one opined, without heat. "Just kill us now."

"There ain't no easy way out, boys. You done a bad thing. What you got to decide now is how do you want to pay your debt to society?"

Scithe was having fun.

His question was not meant to be answered. Neither villain tried. Both were, now, lost souls wandering a desert of despair.

Tinnie said, "They could probably get some cooperation points if they came clean right now, couldn't they, Senior Lieutenant?"

I took a closer look at Scithe. Sure enough, he was sporting senior lieutenant's pips. He was bounding up the law-and-order ladder.

The man had a knack for something besides mooning after redheads. He could get villains to keep him happy by confiding in him, urged along by his implying that he could provide something they wanted badly: a way out.

"Gentlemen, you have to give me something. I know you aren't stupid." Which was a bald-faced lie. "You know how the system works. You'll go to the Al-Khar because I can't not take you in. We have to see if you're on the wanted book for something ugly. If you have no majors there, you could walk out under your own power." In chains, headed for the swamp. "You know we do let folks go to encourage the rest of you to cooperate. So far, here, all we've got is a jimmied lock and some folks who aren't happy about getting waked up in the middle of the night. So why not tell me? What's the story?"

The elder brother thought he'd give cooperation a chance. Condemnation to the Little Dismal Swamp project amounted to a death sentence. Though some prisoners might complete their sentences, someday. None have yet but the project isn't all that old.

"We was supposed to catch the woman and take her someplace. The guy wasn't supposed to be here. If he was, we was supposed to bop him on the head and get out. With her."

That sparked interest all round. None of us expected Tinnie to be a target.

Scithe can be blisteringly obvious. "Why?"

Shrug. "We didn't get paid to ask questions."

"You did get paid?"

Tin whistles looked at me like I knew what this was all about.

"Talk to him," I grumbled. "He's the one with the answers."

Here was one now. "Forty percent. The balance on delivery."

"Let me get this straight." Scithe was having trouble getting his mind around something. "You were hired to kidnap Miss Tate."

"Ain't that what I just confessed?"

"You did. Yes." Scithe took no offense, nor did he argue, however senseless the villain's statement. "Who might be so starved for Miss Tate's company that he, or she, would enlist your assistance in arranging a date?"

Both bad boys frowned and wrestled with that. The younger one worked it out. "Jimmy Two Steps hired us."

I gave Tinnie a dirty look. I was so out of touch I didn't know who Jimmy Two Steps was. Then me and the minions of the law exchanged eyebrow lifts. They didn't know Jimmy, either.

Neither did Tinnie, who said, "I don't know anybody named Jimmy."

Mysteries. We got mysteries. We got off-the-wall mysteries.

It was the way things started. There was a smoldering hottie underfoot. But, Tinnie? It was usually a personable wench from the grass-is-greener side.

I told myself, "This isn't something getting started. This is just random." But even clicking my heels didn't convince me.

4

After turning up Jimmy Two Steps, the brothers gave us nothing more. A lot of clever questioning went to waste. I told Scithe, "Take these guys over to your shop. Tomorrow I'll check with my old contacts and see if somebody doesn't know where to find Two Steps."

Tinnie blistered me with a look because she was part of the subtext of what I'd said. I didn't feel the heat.

Once the brothers dropped the name they stayed busy whining about how they knew Jimmy only from drinking with him at a place called Raisin's Bookshop.

I remembered Raisin's Bookshop. It was the lowest of low-life bars. The kind of place where our night visitors would hang out. Nobody knew why it was called the Bookshop. If somebody named Raisin was ever connected with it that was so long ago nobody remembered that, either.

Scithe suggested, "Garrett, stick to your job as a security specialist. You try to pick up where you left off, you'll find out how much you don't got it anymore. Miss Tate? He's in your custody. Keep reminding him that TunFaire's Civil Guard handles these things these days."

"I will." I had no doubt that she would—often, and strongly.

My natural-born cynicism failed me. The tin whistles had been amazingly effective, lately. I took the lieutenant at his word, thinking the Guard *would* wrap the mess in a day or two.

"All right. Do your job. Just don't leave us twisting in the wind. Let us know why these cretins were after Tinnie. In case we need to be ready to entertain another clutch of numskulls."

Tinnie gave poor Scithe a look that made him forget he'd been happily married for years to a perfectly wonderful but ordinary woman. "I'll do that," he promised. "I'll do that for sure."

Tinnie turned on the heat in the distractions department as soon as I got back from making sure our guests had actually left the premises. "I know what you're going to say, darling."

"Which would be why a roasting holiday goose is usually better dressed than you are right now."

"I can't fool you for a minute, can I?"

No, but she could do a damned good job of diverting me, after which, to be contrary, I didn't have anything to say. I lay there and brooded till I woke up in the middle of the next morning.

5

I asked, "You recall last night?" Tinnie was trying to make breakfast. Trying hard. She wanted to do good. She had nothing else left in her arsenal of distraction. Sadly, she's much better at looking good than at cooking good.

"Yep. Yep. I remember."

Ha! Nervous. Maybe even feeling a little guilty, though the Guard's inquisitors wouldn't get her to admit that.

"The sausages aren't as bad as they look," she promised. "And the toast will be fine if you scrape it a little with your knife."

"Kip Prose has a thing for making perfect toast." I let it go, though. She had used one of the prototypes to burn this toast.

"I just wanted a normal life."

I said nothing. Let her have the argument with herself. Of course, silence is my best tactic in this sort of situation, four times out of five. I let her ramble where she liked.

She ran down. She glared at me. Then she got her second wind. "Gods damn it, Garrett! I know what you're thinking. It wasn't you that those thugs came for. It was me."

Admitting that cost her. Getting any Tate to admit being wrong about anything, even obliquely, is more rare than hens' teeth. And certainly more precious. Having one 'fess up without provocation, voluntarily, is rare beyond compare.

I soldiered on, keeping my big damned mouth shut, a skill I'm still having trouble mastering. Had I done so years ago, I could've saved myself a lot of hard knocks.

"All right! You're right! It never would have happened if I

hadn't insisted that we live up here. The Dead Man would have wrapped those idiots up before they damaged the door."

They might not have come at all. Hardly anybody is stupid enough to take a chance with the Dead Man anymore. They would have caught Tinnie somewhere else. They would have made her disappear quietly.

Which they should have done anyway. Why try for her here, at night, when there was such a damned good chance that I would get involved?

They wanted me involved. Had to. Or whoever sent them did. Ha! Butch and his brother hadn't been well briefed on what to expect before they set off to capture the savage red-head.

Maybe Jimmy Two Steps hadn't had a clue, either.

That is the way I would have worked it if I was in the villain trade. I'd make Jimmy a cutout.

I put some toast and sausage down and did not gag. I took a relaxing breath, announced, "I'm going to visit Singe and the Dead Man."

Tinnie stopped rattling pots.

"Singe won't know Two Steps but her brother might."

"You told Lieutenant Scithe that you would let it alone."

"The Dead Man might have a perspective that I over-looked."

"You promised."

"I'll stop by Morley's place and see what he thinks, too." Morley Dotes is my best friend.

"Garrett, you aren't—"

"He should be able to get word out that it won't be healthy to mess with my number-one girl."

Tinnie chomped some air. That made it all about her. Further argument now would make her look petty.

Not a failing she has concerned herself with much in the past.

"Nobody is likely to come after you here, now." She has a raft of draft-age male relatives. Two were outside as we spoke, illegally armed and ready for war. "Stick to business and you'll be fine. No bad guy will ever make it as far in as the financials office."

I wasn't seeing the full picture. Tinnie way far more than

normally insecure. And every word out of my mouth was one she didn't want to hear. Including, "You are supposed to be getting the books straightened out today, aren't you?"

One of the draft-age cousins, Artifice, redder in the head than Tinnie, walked in without a knock or an invitation. "There's somebody out here wants to see you, Garrett." He seemed nervous. He evaded Tinnie's basilisk stare.

I made the head knocker at home in my hand. "Duty calls, my love."

My love sent me off with the kind of language used by men in combat. Then decided to come along and see what was what.

She began showing fierce verbal skills once we stepped outside.

My sweetie isn't one hundred percent contrary. There are times when reason will take hold. Times when she will accept a valid argument without herself arguing for the sake of being difficult.

This was not going to be one of those.

For half a minute she was incapable of doing anything but sputter vile accusations.

6

A big black coach sat twenty feet from our door, just up Factory Slide, the broad street running along the northeast face of the Amalgamated manufactory and the Annex that had been thrown up during the war with Venageta. Factory Slide saw very little traffic not involved with Amalgamated.

This coach had nothing to do with the manufactory.

There was only one coach like it. It belonged to an acquaintance. I hadn't seen her in a long time. I didn't want to see her now. Especially not when Tinnie would know I was seeing her.

Belinda Contague, empress of organized crime, deadly sociopath, one-time girlfriend, briefly, and, theoretical current friend, owned that coach. And was the kind of friend you might wish you didn't have because they can complicate your life to no end.

Two armed men perched atop the black behemoth, behind a six-horse team. A brace of armed horsemen preceded it. Four more waited behind. Not a one looked pleased to see Mama Garrett's number-one son.

Though she had a few quiet shares in Amalgamated, Belinda was not here on business.

The beautiful madwoman herself opened the near side door. "Hop in, Garrett. I'll give you a ride." From the gloom inside, louder, she said, "I need to borrow him for a while, Tinnie. I won't keep him longer than I have to."

Tinnie outdid herself. For a moment I was scared there would be a skirmish between Belinda's thugs and the draft-age cousins. That would not go well for the cousins but would be bad news for the thugs in the long run. The Tates have a lot of pull.

But my honey was not as far out of control as she put on, which was often the case. She was fond of putting on the drama. This scene, though, could lead to some really unhappy reviews.

Belinda seized the day. She announced, "Someone tried to kill Morley Dotes. He's hurt bad. He may not make it. I need Garrett to help look out for him."

That fired Tinnie up all over again.

"Who is going to look out for me? It's his responsibility to look out for me. Garrett! I want . . ." She went on and on.

I asked Belinda, "Is he really that bad hurt?"

She whispered. "Yes. I really don't think he'll make it." She surprised me by choking up a little as she said that. "Worse, I think there's a better than even chance that somebody might try to make sure that he doesn't."

It could be argued that the Outfit was capable of handling that without me. But if Morley was on his way out, I had no choice. He was my best friend. I had to be there.

I went back to Tinnie, took hold of her shoulders. "You're going to be all right. This is something I have to do. For my friend."

My attempts to make her understand didn't have much success.

She wasn't going to let that happen.

She was mad and she was scared and she was thoroughly accustomed to being the Tate princess who got whatever she wanted whenever she wanted it, even from me. She was the ruling goddess in her own little universe. Right now, because she was unhappy, the wants or needs of others had no meaning.

This was not the first time I had seen her this way. Talking wasn't going to do any good. Only time would have any effect.

And she couldn't get any more angry.

"I'll be back as soon as I can, darling. Midge, take good care of her."

The cousin who had not come inside nodded. Sweat fell from his forehead. He gave up a huge sigh of relief, suddenly sure that he would not have to become the first casualty in a war so small it wouldn't be noticed while it was going on.

I tried to kiss Tinnie. She wouldn't have it. I backed away. "I do love you. But you can't own me."

She managed to keep from saying something really awful.

I got in. The coach rolled before I settled the back of my lap on the plush opposite Belinda.

Time had been kind. She was as striking as ever. Her best feature was her long, glossy black hair. It accentuated her pallor and the red she used to paint her lips.

But today her hair was unkempt, stringy, in need of washing. Her complexion had gained a sickly yellow-green cast—though maybe that was the light. She did not wear any of her usual makeup, crafted to create a vampire look. And she had given little attention to her clothing.

I guessed she hadn't changed in days. She had that air.

Being an accomplished observer, I sensed that she was deeply upset. "Talk to me."

"Somebody took a run at Morley Dotes."

"You said."

Morley had been my best friend for so long that I couldn't recall when he hadn't been. Well, not before the war. But almost forever. I hadn't seen much of him lately. Tinnie didn't approve. Her disapproval was not ethnic, or social, but intellectual. Morley Dotes had the capacity to distract her special guy from what she wanted him focused on: Tinnie Tate.

I appreciated the courtesy of being informed but wondered why Belinda would involve herself in Morley's affairs. Maybe because she was the silent money behind his very successful restaurant enterprises.

"I'll tell you what I know. Three nights ago he staggered into one of our knock shops on the edge of Elf Town. He was full of holes but not so full of blood. The backstairs crew was turning out his pockets when somebody recognized him and decided to keep him alive till they tracked me down. I went there the night before last. He was six inches short of dying. I waited around but he never came to."

"What was he doing up there?" And why had she gone running to a cathouse when she heard? "Rhetorical question. Thinking out loud. I have no idea what he was up to these days. We don't get together much anymore."

"I understand. Red hair."

I doubted that she did. She had no one special in her life. She couldn't possibly know . . . "My god!" Could it be? It couldn't be.

Morley's First Law is, never get involved with a woman crazier than you are. But . . . There it was, between the lines. Something was going on between the Queen of Darkness and my best pal.

"What do you need from me?"

"Stay with him. Make sure nobody helps him spring any more leaks. When he comes around, find out what we need to know."

Which meant, find out who to hurt.

"All right." She was saying plenty without stating it direct. There were ears up top and she wasn't in a trusting mood. She counted on our shared experiences to convey what she wanted me to know. For example, that she couldn't count on her own people to protect a boyfriend they didn't approve. "But I have my own problem." I told her about my visit from Butch and his brother.

"Tit for tat. I'll look out for Tinnie. Any way I could get my hands on those two?"

"What for?"

"To ask if there's a connection."

Stranger connections have turned up in my life. "They're inside the Al-Khar. You could ask General Block but I don't think he'd cooperate. Go after Jimmy Two Steps."

"Two Steps?"

"That's the name they gave up. You know it?"

"I don't. But there are too many of them to keep track. TunFaire is like a dead dog and they're like flies."

"There was mention of Raisin's Bookshop."

Belinda frowned. In that light, doing that, she looked much older. "A bookstore?"

Carefully, I said, "Think back to when we met. That was one of the places."

She had been hard at work committing slow suicide in the worst dives TunFaire boasts. The Bookshop was one where I interfered with her self-destruction.

"I must've been all the way to the bottom. I don't remember it at all."

"It's bad news on wheels."

"Not part of the family enterprise?"

"It wasn't, then. I doubt there's been any reason for that to change."

"It's a place to start." She thumped the wood behind her head. "Marcus!"

A panel slid aside. A guard showed his face. "Ma'am?"

"How much longer?"

"A minute. Two, tops."

"Excellent." Of me, she asked, "Do you know a place called Fire and Ice on the north side?"

"No. I've been weaned off any such useful knowledge."

"You'll find it. Take the Grand Concourse north. Stay with it after it turns into an ordinary street. When you get close to Elf Town, ask. Somebody will know it."

"I'm going there because?"

"That's where Morley is. I don't want to move him till he can do it under his own power."

He was my pal. I ought to be all over this. But I wasn't sure I was getting the whole truth.

Belinda understood. "I'm not working you, Garrett. You take care of Morley. I'll take care of Tinnie. And her family if it's a trade dispute."

That hadn't occurred to me. There were magnates capable of such shady tactics.

The coach stopped. "We're here. You need anything up there, you tell them. They'll handle it. I'll see you as soon as I can." Before I could protest her presumption she opened the door and gave me a shove.

Belinda is one of those people whose expectations become unspoken commands.

7

I turned an ankle, not badly, when I landed on the cobble-stones of Macunado Street in front of my old house. It was still my place, I just didn't live there anymore and had not been around to visit for a while.

The place had gotten a face-lift: paint and some tuck-point-ing. The cracked window pane on the second floor had been replaced. There were new curtains up there. And there were planters on the front stoop with unstolen flowers in them.

The siege of law and order had become quite epic.

I stood there considering, wrestling a dread that when I went inside I would be entering a foreign country. I climbed the steps. I didn't feel the Dead Man.

I dug in my pocket for a key I wasn't carrying, then knocked my personal "I'm not here at knifepoint" knock. I waited. I ex-amined the brickwork to the right of the door frame. The hole into the voids inside the wall had been sealed with mortar and a chip of brick. Which explained why, on a fine, warm day, I didn't have pixies swarming around me.

I'd have to get the story there. Melondie Kadare and her mob had been handy friends, if a little rowdy and unpredictable.

The door opened. The lady of the house stepped aside so I could enter.

Pular Singe had matured. She had put on a few pounds and was both better and more carefully dressed. I had nothing ready to say. "How's business?"

"There has been a slowdown. That is Director Relway's fault. But we get by. Dean is making fresh tea. Come into the office."

Her office was what we had once called the small front

room, in the front of the house on the right side of the central hallway. It hadn't been used much before Singe cleaned it up and made it our bureaucratic headquarters.

"What happened to the pixies?"

"Melondie Kadare died."

"They don't live long but she wasn't that old."

"She got run over by an oxcart. She was drunk. She flew into something, bonked her head, fell down in the street. The wheel got her before anyone could drag her away. Afterward, the colony moved. I will find out where if it matters."

"It doesn't. Not right now." I settled into a chair. She had gotten some comfortable furniture in. I considered her.

Pular Singe was a ratgirl, a touch over five feet tall when she stood as upright as she could. Her sort—there are several species of ratpeople—were created by experimenting sorcerers several hundred years ago. The majority aren't very bright. They subsist at the lowest social level, doing the meanest jobs.

Singe is a freak among freaks.

She's a freak because she's a genius—not just among her own kind. She's brighter and more clever than most humans, too. So, a freak.

She scares people. Sometimes she scares me.

I adopted her, more or less, while working with her, when I realized that a dramatically fine mind would go to waste if she remained in the paws of the villainous ratmen exploiting her then. She'd been an early adolescent at the time.

Dean Creech, ancient live-in cook and housekeeper, arrived with a tray bearing tea, cups, and sandwiches. He had been generous constructing the latter. He said only, "You're looking fit."

"More exercise and less beer. It's hell." He headed back to the kitchen. I noted, "He's moving slower."

"We all are. What's the trouble?"

Singe knew I wouldn't be home if there wasn't something. That stirred her resentment. She didn't really like me walking in like I owned the place now that she was running it. But, more deeply, she did not like Tinnie telling me who my friends were and when I could see them.

I explained what had happened to me and what Belinda said had happened to Morley.

"Is there a connection?"

I shrugged. "Not logically."

"But you have no faith in the power of coincidence."

"True."

"First thing we will need to do is get Morley moved in here."

That hadn't occurred to me. I did see her reasoning. There couldn't be a safer place to stash him.

"Belinda says he's too badly hurt to move."

"You will be with him. You will know when he can take it."

I nodded.

She stared into nothing briefly, then said, "I am considering knocking out the wall between this room and your old office. Any objections?"

"Only emotionally. There are a few thousand memories haunting that room." It was the smallest in the house. I used to describe it as a broom closet with delusions.

"We will be too busy to have workmen in, anyway. The Dead Man is asleep. If you were hoping to consult him."

"I figured. He hasn't been harassing me." I surveyed some shelving she'd had installed. "That's a lot of books."

"Some days I do not have much else to do. The only call for trackers anymore comes from the Guard. They have grown so effective with their law-and-order scam that they have people turning themselves in after they have reflected on whatever seemed like a good idea after a half dozen pints. The penalties are less painful. I do some bookkeeping for Humility. I manage his investments. And yours. I study. And that is it."

I had investments? How come I didn't know about that?

Because I would have spent the money instead of investing it.

Another female doing my thinking for me.

"You are doing well with your investments."

"Especially Amalgamated?" I had a small percentage but never considered it an investment. I hadn't put money in, just me.

"Especially. But I put some of your cash into other things. You will continue to have an income stream if Amalgamated comes apart."

I wasn't paying attention. I mostly saw a ratgirl when I was with her. I didn't look for signs that she might be making sure

I'd be all right if Tinnie, Amalgamated, and I had a falling out. I would get it later, though.

"I see." We had begun talking about stuff that didn't require us to confess how much we missed each other.

Dean came back. He brought his own tea and cookies. He took an empty chair. "Are you back, Mr. Garrett?"

8

I wandered around the house, cataloging changes and remembering some whens. The changes consisted of paint, new wall finishes, and new furniture.

I lugged a big mug of beer. There was a supply.

I had thought there would be. Singe was a fan.

"You haven't been bringing guests in?"

"No one but my brother, some workmen, and the Dead Man's students. Humility only comes on business since I stopped his beer privileges."

Her brother, real name Pound Humility but known on the street as John Stretch, was chieftain of the biggest ratman gang in the city. He was of a different litter so they shared only the same mother, but their relationship was surprisingly tight.

Singe said, "He just could not help being a rat. He took advantage."

"Don't piss him off. He's a handy guy to know."

"Garrett."

"I'm sorry. I can't help fussing."

"And yet you resent it so much when people do it to you."

I shrugged. Being consistent is a sign of a narrow mind.

That was the moment we first stepped into the chill of the Dead Man's room.

One small candle burned in a sconce outside the door. It didn't cast much light when I took it in. It wasn't there for that. It was meant to fire lamps when His Nibs had people in who needed the comfort of the light.

I raised the candle high. The Dead Man was right where I'd left him. Where he had been since I bought the house, seated in a massive wooden chair, looking like a badly rendered idol featuring an anthropomorphic elephant god. I said, "Cold in here."

"Yes."

"*Really* cold in here."

She explained the mix of spells, leased from the same supplier as those chilling the cold well in the kitchen. "Kip Prose designed the suite. It does not cost that much. It will make sure he is with us for a lot longer."

"Kip Prose. Of course. He's into sorcery, now, too?"

"No. He could not make a rock fall down if he had to use magic. He can come up with mathematical models to make spells work more efficiently, though."

The last contractions had dropped out of her speech. She was talking slower. She had begun to show a little of the rat-man lisping accent.

She was nervous.

"How much *is* the cold costing?"

"Less than you might think. It is an investment in our future. We can keep food fresh in here, too."

I do fuss about money. Someone has to make people think a little before they empty my pockets.

I was the despair of Dean and the Dead Man, and of Singe after she helped herself to a place in my life, because I am disinclined to work any harder than necessary to avoid ending up ranting on the steps of the Chancellery in hopes somebody will be amused enough to toss a coin into my tips box.

I heard harsh talk about poorhouses as those fine business minds missed the fact that the poorhouses were shutting down. Without a war there was no need for sweatshops to make things soldiers needed.

Life, I will confess, has been generous to me. Big bags of money have wandered in just when they would be most welcome. I bought a house. I have investments that generate income enough to keep the place up and to house its occupants in comfort—though that is mostly Singe's fault.

Singe is a big part of my luck.

I got no sense that the Dead Man was remotely close to awake.

Singe asked, "You're going to do what Belinda wants?" Her crisis had passed. Contractions were back. She was an amazement. Ratpeople voice boxes aren't made for colloquial human speech.

"It's Morley, Singe. I have to."

"And Tinnie? This could poison . . ."

"I have to. If she can't understand, we've both been wasting our time."

"Wow."

Yeah. I was terrified. That might be the case. Tinnie turned into a different woman once she was sure she made herself the only woman in my life.

Things men associated with the dark side of a redheaded woman became exaggerated immediately.

I will stipulate that the plus side remained as marvelous as ever.

"All right."

Singe sounded like she was having trouble believing what she heard. "Since I know you will head straight for this Ice and Fire place, I'll handle Tinnie."

I started to protest, then grinned. People don't handle Tinnie. Tinnie handles people. "Wrangle away. And good luck."

"Are we likely to make money out of this, Garrett?"

"No. This time is for love."

"That is the way you think most times. Maybe we'll get lucky this time, too."

9

Singe made sure I was armed and ready for the older, less friendly TunFaire before she let me leave. "I will pray to the human gods that the Civil Guard doesn't roust you. You aren't a good liar. They'll pat you down ten seconds after they stop you."

And my record as one of the finest subjects of the Karentine Crown would not tilt the balance away from an arrest for possession of proscribed weaponry.

Singe would not let me go with anything less. And, "Even though this does not look like a situation where we will need the Dead Man, I'll try to wake him up."

"Singe, you are a treasure."

That was a wonderful straight line. I regretted it before I finished saying it. Singe, however, confounded heaven and earth by disdaining her opportunity. "I know. I have trouble imagining how you have survived without me. Get along. No! Wait! What about your other friends?"

Symptomatic of my reduced status, I asked, "What? Who?"

"Saucerhead. Winger. Playmate. Half a dozen others."

"Oh. Them." At the moment Mama Garrett's boy didn't have much of a positive attitude toward her second favorite son. I had done so little to keep in touch. "I guess you could, like quietly, let them know there's a situation. Without mentioning what happened to Morley. But I don't think we'll be asking them to get involved."

Singe just shook her head.

I needed to get out there and make my special ratgirl happy by finding the real, missing Garrett.

10

Fire and Ice wasn't hard to find. It was a well-known establishment on the frontier of Elf Town, serving the needs of the successful working man. Meaning it wasn't quite the upscale hook shop I expected but it wasn't rodent's belly nasty, either. It was a place where shopkeepers and skilled tradesmen could relax of an evening. A throwback kind of place, actually, because it didn't make its money on volume, nor entirely on marketing its keystone service.

I expect the relaxed atmosphere was one way the house competed for scarce disposable income—much of which, these days, ends up in TunFaire's gaudy theaters.

Play-going was all the rage, in part because a man could take his wife. And the wives knew that.

I gave my name at the door. It was no shibboleth. I tried Belinda's.

There was the magic.

A veteran brunette—absolutely a heartbreaker not long ago—turned up quickly. She had something special going. I was tempted to fail to remember that I was taken.

"You came from Miss Contague?"

"She asked me to keep watch on your injured guest."

She considered my claim. She considered me. She consulted some recollection. She decided that I was the real thing, though she was not prepared to be impressed. My feelings were bruised. I was willing to be impressed by her. And I was as fine a specimen of former Marine as you're likely to find still vertical. I had my dings and scars but they just let you know that I was the genuine article.

"All right. Come with me." After a glare that dared me to even think about running with that.

We passed through the fancy public lounge works, entirely uninhabited at the moment. Potential witnesses had been cleared out. In the back, where delicacies comestible and sensual got prepared, I spied several toothsome lasses enjoying a light repast and steadfastly taking no interest whatsoever in anyone passing through. Two appeared to be full-blood elf girls. The others were nearly as gorgeous.

"Stop slobbering on the carpet."

"Sorry. I don't get out much anymore."

"Here's a suggestion. Keep your hands to yourself while you're here." Then she snorted. She was one of those people who can't keep their laughter out of their noses. It took me a few seconds to get the joke.

"I'm taken," I said stiffly.

"Most of our clients are." We came to a narrow, steep back stair.

"I'm Garrett," I said, though my name had failed to awe anyone yet.

"I know. I've heard of you. I'm aware of your reputation."

"Damn! I didn't know I had one. It's probably all lies and exaggerations. Who are you?"

"You can call me Miss Tea. If I find out that you're tolerable, I'll let you call me Mike."

"Mike?" One of those? Here? "I had a brother we called Mikey."

"For Michel." That was a hard "ch." "He didn't come back?"

"No. It broke my mother's heart." She gave up. She'd already lost my father and hers, and some brothers, to the terrible beast of war.

Mike turned a little less hard-ass. Very little. Like almost every human in Karenta she shared the experience. "You were luckier."

"I was. Most of me made it home."

She looked me straight in the eye. "And now you're stalling so I'll go up the steps first. So you can be behind me and watch my ass."

"That hadn't actually occurred to me, but now that you mention it, sure, I'll be a gentleman and let you to go first."

"Living up to expectations so far. Enjoy the show. It's the best you'll get around here."

Did I threaten her somehow? Was she a secret agent of the redheaded Tate? "I'll do that. It's a sin to ignore what the gods generously set before us."

"And me without my work boots." She started up the stairs and laughed mockingly as she went. And, hard as she might have tried, she could not help putting a touch of flounce in her step. "And you said you were taken. Hypocrite."

"Are you my conscience?" I was a tad flustered and confused. So I did try to lean back and enjoy what the gods set before me.

I began to suspect that Misty was not entirely disinclined to have her assets appreciated. And that she considered her behind to be the best of those. And I thought she might be right, seen from where I was standing.

11

They had Morley stashed in a second-floor bedroom at the back of the house. I stuck my head in long enough to make sure he was breathing. He was lying on his back in a big, comfortable bed. He had bandages all over. He was having trouble breathing. A punctured lung?

Two house operatives were there with him, looking decidedly rough, as though standing a deathwatch over their one true love.

I wanted to hop in and give my dark elf buddy a good swift kick. He was out of it, trying to die, and still he had women swooning.

"What are you doing?" my guide demanded when I didn't rush right in.

"Scouting ways somebody might use to come after him. In case the folks who put the holes in him want to add to his collection."

Madam Mike didn't follow my reasoning but indulged me.

There were three ways to get to Morley. Up the front stairs the clients used. Up the back stairs from the kitchen, the way I came. Up the outside of the building, then through a window. That would require a small, skinny assassin. The window would open only six inches.

For the villain with gaudier ambitions there was the time-honored option of burning the house with Morley inside it.

While I examined the window my guide evicted Morley's caretakers. She promised them they could handle communications between the room and the world.

After they left, I asked, "How old are those two?" They seemed a little fresh to be in the life.

"DeeDee is twenty-nine. She has some elf in her. She's just gotten to the point where we can't auction her virginity. Her daughter Hellbore is sixteen."

"Hellbore?"

"Really."

Both were legal, then. I couldn't imagine the older one having weathered the vicissitudes of her career so well.

I said, "I'll settle here. If you have something like a field cot, I'd never have to leave."

"That would be useful. Business has been slow. I don't want what clientele we do get scared off by you."

"By me? Come on!"

"You're so straight-arrow a blind man can see it. They'd think you were spying for their wives. Or you were a Runner collecting stuff for the Unpublished Committee's files."

The Unpublished Committee for Royal Security were the secret police. "I'll be good. I'll stay in here with my boy, making my list and checking it twice. Been a pleasure meeting you, Misty."

Flirty brown eyes flashed. "Not Misty, dolt! Miss Tea. As in the capital letter. For Teagarden."

I gave her my special raised eyebrow, the one that gets the nuns salivating. Miss T came close to slamming the door as she left.

I had been out of circulation too long. I needed to sharpen my tools. Unless she was one of those lesbian types. That would explain her natural resistance.

I paced. I watched the world outside the window. I studied Morley and felt bad for him. I paced some more; then I inventoried chamber pots, bedpans, pitcher of water and bowl. Then a second pitcher and bowl on a small table in a corner, accompanied by a bar of soap and a stack of towels.

Of course there would be towels and soap. Necessary to the trade in an establishment like this.

I decided to ask for a cup or mug so I wouldn't have to drink straight from the pitcher, using a ladle.

The door opened after a perfunctory knock. DeeDee and Hellbore lugged in a mildewed cot. They dumped that, made sure I hadn't let Morley die while they were gone.

Miss T followed, pushing a small cart. "Food. Drink. Other

stuff you'll need. Crush or DeeDee will come around regular. They'll bring whatever you need brought and take away whatever you need taken."

"Crush?"

DeeDee said, "She don't like her real name."

Hellbore/Crush, a foot shorter and ten stone lighter than me, gave me a look that asked if I wanted to make something of that.

"All right." I tried to get DeeDee to chat some. She had a marvelous, breathy way of talking.

Miss T said, "And you a bespoke man."

These women could not be fooled or manipulated. Unless you were Morley Dotes and you were unconscious. Then they would be your slaves.

Oh, well. They were too weird, anyway. The mother was mildly inclined to flirt and had a silly streak. Crush had the cynical hard-eye of a twenty-year veteran of the life.

Miss T asked, "What were you figuring on doing while you wait for something to happen?"

"I'll catch up on my sleep. And maybe spend some time worrying about what my woman will say when I come wandering home."

"Are you a reader? We have a few books. Mostly for decoration. Ask Crush. She's read them all. She might recommend something."

I looked at Crush, who did an outstanding bored teenager's "whatever" shrug. "Thank you, Crush." Meantime, DeeDee gave me a suggestive look. The new, improved, extra-mature me thought that might be a marvelous pastime, especially if the excellent Miss T would join us, but then I'd still have to find something to do the other twenty-three and a half hours of the day. And somebody would put a bug in Tinnie's ear before I got my shoes off. So I stuck to, "Yes, I can read. This would be an excellent time to broaden my mind. So if Crush will bring me something, I'll be happy."

At that moment I was still thinking in terms of minutes, hours, and, at desperate most, a couple of days.

Miss T herded the talent out of the room. I watched them go, wondering if they weren't running a scam. The purported mother not only acted younger, she looked it.

Miss T said, "My obligation to the Contagues leaves me no choice but to give you whatever you want. Indulge me. Be reasonable. And, really, stay out of sight."

I blew her a kiss.

She gently slammed the door.

It set my cot up against it.

As long as I was sleeping, loafing, or reading, any intruder would have to knock it over to get in.

12

Waiting for Morley to get better got really, really boring really, really fast. Being Tinnie Tate's boy toy had stripped me of my knack for enduring endless do-nothing.

Tinnie was not patient. She had rubbed off.

Crush's taste in reading was unusual. The first thing she brought me was a collection of plays written by Jon Salvation, including the still running *Rausta, Queen of the Demenenes*, in which Tinnie had had a featured role when the play first went on in Max Weider's World Theater.

"You're a fan?"

"He tells wonderful stories."

The wildest were the ones he made up about himself. "I know him."

"He's a friend of yours?"

"No. He comes with a woman named Winger who is my friend." Sort of. When temptation doesn't get in the way.

"Wow. I'd like to meet him."

Suddenly, the girl had a new attitude. I stifled a cynical smile. "Maybe someday. Once this is done." I noted that Crush wasn't interested in Morley when her mother wasn't there. I asked, "Did you know Morley before they brought him here?"

"Not me. DeeDee did. I think."

She called her mother DeeDee.

"Is there anything to read besides plays?" I wondered who was putting those out there, and how. I'd had a scheme, once, but it had involved using hundreds of ratpeople to make copies.

Kip Prose could, probably, tell me how it was done. If he wasn't responsible.

"There are some history scrolls. Tedious stuff about the olden times. Somebody left them when he couldn't pay his tab. Mike never got around to selling them." The kid leaned closer, whispered, "She gets airs sometimes, she does. Gets above herself."

All interesting. Grist for the mill. Me soaking stuff up, getting the old ear back.

When I worked up a good case of cabin fever, I tamed it by rolling the sheet back off my friend.

Morley had suffered eight deep stab wounds. He had an additional dozen cuts. And he had a fine collection of bruises and abrasions from having been kicked, clubbed, and dragged.

I hoped that Belinda would have her ear to the ground listening for the brag of the sort of idiot who can't help telling somebody what he did.

People tell me I think too much. Most of the time things are exactly what they seem. Trying to make more out of them is a mug's game.

I say that when you stop believing in weird conspiracies that involve scores of people who never break faith, you're fully ripe for the weird to come get you.

I was thinking that kind of stuff and, alternately, trying to dismiss it or get it to make some kind of sense if I entered Morley into the equation. I couldn't get anything rational to fall together.

There was nothing to do but wait on the man himself.

13

Somebody shoved against the door to the room so hard that the impact against my cot wakened me.

I got my feet under me. I stood the cot up against the wall. I was not in a good temper when I opened that door.

Miss T was my antagonist. I blurted, "What the hell? This isn't any time when a rational being . . ."

I sniffed. Something smelled odd.

"Stuff it, Garrett."

Miss T had not come alone. That was Belinda Contague.

The smell came from behind me. I glanced at the window. It was dark outside, except for a three-quarters moon. "What the hell?"

One curtain bottom had been pushed a foot aside. Enough for me to see the moon in a cloudless sky. The window was up about three inches. I had left the curtains closed and the window shut.

The smell came from outside.

I forgot about the rude folks in the hall. Something more sinister had been going on. I might ought to be grateful that they had wakened me.

I went to the window. It would not open enough for me to lean out. Every shadow across the street, though, felt like it was hiding something rotten.

I said, "I'm way off my game. I might not be the man for this job, Belinda. Let me ask, less irritably, what's the occasion?"

Belinda took in the situation with the window. "I brought a healer." She and Miss T moved aside.

A small, well-rounded, bald-headed man passed between them. He sniffed the air. "I hope that's not your patient."

The healer wore dull black clothing in a style declared defunct a hundred fifty years ago. Deservedly. Clotheshorse Morley should have shrunk away even in a coma.

The healer belonged to a cult called the Children of the Light. Of the Dying Light. A prime tenet was no sexual conduct. They were militant pacifists, too—the kind willing to pound the snot out of you if you tried to claim that war might actually solve something. They were born-again do-gooders, as well, but so smugly self-righteous that most people loathed them. They ran soup kitchens. They ran shelters. They ran free clinics. They had made a bid for control of TunFaire's grand, totally corrupt charity hospital, the Bledsoe. They did a lot of good for a lot of people. Their healers were minor magic users. The Hill turned a blind eye to their unlicensed operations because they confined themselves to charity work.

Cynicism being my nature, when I thought about the Children, I mostly wondered where they got their funding.

Saving the life of a friend of the Queen of Darkness might shake loose a serious donation. Unless she decided to have the healer drowned so he wouldn't talk about Morley's condition or whereabouts.

"Excuse me," nameless round character said. Nobody made introductions. He pushed through and plopped his carpetbag down near the head of the bed. He began examining what was left of my friend.

I urged Belinda over to the window. I used my left thumb and forefinger to measure the gap before I shut it again. "As soon as he can survive it, I want to move him to my place."

"Factory Slide or Macunado Street?"

"Macunado. Nobody will come after him there."

"I'd rather move him out to my place in the country."

I didn't argue. There's no point with Belinda. She would go on doing things her way while empires collapsed around her. This time, though, she could be right. The Contague residence didn't have a live-in Loghyr but it was a fortress. The facilities and amenities were superior.

"It could be a long time before he's in shape to travel that far."

I have visited the Contague digs under a range of circumstances. A man could live comfortably there. He could also go in and never be seen again.

Belinda told me, "He won't go anywhere before he's ready." One pallid finger, tipped by a long carmine nail, tapped the windowsill.

I nodded.

A patch of something lay there, glistening. Something drying out. It reminded me of the trail left by a migrating slug.

I whispered, "Send me a pound of salt."

She might have been Belinda Contague but she was a girl. She didn't know about salt and slugs. Puzzled, she said, "All right."

The healer announced, "I've done what I can. He won't die. But he will be a long time getting back to normal. He may have been stabbed with cursed blades."

That smelled religious, which made no sense. Morley had enemies who would happily poke him full of holes if they could get away with it. They weren't religious wackos, nor were they so abidingly nasty as to go after his soul as well as his life.

Belinda concluded, "Must be a woman." No man was that vindictive.

"I don't know what's been going on in his life. I see him only when we stop in at the Grapevine after a show. You know my situation."

"I tried to talk to Tinnie. I wanted her to know what's happening."

I didn't like her tone.

"I was polite and respectful, Garrett. She was not."

I really didn't like her tone. Tinnie could get hurt. "She's really insecure . . ."

"I just tried to explain the situation. She didn't endear herself. It wasn't about her."

Almost certainly my dearly beloved had failed to become more intimate with fierce pain primarily because she was my dearly beloved. Could she be made to understand that anymore?

Tinnie couldn't have changed that much. How could she? She was brilliant. She understood the real world. She had shared its harsh realities with me. She could figure things out. She had discovered, years ago, that Tinnie Tate was not the center, fulcrum, or favorite child of the universe.

I had this chill like it was midnight on the boulevard, and I was fixing to whistle my way past the graveyard.

I had an epiphany. "We're seeing symptoms, not the disease."

Belinda grunted, more interested in watching slime dry.

I stopped worrying about my troubles and checked my pal. His color and breathing had improved. He looked ready to wake up.

The round cultist went away. Belinda and I looked at each other. We wore big, goofy grins.

I went right on having trouble believing there could be anything but business between her and Morley.

14

We were alone. The three of us. Morley fought the good fight,
trying to escape his nightmares. I wandered my own realms
of fear, where my ill-defined love for a friend might have cost
me everything else I held dear. Belinda sat beside me on the
cot. We leaned back against the door. She was so far gone off
somewhere else I wondered if she could get back. Maybe she
was trying to find Morley so she could lead him home.

She blurted, "I didn't get there in time."

"What? Where? In time for what?"

"Raisin's Bookshop. In time to round up Two Step Timmy."

No point correcting her. Her heart was in the right place,
though maybe oddly shaped, hard, and cold.

"Made a run for it, did he?"

"Straight to the Al-Khar. The tin whistles beat me there."

"They get more efficient by the day. Hard on both of us."

"A few still appreciate a generous tip."

"Good to know. You get anything interesting?"

"Two Step said his interlocutor was a woman."

"Damn. Look at you. You been taking a class? Interlocutor?"

"Oh, yes. Look at me. Damned near as smart as your ratgirl."

"I'm too tired to squabble. I've got redheads on the brain."

"You'd salivate if you met this one. If Timmy told the
truth."

Not many guys lie once they're inside the Al-Khar, and the
truth is the only key to getting out.

"No more redheads."

"I'm talking red hot, not red hair. Young and with a flair for show. Two Step says she wore skintight black leather."

"You naughty girl."

"Not me, dolt. Not anymore. I sag in too many places to make it work."

Golden-tongue Garrett conceded, "I know that." And he didn't even realize he'd stepped in it.

"Oh, yes. That's why I love you. You say the sweetest things."

"I wish your whole species would dispense with that stuff. Can't talk about the damned weather without it turning into . . ."

"Can it, Garrett. What Two Step said could mean we have a bigger problem."

"I'm listening."

"The one witness to the attack on Morley told me that a well-assembled girl in skintight black leather directed the creatures who stabbed him. She had about a cubic yard of bushy blond curls. The girl Two Step met was a short-haired brunette with intense brown eyes. The blonde, no telling about the eyes."

"Creatures?"

"Men in tight wool costumes with big gray eggs for heads."

"You didn't bother to tell me before?"

"I couldn't tell you what I didn't know then."

I got that. "Go see Puddle and Sarge. They might know what he was into." She didn't respond. I had just said something dumb. I guessed, "They didn't know anything."

"You are correct, sir. Morley walked out of the Grapevine after the late play rush. They never saw him again. And that was all they knew."

I had no trouble believing it. That was Morley Freaking Dotes, total individualist. "I guess all we can do is be patient and hope he gives us something when he wakes up."

"You're a screaming genius, Garrett. I'm so glad Morley and I have you for a friend."

"I am a special kind of guy."

15

The sun was up when I awakened. So was the queen of crime, in a good mood despite being caught in the inelegant process of riding a chamber pot. She pointed. "Look there."

"What am I supposed to notice?"

"We closed the curtains and the window."

Oh.

The curtains had been pushed aside. The window had been raised four inches. And the sill glistened with more dried slime.

"I never liked the kind of window that slides up and down."

"I don't know why I woke up when I did. I don't care. But when I did I saw what looked like a python oozing through the crack. It was about a yard in. I guess it was headed for Morley."

I eased over, studied the window close up. That allowed her some dignity at the same time. "A big snake? Really?"

"Not exactly. You saw real giant snakes when you were off in the islands. You probably wouldn't have been impressed. But that's what it looked like to me."

"It went away once it realized you were awake."

"After I hit it about twenty times with your club."

The woman was gorgeous and brilliant and evil, but she was no connoisseur of personal-use nonlethal defensive instruments. I carried nothing so mundane as a club.

"Why didn't you wake me up?"

"I hollered. You didn't even roll over. Then I was busy slamming the slime out of that damned thing."

"You should've poked me with the stick."

"I was distracted. I didn't think of that." And that was right in character. She hardly ever asked for help, even when she had no choice. This thing with Morley was a wonderment.

"All right. Tell me how it happened. In order. Exactly."

"I told you. There was this snake thing. I pounded on it till it pulled back. The shiny stuff is what it left. And, yes, I know we have to move Morley now because we can't totally protect him here."

Morley made a noise. I thought he wanted to say something. I was wrong. He had a problem with phlegm.

"That's a good sign, isn't it?"

"I think so." For a few seconds Belinda was the woman she could have been if she had chosen different parents and wasn't a flaming sociopath.

"You got anybody set up around here besides me?"

"Outside. You're my inside guy. You're the one I trust."

Somebody tapped on the door. I couldn't help myself. "What's the password?"

"How about 'Breakfast,' nimrod?" That sounded like Dee-Dee.

Belinda collected my head knocker and got ready to brain an intruder clever enough to mimic DeeDee's twang.

I cleared the bowl and pitcher off the nightstand. DeeDee parked the tray she carried. She turned on Dotes. "It worked! He looks a thousand percent better. He's coming back. He's going to be all right." She bounced and clapped her hands like a girl younger than Crush, then bolted out.

I asked, "What's the story there?"

"I don't know. It may be best that I don't."

I hadn't meant DeeDee's connection to Morley. I'd meant DeeDee and Hellbore. On reflection, though, there was no reason for Belinda to know anything about employees so far down the food chain that they dealt direct with the folks whose money fueled the Combine engine.

"She brought food enough for us and our childhood invisible friends. Let's do some damage." I hadn't eaten since I left Macunado Street.

DeeDee came back with Crush before we were done. Crush jumped all over me. "You weren't supposed to eat the cream of wheat!"

"The what?"

"The mush, nimrod! That was for him. The heavy stuff was for you."

The invisible friends must have gotten that. I hadn't seen

anything I considered part of a hearty breakfast. "The nearest thing to a real breakfast . . ."

Belinda squeezed my left elbow. She had some grip for a girl. "Garrett, your job is to keep your mouth shut, look pretty, and break the legs of anybody who tries to hurt Morley."

I could do two out of three blindfolded but the mouth thing has been a lifelong challenge.

"Belinda, silence is too hard." I was always chock-full of words that want to be free. Some even coagulate into rational . . . somethings.

16

Good thing Crush and DeeDee were dedicated to Morley's welfare. I was still wondering if I had what it took to feed him when they finished that and got to work dealing with the consequences of giving an unconscious man food and drink.

He needed bathing. His bed needed changed. I opened the window to the max during the process.

Belinda said, "You have to get more water into him. He's hot but he isn't sweating the way he should."

What would she know about dark elf fevers and sweats? Shrug. I have made a point, lately, of not hearing anything interesting about Miss Contague.

Some would say that I'd made a point of not hearing anything interesting about anybody who lacks red hair.

I wondered how Tinnie was doing.

I said, "My gut is full. While you're all here I'm going to look around outside."

Belinda gave me a dire look.

"Fear not. I won't make a run for it." I reclaimed my stick and got out, just to stretch my legs.

Belinda's watchers were easy to find. They all recognized me. They had been with her when she collected me on Factory Slide. They had nothing to report. Two were so bored they would have talked about anything with anybody.

The last one, though, had nothing to say. He had seen something interesting. Something interesting had seen him, too. He looked like he was napping at the top of a stairwell to a cellar. He had been dead long enough to cool down.

A few years ago that would not have moved me. Back then

every night produced its crop of corpses for morning harvest. But our great city is fraught, entangled in the throes of change. Casually created cadavers have become uncommon. Director Relway's winnows have been harsh.

I considered the scene with time-dulled mind and senses. This was not one of Belinda's coach crew. He had not died fighting so had not been alarmed by the approach of whoever did him in.

I crossed over to the wall beneath Morley's window.

That was redbrick. It glistened. There was dried something on the cobblestones, too. A pile of goat scat marbles lay a few feet south of the glisten. Flies were feasting.

I marveled at all the quiet. Senior management at Fire and Ice had to know the true names of some well-placed clients.

True names weren't just useful in the sorcery game, they were invaluable in politics and the blackmail game. Even the passive sort that assures localized maintenance of public works and a useful police presence. Or absence.

The streets were in perfect repair. Night lamps were in place and unbroken. There wasn't a red top in sight.

There wasn't anyone in sight. Which explained why a dead man could cool down without an uproar.

I made a second round of Belinda's watchers. Then I went back to report.

DeeDee and Crush had finished. I met them in the hallway. I found Belinda seated on the edge of Morley's bed, holding his hand. She started, pulled away, looked slightly guilty.

I ignored that. "He does look like he's coming back."

"You don't look good. What happened?"

"Somebody killed your man who was watching the window. You want to see, look to your right, far side, at the top of that cellar well about forty feet along."

Belinda looked. "Oh. I see him now. Looks like he's sleeping."

"Which is why nobody noticed till I tried to wake him up."

Belinda went from concerned to grim in a heartbeat. She nodded but just stared at the dead man. Bodies and parts thereof would begin skewing Director Relway's violent crimes statistics real soon.

"Let me guess. Those idiots never saw a thing."

"No. They did. But I had to ask twice. They only thought

they hadn't seen anything. Once they heard that a friend was dead they remembered an old woman with a goat cart passing through, headed toward downtown."

"What's the kicker? I'm in no mood for guessing games."

"It took her over an hour to get from the guy in the north to the guy in the south. It should have taken five minutes. The guy who saw her first said he heard her going. The man on the south side said he never heard anything. Bam. She was there. She scared him. He says her cart smelled."

"That's it?"

"That's it."

"There wasn't a cart out there when I looked. After I hit that thing with your club."

I got up to the window. "If it was next to the wall you wouldn't have seen it."

"I'll go get writing stuff."

"Uh . . ."

She was ahead of me. "I need to send a note to Pular Singe. An offer of employment."

"But . . ." I didn't want my little ratgirl involved in something deadly. Not again.

Belinda set a brisk pace when she had a goal. She returned with the essentials for letter writing before I finished inventorying improvements in Morley's condition.

"I brought extra paper. I'll write a letter of my own, for Singe to pass on to John Stretch. I may have work to subcontract."

She was in the red zone. Somebody was going to get hurt.

I hoped that wouldn't be her. Or Morley. Or, especially, me.

"I should send a note to Tinnie, too."

17

I did write a letter. It seemed futile once I finished. I didn't have it delivered. Tinnie knew what was going on. Anything I said wouldn't change her mind.

My dearly beloved had become fixed in her attitudes. She didn't let facts get in the way of her making up her mind. My friends thought that was my fault. Tinnie and I had a long history. When I stood up on my hind legs she would pack the attitude in. But I did let stuff slide because it was easier to go along.

I was supposed to be guarding someone, not known to be alive, in a hideout where nobody would think to look. The engineer of the hidery hadn't been successful. Somebody had tried the window already. A guard had lost his life. Then, scarcely an hour after Belinda went away, the last person I expected to see ambled into the room.

DeeDee and Crush were with me, DeeDee worshipping Morley with her too-young eyes, while Crush plotted some means of getting the best of her mother once Morley came around.

I got into weird stuff but not this kind of weird, where a mother looks younger than her daughter and acts it, both of them being professional ladies, fiercely competitive, and desperately eager for positive feedback from a man claimed by a bad woman from far above them in the food chain.

I finished nailing the window shut. "Most excellent, Garrett. A job well-done." I heard the soft scrape of a foot on hallway carpet. I turned.

Deal Relway came in. The Director himself. The terrible

swift sword of the law, older and more worn than when last I
saw him. I had heard that he never left the Al-Khar anymore.
Too many outsiders wanted to break his bones.

He was a little guy, and ugly. Sometime way back an impu-
dent dwarf had taken a climb through the family tree, plucking forbidden fruit. Additional members of the Other Races
had contributed over the generations.

Relway's minions were too efficient. He had arrived with
no more warning than his shoe brushing the nap of the carpet.
He looked around, said, "About what I expected. You ladies
finish what you're doing and go."

They had no idea who he was. I told them, "It's all right.
He's no enemy."

Frowning, unsure, they drifted out into a house saturated
with red tops.

Relway studied Morley. "Hard to believe."

"Bad luck can catch up with anybody. What brings you in
out of the smoke?"

"The hope that I might learn something helpful in dealing with a problem that's been nagging me almost since you
dropped out." His tone and mannerisms were casual. He was
more comfortable than when last I had seen him.

"You do understand where you are? Whose place you've
entered without invitation?"

"Not something that concerns me. Her interests and mine co-
incide right now. Down the road I'll probably shut her down."

"It's good to be confident. But you, sir, are going to die
young. And when you do you'll refuse to believe that it could
happen to you."

Relway was neither devastated nor confused. I kind of felt
sorry for him. I didn't know what I was talking about, either.

"You've been out of action for a while, Garrett. The para-
digms have shifted."

"Many casualties? Much property damage?" I wasn't sure
what a paradigm was. He didn't look likely to explain. "Good
for you. But what about right here, right now?"

"Let us readjust and reassess. At the moment I have no
interest in what Mr. Dotes may be doing with his life. I'm even
disinterested in the fell Miss Contague. I *am* interested in
making contact with whoever or whatever was responsible for
Mr. Dotes' condition."

"Why is that?"

"I am pledged to protect King and Crown. Something out there means to attack both. Your friend may have stumbled into it."

So. He felt threatened because he wasn't on top of everything happening in our marvelous city.

We talked, though not about much of consequence. Half an hour later we parted, me thinking that neither of us had profited, till I realized just how far out of trim I was.

He had learned plenty by listening to what I didn't say. As in not asking what he had learned from Jimmy Two Steps. I must know already, despite being holed up here, seeing no outsider but Belinda.

The runt had peeked through the curtains of my dreams.

Given time, I relaxed enough to realize that Relway had come fishing. He hungered for information on something that troubled him deeply—and I hadn't helped despite my honesty.

Relway's crew left Fire and Ice in stages, careful to protect the Director. So Crush said when she brought lunch, once the scary little man was gone. I loathed myself for my idiot response to a girl her age—while aching because a girl her age considered a guy my age a bad joke.

But she could go cow-eyed over Morley Dotes, thinking it somehow wondrous that she had gotten to change the diaper of a bad boy dark elf a whole lot older than me.

Crush was indifferent to Garrett the man. Our basis for interaction was Morley. She admitted that she had no idea who he really was. DeeDee might know him, though. The whiny guy inside asked, "So why are you drooling all over him?"

She rose dramatically in my estimation. She gave my question some thought. "I don't know. Not when I try to logic it out. Is he a sorcerer?"

"Your guess would be better than mine. You're female. I've never figured it out. Maybe he gives off a smell because he's a vegetarian."

"I doubt that. Anyway, with me it's probably about competition with DeeDee. And he has an exciting reputation. He's bad, he's beautiful, and he has been connected with some famous women. Strip everything else away, there's still bare-naked curiosity. What did those other women find so special?"

I considered Morley sourly. He had told me once that he had worked hard crafting his reputation. By building it and broadcasting it, he guaranteed himself a bottomless pool of ladies wondering what the excitement was all about. He had insisted that there was no trickery involved. He was providing excuses so women could pursue their own wicked desires.

Crush finished her work. She had no excuse for hanging around. She left without an apology, a farewell, or a broken heart.

I shut the door, pushed my cot against it. I lay down for a nap that didn't last but two or three hours. Then I was wide awake again. I took advantage of the chamber pot, then checked the window.

It was still nailed shut.

On the other hand, it was glass. Glass could be broken.

18

Sound came from the bed. I dropped Jon Salvation's omnibus of masterpieces. I thought Morley was choking.

He was. On words. His eyes were open. He was trying to talk.

His eyes were wild. He did not want to know where he was or what was happening. His latest memories were of being stabbed. Seeing me did not help. He did not recognize me.

Time was on my side. He wasn't going anywhere. He had neither the strength nor the will to do so. He was feeling every wound. One try to get up left him clear on how he would spend his next few weeks.

He didn't quite scream. He wasn't loud enough to bring on the rest of the house. He lay there panting, collecting himself. He did recognize me now.

"You finally irked somebody a little too much. Maybe laid your blessings on the wrong wife or daughter."

He made a sound of negation.

"Then it's business or your past catching up."

He did not respond. He turned thoughtful. Since he was supposed to be an honest restaurateur these days, I surmised that he was mining memory for a connection.

He continued not to respond.

Should I put aside the notion of a vengeful revenant? There would be few such who remained alive and dangerous. The Morley I knew when we were younger didn't leave live enemies behind.

He lapsed into sleep, then wakened again a few hours later still unable to speak. He did make me understand that he was thirsty.

He was asleep when DeeDee and Crush came for the evening cleaning and feeding. I did not share the good news. I wanted them out of the way quickly.

Miss Tea looked in during the cleanup but left without saying anything.

Morley went for a long, deep doze. When Jon Salvation became too much for me—I kept hearing his irritating, whiny, scratchy voice as I read—I turned down the lamps, sprawled on the cot, and got busy doing some snoozing of my own.

At some point I halfway wakened with the vague notion that Morley was trying to say something. Very mechanical and as clear as a falling-down drunk speaking his native tongue. Later still, I halfway wakened thinking something was trying to open the window. The glass squeaked. The frame creaked.

There was a flash and bang outside, followed by yelling and screaming. The shrieks of Civil Guard whistles followed. I saw nothing when I got to the window. There was no light. There was a heavy overcast.

I heard nothing more till early birds DeeDee and Hellbore wakened me by banging the door against my cot.

Hellbore. Wow. What a marvelous name. I would honor her preferences and call her Crush.

19

This time Morley woke up while the women were ministering to him. I got to witness another of those fascinating, inexplicably repugnant things that happen around him.

Two professional comfort women went red with embarrassment when he opened his eyes.

I just leaned against the wall, out of the way, and marveled. Un-bee-leave-a-bull!

DeeDee was in a charitable mood. Or needed to overcome her shyness by diverting her attention toward an unthreatening target. "There was some excitement out there again last night."

I'd almost convinced myself that I had dreamed it. "I hope it was less deadly than before."

"I think it was pretty ugly. You should talk to Miss Tea about that."

"I'll look forward. Moments with Mike are more precious than pearls."

DeeDee would never be an aficionado of my special humor. She looked at me blankly, not even wondering if I was poking fun.

Crush, though, rolled her eyes. She awarded me a sneer that said she got me and I was lame.

Morley made noises that sounded like they belonged to the family of questions most frequently asked upon awakening in strange circumstances.

I told him, "We're hiding out on the second floor of a hook shop called Fire and Ice, a subsidiary of the Contague family enterprise. We're here at Belinda's behest. She thought this would be a safe place to hole up till you heal enough to move to her place. Your lovely attendants are DeeDee and her daughter Hellbore, who prefers to be called Crush. They have been tending you since you were brought here. What, four days ago? Ladies?"

DeeDee counted on her fingers. "Yep. Four." Then she actually curtsied.

Crush rolled her eyes.

Morley made noises. I translated. "He says pleased to meet you and thank you for all the care you've lavished upon him."

Crush said, "Didn't sound like that to me."

Nor to me. "He might have expressed himself a little less elegantly. A man with deep stab wounds tends to be curt and cranky, especially when he's just wakened and the pain is catching up. But those were the core sentiments he wanted to convey. Deep down in his heart of hearts."

Crush said, "Man, you are full of it."

"It's one of my most endearing qualities."

She snorted.

"I'm really a big old lovable stuffed bear once you get to know me."

Another snort, dismissive but not derisive. "That isn't going to happen. The Capa left very specific instructions to the entire house. Not even DeeDee is dim enough to confuse them." She eyed her mother. Who kept right on looking like Crush's happy younger sister. "Or maybe she is. But she's already fixated on the bad boy."

"In another place and time, under different circumstances, we could have been great friends. I like the twists your mind takes."

That left her speechless. I indulged my evil laughter. I hadn't had a chance in a long time. Then, being a trained detective, I detected. "You guys didn't bring breakfast with you this morning."

DeeDee told me, "It wasn't ready. There were problems in the kitchen on account of some of the staff are late."

My paranoid bodyguard side went on alert.

Needlessly. DeeDee explained, "Mostly they're late because they have to get through all the tin whistles and whatnot that are out there. But some are fighting hangovers and stuff, too. The chief cook's daughter got married last night and that idiot paid for an open bar after. There'll be all the food you can eat once they get rolling."

Crush rolled her eyes again, this time for no obvious reason.

Morley stayed quiet. He listened, building mind pictures of character.

I said, "I'll need one of you to help feed him when the food does come."

DeeDee startled me. "That should be Crush. She does it better than me."

Crush shook her head. She didn't want the job if her mother didn't want it.

I opined, "Maybe we ought to let Miss Tea decide." Because that worthy had arrived. A wondrous medley of breakfast aromas pursued her. A previously unmet young lady deposited a tray on the nightstand. It was beginning to get crowded. If I had been between twelve and twenty-nine, I would have been in heaven. But I was a big boy now, no longer allowed to think that way. And the stench off a side of bacon was a total distraction.

Miss Tea said, "DeeDee, you and Crush go down and help serve. I'll feed Mr. Dotes while I talk to Mr. Garrett."

"Serve?" Crush asked.

"I opened the grand parlor to the Civil Guards. Serving tea and sweet rolls. A goodwill gesture."

"Always helps to be on good terms with the local red tops."

"It is. Move along, ladies. Garrett, before you pig out totally, hand me that glass and the long spoon."

"That glass" contained a greenish sludge made from something a starving pig probably would refuse but which might be good for a guy full of knife holes. Miss Tea said, "Some water, too."

That got to Morley via a reed, Miss Tea trapping a small quantity by holding a thumb over the reed's upper end, then releasing the dribble into Morley's mouth. It worked better when he was awake.

He was very thirsty.

Miss Tea fed him patiently, in little bits. "There was more excitement last night."

"So I heard. The neighborhood is overrun by red tops."

"They're everywhere. Half my people can't get to work. I try to make the tin whistles comfortable while they waste their time. And mine."

"What happened?"

"The night visitor came back. The Capa had a specialist waiting. And Director Relway had a team of Specials in the area, too."

"I thought I heard an explosion but I didn't see anything when I looked out the window."

"There *was* an explosion. Why don't you go down and see for yourself while I do this?"

"Sounds like a plan."

"Here." She pulled a slip of parchment from its nest in her cleavage. It was warm and lightly scented.

"What's this?"

"An employee pass. It will get you in and out if you have to deal with people who don't know you."

"Thank you. That should be useful." For a moment I wished I could spread the brag amongst my circle. I had written proof that I was a bona fide employee at a top-level brothel.

On reflection, though, it might be better to keep it to myself. I would hear every possible bad joke from people determined to undermine my dignity. Towel boy would be the most generous accusation I'd hear.

20

The pass proved unnecessary. Several tin whistle sergeants remembered me and had been tipped that I had semiofficial standing. This one time only, my presence within sight of a crime scene was to be tolerated.

Barry Berry was a humorless man but a good guy. He attached himself to me like that was his special assignment. He took me on a tour. "Everything is right where it fell. The Director and General Block want to see it all for themselves before we start the cleanup."

There would be some of that to do. The neighborhood had been blessed with five corpses. Two had been Civil Guards. Another had been one of Belinda's men. The remainder were unknowns presumed to have been companions of the perpetrator. They wore tattered gray wool. They had wooden helmets encasing their heads.

I observed, "Somebody believes in living on the edge."

"The prevailing theory is that it's somebody who can't make the connection between actions and consequences. We got a sicko out there, Garrett. A huge sicko."

A race was on, now, between the Outfit and the Guard. Honors to the winner would be first chance to have a long, painful sit-down with whoever was behind these deaths.

The mystery men in gray had fallen in the street on a line from under Morley's window to the place where Belinda's watcher had perished earlier. The force of the bang had hit them from behind, hurling them a dozen yards across cobblestones. A blood trail said one crawled twenty feet before expiring. The broken remains of a cart and roasted carcasses of two goats marked the beginning of his brief trek. Against the brick wall, below the window, lay a chunk of something that put me in mind of squid. There were no tentacles or anything, it was just that the skin on the uncooked side had a texture that stirred the squid notion.

Berry said, "Most of the guys were reminded of snails. I guess because of the crust on the brick."

"No shell."

"No tentacles, either."

"That's true. Do we know what happened?"

"We know exactly what happened, minute by minute."

"Give me the highlights. If you would be so kind."

"The goat cart showed up just like it did before. Like whoever was bringing it had no idea that we might be watching."

"But with two thugs along."

"Stupid. Totally overconfident stupid. Miss Contague had a friend off the Hill tucked in to watch, same place as the guy who got waxed. He used a stealth spell that wasn't completely effective. The villain didn't notice him right off. When he did the Hill guy unleashed the lightning."

"And that caused all this?"

"It did. Miss Contague used somebody from the first string."

"Where's the villain?"

"Got away. Come over here." Berry led me past the wreck of the cart to a patch of what looked like candle black fifteen feet across. At its center was a circle of perfectly pristine cobblestones a yard across. The black around the circle was an eighth of an inch thick. Small footprints left, passed all the casualties, and headed toward downtown. "There was a running fight. That's when we lost our guys. And the Outfit soldier."

"No wounded. Just dead."

"Yep."

"And the sorcerer?"

"The one who made the bang? Too old and fat to keep up."

Surrounding buildings were too tall for me to see far but I thought the villain's line of flight might parallel a crow's toward the Hill. I didn't mention that. I didn't need to. That angle would be getting a hard look already, not just by the red tops and Outfit but by key people on the Hill. They don't like rogue behavior likely to attract more animus than they already enjoy.

"This is a puzzlement, Sergeant."

"It is indeed. Dotes said anything yet?"

Ha. Here was why I had my very own red top tour guide. "Not yet. Believe me, though, I'll have a book full of questions when he does wake up."

"If he does?"

"He's my oldest friend, Sergeant. I'm bound to think positive."

"Was I you, I'd do my best to *be* positive. After last night people all the way up to the Crown Prince are going to want to ask him what's going on."

I made one of those intuitive leaps for which I'm not well-known. "I'll bet an angel right now that he won't have any idea."

"He's going to clam and try to handle it himself?"

Morley's mind would work that way. "Not what I meant. I mean I'm willing to bet he knows less about what's going on than you or me."

"But somebody wants to kill him."

"Maybe. But maybe the somebody who was here wasn't the same somebody who turned him into a pincushion. Maybe this somebody wants to find out what that somebody was up to." I was brainstorming. That notion arose from the fact that there had been no sorcery involved in the attack on Morley. "Mistaken identity might be involved. Or somebody thinks Morley knows something that he doesn't. I could come up with this stuff all day. It's just speculation."

"Sicko."

Probably. Undoubtedly. In the spirit of open cooperation, I began to quiz Berry about crimes that might have been related to what had happened here. Relway had mentioned a deep interest in a pattern of ugliness.

I did not get to run with that. After discovering that she could not open the window to yell at me, Miss Tea began pounding on glass to get my attention. She beckoned vigorously.

"Got to go, Sergeant. Thanks for everything."

21

Miss Tea did not give me a chance to ask what was happening. "I didn't tell you to take the rest of the day off, I'd cover for you."

"The red tops gave me the first-class tour. I've never seen them this serious. We may have Prince Rupert himself up here later."

She wanted to go on being irritated but put that aside. A visit from the Crown Prince had a ton of meaning. "I see."

"Our own prince say anything while I was out?" Dotes was sound asleep again.

"He proposed. A two-hour common-law marriage. After he gets on his feet again. I'm thinking about it."

"Another sign that he's recuperating."

Miss Tea scowled at me and grumbled something I don't think Morley would have found endearing. She absented herself in quest of more important duties. She didn't take the breakfast tray. I poured cold tea, put my cot back down, settled, picked up the Salvation omnibus and tried reading *Star-Crossed Love*. The title said it all. The theme animated most of the plays put on in TunFaire's theaters. There were autobiographical elements to this one. The female protagonist, instead of being the usual fainthearted rose, resembled Salvation's girlfriend, Winger.

After a few pages I glanced over, wondered aloud, "What did you get yourself into this time?"

It looked big. That didn't fit. Morley would not do anything to invite the attention of Prince Rupert.

That left me thinking about the attack on me and Tinnie. We weren't involved by choice, either.

I went back to the play. I needed to clear my head.

I finished the first scene in act three, looked over, found Morley looking back, not brightly. "What the hell did you do?"

He gave me a weak smile, said, "Water!" in a raspy little croak.

I dribbled water. When he had enough he went back to sleep, nothing said and no questions answered.

Crush brought lunch and took breakfast's remains away. I told her, "I need more water and a chamber pot change."

"I need a diamond tiara."

Despite the attitude, all was handled quickly.

Morley woke up, drank water, dispensed no wisdom, and went back to sleep. An hour before supper the healer returned, tricked out in his best mourning outfit. I did not care enough to ask why the Children dressed that way. I was getting jaded. And distracted.

Accompanying the healer was a serious surprise from yesteryear, the Windwalker, Furious Tide of Light.

She was surprised to see me, too. And a tad embarrassed, I think. She lowered her big, beautiful violet eyes.

I greeted the sorceress politely, inwardly pursuing a goofy calculation trying to connect a heavyweight off the Hill with a cult healer because of the word Light. I don't have an adequately developed paranoid imagination.

Belinda Contague accompanied them but stayed in the hall, observing. I did some observing myself.

The Windwalker hadn't aged a minute. She remained totally waiflike and utterly delicious but today she was all business. She moved to the window, looked out, paid almost no attention to Morley. I tried to remember if they had met. Those were confusing times. Antediluvian times. I was a different man in a different world, then, not a respectable member of the bourgeoisie.

I couldn't help but snicker. That earned a scowl from all women present.

The healer asked, "What's happening with him?"

"He sleeps and he drinks water. I think he's getting better."

"He drinks water."

"He wakes up, makes a little croak that means he's thirsty. I

use the pipe. He sucks it down; then he goes back to sleep." For
the lady in the hallway, I added, "Miss Tea claimed he made a
pass this morning. She was just trying to get my goat."

"It will be a long time before this fellow sins again." He
examined Morley's wounds while he talked. "He is the luck-
iest knife victim I've ever seen. Some of these wounds are six
inches deep, yet not one cut an artery or hit a vital organ.
There is no infection, either. Don't press him with questions.
He won't be able to answer for a while. Ah! Here he is now."

Morley's eyes opened. He cataloged the crowd, made his
"Water," sound.

The healer produced a black glass bottle the size of my
thumb. It had a clear glass stopper. "Three drops into each
pitcher of water. Keep his water separate. This is for pain. There
is a good deal of pain still, isn't there?" he asked Morley.

Dotes grunted, closed his eyes.

The healer spoke to the doorway. "I've done what I can.
He'll recover. How well depends upon how firmly he clings
to my instructions. No straying from the diet. All the water he
wants. The drops are not addictive. They will cause considerable drowsiness. Keep him clean. Turn him once in a while.
Time is what he requires. There was a timetable in the instructions I gave you, madam. Enforce it to the letter."

Wow! I'd never heard anybody give Belinda Contague orders. This nut was doing it. And she was nodding! She understood the instructions, too. Morley was sure to try going before
he was ready.

Furious Tide of Light said nothing. After the early glances
she ignored Morley. She was fascinated by something in the
street. "Your rat associate is quite clever."

The fit was tight but I managed to join her. Singe was down
below, talking to several senior red tops and a brace of wide
loads from middle management in Belinda's enterprise. I was
pleased to see my little girl getting the respect she was due as
the finest tracker in the city.

"How so?" I asked.

"She means to backtrack instead of trail forward."

Backtrack goats? Easier than following some human who
killed three people while making a getaway. Safer, too. And
more useful. Both incursions had come from the same direc-

tion and had gone on toward the Hill. "The girl is scary smart. What are you doing here?"

"Personal appeal from Prince Rupert."

Ah. A family friend, I recalled. "And how is your dad and your daughter Kevans?"

"We're not getting along at the moment. Let's concentrate on the task at hand. I'm not the woman you remember." She turned her cool, emerald eyes my way. I was afraid I was going to drown there.

"I'm sorry. I'm probably not the man you think you remember, either." I watched some of John Stretch's ratman associates emerge from shadows as Singe moved out with a train of thugs behind. Those hailed from several sides of the law. They stayed back so as not to distract her.

I asked, "You know why this mess is causing so much excitement?"

The Windwalker met my gaze. Her eyes were a striking blue. The shy girl I remembered emerged. "I can comment only from a position of vast ignorance. Prince Rupert is concerned about a possible Hill connection."

I met the Crown Prince once. He'd asked me to be his personal agent. He was as determined as Deal Relway to afflict TunFaire with great gobs of law and order. Someone who failed to acknowledge that rules existed would be a definite black beast to him.

"What I wanted to know was, what are you doing here in this room, with us?"

"I had a notion that, with the healer's assistance, I might learn something useful. I was wrong. Then I was so startled by seeing you . . . I *should* get back to work. I need to be with those people out there."

Tight as it was, she got past me and Belinda without getting intimate. She left me totally rattled. Those eyes . . . I had forgotten those eyes.

22

Belinda gave the Windwalker a short lead. "There something between you two? I thought I knew all the bimbos that came after me."

"Only in her head. Maybe. She took a weak run at me once upon a time. It didn't go anywhere. Though . . . She's a multiple personality type."

"She'd have to be to come down off the Hill to chase you."

Belinda was kidding but was so tired and worried she made it sound serious.

I kept my mouth shut. Belinda wasn't really interested. She held Morley's hand and asked, "Where the hell were you for those ten days?"

I got confused. "Ten days? There some things you haven't shared with me? The backstory changes as we move along?"

"What are you yammering about?"

So I thought back. And decided I was a dumbass. All she had said was that he had been laid up here three days before she brought me in. "I don't know. I'm having trouble getting my mind into fighting trim. You did wait three days before you came to me?"

"I was rattled. You, of all people, understand that we do stupid things when we aren't thinking straight."

"He could have died."

"But he didn't. And I did get around to you and the Children of the Light."

"Sorry for barking."

"I had it coming." Belinda looked at Morley with the same cow eyes I have seen on a thousand other women. I took a short ramble through the realm of intuition.

"Belinda?"

"Uhm?"

"Were there any weird events around here before I showed up?"

Sometimes Miss Contague is a mind reader. "You suggesting that they suspected he was still alive but didn't know where to look? So they watched you. They raided your place to get you moving . . . No. That doesn't hang together."

"They watched you till you contacted me. Then they watched me. That's how I would've done it. How come they're so desperate? Where did it happen? What did the people who found him say?"

"I don't know where, yet. I'm supposed to go look at a place. They found him dying. That's about it. It was obvious he wouldn't need his stuff anymore so they started turning out his pockets."

"And found something to connect him to you. So they did the right thing."

"They did what they thought might put money in their pockets."

"Did they bet wrong?"

"No. That's just good public relations. You feed the beast sometimes."

"Did you get his stuff back?"

"I did. I thought he might have been hit because of something he was carrying. He had nothing on him. But he might have been cleaned out where he was attacked."

"How about dead attackers? Nobody could do this much damage without Morley doing some damage back."

"The place I'm going to check, there was some blood and others signs of a big fight. But no bodies. My people found two wooden buttons, a scrap of gray wool cloth, and a broken wooden mask with cast glass eyehole covers. Weird, huh? I hoped Pular Singe could do something with them. She said it's too late. That trail is long gone."

"He was missing for ten days?"

"Yes. Again."

"He really never told Sarge or Puddle or any of his mugs anything?"

"No. I went there even before he turned up full of holes. We talked about this already."

"I have to ask over and over. You had a witness."

"One who can't be found by anyone anymore."

"Put away for safekeeping." In the river, with big rocks for shoes.

"I'm thinking ringer. Not based on any evidence, just intuition."

"No marvelous body in tight black leather?"

"Not him. We'll find him eventually."

We would, of course. "I can't see Morley wandering off for that long. For one night, maybe. But he's a hands-on guy with his business."

"You're not producing original thought."

"I'm not trying. I'm musing out loud. But here's a question of personal interest. How close are you working with the Director?"

"We pretend not to see each other poking around. Communication between foot soldiers will be overlooked."

"Last time our paths crossed, Relway was putting together teams of specialists. One was supposed to do forensic sorcery."

"The Specials. There are a dozen squads, now, and more to come."

"If the forensic sorcery group is up, maybe you can get Relway to check out this place when you visit it."

"I'll suggest it. But the red tops don't give a shit about Morley."

I eyeballed Dotes. What secrets would we prize forth once he could sit up and talk? He looked more relaxed. The drops in the water must have been working.

"There is one obvious answer to *why* Morley was missing for ten days."

"He was a prisoner."

"Fits what we know. And might explain why someone tried to kill him, assuming he escaped."

"He showed no signs of having been restrained."

I picked up a hand, looked at the wrist. Nothing, of course. "Meaning he wasn't kept in chains."

Belinda stood at the window and watched the street, likely not seeing anything. "I'm considering changing my mind."

"About?"

"Moving Morley to your house."

"Really?" Warily.

"Two birds, I think. He wouldn't be safer anywhere else. And your partner could find out things we need to know."

Belinda is ever-capable of doing the startling thing.

"One problem. Old Bones is dead to the world right now."

"You always say that."

"This time it's true. Actually, it's almost always true."

"And you're here. The one man able to stir the relict out of his dreams."

Marginally true.

Crush and DeeDee arrived.

23

As mistress of an empire spanning the full underbelly of TunFaire, employing more than a thousand people, Belinda had obligations outside Fire and Ice. And she had digging to do. Yet she just sat there staring at Morley, muttering, while seated on a hard folding chair, courtesy of the genius of Kip Prose and the production acumen of the Amalgamated Manufacturing Combine.

Miss Tea had brought four chairs. They took hardly any room when folded. No doubt they cost a fortune. And cheap knockoffs would be available within weeks if I remained unavailable to fight for Amalgamated's intellectual property rights.

There are laws but we have to enforce them ourselves.

"Belinda?"

She did not respond.

"Hey. Girl. Listen up. Investigator working here. Let's get on with the questions and answers."

She turned weary eyes my way.

"A long time ago, two days and a few hours, you told me some things about Morley's situation. There have been changes since, all moving toward the less specific and more ambiguous."

"That can happen when you talk to witnesses."

"True. You had an eyewitness. Now you don't?"

"Like I told you, he disappeared. His story didn't hold water, anyway."

"A ringer."

"Looking back, I think he was fishing for a trace on Morley. I wasn't thinking clearly. I didn't hide the fact that he was alive."

"Could he have been the villain himself?"

"I don't know."

"Sergeant Berry insists that we're up against a sicko. Could he be one of those who feeds on the action around his crimes? Some even try to get in with the tin whistles so they can tag along during the investigation."

"Could be. I'll bet this one is sick in more than one dimension."

"Remember what he looked like?"

"If I was an artist I could paint his picture."

"You have trouble drawing stick figures."

"I do."

"We could recruit an artist."

"I don't think . . . Hell. I *know* my powers of description aren't good enough."

"I was thinking we could have the Dead Man capture the image and pass it to a skilled painter. We have some good portraitists in TunFaire."

Belinda glared like she meant to cause spontaneous human combustion through sheer willpower.

"I thought you'd be too paranoid to do it the easy way."

"Paranoid? Me? You're the loon if . . ."

"Suppose he did rummage through your head?"

She did not answer. The idea terrified her.

"He's done it before. You survived. What would he do with anything he found? Besides sit around radiating smug because he'd gotten a peek up your skirt?"

She had no ready answer. The arrival of a flustered Miss Tea saved her the need. Miss Tea gushed, "You better come down, ma'am. The bloody, frigging Crown Prince his own self is here."

Belinda said, "Looks like I'm needed."

"Want me to come with? I know the man."

"Bullshit. You don't even ooze between the toes in his circle, let alone run."

"Bet that and you'd be wrong. He asked me to be his own personal, private investigator one time." And I turned him down. I like being my own boss. As I have been since I told him, "Sorry, no." The job had gone to a clever rascal called Lurking Felhske instead.

Felhske was sure to meet a bad end. So I told myself while

stalking the floors of Amalgamated's manufactories, hoping to intimidate the rare fool who would steal from his employer at a time when people starved if they lost their job. Amalgamated and Weider Brewing were the only employers creating jobs, these days. And I worked for both.

Sitting there in the waning hours with the queen of crime and a best friend who couldn't show me his mocking smile, I had no choice but to look at who and what I had become. Which left me a little embarrassed.

Belinda told me, "You stick to your job. I'll charm Rupert."

"Try not to hit him. If you do, though, try to pull your punches."

"Wiseass. I keep telling you I'm not that girl anymore."

Yes, she was. She just hid it better. And she was about to go into the presence of an abrasive and condescending personality.

For all his high-mindedness and determination to do right for Karenta, Rupert was a dork. He was a hard case about his good works but did not have a ghost of a concept of royal subjects being anything but social and mental inferiors.

He was a shepherd oath-bound to shield his dumb animals from danger.

"Good luck then, darling," I told Belinda.

24

Crush came up late, bringing water and a pound of salt. "We had to send out. The cooks wouldn't give theirs up." She moved gingerly. "You probably won't see me or DeeDee in the morning. We need time to recover. Those Guard assholes all want the young stuff. And they're lousy tippers."

What could I say? That you have to deal with assholes whatever your line of work?

I did try to look sympathetic. "Next time you do come, I could use something else to read."

"If I can still walk. Or you could go down and get something."

Wonder of wonders, the excitement faded away. However bold they were, the baddies figured out that it wasn't cost-effective to come after Morley at Fire and Ice.

Night after night I sat there waiting for him to do something more than drink water and poop. It was like having a newborn, only I wasn't the one who had to change his diapers.

I wondered about Singe's tracking expedition. I wondered what Relway was doing, what the Crown Prince was up to, and what Belinda had found out. And, more than anything, I worried about Tinnie. I hoped she was better posted than I was. The only people I saw were Miss Tea, Crush, and DeeDee. Miss Tea helped some while the other ladies dealt with the upswing in demand for the house's principal product. Miss Tea did not pitch in with that. Nobody said anything about anything happening outside the house.

I did get all the dirt on those who made Fire and Ice special.

I sat in that room with that man and slipped ever nearer the bounds of explosive lunacy.

I needed to rediscover patience. There would be a long training period once Morley climbed out of that bed. It might take him a year to get strong enough. Then we would go get whoever hurt him.

Crush came in. "This is the last book we've got. And the most boring." She passed me a ragged old thing from the last century, well into its senior years. It was tied round with ribbon to keep loose pages from getting away.

"What is it? Maybe I won't need to figure out these knots." Crush had decided I wasn't that awful after all. I was unthreatening. Avuncular. The kind of uncle who keeps his hands to himself. We could talk about stuff. Bookish stuff, but not for long. She was a popular girl with an extended list of regular clients.

This book was a history of TunFaire's early years, up to the establishment of the monarchy. It was a copy of a copy. It was a slow read because the language was old-fashioned.

I was excited because several chapters covered times when the Dead Man was still alive. He might get no mention but I could peek through a window into the age that shaped him.

"Crush, how long you figure on staying in the life?"

"What kind of question is that?" Instantly defensive.

"A serious one from somebody who thinks your mind is wasted here."

"The mind may be. That's not the business we're in. The body is getting pounded so hard I mean to walk on my twentieth birthday. I shouldn't ever have to work again. If my investments are good. I might take DeeDee with me—if she can learn to live without the attention."

DeeDee was the star of the house. Normally, she dealt only with select private clients. She was a blonde, none too bright, part elf, extremely sensual when she was so inclined, and, rumor said, thoroughly enjoyed her work. That was unusual in her trade. She craved approval. She got all she needed here. Crush was afraid she would refuse to give it up.

Crush was brighter than she pretended. In time I realized that all of our conversations came round to what we were working on at Amalgamated.

Why? Amalgamated is a company but you can't buy in.

Different people have different percentages but every fraction is fixed. If a founding partner wants out he has to offer his points to the other investors first. So far nobody has shown any inclination toward getting out.

Amalgamated was designed to make us all rich by bringing the fruits of Kip Prose's genius to market. The big shareholders are Kip and his family, the Tates, and the Weiders of Weider Brewing. I have a few points for having kept Kip alive through hard times, and for having had the wit to put him into the company of rich people content to let him tinker and fiddle and make them far richer than they already were.

Subjectively, I spent half a lifetime at Fire and Ice. On the calendar it was four days. My best pal kept on sleeping, waking up for water ever less frequently. I wondered if his medication didn't do more than just manage pain. Keeping Morley in Nod seemed like a good idea, medically. It was less optimal for those of us who are naturally impatient.

I kept thinking that if that was me I would have been up and running already—if somebody didn't fix me so I couldn't.

Belinda's doing. Had to be. She thought it was more important for Morley to heal than it was for us to get out and mix it up with villains.

I was thinking stupid and knew it. And was afraid that just sitting watch over Morley would end up with me hating him.

Miss Tea invited herself in occasionally. She did not become less antagonistic. Finally, though, she turned up in a less gloomy mood. "The Capa says it's time to move him. After his supper and evening cleaning. If you need to make special preparations, tell me now."

I mentioned a lamb-and-rice dish that I liked, chattered about how I would miss the place that had been home for so long.

"You've been here less than a week."

"It feels like so much longer."

"It did to us. But you're just being a wiseass. I have the Capa's promise that I don't have to put up with any crap."

"Uh-oh."

"Exactly. Get your stuff ready. I especially want that arsenal under the bed gone before somebody takes legal notice. The books stay home."

"I'll see if I can't send up a few that are more interesting."

"Now you're being a dick."

"I can't help it. It's being cooped up in here."

"Now you're going to blame your personality defects on us, too?"

Ouch! "Good thing we still love each other."

Ghost of a smile. "Will where you're going be any better?"

I restrained myself. Maybe not. My responsibilities wouldn't change. "I don't know. Come by some time and see."

25

As promised, Belinda turned up with several burly henchmen after supper. DeeDee and Crush got Morley back into the rags he was wearing when he showed up. Most of the blood had been scrubbed out. The holes hadn't been mended. Mixed feelings floated around. DeeDee and Crush were sad to see Morley go, though neither ever exchanged a word with him. Despite all the attitude, Miss Tea was unhappy, too. She turned out the off-duty staff to move Morley and my stuff.

"A hearse?" I asked Belinda when I got down to the street. "You're taking him away in a hearse?" Where did she even find one? There can't be ten in the whole city.

"Yes. Put on the hat and coat that Joel has for you. Then climb up and take the post position."

"What are you talking about?"

"Get up on the seat beside the driver. Try to look like a professional."

"A professional what?"

"That's always the question with you, isn't it? Move! We don't have time for games."

Four men emerged from the back door of the hook shop. They behaved exactly like men sneaking a corpse out of a place where it shouldn't be found. I considered leaving Miss Tea with a buss on the cheek and Crush with a promise to visit soon, decided to be more mature, walked away from what would have been signature behavior a few years back. My best pal was on that litter, under that black woolen blanket, and several people, including me, were counting on me to get him where he needed to go with no damage added.

I hustled over for a costume fitting.

Joel was a slim hard case with zombie eyes. He put me into a long black coat and a semierect black hat, like a soft cone, nearly a foot tall. With the hat I acquired the long, twisted sideburn curls of the morticians' guild. The hat had wig elements built in. Joel said, "Quit grab-assing and get up on the post. And, yes, the hat is real. Move!"

Maybe that was why you never recognize a mortician when he isn't on duty. He wears a disguise at work.

The coat cramped my shoulders. It hung to my ankles. The climb to the seat was difficult. The goofy damned hat slipped down into my eyes.

I settled to brood and nurture my resentment of the man who had overturned my life by getting himself all stabbed up. If the damned fool could've skipped that I'd have been snuggling with my favorite redhead.

The hearse was not a tall wagon, though the seats were high. The driver, seated to my left, asked, "You heeled, Slick?"

"Lightly." I showed him my head knocker. "The character with the ratty ginger hair put my heavy equipment in with the client."

The man chuckled. He was an old, long drink of water who looked like this might be his true calling. "Client. I like that. Nice stick, too. Good enough for tonight. Won't no resurrection men mess with this mob."

Two mounted men led, followed by Belinda's coach with thugs all over it. Then came another armed rider, the hearse with the mighty Garrett in the post and an armed thug on a running board to either side. One of those was my new pal, Joel. Behind the hearse were two more horsemen.

"What might resurrection men be?"

"Body snatchers. It's a problem lately. Somebody is buying youngish corpses that're in good shape. Where you been, Ace? Out of town?"

"So to speak. Stealing corpses, eh?" This was the first I'd heard about that. But there had been no reason for the subject to come up while I was babysitting. And less so before that. Nobody had a reason to keep me posted. My business was to protect Amalgamated from the larceny of its workers and the predations of intellectual pirates. Ditto for the Weider breweries.

The hearse jerked. I slammed against the back of my seat.

The driver said, "You got to pay attention, Stretch. You're supposed to be looking out for me and him inside. Him being dead and all, he probably won't come back on you if you nod off and the boogie boys get him. But your old pal Cap'n Roger, here, he's gonna come back hard. Especially if'n he gets kilt."

"I have problems paying attention." Problems I had not had in ante-Tinnie times. "You notice me getting glassy-eyed, give me an elbow in the ribs. I'm hell on wheels when I am paying attention."

"I sincerely hope I don't get to see you in action, Bud."

I guessed Roger to be about sixty. That meant he had done a turn in the Cantard and had made it home. Which meant he remembered guys who couldn't focus. All of us who made it back remember guys who couldn't focus. Their bones decorate the desert down there.

The convoy headed south, swung onto Grand, then took that down to my home neighborhood. The streets weren't busy. We didn't attract an unusual amount of attention. I strove valiantly to stay alert, for the sake of my best pal and my new friend Cap'n Roger. It took about half an hour for Roger to decide I was ready for an elbow.

I could not turn off my mind. Calm just would not come.

Cap'n Roger's elbow wakened me as the parade neared my place in Macunado Street. I settled into reality with the suspicion that I'd had an epiphany that I could not now recall because I was too dumb to pay attention at the moment of revelation.

Since I mostly worried about how Tinnie and I were getting along, I guessed that I must have lost a surefire means of dealing.

The hearse stopped even with the steps to my stoop. As I dismounted I noted the neighbors coming out. The door opened. Singe and Dean came outside. Then I felt the reassuring presence of the Dead Man, awake and deeply interested.

Thank you Singe, you wonder child.

In moments I felt more at home and more relaxed than I had for a long time.

26

I would like to say that the depth of Belinda Contague's commitment to Morley was reflected in her willingness to walk into a place where her thoughts could not be kept secret, but . . .

Her willingness is tempered by a cautious application of technology.

"What?"

Once upon a time a band of junior sorcerers, amongst other sins, created a mesh able to keep me from seeing their thoughts.

I remembered. I considered Belinda more closely. "She isn't wearing a wig."

I was in the hallway, adding to the congestion. People were everywhere, getting in each other's way. Morley was supposed to go into what had been my office, back in antiquity. Singe had cleared it out, then had installed a bed, chairs, and a few other bare-bones amenities. The guys with the litter couldn't figure out how to make the turn through the doorway.

This room was smaller than the last but here I would not be confined to one space. I could roam from room to room and floor to floor, and even go down into the cellar. Wide open spaces, compared. And Singe would be more interesting company than the surly folk at Fire and Ice.

I backed into Singe's office while the litter boys twisted and shoved and argued. Joel and Belinda barked advice that only added to the tumult. I wondered what the neighbors thought. You don't often see the morticians make a delivery instead of a pickup.

The mesh is next to her scalp, embedded in her natural hair.

"That's a lot of work gone to waste." If any of these brunos knew something Belinda wanted kept secret.

Too much was happening at once. I couldn't keep an eye on it all. The Dead Man had to make sure nobody collected souvenirs or hid in a closet.

It all worsened when Belinda went from the advisory to the imperial edict stage.

"Hey, woman! Yes. You. The pretty lady who forgets where she's at. Calm down. And get those extra bodies out of here." Her thugs had gotten Morley into his new quarters and established in his new bed. At which point I realized that we didn't have Crush and DeeDee to feed and change him anymore.

Belinda gave me the hard-eye. Then she did remember where she was, what she was doing, and who was there behind her, out of sight but maybe not quite out of mind. "Yes. All right. Joel, get the hat and coat from Mr. Garrett. The rest of you, go to Durelea Hall. Wait there. Joel, pay Roger and thank him for the use of the hearse. Worden, tell my coachman to wait at Durelea Hall, too."

I said, "I hate to give up the coat. I like the look." But I handed it over.

Joel said, "See Cap'n Roger. There's always openings in the mortician trade."

"I left some tools in the hearse. I'll need them. Would you be so generous as to run them up to the door?"

Belinda inclined her head slightly. Joel took that as an order. Off he went. The Dead Man touched me lightly, confirming my suspicions. I asked Belinda, "You spend much time around Joel?"

"Not really. Why?"

"He's got the bug bad. And he smells like the kind of guy who could get weird."

Belinda stared like I was a raving lunatic. Like I had accosted her on the street, insisting that she hear my theory about the royal conspiracy to conceal the truth about the mole people who lived in caverns deep under the earth. "You saw something that I missed?"

"I could be wrong. But the way the man watches you, when you don't know he's watching . . . I'd say it's close to obsession."

"Good to know. I think."

Truly a human shark.

"You can still get a solid read?"

Not if you ruin it by talking about it.

Always a problem, me verbalizing my half of our conversations. "I'm out of practice."

An understatement.

After his appearance out front Dean had fled to the kitchen. He remained in hiding whilst the old homestead swarmed with villains, not out of timidity but to avoid being trampled. He emerged now. "Is the rush over?"

His great dread had been being told to feed the horde. He was irked enough because Belinda and I were still on scene and special needs Morley was lurking in my old office. "I'll need to do some serious shopping if there are going to be extra mouths to feed."

Singe told him, "Make a list. I'll have John Stretch deal with it. None of us should go out. It might not be safe."

Dean shrugged. He did not ask my opinion. He was used to Singe taking charge.

I caught on. Danger wasn't relevant. Singe was giving an old man an excuse to let someone else do his running.

Dean's years were catching up.

I said, "We need to decide how to handle Morley. Belinda, you'll be busy back in the world. Singe and I can, maybe, muddle through an occasional feeding, sponge bath, or linen change, but we aren't qualified to do it regular. We'll need somebody trustworthy." Because he or she would not be live-in. There was nowhere to put anybody.

Singe said, "Taken care of, Garrett. Some of John Stretch's women will handle it."

Singe had everything covered already. There was no need to fuss.

Belinda said, "I'm not needed here anymore."

"Don't go," I said. "We haven't talked about what you found out the last few days."

"Nothing, basically."

I waited for an opinion from the Dead Man. None came. "Nothing at all? That's hard to believe."

"What you believe is up to you. I'm going, now. I'll check in occasionally. If the lazy dick does wake up, send a message." She headed for the door, striding manfully.

The Dead Man touched me lightly—just a gentle suggestion that I keep my mouth shut till she was out of the house.

27

I shut the door, did a quick mental catalog of the faces I had seen watching. There were dozens, still, even with the hearse and coach gone. Some were Belinda's bodyguards. None of the others tripped an alarm. None made the Dead Man wonder, either.

Mr. Dotes' presence will not remain secret. A clever questioner could pluck a detail from this dim witness and that and assemble an approximation of our situation.

"And? So what?"

That was me being too sure that I was untouchable inside my own house. My watchful partner brought my overconfidence to my attention.

I am ever most effective when my presence and abilities are unknown. One would think that you had worked that out for yourself by now.

I was about to spin a big argument. He cut me off. *How would you deal with me, given the knowledge you have?*

A couple notions popped into mind immediately. And I limit my options by failing to be as ruthless as some.

You see. It is all in knowing what you are up against. Which is why my people never reveal all there is to know about us, to friend, foe, or sibling.

Wisdom with which it was hard to argue. At the moment I was thinking the best way to get him and Morley at the same time would be a swarming attack with firebombs. Light the place up and burn everybody inside.

There are people out there able to do that and sleep like a baby afterward. People who would do it for the price of a quality high.

Director Relway doesn't always seem like a bad idea.

*You begin to see. We are most vulnerable to those who know
who and what we are.*

No doubt he meant that on multiple levels.

"I see. In fact, I see so clearly that I'm sure Belinda made a
mistake by moving us here."

*Let me suggest some possibilities. Perhaps she does not plan
to leave Mr. Dotes here long. This may last only until it lures
someone into range.*

"We're bait?"

*Possibly. She might, in addition, be pleased if I could excise
a clue or two from Mr. Dotes.*

"About?"

*All of the great questions. Who? Where? What? Why? When?
How? And who to? Or anything else that might lead to the cut-
ting of selected throats. I am inclined to agree with Miss Contague about the potential value of the dig. Which will be difficult
work. Exploring an unconscious mind, counterintuitively, is
much more difficult than rummaging through a mind that is
awake, aware, and trying to hide.*

"I'll take your word for it. You being the self-declared expert."

*Indeed. At this point you should find someone else to pester.
I need all my minds to winkle out those things that Mr. Dotes
does not know he knows.*

28

One custom had not changed since my move to Factory Slide.
Singe had kept up the payments on the cold well in the kitchen.
Currently, that contained a keg of Weider Pale Ale, a Pular
Singe favorite. My taste runs to something slightly heavier but
the pale ale was plenty good after several days dry.

Singe and I both drew big mugs and backup pitchers before
we headed for her office, leaving Dean preparing a meal obviously meant for more people than me, Singe, and Morley. We
settled into the wonderful new furniture and began to scheme
out how this thing would go.

I said, "First thing, I want to catch up on what you did last
week, up on the north side." I took a sip of the pale. Tasty! "I
saw you. They probably didn't tell you what was going on."

"Not a lot, no. I took the job because you asked me to in
your note."

"And?"

"And what? You need to use small words and be very clear
with us Other Races."

Was she serious? Or just messing with me? Most of my
friends did. Singe had been an exception. "The tracking job.
Where did that take you? What did you find? That might give
me some clue about what I need to do to help Morley. I know
you found something because you're you, Pular Singe, the best
there is and maybe ever was."

"Wow! Doesn't that make me feel special?"

"Singe! Please."

"I keep forgetting that you're a gelding now. All right. Miss
Contague asked me to backtrack a team of goats. I did, into

Elf Town, to a small warehouse, where we found some totally ridiculous stuff."

"Meaning?"

"I can't think of a way to say it better."

"So just tell me."

"All right. The warehouse was maybe forty by sixty feet, two stories tall, all open inside. The goat cart left the warehouse through a pair of doors, each three feet wide and of normal height. They were barred from inside when we got there. Miss Contague's men broke in while Director Relway's Specials looked the other way."

Pardon me, children. I can make this easier for you both. It is a significant event that Garrett has no knowledge of beyond the fact that Miss Contague wanted that cart backtracked.

Singe said, "She knew goats are more pungent and persistent than people. Tracing them would be the easiest way to get a handle on our villain. May I get on with my report?"

No. Too much will be lost if you do it verbally.

Vaguely, I heard Singe use language unladylike even for a ratgirl, then found myself living a memory, riding behind her eyes from the moment she started the trace. Initially, there were flashes, excised moments, as the Dead Man skipped me along like a flat stone across a pond. The stills came closer and closer together. Then I was outside the aforementioned double doors. They had been painted recently, a repugnant flat olive with a repulsive odor.

Red tops stared the other way while Belinda's thugs broke through. Nobody came to protest the violation. Because the doors were standing open when they arrived the Specials were free to pass through and see if crimes were in progress inside.

Nobody was home. Belinda's men and the tin whistles alike produced lights, moved fast.

I was fascinated by the differences in how Singe and I sensed the world. For her, visual things were less crisp and weaker on color. Her depth of field was limited. She had trouble seeing clearly things that were more than fifty feet away. But the smells!

She lived in a rich, rich world of aroma.

Her brother once told me the sense of smell was dramatically more important to rats than to humans and most of the Other Races. I had believed him but not to this extent. The smells were overwhelming.

And, inside that place, they were not good. They were the smells of corrupting flesh, of chemicals and poisons, smells implanted in ratkind racial memory. A place that smelled like it was where Singe's ancestors had been created. That thought hit her the instant she stepped inside, before the first lamp shed light.

Light only confirmed truths evident to her genius nose.

I could be a little parasite swimming around in Singe's recollections but I could not fully appreciate her experience. My senses acknowledged much different priorities.

Once the raiders made light I saw that the place conformed to the dimensions Singe had reported. There were no internal walls except for the far corner on the left side where a space eight feet by ten was isolated behind partitions eight feet high. There was nothing overhead but framing for a peaked roof, the rooftree of which was twenty feet above the floor.

Ahead were numerous glass vats big enough to hold a human being. Several did. They could have been blown only by an artist with a knack for sorcery. Every thug and tin whistle instantly decided that discovering the provenance of the vats would lead them right to the devil who had created this abomination.

The intruders moved deeper into the warehouse. The stench of corruption grew thicker. Scores of dead flies floated in the solution in those vats without closed tops. There were no active flies. They came in the front door but did not make it all the way to the rotting flesh.

That did come from dead people. A twenty foot long, massive oak workbench stood against the back wall. It boasted three corpses in the process of disassembly. Extra parts lay scattered about. At the right-hand end of the bench sat the biggest vat in the place, only as tall as the table but three feet wide and six feet long. Scrap pieces could be swept off into a solution that had to be something ferocious—though becoming slightly diluted. There were chunks of inadequately consumed big bones in there.

Singe had shut down all but the observer part of her mind.

She handled the horror better than I would have. Certainly better than Belinda's soldiers and the tin whistles did. Several left and would not come back. Others did return but absent their latest several meals. Only the Windwalker, Furious Tide of Light, seemed unaffected. She moved through the place slowly, examining everything.

Experiencing all that through Singe's nose was no joy, though to the primal rats from which she descended stinky meat had meant food.

Singe paid little attention to the Windwalker. I was unable to watch the lethal waif saunter about, surrounded by a ten foot come-no-closer spell. Singe was interested only in the manufactory of horror.

That was what she had found. A place where monsters were made from pieces of dead people. It might be the foulest necromantic den TunFaire had turned up in centuries.

I felt frustrated. She didn't just pay no attention to the Windwalker, she didn't poke where I would have poked. Though she did better than I might have, really. I would have focused on the Windwalker. She was remarkable in so many ways, including by being off the Hill, one of TunFaire's top sorcerers. And, once upon a time, she had made it plain that she was inclined to stand very close to a certain professional investigator.

Garrett!

Nothing like a hammer between the eyes to make you concentrate.

Singe left the others for the walled-off section. It had a makeshift door that could be latched from either side. It was ajar. She pushed it open. "Can someone bring a light?"

One arrived quickly. Singe and the light bringer entered the room. The Windwalker followed. She did something mystic to create a better light.

The space was a child's room. Dirty clothes were scattered everywhere. An unmade bed was occupied by a large, tattered stuffed bear. Clutter was everywhere. It included moldy remnants of unfinished meals. The tin whistle with the lantern observed, "Somebody likes stuffed critters." There had to be fifteen of those, mostly large. The clothing was girl stuff, in what seemed to be a variety of adolescent sizes. Singe never actively examined those.

Singe sniffed. The Windwalker began an intense visual examination. The tin whistle asked, "He kept a kid prisoner?" Jumping to the obvious conclusion. "We need to get this guy."

Furious Tide of Light said, "Would you step outside, officer? Watch from the doorway if you like. Our first task will be to find out who lived here." She let Singe stay. Singe was the miracle girl.

The miracle girl didn't pay attention to what the Windwalker was doing. Near as I could figure, the woman was doing the same as Singe, only sniffing for magic.

And that was that. Furious Tide of Light decided that the place ought to be evacuated and cordoned off. A guard would be posted and no one would be allowed in except at Prince Rupert's direction. Singe learned what she could but had to leave with everyone else. She reported to Belinda, then came home. Nothing more had been heard.

Amongst the things I found while Miss Contague was with us was an angry recollection of being asked to drop her private investigation by the Crown Prince.

29

I said, "That was amazing stuff. But what does it have to do with Morley?"

For that connection you must be patient. I have begun exploration but the work goes like trying to fell a tree by gnawing through the trunk.

Singe rubbed her temples. "That was no fun. I hope that is the last time we will go over it."

I have it memorized, now. I can relive it whenever I want. I will not trouble you again.

I started asking questions. I have that habit. Singe said, "You saw what I saw. You have every scrap of information I did. I need to see my brother before I get too giddy."

"Speaking of John Stretch. Some of his people were outside the henhouse with you. What was that all about?"

"Belinda planned to use them somehow. And Humility had them there to look out for me, too. Belinda changed her mind and paid them off."

"After she got warned off."

I might want to talk to her about that.

No. She would wonder how you knew. Then she would conclude that her hairnet is not infallible.

Singe got up. "Shut the door behind me." And, "I won't be long."

She wasn't. I was still standing there, enjoying a mind-sharing experience with the Dead Man, cataloging faces in the street. I watched Singe approach with two brawny ratwomen. Old Bones told me, *Nothing remarkable out there. One watcher from Miss Contague's enterprise whose sole task is to see who else is watching.*

"That's it? There's nobody from the Al-Khar?" I opened up for Singe.

Does the woman up the street still maintain a Watch outpost?

"Get with the times. It's not the Watch anymore. It's the Civil Guard these days."

And the answer to the question? The woman up the street?

"Mrs. Cardonlos? Singe? Is Mrs. Cardonlos still a stringer for the red tops?"

"Yes. But since you have been gone she does not have a regular team staying there. She rents rooms for real, now. Let me get these two started on Mr. Dotes."

The burly, badly dressed ratwomen looked at Singe like she was a goddess. They'd never seen a ratperson in a conversation of equals with a human. And Singe was female!

One eyed me like she thought there was something wrong with me.

I followed but stayed in the hallway while Singe explained the job. The ratwomen had done this kind of work before. They had no trouble understanding. Cued by the Dead Man, Dean brought a tray with food for the help as well as Morley.

Before he went back to the kitchen Dean offered a wan smile and said, "The excitement is back."

Not really. We were going to sit here and do every bit of the nothing we had done at Fire and Ice. Everything else would be in the hands of others. Professionals. And criminals.

A warn-off by the gods themselves would not keep Belinda from digging.

I hoped no one on the law-and-order side pushed her. She was crazy enough to push back.

Dean went to bed before the ratwomen finished. I helped Singe clean up; then we resumed gossiping and honoring Weider's beer.

It didn't take much of the latter to slow me down.

I meant to quiz Singe on how I could handle Tinnie. But I stayed sober enough to realize that was stupid. Singe was barely an adult. She wasn't human. And Tinnie was unique, possibly unfathomable by Tinnie Tate herself.

Eventually I dragged myself upstairs. My room was the way I had left it, except that somebody had cleaned it and had made up the bed with fresh linens.

Singe was altogether too efficient. And was, probably, resenting my intrusion into her quiet, orderly world.

30

There were four sleeping rooms on the second floor of my house. The biggest, stretching across the front, was mine. Dean's room spanned the house in back, except for a storage closet and space taken by the stairs. Singe occupied the largest of the remaining rooms, which sat on the west side of the central hallway. In area, it almost matched Dean's. The fourth room—our guest room—contained a seldom-used bed and lots of stuff that should have been thrown away. We used to hide somebody there once in a while.

There were two real, glazed windows in my room. They were not barred because there was no easy way for villains to get at them. Both looked down on Macunado Street. The one to the east might as well have not existed. I've never opened it and seldom looked out it. The other, beside the head of my bed, had seen some action. Once upon a time I would stare out it while I ruminated. Tonight, as always in warm weather, it was open a few inches so cool night air could get inside.

I liked sleeping in a cool room.

I had the opportunity that night. The temperature plummeted after sundown. At one point I wakened and added a light blanket to the sheet that had been adequate earlier. Later, I wakened again and used the chamber pot, setting some beer free. Then I wakened a third time, needing a heavier cover and with my bladder ready to explode.

The sky had been overcast during the afternoon and evening. That had cleared. The light of an unseen moon splashed the rooftops and turned them into a weird faerie landscape.

My aim was less than perfect. I missed the pot completely

to start. Disgusting. I gobbled something incoherent meant to be an appeal to the Dead Man. No telling what I thought he could do. I got no response, anyway.

Then I saw the ghost.

The specter drifted down out of the night and came toward my window like a vampire in a dream. "But vampires don't really fly," I reminded myself. "They just jump really far." Vampires can leap for altitude or distance but they don't flit like bats. Nor do they turn into bats, much as they might want the prey community to think they do.

I calmed myself, completed my business, formulated a plan for cleaning up before Singe or Dean discovered the evidence. Then I checked the window. And nearly panicked.

The flying woman was still there, hair and clothing streaming in the breeze. Her dress was something light and white that, in moonlight, made me think of fashionable grave wear. And reminded me of what I had seen vampire brides wearing in the nests in the adventure where I first butted heads with Tinnie Tate.

My ears kicked in. I heard my name. Then my brain shed sleep enough to put it all together. That was the Windwalker, Furious Tide of Light. And she wanted in.

So, naturally, I remembered that vampires, like most evils, have to be invited in the first time. And I recalled my reaction to this woman last time our paths crossed.

She didn't look like she had seduction in mind. She looked troubled.

I raised the window as high as it would go, which was not much. I turned up my bedside lamp. The Windwalker, being a wisp of a woman, drifted through the narrow opening.

I settled on the edge of my bed, waited, hoping she would feel no need to pace over there by the chamber pot. She glanced around, shoved my dirty clothes off the only chair, settled. She turned the lamp back down. "A watcher might wonder."

Assuming he failed to notice a flying woman in her nightgown sliding in the window. "You didn't ride anything this time."

"A broomstick isn't necessary." She noted my interest in her apparel. "The King held a ball at Summer Hall. I was invited. He has aspirations." She spoke softly.

So. Not a nightgown. "I see." I matched her soft voice. Singe would invite herself to join us if she heard us talking. "And now you're here."

"Yes. It was on the way."

Only by the most circuitous route.

31

"I'm frightened. Strange things are happening. They're outside my control. I don't deal well with that sort of circumstance."

She spoke like she wanted me to understand, not like she wanted to be comforted, which was how my head worked when she was around.

"I'm lost but I'm listening."

"Otherwise, I'm not sure what my problem is. Actually, I just know that one is shaping up. Besides being able to stroll through the air I'm strongly intuitive, but randomly. I can't control it and don't dare rely on it. Right now I intuit that something abidingly dark is afoot. Powerful people are trying to cover it up. I can't understand why."

"You wouldn't be one of those yourself, would you?"

She seemed genuinely confused. "What do you mean?"

"Last time I was involved in weird goings-on involving secret labs and illegal experiments, your daughter and her friends were in the middle of it. You and your father went balls to the wall to make sure they didn't get eaten alive for their foolishness."

"Kevans isn't involved this time. I don't think any of the Faction kids are."

Kevans' gang of misfit genius friends called themselves the Faction.

"How come it sounds like you're trying to convince yourself?"

"I admit it. Kevans does lie to me. When I see her. Which is hardly ever anymore."

"She's not living with you?"

"She has her own place. I don't think she learned much last

time. And I'm scared that some of her other friends might be involved. Or might know who is. And Kevans wouldn't say."

"Teen solidarity. But, involved in what?"

"Exactly."

"Teen solidarity usually collapses in the face of real consequences."

"I don't think Kevans is involved." She was waffling based on wishful thinking. "But she might be close to someone who is. I don't want to press her. Our relationship is complicated and fragile."

"I know. But how come you're here?"

"Let me tell you about my week." Which she did, wasting few words. "When the business on the edge of Elf Town broke Prince Rupert asked me to investigate. That ended after we found the warehouse where somebody was using parts from dead bodies to assemble custom zombies."

"Singe told me."

"I thought she would. She got warned off before I did."

"Uhm?"

"What did she tell you about that hellhole?"

I sketched Singe's report.

Furious Tide of Light said, "The girl who stayed in that room and slept with that stuffed bear was no captive."

Singe was sure the room's inmate had been a girl, too. "Singe said she was young."

"In terms of socialization, possibly. But no child would have the strength and knowledge to do what she was doing."

I ruminated briefly, then said, "An old woman. A goat cart. Something that behaved like and might have been a giant slug. Two dead men, cut down by sorcery . . ."

"Who have vanished. I was kept away from them. The old woman vanished, too. Cart and goats have gone the way of the dead men."

"And nothing has happened since." I guessed because I hadn't even been fed what the mushrooms get.

"Nothing."

"But you're worried about Kevans. You've developed some disturbing suspicions."

"Not really. I have some fears. I've been unable to support them, which is a good thing. I am intuitively convinced that we're dealing with someone young, female, powerful, rogue, and entirely amoral, though."

"I see. But back to basics. How come you're here? What do you want from me?" I was determined to make a fully adult effort to remain faithful to the redhead in my life.

"I want to hire you. I think. I remember you from before." The lighting was feeble but it was enough to reveal her embarrassment.

"I'm taken."

Wan smile, without comment, in a manner that said exactly what she was thinking. My defenses were male defenses. And she did have a power besides intuition and flight. She could excite the statue of a dead general if she chose to turn it on.

I had seen her reduce a crowd of skilled tradesmen to drooling idiots with no conscious effort.

But tonight she was totally serious.

I wished I knew her situation better. She said she was estranged from her father and daughter. How much so? Her father had run every detail of her life, back when, despite her being one of the most powerful sorcerers in the kingdom. She had not been long on social skills. I couldn't imagine yesterday's Furious Tide of Light surviving on her own.

I shifted the subject. "What about the other Faction girls? I don't recall them that well. Could one of them be our resurrection man?"

"I only knew the ones that came to our house. They were all odd. There were more than I saw. Kids came and went. Some never really belonged to the clique."

"And some were cross-dressers. Including Kevans."

"That, too."

"Any of those kids connected to the Royal Family?"

She shrugged, not surprised. She had considered the question. "Not that I know of."

"What's the mood on the Hill?"

She frowned. Maybe she hadn't thought about that.

"This will reflect on all of you. You want to police yourselves. This makes it look like you need outside help. The villain fled to the Hill twice."

"No. Toward the Hill."

I had to give her that. The monster may have done that as misdirection. "What are your neighbors saying?"

"I don't know. I don't have much to do with them. I'm not comfortable with the ways they think."

The mental work behind the mad laboratory only exaggerated the attitudes of most Hill folk. Furious Tide of Light was the most sane and least dangerous of any I'd ever met.

"All right. Let's lay it out. Straight up honest. What do you want?"

"I don't want to be shut out. I guess Prince Rupert doesn't trust me after the thing with the giant bugs."

"Understandable. That involved another secret lab."

"I know. I see why he might think what he's thinking. That doesn't change what I feel. I want you to help find out what's really going on."

"All right. You're worried about your daughter. But why not stand back and let the professionals do their job?"

She did not offer an answer.

"So. You're not just worried. You want to be a step ahead so you can cover for her again. Even if she's behind the ugliest criminal incident we've seen in years."

"Yes. Sort of."

"Then Prince Rupert did the right thing when he shut you out."

"She's my baby, Garrett. I can't just let her . . ."

"And you can't keep covering. If she can't get a handle on the concept of consequences she'll just keep getting into trouble. You saw the inside of that warehouse. And six people died in two days. You can't make excuses and cover up something like that."

She shrugged. She was near the point where many women turn on the waterworks. She refrained.

32

A tree fell in the wilderness inside my head. Lucky me, I was there to hear the thud. "You've been thinking about this since you saw that stuffed bear."

She admitted, "Your ratgirl friend made me think you were more involved than you said."

"Singe was working for Belinda Contague. She's an independent operator. I don't live here anymore. Which you know. Because you checked up."

She nodded.

"Then you know my real part in everything."

"You're really babysitting your friend."

I nodded.

"Don't you want to know who did it?"

I nodded again. "But I've gotten patient in my old age. I won't do anything till Morley is ready. If the Guard or the Syndicate haven't dealt with it by then we'll see what we can do. It seems odd for you to be pushing revenge when you're afraid your daughter might be involved."

"I don't know what I'm doing. I'm scared and out of my depth. You're the only one I know who does what you do."

I believed her. Including that she would hire me when I might head straight for the kid she wanted to protect. She had been sheltered her whole life.

"So you figure on defying the Prince—for Kevans' sake, even though the best thing now would be to let everything take its course."

"I don't know what I'm doing! I never learned how. All I've ever had to do is be the Windwalker, Furious Tide of Light. I can do that. I can scatter an enemy regiment. I can bring down a castle. But I never learned how to raise a daughter. I never dealt with the quotidian world. Barate handled that so I could focus on being a prodigy."

I wanted to ask about her father but suspected that he would be an unwelcome subject.

"Let's back up to when you got the idea that Kevans—or the Faction—might be involved." I would be covering ground already trodden but she seemed inclined to lurk in the shadow of the truth, now.

"In that warehouse. In that room. That stuffed animal belonged to Kevans. Though I haven't seen it for years."

"You're sure?" I reminded myself that the simplest and most obvious explanation is usually the right one.

"There were other things that reminded me of the Faction. Rupert got the same feeling." So she had seen the Prince at her party.

"You need to talk to Kevans. Straight up, woman to woman, no drama. Then see Rupert again. Be square with him. He'll be square with you if he's really a friend. You might even talk it over with Barate. You're operating on emotion right now. Mostly on fear. You need good information. And you need to decide where you stand on the crime itself, personalities aside."

"I hoped you could gather the information."

She wasn't hearing me. "Don't take the dark side in this. It will just destroy you."

Her jaw tightened. She was going to get stubborn.

"Talk to those people. You have to realize that they'll go hard after whoever created that lab. The Hill is probably a turned-up ants' nest. Nasty people are going to start poking haystacks and turning over rocks."

Her expression told me that she hadn't really considered the reaction of her own class. Those people take a dim and lethal view of rogue sorcery.

"You're sure you won't help me?"

"I can't. Not how you want. Not however much I would like to. I have to stay here, with my friend. That goes to the bedrock of who I am. I'm here even though it could mean the end of my relationship with a woman who . . ."

She cut me off. She didn't need to hear that. "All right. I won't put you in harm's way. I'll do the digging and use you as a sounding board. You just tell me what to do and how to do it."

Startled, I realized that we were not alone. I'd caught the ghost of a sense of amusement from down below.

"I've told you the first thing. The most important thing. Talk to people. An honest exchange could save us all a ton of trouble."

She didn't like that idea.

"If this is going to happen you have to put aside your quirks. You have to gut it up and go face-to-face. Promise me you'll see Rupert, Barate, and Kevans if you can, tomorrow."

I felt a ghostly touch of approval.

This would be interesting. I could play Dead Man in the web, directing the hoof work while I crocheted doilies.

"All right. I can't go out but I can help. You ready to put money into this?"

"As much as it takes."

"Curb the emotion. Emotion won't solve anything. Besides seeing the Prince, Barate, and Kevans, here's what I need you to do."

The intensity with which she listened was embarrassing.

33

I was groggy from lack of sleep when I toddled down for breakfast. I missed a step, lost my balance, and might have busted something if my flailing right hand had not snagged the rail on the left side of the stair. I ended up on my belly, shaking, aching in one bruised knee and embarrassed when Singe appeared at the foot of the stair.

"You all right? What happened?"

"Gravity ambush. I think I'm good. Though I might end up wearing a peg leg." I was starting to hurt where I banged my left hip on the edge of a step. "Let's see if I can make it the rest of the way without killing myself." I turned loose of the rail.

"If you are going to kill yourself, don't do it here. I'm too weak, and Dean is too feeble to shift a corpse."

I sensed amusement from old butterbutt.

Dean had come out to investigate. "We could cut him up into smaller pieces."

"That would make a mess. But we could infiltrate him into the resurrection scheme that's got everybody excited."

"Everybody?" I made it down without further mishap.

Dean said, "Tea's ready. Sausages and rolls are warming." He slipped back into the kitchen.

Singe said, "Good thing you weren't carrying your pot when you did that."

"Yeah. Good thing. But why would I be . . ."

"Because Dean is having trouble getting up and down. He needs to keep both hands on the rails."

"Got it. Now tell me about everybody being excited."

"The news about the murders and the resurrection lab got out."

Not surprising. Too many people knew. Which I mentioned.

"You're right. I hear the public reaction has been strong. Maybe that's because they've gotten spoiled, shaded by the Civil Guard and the Unpublished Committee. Unorganized crime isn't a commonplace anymore. Something like this spooks people. They want it fixed. Fast."

We moved into the kitchen. Dean was just settling my breakfast onto the massive little table. He placed a bowl of stewed apples opposite me, Singe's favorite food. My hip bone barked when I sat down.

I asked, "How is Morley?" I'd drop in as soon as my belly was full.

"Unchanged. But healing. Doing well, physically."

"But?"

"Something inside doesn't want to come back. So I'm told."

"He did try, early on, at the other place." I had a momentary notion about him getting lost in Faerie, a willing captive of illusion.

"And then he decided not to try anymore."

"Is *he* working on it?"

"Of course. He says it might take a long time. It's some of the finest, most delicate work he's ever done. What do you think of the rolls?"

"I like them. Spicy. Sweeter than I'm used to."

"They're from a specialty bakery I found in Fointain Lane. Looks like you're done. Get on with your chores. You slept in so you've only got an hour before the meeting."

"What chores? What meeting?"

"We talked about this. You need to make up your room, deal with your pot, and gather your dirty clothing so it can be laundered. Then you have to deal with the trash. The dustman's wagon will come through the alley this afternoon."

Changes, changes. They come in a blink of the eye these days.

My eyes must have been the size of saucers. I got the sense that Old Bones would have busted out laughing if he wasn't so far gone he no longer exercised a respiratory function.

Welcome to the new regime in the house on Macunado Street.

Like the new regime in TunFaire as a whole, writ small.

"What meeting?" I asked again, maybe a little too plaintively.

"I sent for some people who can help the Windwalker." I had not breathed a word about my night visitor. "You'll have to acquaint them with the facts of the situation. And you'll need to make sure they understand possible ramifications if they do get involved."

"All right, you. What have you done with Pular Singe? And what *are* you talking about?"

"I just told you."

"But . . . If I wanted my life all planned and managed I could've just stayed on Factory Slide."

Oh, my! What did I just say?

"I am not running your life. I'm making it move more efficiently. This meeting had to happen, sooner or later. You would have gone at it piecemeal, catch as catch can."

"Exactly what I mean. Running my . . ."

Children, enough! Garrett, please resist becoming all macho-male excited because someone is thoughtful enough to ease your burdens. He put some power behind that. It was a command. *Pour yourself a fresh mug, then join me for a moment before you start your chores.*

This was not going to be a good day. I resented every minute already. I'm not self-employed because I care about efficiency. I'm interested in not having to do more than it takes to get by. Which was why I moved out of my mother's house as soon as I could.

Was that why she always favored Mikey?

Could be, come to think.

34

"Tell me something that makes sense," I told the Dead Man as I settled facing him. Shivering. My teacup sent up clouds of steam.

Life and afterlife have become more structured. Only you seem to consider that a bad thing.

"The world hasn't changed *that* much, has it? Everybody still wants to unload on me."

He was amused. He did not argue. I heard my mother telling me I had a wonderful mind. Why couldn't I just *try* to live up to my potential?

The amusement deepened, still absent comment.

"Did you find anything interesting in the Windwalker's mind?"

She believes you would make an excellent husband.

"What?" There was a hit from the blind side.

I know. If she can delude herself that deeply in a personal matter how can we possibly credit anything else inside her scrambled brain?

That was not what my expletive meant. "Are you making up for time lost?"

No. We have no time for amusements. You have chores that need doing. Pay attention. Feel sorry for yourself later. The Windwalker was, overall, as honest as she could be. She is frantic about her daughter. She is in the cleft stick of a quandary that no parent should have to face. Her only child may be a monster in human guise.

I could see the quandary. It might take a stronger spirit than mine to roll over on my own family, though that would save the lives of strangers.

You have done the equivalent. You have the strength to champion the right. The Windwalker's deepest fear is that her daughter may not only be a villain. She may have created corpses for her experiments.

What could I say to that?

Young, undamaged corpses would be at a premium. Many lost souls roam the byways of this city and are unlikely to be missed. Mr. Dotes could have stumbled onto the harvesting in progress. Nothing I have found in his mind rules that out.

"Look, I remember that kid. Her head was messed up because of her family situation but she wasn't homicidal. She was creative. Weird creative, like Kip. Not deadly weird."

You are correct. To that point. But people can change. When they do, it is usually for the worse.

"I take it you haven't had much luck with Morley."

Very little. He is remarkably closed. If he were an animal I might think he was hibernating. Inasmuch as he is intelligent I have to believe that something was done to keep him untouchable.

"He might never come back?"

He will be back. I promise. As the challenge grows bigger I become more determined. I will build him a path of escape. Henceforth, do not be startled if I reexamine every second of your recollections of your time together before you came here.

Clever Garrett got it in one. Morley had started to wake up. Then he had gone away. "Belinda's healer. We need to find him."

Yes. Though I was thinking about what tried to get in through the window.

"Maybe he just decided to dig a hole and pull it in after him."

That would not be in character. Enough. Do your chores. I have a visitor arriving momentarily. She is not comfortable in your presence.

That had to be his pet priestess, Penny Dreadful. He had taken Penny under his intellectual wing when she was little more than a toddler. He had mentored her ever since.

I considered lying back in the shadows at the foot of the stairs just to get a look but thought better of it. I was upstairs being domestic when Penny arrived.

35

I was still upstairs, taking a nap. Singe invited herself into my room. She poked me with a stiffened finger. Impossible! It couldn't be! Not across species as divergent as redheads and artificially intelligent rats.

"Ouch! Once was enough."

"Drag your lazy ass out and go downstairs. People are waiting. Their time is valuable, too. Look at this mess. You didn't do anything."

"I made the bed."

She snorted derisively.

"And I considered the possibility of changing the lock on the front door," I grumped, sourly enough for her to take me serious for a second. "That might get me some peace."

"I despair of seeing you grow mature and responsible."

"I don't. It isn't on my agenda."

"Be that as it may, you need to go downstairs. Otherwise, those people will drink all the beer and eat everything in the pantry."

"A blatant provocation of my natural inclination toward frugality."

"The correct word is parsimony, but if you prefer the illusion of thrift, indulge."

I was out of practice. I had to settle for being proud of me because I did not let my frustration overcome my self-control. I swung my feet off my bed, planted them firmly on the floor. "Look at me. I'm on my way. Now would be a good time for you to get yourself a head start."

Clever Singe realized this was not the best time for further nagging. Maybe she got private advice from the Dead Man. She scooted out.

I saw Dean leave the kitchen with refreshments as I descended the stairs. He staggered under the weight of the provisions. An absence of cups, mugs, plates, milk, and sugar bowls suggested that this was not his first run. The natural parsimony that Singe had mentioned kicked in—as she had intended.

A dull roar of conversation came from the Dead Man's room.

I followed Dean, wondering if I hadn't made some mad, long-term mistake when I took Singe in.

The Dead Man's room was wall to wall with bodies and faces. There was Saucerhead Tharpe, showing a touch of gray, with an extra layer of muscle around his midriff. There was Singe's brother Pound Humility, better known as John Stretch, gaudy in the latest ratman style. Jon Salvation was there, looking cocky and prosperous. Why the hell was he here? Looking for an angle for a new play? Sarge, one of Morley's oldest henchmen, stood alone, vaguely confused. Playmate looked awful. He had lost a hundred pounds. He was as gaunt as a man dying of starvation.

There were others, in disguise, maybe to avoid being identified by watchers outside.

Belinda had done a creditable job of turning herself into a slim, handsome dandy with a dark dash of a mustache, reminding me of the chap squirreled away in my old office.

General Westman Block looked like a wino who had wandered in unnoticed while the door was open. He looked confused. He was not well-known but everyone here had run into him before. No one seemed troubled.

There were people I did not recognize. I took it on faith that the Dead Man needed them.

I looked for a special one with red hair and came up with a count one short. Singe saw me checking. "I sent word. Maybe she'll come later."

I got no chance to respond. My own respite from recognition ended. People swarmed me. Saucerhead said, "Man, I didn't hardly know you, all dressed weird, and shit."

Jon Salvation stroked his pointy little beard, which wasn't the same color as his hair, and said something about me having adapted my fashion flare to something showing a distinct feminine influence.

A third kind soul mentioned that I was developing a pot. Someone else said, "That happens when you don't got to work for a living no more."

To which Saucerhead responded, "Garrett never did do no more work than it took to keep from starving. He just had a run of luck." Stated with a touch of envy. Like me, Tharpe worked as little as possible but his luck never shined. Too often he had nothing more than the clothes on his back.

36

Amongst those people who stayed quiet and didn't move much were Sarge and Playmate. A good look at Play left me shocked. Not only had the man lost a huge amount of weight, he stooped to where he was no taller than me. He looked like he had to deal with bad chronic pain.

He does. Had I been aware of his situation I would have made something good happen for him, long ago. Without you here these people never visit. I remain unaware of what is happening in their lives. On a positive note, I have gotten Miss Contague to send for the healer who worked on Mr. Dotes.

"Clever. Two birds."

Probably just one. Playmate's cancer appears to be advanced.

I could say nothing more out loud.

I shook hands, slapped backs, exchanged hugs. I asked Jon Salvation where his shark woman was. He astonished me by reporting, "I don't think she was invited."

"You came anyway?" I blurted.

"I do things like that these days. You'll find me more independent than the Remora you remember." He had been called the Remora because he swam in the slipstream of his girlfriend, Winger, betraying no personality of his own. "I expect she'll turn up anyway. She'll be sure the lack of an invite was an oversight."

I looked over at Singe. She was doing a credible job of being the lady of the house, seeing to our guests while being smoothly sociable. Even the prejudiced were unable to consider her as just a ratwoman.

Neither Belinda in disguise nor General Block in disguise

did any socializing. With the exception of brief exchanges with John Stretch, neither spoke to anyone.

The more I looked around the bigger the crowd seemed to be. I kept spotting people I didn't know. I saw John Stretch associates helping Dean with the refreshments. I saw people I did know but would not expect at a let's-decide-what-we'll-do party themed round Morley Dotes.

Singe's office was open to the crowd, too. People drifted back and forth in search of conversation. Morley himself had been declared off-limits. Three of John Stretch's worst villains were in there and had permission to hurt people who wouldn't take a hint.

There were exceptions, one-on-one and closely watched. Sarge. Saucerhead. Belinda. Me.

Once I lost my appeal to the mob, Belinda and the General drifted closer. Block shook my hand, told me I was looking good, then said how wonderful it was that I was showing some civic interest again. I kept a straight face and did not ask when he thought that I ever demonstrated any civic mindedness. He asked, "Can we slip into your kitchen for a second? This isn't private enough."

"How can I say no?" Though there wouldn't be much privacy back there, either, what with Dean and his ratfolk assistants underfoot.

This may be important. Do not waste time fencing, Garrett. I sense the imminent arrival of someone who may be Miss Contague's healer. He is very closed. Also, the population of loafers has begun to grow out on Macunado Street.

We stepped into the kitchen, conveniently as Dean and his helpers trained out with trays that looked like each ratman was carrying his own weight in drinks and treats.

I began to suffer grim thoughts about how the Dead Man better not be only plundering minds, he had best be bringing the right people together to talk about what needed doing. And he had better be putting the right ideas into the right minds while he was at it. Because this was going to bankrupt me if it went on for long.

I drew a mug, asked, "Fill you up?" Headshakes. I settled at the overloaded table. "Talk to me."

The General seemed disappointed.

He had changed. The weary but determined middle-aged functionary had become a worn-out elder bureaucrat.

"Garrett, I don't know what to say. I hear you've changed. I'm told you've turned into a model subject of the Karentine Crown."

"I always was."

"Pardon me? You were always a stubborn, obstructionist asshole. You had no interest whatsoever in forwarding the welfare of the commonality."

What the hell? "You mean I wasn't excited about 'forwarding' the cause once Deal Relway defined it for me."

Do not argue. Accept. From his viewpoint he is stating one hundred percent truth.

Meaning he got to define the welfare of the commonality. "I love you, too."

No two people see everything the same. You know that. At the moment it is important that we not antagonize our allies simply for the pleasure of being difficult.

Hang on. Even my partner thinks I refuse to cooperate with the tin whistles, and hold back information, just to tweak them?

"Garrett? You here?" the General asked. "Or have you died and gone to hell?"

"I'm sorry. I was in the throes of what might have been a grand epiphany." On the other hand, it might have been breakfast backing up. "What do you need?"

"We Guardsmen have a morale problem that is becoming a moral problem."

"I hope that's not contagious."

"Exactly. All the good we've done could start to unravel if this mess keeps on the way it has been."

"You lost me."

"Will you . . . ?" He glared in exasperation.

"Ever since we met you've accused me of stonewalling or deliberately holding things up. You were right. When it was in the interest of my client. Maybe one time in ten. I knew why you were barking, then. This time I don't. All I'm doing is protecting a friend who came within a frog's feather of getting himself stabbed to death. In case somebody tries to finish the job. I've been told by half the people here and some who aren't that this is all I'm allowed to do. It's all I intend to do. And at least one woman doesn't want me doing that much."

"Touchy."

"Damned straight."

"Why do you have all these people here, then?"

"I don't. I didn't invite them. Did you get an invitation from me?"

"No. But this is your house."

"It's a place where I'm staying because I thought Morley would be safer here than anywhere else."

He gave me a dubious look.

"The first I knew about this was just a while ago when Singe woke me up from a perfectly beautiful nap and told me to come help."

"You always blow a creditable cloud of smoke."

"Again, what do you want?"

"We've been warned off this case."

"You're going to let it slide? You lost people."

"Garrett, can the shit. For the rest of us this isn't about Morley Dotes. About him and his problems I don't much care."

"Tell him that."

"Gladly. Is he up for an interview?"

"He's in a coma."

"Too bad. But his testimony isn't critical. What is critical would be our incorruptibility. When we started out Deal and I were promised that no one would be above the law. Not even the Royal Family. Prince Rupert stood behind us when we stepped on sensitive toes. But this time he's telling us to back off. We have to let it go. The same word has gone out to the Syndicate."

"Who has the drag to bully the Crown Prince?"

"Exactly. We mean to find out."

"You're not going to back off?"

"We're going to be less obviously vigorous. Unobtrusive. But the more pressure we get the more we'll dig. Same pertains for the Syndicate, I suspect. You push the Contagues, they push back."

"You think dread of an explosion in production of dead bodies might be why the Prince wants to stand down?"

"No. I think somebody on the Hill, somebody who can

make even Rupert shit his knickers, wants the thing left alone.
I'll even go so far as to guess that the Hill as a whole wants it
left alone."

"Because the villains might be some of them?"

"In part. But more because if we poke our noses in very far
we're likely to turn up all sorts of things they don't want the
public to know."

I poured myself some tea. Dean was outside the kitchen
door telling me to hurry up. He had to get back to work.

I raised a questioning eyebrow.

Block said, "I'll stipulate that most Hill folk are as dis-
tressed by the warehouse as the rest of us. But they want to
handle it themselves."

"So let them."

"And next time somebody wants to shut the Guard out?
Next time somebody wants to handle justice privately?"

Block had a fierce case of the same disease that ruled Relway. Most of the time it did more good than bad.

"All I can do is wish you luck. I'll be right here babysitting."

He didn't believe a word.

Sometimes there's no point trying to communicate with
some people. They live everything inside their heads. Outside
things that don't fit get ignored.

Westman Block was a good man. I liked him. But he could
frustrate me like almost no one else but Tinnie.

"Come on in, Dean."

Dean burst in and got cracking. He was determined to ren-
der me destitute before the sun went down.

37

Belinda isolated me, in with Morley, amongst the deaf ratmen. "They insist that we back off. That we have to let this alone."

"They? We?"

"Don't play word games."

"I'm not. You know what I mean. Nobody has told *me* not to do anything. And the only *we* I'm part of is me and Morley."

"Then I'd have to ask why most everyone you know by name is here. I even saw that poisoner, Kolda, a minute ago."

"He's not a poisoner." Distracted. "I don't know why you're all here. I had nothing to do with that. Like I told the General."

She didn't believe me either. Someday I'll make a huge score because nobody will take me at face value. I could loot the Royal Mint, then run around yelling about how it was me that done it.

I did know what was going on. Singe and the Dead Man had cooked a plan to investigate out of my house. They would use people we had worked with in the past. I found it disconcerting that they weren't troubled by a Hill interest potent enough to make Prince Rupert back off. Old Bones must have seen a way to get away with defying that which must not be defied.

This was shaping up to be what I'd had in mind when I'd visited with the Windwalker. Who was not around today.

I asked, "Is that healer ever going to come?"

"Are you kidding? After what I paid him before?"

"And he isn't worried about my friend in the other room?"

"He doesn't know. I told him you spilled the medicine. That

we'll want more. But first he has to take another look at Morley. I'm pretty sure there's something more wrong than what he thought before."

"And if he's a villain?"

"We'll know that straight off, won't we?"

We contemplated our mutual friend. Morley looked as peaceful as a man in a coffin.

I kept wondering why it was taking the healer so long to show.

He is out there. All the traffic makes him nervous. He does not like that but cannot shake his greed. He will come into the trap eventually.

My impatience faded. I just worried about Morley. Till my mind wandered off to Factory Slide.

An unexpected voice asked, "Garrett, are you all right?"

I looked up. "Gilbey?" Manville Gilbey and his recently acquired wife, Heather, were framed in the doorway. Gilbey was the number-two man in the Weider brewing empire. He seemed concerned. "I'm all right."

"We haven't seen you at the brewery lately. When I heard about your open house I thought we'd stop by and see what your situation is."

"It's marginal despair." I glanced at Morley. "What do you need to know?"

"Nothing, now. We've been circulating long enough to get a flavor. Max will stand behind you."

Of course, because Max Weider didn't like folks involved in illegal experimental sorcery. Several of his family were murdered by shape-shifting things created in abandoned beer vats. Max wouldn't mind exterminating the whole tribe of sorcerers.

Heather Gilbey was usually more forthcoming and social, naturally, than Manville, but today she just smiled and kept her mouth shut.

Gilbey told me, "Take care doing what you need to do, Garrett. We value you." He eyed Morley, then the ratmen with illegal weaponry. He knew Morley. Morley's restaurant was across from Max Weider's World Theater, where Heather was manager.

Heather gave me a slight smile before she stepped out of sight. I liked her fine but she was high on Tinnie's list. Tinnie had acted in several Jon Salvation plays. She had gotten a big head. A huge head. Heather wasted no time letting her know that her talents might be better appreciated elsewhere, a fierce stroke since the World is the only theater where female actresses are not expected to have other commerce with audience members.

Tinnie is not accustomed to failure and has almost no capacity for accepting criticism.

38

I had some quiet time with my friend, then, sharing the space with John Stretch's goons. I stared hard, willing Morley to come back.

Belinda stepped in. "No change?"

"None. There's definitely something not right."

"We should learn a lot from the healer."

"You sure he doesn't know about Old Bones?"

"Believe it or not, Garrett, almost nobody outside your acquaintance does. Particularly since you've been inactive for so long."

Things do get forgotten quickly in TunFaire. Maybe that's an urban survival skill.

"The Dead Man is barely a spook story. He's something kids scare each other with. Nobody really believes that he exists."

"Interesting."

"I have to go soon. But not right away. I want to be here for the healer."

"If he ever gets here."

"He'll show up. He might not come inside if he doesn't see me."

He would—unless he could shake off Loghyr mind control.

The healer is close now but is very uncomfortable. He is not a people person.

Belinda did not react. He had not included her. I told her, "His Nibs thinks the healer is finally here." Old Bones would avoid direct contact till it was too late for the man to get away. And, maybe, Belinda would go on believing her own thoughts were inviolate.

I felt a tickle of Loghyr amusement.

I told Belinda, "Your man is really nervous. Get him before he spooks." And, "Let's don't jump him before we lock the door behind him."

I got a hint of something like the old saw about teaching grandma to suck eggs. At the same time Old Bones used a gentle influence to move our guests into his room or Singe's office.

Moments later I said, "Doctor. There you are. I'm getting really worried about my friend."

The healer gripped his bag in front of his chest. He stared at the three ratmen. He looked like he had just been sentenced to hang.

"Are you all right?"

His mouth open and closed. Nothing came out. Belinda filled the doorway behind him. She did not keep her expression benign.

I said, "Don't mind these guys. They're here to protect Morley."

Almost inaudibly, the healer asked, "You spilled the medicine I gave you before?"

"Yep. Fumbled it when I was opening it. It hit the floor and rolled under the bed. It was empty before I could fish it out." He relaxed slightly. I grinned. "No, not really. That was a lie. We thought having you think that would help us get you here, you villain."

His eyes got big. He managed to turn even paler.

His attempt to flee failed totally. Belinda didn't move.

Oh, yes. He is guilty. The medication he provided was designed to keep Mr. Dotes unconscious. Our villain is greedy but he is not a murderer.

I told the little man in black, "Friend, you have reached a crossroads. This is the pivotal moment of your life. And it could be fatal."

Take care. He believes he still has options.

"The lady behind you isn't happy with you. She paid you to heal this man. You poisoned him instead. The gentleman behind her is General Block of the Civil Guard. He wants to ask you some questions, too."

Easy, Old Bones sent. *Stop pressing. I have to get control of his body functions, especially his heartbeat. He could die if I do not.*

I started to ask a question.

Silence! His heart is about to burst.

I'd heard of that in mice and horses but never a human being.

I raised a hand to Block and Belinda. We had to let the Dead Man work his magic.

Old Bones stilled, calmed, and reported, *He was prepared for entrapment by a master hypnotist who was unaware that he might encounter someone like me. I have undone the commands driving him toward heart failure but I have failed to discover who placed those commands.*

Inspiration. "Belinda, why did you choose this particular healer?"

"I went to the Children of the Light. I asked for someone. Then I proved that I could afford them."

Maybe that inspiration was halfway a dud. "How long did it take them to decide to help you?"

"Oh. Several days. More than three."

"You went to them before you came to me." Which didn't hurt my feelings. My skills as a healer are slightly inferior.

Old Bones sent, *This one was given the assignment by lot. He was suborned between his first and second visits to Mr. Dotes. A great deal of money was involved. He has done wicked things before. This is the first time his perfidy has been detected.*

The old devil was gleeful.

Belinda said, "You have a lifesaving opportunity, healer. That life being your own."

The Dead Man stabilized the healer's vitals, denying him the escape of death. I'm sure he plundered the man's memories at the same time.

I said, "I'm feeling generous. I'm going to offer you a chance to save *two* lives." Playmate was asleep in a chair in the Dead Man's room. I would make this greedy idiot heal him after he turned Morley around.

This is remarkably difficult, the Dead Man sent. *I cannot negate the full regime of posthypnotic commands. What we want we will have to get quickly. The self-destruct sequence has only been stalled. I may not be able to hold it off indefinitely.*

I looked at Morley, at the healer, at Morley again, and could not find in myself any sympathy for the healer.

39

I called General Block back. He had drifted away, seduced by the siren of free food and beer. Plus, for the moment, he was a celebrity. Even he craves admiration.

"See if Kolda is still here."

"The poisoner?"

"He's a chemist. An apothecary. A natural extracts guy." Why was I making excuses for Kolda? Because I kind of liked him? He did try to poison me, once upon a time.

"Whatever."

"Never mind. Skipper, find Singe. Tell her I need Kolda."

One of the ratmen left. While I waited I filled Block in on what we had dredged out of the healer while he was away enjoying his back-patting. He was aghast. "And now he's doing his damned best to die before we can get anything else. While he's practically begging Old Bones to save his ass."

Block lost color. He swallowed a few times. That one of the Children of the Light could be so twisted was a shocker, apparently.

In this mean city we should find nothing darkly amazing. Even in the age of police protection.

Block gurgled, "He's awake. I thought he was asleep. I was promised that he was in a full, deep sleep."

I got it, then. It wasn't the twisted healer. It was the Dead Man. I laughed. "Somebody lied. But not to worry. He doesn't poke around inside people just because he can. And when he does he passes on only what is germane. In this case, what this man knows about what was done to Morley Dotes. Meantime, we're going to lose him if he carries out the hypnotic instructions driving him."

"That can't be. I know a little about hypnotism. We use it in interrogations. You can't make somebody kill himself."

"Old Bones tells me you can if your victim doesn't know that's what he's doing. You make him think he's doing something else."

Whoever prepared this man was a genius. He started with a typical healer and made the man over into an assassin without triggering any serious conflict.

"And quick enough to prep him for Morley?"

Pay attention. We have established that this man has committed other crimes. I suspect that similar mental manipulations were used on Jimmy Two Steps.

"There *is* a connection?"

Information in General Block's mind, compared with facts in the healer's, makes that seem likely. The puppet master evidently agrees with the Al-Khar about you. You need to be kept away. You are a wild card. The cascade of events so far suggests that they might be right.

"Interesting." I began making further connections.

Yes. The attack on you and Miss Tate took place soon after Miss Contague decided to ask you to protect Mr. Dotes. Then, on successive nights, attempts were made to get you at Fire and Ice.

"Me? Not Morley?"

You, I am certain. Mr. Dotes would be useful collateral damage but would be neutralized anyway once he started his medication. You, however, have a history of stumbling around and causing avalanches of unexpected consequences. It is what you do. Particularly in the mind opposing us.

"This is someone we've run into before."

I expect only obliquely, if at all, with us taking no notice. Aha! I broke the code. I found the key to the sequence.

"Huh?"

The healer. I can save him. I have cracked the progression of suggestions laid into his mind.

"Good. Once you have him calmed down and set to go, turn him loose on Playmate. Accept no excuses."

Of course.

Block asked, "Interesting private chat?"

"Yes. He figured out how to save our healer assassin from himself."

"Excellent. I do have some questions for that man."

"Go through His Nibs. Otherwise, you'll be wasting your time."

Block did follow. He nodded, admitted, "This isn't the first bad guy to turn up with no notion why he did what he did and no idea who told him to do it."

Intriguing. The General is reflecting on thefts of chemicals that turned up in that warehouse.

"Bring them around, General. Let Old Bones chat them up. Meantime, how about you see the Children of the Light about this guy? They might be able to shed some light."

He refused to acknowledge my clever word play. "Ooh! That sounds like fun. Deal will be all over that. We wouldn't even be breaking any recent rules. This would be a separate case. An attempted murder possibly connected to successful murders that had no obvious connection with a warehouse in Elf Town."

I started to ask if the Guard had canvassed the neighborhood. I got a caution from the Dead Man. That had been ruled out by Prince Rupert.

"How about hunting the resurrection men? Has that been disallowed?"

Block smirked. "Not yet. But they're damned hard to find. They've been told to lie low and keep quiet by somebody who scares them more than we do."

That figured.

Belinda leaned into the doorway, which was the best she could do because of the crowd in the room already. "I got Kolda. It took a while. We had to run him down."

40

Block had arrived looking for one thing. He went out with something else in mind, but happy and eager to get to work.

The Dead Man would give him additional information. Soon the Al-Khar would be a-bustle. No one but the Director and the commanding general would know that the Guard was violating the spirit of their orders.

Kolda joined me in with Morley. He was nervous. Our history, while limited, left him no reason to think that he was in a good position. I told him, "You're an expert in chemicals and exotic herbs. My friend, here, has been poisoned. It's not lethal, it just keeps him from waking up. And it makes him heal really slow."

Kolda gave me a big-eyed, frightened look but didn't say anything.

"The pudgy character with Dollar Dan's paw tangled in his collar delivered the poison. That was given to him, along with a lot of money, by a third party, after Miss Contague engaged him to heal my friend. She gave him a lot of money, too."

Kolda had a worse flair for fashion than me. He couldn't keep his hair combed or his shirt tucked in. He was always nervous. His social skills were negligible. But he was a genius in his field. And he owed me.

I had insisted, to Block, that Kolda wasn't a poisoner. But he did poison me, once upon a time. I'm still breathing and complaining. The evidence suggests that I found the antidote.

I said, "Healer, give this man the bottle you brought today. Then Dollar Dan will take you across the hallway. Your redemption begins when you start work on Playmate."

He didn't want to do that. Freebies went against the code of the Children of the Light. "I understand." His voice was slow and toneless. He dug out a little bottle identical to the one he had given us during his visit to Fire and Ice.

I asked the air, "What are the chances this bottle contains the same ingredients as the first one?"

Indeterminate. Ten seconds passed. *Clever catch, Garrett. He did, in fact, consult a contact after he heard that you needed more medicine. The excuse we provided was of a sort to excite the suspicions of a paranoid supplier.*

"We do still have the original philter. Kolda can compare them."

The healer surrendered his new bottle. Dollar Dan hustled him across the hall.

I gave Kolda the original bottle. "This stuff goes three drops to a two-quart pitcher of water."

"Potent, then." With commendable caution he unstopped each bottle and took a gentle sniff. Of the new bottle he said, "This is vanilla, a touch of clove oil, another of castor oil, in wood alcohol. There is something more that I don't recognize." After sniffing the original bottle, he said, "This includes everything in the other bottle, with less of the unknown odor and more of something that smells like death."

"Definitely different formulas, then?"

"Yes. But subtly. Both would be deadly, in different ways."

I asked the air, "What do you think?"

You may be on the right trail. Neither oil of clove nor oil of castor ought to dissolve in cold water but their presence, with the vanilla, might be there to suggest that the concoction is medicinal.

"The poison has to be something that is effective in amounts so small . . ."

The beans from which castor oil is rendered. They contain a poison so deadly that infinitesimal amounts can kill scores. The poisoner's dilemma has always been how to remain unpoisoned himself, then how to disperse the poison in an effective manner. It would appear that someone has found a way to use it, one customer at a time.

Ah! Friend Kolda has begun thinking along the same lines. I will spare you the admiration he has for the genius of his fellow chemist.

Kolda said, "Someone has done the impossible. Someone has achieved an unbelievable breakthrough."

I asked, "What do you mean?"

"Someone has found a way to extract the poison from castor beans."

"You dud. That's been known for years. What nobody does know is how to use the poison safely."

Kolda gave back an unhappy grunt. He might not be as ignorant as we hoped.

He *was* ignorant about the Dead Man. I'm not sure I approve but last time we crossed paths Old Bones added some trapdoors to Kolda's memory.

Kolda will never remember anything he learns while visiting us.

I was beginning to think my partner wasn't as swell as I claimed he was.

I felt a touch of amusement from outside.

41

With Kolda and the healer gone to see the Dead Man there wasn't much for me to do with Morley. And it was almost time for the ratwomen.

I decided to cultivate my atrophied social skills. But only a handful of guests remained. The healer, Kolda, and Playmate were in with the Dead Man. The rest were in Singe's office. Jon Salvation was talking up his next play. I checked the corners and under Singe's desk. Still no Winger. How did he manage?

The Dead Man's special student, Penny Dreadful, hadn't fled when I turned up. There had been enough witnesses for her to feel safe.

My, how she had grown!

You notice these things when you're male and still alive.

Morley's longtime associate Sarge was there, too. He looked lost. He looked like somebody just poisoned his kitten.

I snagged the last available chair, beckoned Sarge, indicated my willingness to share the contents of a pitcher clearly in need of refurbishing. Sarge was slumped on a chair in a corner not occupied by Saucerhead Tharpe's or Singe's office furniture. He brightened slightly and dragged his chair over.

"How is the restaurant managing without our boy?"

"We don't need no barkin' from Morley to make dat work, Garrett. We been in da racket so long da business rolls on like a mill wheel turnin'. But he's our frien', too. An' none of us know what we'll do if'n he don't make it t'ru dis."

"Belinda has probably made you crazy trying to figure out what Morley was up to when he got hurt, but . . ."

"Dat's for sure. But she don't listen to what nobody tells

her so she ain't never gonna get nowhere. She's one a dem
people what figures out ahead a time what dey're gonna believe, den dey don't never hear nothin' dat disagrees."

I'd known Belinda longer than I liked to remember and
more intimately than the world needed to know. She had
huge intellectual flaws. Willful disdain of facts was never one
of those. "For sure? Like how?"

"Well, you know, Morley don't got a lot a use for his et'nic
roots. He's a dark elf, but, yeah? So what? He's in business in
a human city an' half da people dere, dey don't know dat, can't
tell dat, an' maybe don't need ta know dat if'n dey're da kind
what gives a shit about dat."

I nodded. Sarge's dialect was thicker than usual but I was
following him. He was saying Morley wasn't one for living in
the past. "Did something change?" He *had* been found in that
zone where greater TunFaire fades into the neighborhood
known as Elf Town. Folk there, who never saw a house in their
home country, live in tenements twelve to a room and insist
that they'll never put the old ways and old tongue behind
them.

"Sumptin' did. Maybe dat bint what his folks arranged him
ta marry came ta town."

"I thought he bought his way out of that a couple years ago."

"We all t'ought dat. Maybe he just wished he did."

Jon Salvation joined us, uninvited. He planted himself in
front of me, hands on his skinny little girl hips. "Garrett, you
have to help me."

Story of my life. "I can't afford to invest in one of your
plays. And I'm busy, here."

"I don't need investors. I have people lined up to buy into
anything I put on. I stick with the Weiders because they give
me artistic control. But you're the only one I can count on to
make my next project a success."

I forgot Sarge and Morley briefly. Pilsuds Vilchik had pre-
sented me with a grand conundrum. No way could a street
operator like me assure the success of a stage drama. Unless
he wanted me to sell seats at knifepoint. Or maybe he wanted
Winger kept out of his hair.

"Where is Winger?"

"Getting into mischief somewhere." He shrugged. "What I

want is for you to get Tinnie to come back. She's perfect for the lead in *The Faerie Queene*."

"You want to cast Tinnie as a fairy? Man, that's a stretch. She is way too substantial." That wisp Furious Tide of Light was far more suitable.

"That's the point. I'm not doing fairy-tale fairies. They won't be ethereal. They'll be like elves, only from a realm at right angles to our own. Tinnie's coloring and attributes, her stature and sharp attitude, even her freckles, make her the perfect Mathilde."

"Will this go on at the World?"

"Main stage, expanded. This will be my biggest hit yet, Garrett."

"Tinnie doesn't get along with Heather Soames."

"I'll make them get along."

I liked his confidence.

He said, "Tinnie *is* Mathilde but I will send her packing if she behaves the way she did before. You don't need to tell her that. I'll make it clear at first rehearsal."

Interesting times were headed our way. "Look at you getting all self-confident and assertive. What happened to the Remora we knew and loathed?"

"He found his passion. Are you going to pitch Mathilde to Tinnie?"

"No."

"What? Why not?"

"I'm committed to my own passion. That will keep me here with my injured friend. If you want Tinnie, head on over to Factory Slide. Or, better, catch her at work. Go in the afternoon. She'll be sick of accounting. I can give you a letter to get you past the guards."

"If that's the way it has to be. Would you be interested in a small role? I need a banged up hulk to play the faithful old soldier . . ."

"Jon, you need to come at me some other time. I was involved in an important discussion with Sarge when you horned in."

The playwright goggled. He had lost his appreciation of direct talk.

People did talk to the Remora that way, back when. They

talked to Pilsuds Vilchik that way in the once upon a time. They didn't talk that way to the town's hottest celebrity today.

Sarge volunteered, "I'd make a good fait'ful old sojer what's been banged aroun' enough ta have some character."

And there was another reason Jon Salvation felt free to unleash his inner dick. People put up with it because he might cast them in a play.

42

Salvation did not get in a huff. He just went away, no doubt deleting my name from his roll of potential character actors.

"Sorry about that, Sarge."

"He ain't timid no more."

"No. Unless he was on the street."

"No shit dere. Dat attitude don't cut no nutin' wit' da brunos. If dey was any dat da Director didn't already ship off ta da work camps."

An interesting notion, that law and order had become so ubiquitous that smarmy little peckerwoods like the Remora could turn snotty and not have to pay with bloody head wounds.

What did Deal Relway think of that unintended consequence?

"Anyway, you were telling me that Morley's country fiancée might be in town hoping to dip into his pockets."

"Dat's just one t'eory."

"Are there others?"

"Probably. You gotta ast da Capa. Me, I don't t'ink so fast so I jes' follow along."

"I see. Don't put yourself down. You have a knack for doing the right thing at the right time." He saved my life, once upon a time. "Did you hold back anything from the Capa? Something you guys thought might upset her?"

A downside to being a sociopath, like Belinda, was that people walked on eggshells around you. They didn't tell you things that might upset you. You ended up operating in a bad news vacuum.

Belinda was smart enough to see that. She created ways around the standard distortion. But those ways would not work inside a closed and loyal crew like Morley's. Belinda might suspect that they were blowing smoke and leaving things unsaid but that would be outside her imperial reach.

"Any other time, Garrett, an' you'd be right. If Morley survivin' wasn't involved, we'd mix up a whole stew a half-troots an' misleadin' troots. We wouldn't let her know what was really what. But dis time it was himself as da table stakes. Dis time we had ta tell her true."

The dialect had weakened. I understood every word.

Morley's crew would not hold out on Belinda while she could do their friend and employer some good.

They would turn loose nothing that didn't bear on the immediate problem, though.

"You didn't hold anything back?"

"Nut'in'! We gotta get our Morley back—which I guess we sorta got, if'n he ever come outta dat coma—an' we gotta have a shot at fixin' whoever done whatever got did ta him. We figure you an' da Capa tagether are gonna see the blood spread where dat's gonna do da mos' good. An' I t'ink I better get on back down ta da place, now. Dey're gonna need me. Dis is da busiest night a da week."

"I wouldn't want to interfere with business. Get going. If something turns up that might interest me don't waste time letting me know."

Sarge nodded. "He's gonna make it, ain't he, Garrett?"

"I'm sure. Tell the others. Morley will be back real soon."

"T'anks, Garrett." He stared at me for several seconds. "Maybe you ain't da complete sponge we always t'ought."

Sarge, Puddle, and others of Morley's bunch had, back when, treated me like I carried a social disease. They had kept it in check only when Dotes was there, watching.

"I'm pleased to hear you say that, Sarge. It means a lot. Now go back to work and make Morley rich."

As Sarge headed out I realized that I could not remember what Morley called the place he had opened across from the World. What was wrong with me? Tinnie and I had eaten there several times.

43

A quick census revealed that the Garrett household had shed most of its visitors. Some, when the Dead Man showed me the roster, were folks I'd missed. Some I didn't know. "Tinnie never showed?" I asked Singe.

"Which means nothing," she told me. "She was informed that important matters would be discussed but this is the middle of the workweek and Amalgamated still suffers from explosively good sales. Note that the people who were here mostly aren't the kind who have ordinary jobs."

Yeah. True. She made it sound plausible.

Those who were still around sure fit. Saucerhead Tharpe, maybe passed out drunk, looked pathetic snoring in a corner. Jon Salvation was bold enough to use Singe's pens and inks to scribble in the bound book of blank pages he carried everywhere.

Then Salvation was up and reminding me, "You said you'd write a letter that would get me in to see Tinnie."

"So I did. Help me swing this desk around and I'll get on it."

I created a three-hundred-word masterpiece that would get Tinnie salivating over the prospects of what Jon Salvation might want to discuss. I kept me out of it. I said nothing about where I was, what I was doing, why, or even my state of health. She could squeeze that out of the Remora if she wanted to know. And he could let me know how interested she was.

If it went right I might try to sneak away for a peace conference.

And then we were down to Saucerhead, a few ratpeople, and the folks over there with the Dead Man. I complained, "I never got a chance to talk to John Stretch. I wanted to catch up on his adventures."

Singe said, "He's doing fine. Outstanding, considering he's still the boss of bosses in the rat underworld. After all these years."

"That would be about three, wouldn't it?"

"Only one as boss of bosses. The first of his kind, really."

She glowed with pride. Her brother was the undisputed overlord of crime amongst her species.

Her look dared me to disrespect her pride.

I'd never do that. Not to Singe.

Garrett. Please join us.

Though I did not hear Singe mentioned I was not alone in migrating.

It seemed there wasn't just one corpse in the cold room when Singe and I arrived. Nobody moved. You'd expect that from Old Bones but Kolda, Playmate, or the healer should have been doing something.

Singe went straight to Playmate, who, definitely, looked dead.

I had Mr. Kolda give him a measure of the medication meant for Mr. Dotes. We will put a bad thing to good use by keeping Playmate under while I battle the monster devouring him from inside. Singe, engage one of the Kerr tribe to take a message to the brother-in-law managing Playmate's stable. He will need to understand what is happening. Do not give too much detail. Do not suggest that we have any great hope. The brother-in-law will, almost certainly, find the prospect of Playmate's recovery disheartening.

From what I knew about Playmate's brother-in-law, I reckoned the Dead Man was spot on. Play's sister was his only heir. The idiot husband probably had a buyer for the stable lined up.

"So what are you actually doing?"

I am working inside Playmate's brain to shut down the pain that distracts him from handling the rest of his life. In parallel, I have been scanning Mr. Kolda's herbal knowledge in hopes of discovering a specific for Playmate's cancer.

"Any luck?"

Possibly. But it comes from the mind of Brother Hoto instead. He knows of a reptile venom that attacks tumor tissue vigorously.

"Where do we find the poison lizard?"

It is a tropical species. A flashily-clad critter something like an iguana with saber teeth appeared in my mind.

"I remember this guy from the islands. A bad actor. You went down if he breathed on you."

As always, you exaggerate where there are no witnesses to contradict you. Nonetheless, the venom is potent. A few of the lizards may live in TunFaire.

Somebody in Kolda's racket had a few hidden away. Or maybe the Children of the Light, selling miracles to the wealthy.

They are in the exotic reptile house of the Royal Zoo.

Oh. Yeah. The royals did collect odd critters. One of the princesses had a special building for moths and butterflies. None of us low-life types ever get to see that stuff.

You have a connection with a prince.

I did. Sort of.

Meantime, I am mining Brother Hoto for anything useful in developing an understanding of the who, what, and why behind Mr. Dotes' misadventure.

"Why not just pluck that out of Morley's head?"

Those fruits are not there to pluck. It could be that he was hit with a rock from the sky and will not be able to tell us anything when he does wake up.

"But he will wake up?"

Within two days. Possibly sooner. Assuming Brother Hoto knows his poison. You may go ahead now, Singe.

He had given Singe work without consulting me.

I was getting hungry. I hadn't seen Dean for some time.

You now know what I know. There is nothing you can contribute here. Check on Mr. Dotes. Go to the kitchen. Get some rest.

I took a good look at Playmate before I went. The man was one of my oldest and most reliable friends. We had helped one another countless times. He grumbled when I asked for something but never failed to come through. I would do what I could to be a good friend in turn.

Morley was sleeping normally. There was more color in his face. Dollar Dan told me he had said something, one word, but nothing the guards had understood.

Headway!

I found Dean in one of the chairs at the kitchen table, leaning on his folded arms, asleep.

I downed the last of a collection of tasteless leftovers. I had caught something from one of our visitors, several of who had had the sniffles.

Whatever it was, wherever I got it, it was aggressive. I felt weak as I headed upstairs. At that point I thought it was because I'd put away too much beer. Half dreaming already, I caught the edge of the Dead Man's concerned thoughts. He was worried about something. It was a generalized worry, about all of us, not targeted.

44

I wakened in the middle of the night. A cool breeze came in the open window. The Windwalker, Furious Tide of Light sat cross-legged on the corner of the foot of my bed, on the side where my feet weren't. I was stretched out kitty-corner from top left to lower right. She looked far more the fairy princess than Tinnie ever could.

She looked like the queen of temptation, too.

She had turned the lamp up. There was light enough to reveal her flash of a smile when she saw that treacherous flicker in my eyes. She could have had me then. If she'd wanted.

But I sneezed.

She thought that was funny.

"I can't help it." I prayed she wouldn't turn on the heat.

I had seen her reduce an entire construction crew to drooling idiocy, not even doing it deliberately.

I'm a committed man. I told myself. I can't jump into these things . . .

I sneezed again.

She produced a dainty handkerchief.

"Thanks." My head was full of stuff.

The bright side was, a man sneezing and clearing his head doesn't make that interesting a target for a vamp.

Still, I asked, "How about you get to business before I go crazy?"

Ghost of a smile. She was pleased. She had reassured herself. She *was* desirable.

She had serious issues but none connected to what we were into today.

"Business. Yes. I need that, too." She shut her eyes and

made a conscious effort to become asexual. She wasn't entirely successful but it did get easier to consider something beyond the possibilities of our situation.

I blew my nose again.

She told me, "I visited Prince Rupert today."

"You sound glum. It didn't go well?"

"It went better than I expected, actually. It just didn't go the way I hoped. He named no names and pointed no fingers. He admitted that he's under pressure to stay away from the mess on the north side. He kept up a brave front but he's scared. I think the pressure comes from his brother."

"The King?" I sneezed. This cold could become ugly. The coughing couldn't be far away.

The King seemed an unlikely villain. Since peace broke out he had done little but party all night and sleep all day.

"I know. So, then, who has the power to move the King? I'm top ten and I don't. I can barely get in to see Rupert."

"Why would he go along?" I looked at her and tried to keep my gaze from roaming.

"Bless you."

Yeah. Bless the common cold. My honor saved by mucus.

I turned so I could look at anything but her.

She said, "One good thing came out today. I'm satisfied that Kevans isn't involved."

"I'm happy for you." I wasn't so sure. Her daughter had serious head problems that disconnected her from society and its rules.

"First proof is, nobody would cover for her like this is being covered up. *And* she has alibis for both nights when crazy things happened." She didn't sound happy about that.

She said she was estranged from both her father and daughter. Maybe her dad was Kevans' alibi.

Had to be. And that might not hold up.

The Windwalker really did not want to rely on her father anymore. She had pushed him out of the family mansion on the Hill.

Barate Algarda—who was, in every other way I'd ever seen, as exemplary a human being as you could hope to meet—had instilled in this daughter an insecurity so great she thought that her only real value could be as somebody's sex toy.

Which I was thinking when she said, "I'm one of the ten

most powerful sorcerers in TunFaire." But the little girl inside didn't reckon her worth that way. "I know that here." She thunked her noggin with her fist.

"So the question would be, who scares Rupert more than you do?"

That drew a surprisingly adolescent grin. "Yep. But you need to remember that Rupert will still be his own man. Even if somebody has him wetting his pants. He's kind of like you, that way."

I felt a far, far sense of amusement.

She rambled on. "Without saying so he let me know he hopes I'll keep stirring the pot. He hinted that there are people on the margins who aren't likely to turn their backs because an authority doesn't want them nosing around."

That sounded like Rupert. He would conform to his instructions but would fail to notice insubordination. A toe tap here and there might encourage more noncompliance.

The Windwalker said, "I have to leave. I can't stand the distraction." She eased off the end of my bed, headed for the window more slowly than she could have done. I had no trouble sensing her willing me to stop her. I imagine she had no trouble sensing me wanting to do exactly that.

It didn't happen. It wasn't the time, even if it was fated.

She clambered out the window. A clumsy process, also slower than it had to be. But she turned divinely graceful once she started walking on moonlight.

She said, "There's something about you. . . . When your relationship with the redheaded woman falls apart, I'm coming for you. You'll be amazed. We'll be the talk of the town. We'll have the wedding of the year."

I gulped and gaped as she fluttered away, leaving no doubt that she meant every word. Hill folk do when they make a declarative statement. Even shy, socially inept Hill folk.

Which left me with extremely mixed emotions.

I lay back, sure I wouldn't sleep again for the rest of my life.

45

I've got talents. I've got skills. When my head gets too frothy with what-ifs, I've got a live-in (so to speak) Loghyr who steps in and shuts me down. I slept till midmorning.

Singe came to wake me. I came round in a good mood. "If it wouldn't get us both burned at the stake I'd pro—" My tongue froze. My jaw locked. Old Bones *never* touched me that way.

That he had needed no explanation.

Ratpeople weren't built to frown. But Singe could squint and demand, "What?" in her most puzzled tone.

"Singe, I was going to make a really bad joke that would've been way out of line. I'm sorry. I've been away too long."

Singe was bright but didn't work that one out. Thank God. Or the gods. Or maybe the old dead thing downstairs who saved me the taste of leather in my mouth.

So. Singe was a grown ratwoman and no longer entertained adolescent fantasies about us becoming lovers. She was the wondrous perfect business side of my business. But she still had emotion invested. She could be hurt deeply by what might sound like me poking fun.

By the time you reach two hundred we will turn you into a mature, thoughtful, sensitive adult who thinks before he says ... Oh, sugar!

Oh, sugar? What the h-e-double-broomsticks did that mean?

While the mental stuff happened I dragged myself out of bed. My marvelous business partner, whose feelings I had just so bravely taken into account, sniffed around with increasing agitation.

"You had a woman in here last night!" There was an angry

edge to her voice. After several bellicose sniffs round the bed, though, she relaxed.

Maybe the Dead Man brought her up to speed. Or she worked the whole thing out with her mutant nose. Garrett had avoided temptation.

Oh, sugar, because we are about to have unexpected guests. And you need to be here to help manage them.

An image of an angry band of Children of the Light formed in my mind. They made a big black blot in the street.

"What's the big deal? Ignore them."

I would rather not. More than most who come threatening grief or mayhem, these old men could cause us some discomfort.

Naturally, he didn't explain.

With Singe's assistance I made myself presentable and was ready before the hammering on the door commenced. I used the peephole, saw a lot of black clothing. I let the folks stew till the Dead Man thought they were ready.

My first impression was, wow! I'd better send Singe for Cap'n Roger. Half these guys were going to expire before sundown. Their median age had to be in triple digits. The youngest looked like he started yearning for the good old days when the Dead Man was a pup.

Four had reached my stoop.

"Howdy, fathers. How can I help you?" How had they survived the climb? "If you're collecting for your church I have to tell you we're Orthodox here." By birth. I hadn't been to a service in an age.

"You have Brother Hoto Pepper confined here. We have come to take him away."

The Dead Man sent, *Pull the ugly one inside and shut the door. Lock up, then bring him in here.*

Excellent. We had a plan. All I needed to do was to pick a winner.

Old Bones had no patience. One old man developed a halo. I grabbed, pulled, slammed, locked. Well, Singe did the locking while I held the door shut.

Our victim shambled dispiritedly off to the party room. The Children of the Light outside waxed enthusiastic in their threats. The Dead Man showed no concern.

I asked, "You need me now?"

Not right away.

I headed for the kitchen. I was hungry.

I didn't get far with correcting that.

You may allow our visitors to leave, now.

I pushed back from the table, marched off to do my duty. "You sure?"

There is nothing more that I can retrieve from any of them.

Two old guys in black and the poisoner Kolda—pardon; the *apothecary* Kolda—awaited me outside the Dead Man's doorway.

Kolda will be gone only a short while. He will gather some specifics to help with Playmate. Please make sure that Brother Hoto does exit the premises. He is reluctant to rejoin his own kind. He fears that they will ask him the same questions I did, but using tools.

I expected a hassle from the crowd when I released their brethren. That did not happen. The Dead Man had tamed or confused them. And they had worn themselves out chipping the paint off the door.

I closed up and went back to reacquaint myself with breakfast.

As I passed my former office I noted that Morley's only company was Dollar Dan. The caretaker ratwomen had come and gone. The other guards had gone with them.

We do not need them now that there are no outsiders in the house. Mr. Dollar can go once you finish eating.

I trekked on and in time assailed a stack of griddle cakes. Dean didn't make those often. He was in a good mood. I mentioned it.

"Perhaps because of the excitement yesterday. It took me back."

I looked at him askance.

He didn't change his story.

46

I shut the door behind Dollar Dan. He would come back later, to sit with Morley while I was upstairs snoring.

"And snoring it had better be," Singe told me, remembering the woman smell. She did not like Furious Tide of Light today. I wasn't sure why.

I can't quite work out how Singe decides who she likes and who she doesn't, nor why she will change her mind overnight. Her brain doesn't work like mine. I'm sure her sense of smell has something to do with it.

I settled in near Morley, a pot of tea at hand. The Dead Man filled me in on what he had learned from our visitors, including tidbits from the elders who had come for Brother Hoto. Of interest was the fact that Winger and the Remora were drifting apart, the drift mainly hers. She couldn't handle his success.

We do not know much more about the threat to the city. We do know who has been warned off it. We have eyes and ears watching and listening, now. We know we will get Mr. Dotes back. Additionally, we have set in motion actions that offer a chance of rescuing Playmate from the natural monster devouring him.

That was good news. "Did you get anything from the Windwalker?"

Vague amusement, presumably at my expense. *That woman is the most simple-minded, empty-headed genius I have ever encountered. She can focus her entire being on the moment. You could do far worse.*

"Excuse me?"

As a practical matter. She would provide all the fireworks— and more—with none of the drama of your Miss Tate.

"Uh . . ."

Miss Algarda is ready to grant her devotion. That would be unreserved and absolute. She considers you an ideal candidate. Although she is an immense and formidable power, and a genius professionally, her emotional world is simpler than that of Deal Relway.

"That's scary."

It is. She does not grasp nuance or shades of gray.

The answer to why me might be tucked inside what he had sent. A different kind of sociopath, she would not need time to work things out. Is/is not, with nothing in between. "She would be clever enough not to push me, wouldn't she?"

You could be right in considering her a special kind of sociopath. She is smart enough to show the behavior she has seen in courtships. But she will not be resilient if she is mislead, mistreated, emotionally abused, or blackmailed.

"I believe I get the idea."

Good. You are staring into the eyes of a big responsibility.

I had an uncomfortable notion that I knew what he meant. Dotes' First Law. Keep your hands off a woman crazier than you are. Which I observed in the breach. Furious Tide of Light would be, "You Touch It, You Bought It."

But I didn't believe she was crazy. Not the way girlfriends usually are.

Her head worked different, sure. She had grown up sheltered from life. She coped now because she didn't go out much. When she did she dealt with people she scared so bad they couldn't imagine messing with her.

Hers was a unique emotional realm but it was the only one she knew.

Part of me did find her damned intriguing. It hunted loopholes in Dotes' Law.

That was the part exhausted by squabbling with Tinnie.

"What do you think, Old Bones?"

I think it is none of my business. I think you are an adult now, and I should not tinker—unless, as was the case with Singe this morning, you start running your mouth with no thought to the consequences.

I was stunned. By making that carefully neutral statement he had told me something I'm sure he did not intend. He had doubts about Tinnie. After all this time.

I would have expected him to endorse the redhead and re-
ject the Windwalker. I wasn't in her class and she came with a
whole different drama. (I wasn't in Tinnie's class, either, but a
different definition of class was operative there.)

Maybe he was tired of the drama, too.

Still, I carefully reviewed his communications since he had
labeled Furious Tide of Light an empty-headed genius. I got
a strange impression that he did prefer the Windwalker but
would be careful not to say so.

Off I rambled into my own internal drama land, wondering
what it was about the beautiful but weird sorceress that made
her a preferable mate.

Morley tried to say something.

47

Morley was awake.

His eyes were halfway open, fluttering. He wanted to say something.

Having been in his position myself, I told him, "You're at my place on Macunado Street, being watched out for by me, Singe, the Dead Man, Belinda, John Stretch, the Civil Guard, and the godsdamned Windwalker, Furious Tide of Light. Somebody really wanted to close you down, buddy. Oh. You've been out for more than a week. They tried to poison you, too."

In retrospect, that actually helped. His wounds healed a lot while he was unconscious.

He tried to sit up. He got nowhere. His wounds were not healed enough. He felt them, too. And now had no strength left.

"Water!" was the first word I understood.

Then Dean was there, not only with water but with warm chicken broth. Singe was only a moment behind. She helped lift Morley so Dean could deliver the water and liquid chow.

After the stress level declined and the broth began to work, Morley croaked, "Tell me."

"Be easier for the Dead Man to . . ."

"You tell."

I told my part and what I knew to be true with the precision I used reporting to the Dead Man.

Morley did not seem much interested in who had stabbed him. He was intensely interested in all the whos and what happeneds after he went down. Singe and I added what we had heard from unreliable sources.

Everything given him, I moved on to my own curiosities. "What were you doing in that part of town, anyway? Not that you don't have a right to go wherever you damned well please. But, unless things changed lately, you don't have much to do with those people."

Sometimes I think he was embarrassed by his ethnic background.

He was not yet in any condition for real talk. He eyed me in disbelief. Then his handsome face collapsed into despair. "I can't remember!" Moments later, "*He* couldn't root it out?"

"No. Unless he didn't recognize it because it didn't connect with everything else." That was my theory. Morley had been involved in something else entirely when he walked blind into something deadly.

Morley frowned. I took that to mean he wanted an explanation.

"Sarge thinks you were up there paying off your fiancée's family."

Morley looked puzzled but I didn't feel any honest emotion behind that. I didn't pursue it.

Old Bones could fill me in later.

I did ask, "How do you justify Belinda Contague against Dotes' First Law?"

"There are twelve kinds of crazy, Garrett. Romantic attraction is the worst." His first complete statement, and, probably, one of the truest things he ever said.

I am getting nothing more now than I did while Mr. Dotes was unconscious. There is nothing there. Though it would appear that chunks of memory may have been lost to concussion or that drug.

"A pity."

Indeed. All that can be done now is to protect him till he can protect himself.

"He'll want to get after this before he's physically ready."

Should he be so inclined I will make sure he falls asleep on his way to the door.

I chuckled.

Morley scowled.

I explained. "Not to worry. We're just planning your future. You'll thank us later."

He hurt too much to be amused.

I said, "There's some silliness taken care of. What do you figure on doing?"

"I'm going back to sleep." And he did, just like that. And it was the best thing he could do once he was full of high-potency chicken broth.

Soon he would get full-bodied chicken soup with noodles and bits of bird.

The Dead Man suggested that I forget Mr. Dotes for a while. I should go relax with Singe, who could help bring me up to speed.

That made me feel like I had been cast as a spear-carrier.

I had few options if I wanted to stay close to Morley.

Old Bones didn't mind not keeping *me* posted, but Singe had to know stuff because she managed operations and handled the money.

She commiserated over my problems with the redhead. "Pack up your pride and go talk to her. Morley will be safe."

I hemmed and hawed but I'm no good at stalling while trying to find plausible excuses for avoiding something that could turn out ugly.

"Good gods, Garrett! What are you? Thirteen and an only child? Go talk to her. What's the worst she can do?"

I told her what the worst was.

"After all the time, trouble, training, and emotion she has invested in you?"

"Yes. After all that. She's turned into a pretty selfish girl."

"How did that happen? Who gave her the idea that whatever Tinnie wants, Tinnie deserves and gets it? Garrett, you are a first-class dum-dum. Tinnie has been in your life since my mother was a pup. She came and went a few times but she was always back after whoever was distracting you moved on."

That was harsh but essentially factual. Both ways. Tinnie had had some gentlemen suitors. I had had . . . Maya, Eleanor, even Belinda.

I scowled, hoping Tinnie's man friends had not gotten as close as I had to some of those ladies. Maya had been determined to marry me. She never managed to get me to hold still long enough. She had gone on to do much better. And I had gone gaga for Eleanor despite her having been murdered long before I ever met her. Her ghost and her memory were an important part of my life for a long time.

Singe told me, "You need to leave the yesteryear baggage behind. Get back to Tinnie being who she was when she was your special best friend who happened to be a girl."

I wondered if she was being coached from across the hall.

"Good stuff, Singe. Stuff worth thinking about."

She preened.

"What do you think of the Windwalker?"

"Who?"

"The Windwalker, Furious Tide of Light."

"The sorceress who tagged along when I backtracked to the warehouse where all the horror stuff was? The woman who was in your room last night?"

"Her."

"What about her?" She didn't have much of a ruff but it was up.

"You remember her from the thing with the ghosts and giant bugs?"

Several seconds of silence. "All right. That was the same woman?"

"Singe."

"What about her?"

"Singe, I'm asking your opinion of that woman based upon your exposure, interaction, and magical nose."

"I don't have an opinion. How could I? My personal exposure hasn't been enough to develop one. Probably less than an hour over both our lifetimes. Anything I said would be speculative. So. Why is my opinion important?"

That had a high bull-poop content. I didn't challenge it. "Because she's important to me. Because you're important to me. I'm extremely attracted to her, physically and intellectually. And she says she's going to marry me."

The Windwalker did say that, didn't she? Or did I dream it? No matter. It was out of the bag now.

Singe said nothing for several minutes, though she did spout the occasional interrogative sentence as she discussed this revolting development with our deceased friend.

Singe was, apparently, astonished by the Dead Man's positive attitude toward the Windwalker and his lessened enthusiasm toward Tinnie.

I must say that, though forewarned, I didn't understand him, either. And he offered no explanation.

I needed to think about that. The mix for consideration should include not just what I knew about Tinnie and the Windwalker—whose given name I did not yet know—but, also, what the Dead Man knew and never shared.

I should get Tinnie to visit. Old Bones hadn't burgled her head in ages.

I asked the air, "Do I need to be scared?"

I got no answer. Of course.

Then I got distracted by supper and Kolda's return. Then it was time to supervise the ratwomen who came to clean Morley. They were amazed and amused by a gallant salute that reared up while they changed his diaper.

He was on his way back for sure.

The caretakers gave way to a brace of armed ratmen. Singe's brother came with them. We settled in her office. We drank some beer. John Stretch had become an interesting person in his own right. I wondered how many more geniuses his mother had produced.

I wasted a lot of time wondering about nonproductive stuff.

48

Confusion. A lot of beer went down during the discussions with Singe and John Stretch. Then came bed, me thinking this was like the good old days. All that commotion about relationships was silly-ass fuss with no enduring real-world significance.

Singe had bullied me into reaffirming my commitment to Tinnie. She wasn't hot to have Furious Tide of Light as her stepmom.

So the woman had a few quirks. Didn't we all? The problem she had was breaking loose from her father.

As I noted, the Algardas might be weird and have dark secrets but they were still caring, kind people where others were concerned.

Such was my tangle of thought as I drifted off, not nearly as reconciled to the redhead as Singe hoped. I left the window ajar. I told myself that was because I needed the night air to cool my room.

More than air got in. And had done nothing to cool anything down.

Furious Tide of Light played more fair than most women. She knew she could turn me into a sock puppet with some eye-batting, heavy breathing, and a dash of suggestive dialog. Women understand these things by the time they're ten. Some just don't learn to trust their instincts.

A desirable woman who catches a man in bed in the middle of the night won't need to work hard to have her way.

The Windwalker was gentle, thoughtful, and careful not to unfairly exploit her advantage. She could have made the situation more chaste only by standing off and touching me with a ten-foot pole. Once I woke up all the way, though, I took over. The natural Garrett charm kicked in, made sure she found me completely unappetizing.

I had done honors to a lot of fine beer earlier. It now yearned to be free. My choices were to be embarrassed a little or embarrassed a lot.

I chose the chamber pot over wetting myself. Not behavior accepted in the drawing rooms of the upper classes but not utterly gauche and unacceptable in mine. Elimination processes are natural and necessary. And I was polite enough to step into a corner and face away.

Never mind. The Windwalker woke me up. I did what I had to do. Any romantic notions she brought along got put on hold. Still, she was a resilient fey. She might have bounced back had it not been for the interruption.

I was looking at her, determined to ask why she was here but getting entangled in the fantasy—wondering if I shouldn't have taken a bath—when she let out a baby squeal and slammed a fist down hard on the windowsill.

She had to leap to do it, and when I say hard I mean she shook the house. The wood in the window frame groaned.

A soft curse from the street followed. _And_ I felt nothing to indicate that the Dead Man knew something dangerous had begun.

The Windwalker had not brought the lighting up brighter tonight. Yet. Only a candle burned, its wan light barely potent enough to reveal a blindly groping arm of flesh like the one that had tried getting in through the window at Fire and Ice.

I joined the Windwalker in an effort to punish that. Unhappy noises came from outside. I hurled raging thoughts the Dead Man's way. I slammed the window shut.

Furious Tide of Light used the candle to light my lamps, then applied the business end to the probe still oozing in through the crack of the window.

That caused some excitement.

Sudden as an explosion, an awful, despairing wail came from the street. The arm of flesh went crazy as a snake with a broken back. My friend kept right on attacking it. Something on the other end decided that it did not need to explore my bedroom after all.

Furious Tide of Light leaped into the air, slammed down hard on the double-hung.

A chunk of whatever two feet long and as thick as her wrist separated from what lay outside.

That was most remarkably unusual! Definitely a woman with potential.

I had nothing to say. I fell down on the side of my bed. The Windwalker landed in my lap. Our hearts were pounding. Our attention was on the severed tentacle. I croaked, "They found Morley again."

A shriek of rage and pain ripped the night outside. It did not stop. It headed away, uphill on Macunado, at no great speed.

The Windwalker did not get up to take a look. I did not have the moral fiber to set her back on her feet.

The Dead Man made contact but his thoughts had no form. I got the impression that were he a living being he would be puking up his guts.

His distress took me away from my dilemma, some, though the Windwalker kind of leaned back and made herself comfortable.

Old Bones needed time to pull himself together. Once he did I was in contact with a different being. He had dipped a toe into a darkness even he could not have imagined just a few days ago.

He was centuries older than me. That something contemporary would appear terrible to him scared the pants off me. Did I dare be pantless in the presence of Furious Tide of Light?

If they are not on now, Garrett, get them on. You have to make a census of the people who were supposed to be watching.

I do? "What?"

Your trousers. You are not actually wearing them. Remove the Windwalker from your lap and put on your trousers. I want you both out in the street. Her I want aloft and following the thing that fled up Macunado. It was not traveling at any great speed. Let her catch up. If she can control it, have her bring it back.

I had questions. This was not the time. This was the time to move fast. Response times are crucial.

Singe will come collect the specimen.

"She'd better hurry. The one up north turned to stink and goo."

The Windwalker, prized loose, looked at me oddly.

I told her, "You know about my partner. He's why you're wearing the Kevans mesh. So he can't get inside your head. He wants me to ask you to do some stuff." I relayed the Dead Man's instructions quickly.

She understood immediately.

"I'd better get going. I don't think there's much chance I can control that thing. I don't have those skills. Get that window open."

I'd just finished when Singe bulled in, armed with a bucket and sour attitude. She turned sourer still as she watched the Windwalker float away. Which I wasn't watching because I had turned to face her.

As I pointed out the piece of monster flesh, she demanded, "Why isn't that woman wearing any underwear?"

"Damn! I missed that completely."

Lucky for Singe's peace of mind, I'd had my pants on when she charged in.

49

I went out the front door like people who can't fly. Singe had armed me up, though my lead-weighted head knocker was the only tool of mayhem obvious. I was feeling less confident than I ought, being fully aware that I hadn't done this stuff for a long time. My skills and instincts had atrophied.

The Dead Man filled my head with an itinerary. And, *There will be much to tell once I have had time to reflect. Those things should not have been able to get close. They should not have been able to brush me aside so easily, though it may be a blessing that they did. I cannot imagine the mind of a master vampire being more filled with filth.*

Five men representing as many interests had been posted to keep an eye on my place. No doubt they knew about one another. They might have pooled resources. Old Bones wanted a roll call. Men doing similar work had come to grief up by Fire and Ice.

This was nothing I wanted to do. Which might suggest that I *was* past the point where I should stop doing what Tinnie wanted me to stop doing.

If I couldn't handle the ugliness anymore I should get busy being the neutered door guard I'd seen myself as before this came rumbling down.

Among the Civil Guard, Belinda's friends, a guy from Morley's crew and one from the Children of the Light, I found six of the five people Old Bones claimed were watching. John Stretch's guys nabbed the extra.

First was a red top right across the street. He was uninjured but his mind had gone blank. Which was the story over and over. The last man, a tin whistle posted on the steps to Mrs. Cardonlos' house, was awake but deeply confused.

I found one dead man, a door up the street from my place. Nobody knew him. Probably an unlucky guy who thought he'd found a nice place to spend a homeless night.

I approached the Cardonlos homestead, wakened the widow. She pretended that I was disturbing her rest with my assault on her door. She had not aged well and had not handled that well. She had become a cosmetics huckster's dream, a younger man's nightmare, and an object of derision for attractive younger women.

I've seen so many like her that I suspected a disease strikes women of a certain age. Badly colored hair. Makeup laid on with a trowel. Perfume dense as a swamp's miasma. And a ready, pathetic simper for any man young enough to remember what it's like to stand upright.

She did not simper at me. She recognized me. "It's started, hasn't it?"

"Excuse me? What's started?"

"The death of tranquility." She freighted that with omen, like she was proclaiming the twilight of the gods. "There hasn't been any trouble here since you followed your trollop up the Hill."

She didn't have that right. My trollop was actually a lady. And she had nothing to do with the Hill. "I'm back. You should petition the Director to put you back on full time. Meantime, he needs to know what happened tonight. All his people were hurt. One man died. He'll recall what happened on the north side."

Mrs. Cardonlos gulped some air. She wanted to make that all my fault but didn't know how.

I pointed. "That one down there has lost his hearing."

The veteran lady gulped again. "The excitement *is* back."

"Get word to the Al-Khar. I'll be busy getting the casualties together and trying to help them." Extra info she could include in her report, to encourage a quick response.

Relway would want his troops exposed to the Dead Man as briefly as possible.

50

Furious Tide of Light returned before the Guard showed. She was morose and uncommunicative. I wasted no questions. The Dead Man would winkle out anything of interest.

I did suggest, "How about you help with these guys that got hurt?" I had three pulled together in one place. Keeping them there was problematic. They wanted to wander off.

Singe had gone to find her brother. She returned with a half dozen ratmen who helped collect the other casualties and wrangled those already rounded up. Singe was antsy. She wanted to get on the trail of the thing that had started the excitement. But she restrained herself in front of the Windwalker, at the gentle urging of the Dead Man.

Furious Tide of Light went through the motions halfheartedly, aiding the injured. She must have found something she had not wanted to find, following that whatever to its lair.

When she wasn't being her brother's surrogate on the spot Singe glared at the Windwalker and gave me looks, demanding, "When are we going to get going? The trail is getting cold."

I told her, "I don't think we will."

"Why not?"

"Three reasons. We are forbidden. My mission is to protect Morley. And Old Bones already knows."

She understood. But still she made hissing noises to express her exasperation.

The Windwalker's healing skills were basic. She reached her limits quickly. But she did stabilize everyone.

Nobody else died but the man I had found dead stayed that way.

* * *

The man who came out on behalf of the Guard was one Rocklin Synk, previously unknown to me. He was rational and reasonable. He didn't automatically assume everybody who wasn't him was guilty of something. He didn't treat people like they'd already been convicted of aggravated capital treason with a garlic pickle on the side.

We were headed into the graveyard shift when he showed. We had a smaller audience than seemed likely. Evidently people didn't get out of bed to be entertained by the misfortunes of others anymore.

The time and pitiful audience may have helped shape Synk's attitude. Maybe it wasn't worth the work, putting on a hard-ass show.

Still, any true believer in the Relway vision must start from the premise that anyone who isn't Deal Relway or one of his henchmen is likely an agent of chaos and a harbinger of the coming darkness. Investigations are built on such foundations, their function to find or create support for the initial supposition. Synk was the kind of guy who palled around with you till you handed him the end of the rope he would use to stretch your neck.

I kept him near the house while we talked.

Old Bones soon let me know why this man had been sent.

This is Mr. Synk's first field assignment. His functions at the Al-Khar have involved payroll accounting and personnel management. His task tonight is to learn as much as possible without revealing the Guard attitude toward this case.

Meaning the Civil Guard did have an attitude they didn't want expressed. "I don't care. All I'm interested in is taking care of my friend till he's ready for release into the wild."

By now the Guard had established an overwhelming presence. Ratmen were scarce. The Windwalker got inside before she was recognized. I was outside with nobody but Singe and swarming red tops.

I developed the suspicion that nobody interested in this mess was really looking the other way just because some unidentified entity insisted. Not privately.

I was a gracious host. I repeated my story over and over. Synk insisted that he had to have the fragment of a tentacle. Singe hustled off, brought it out. It was spoiled already. The bucket contained noxious brown soup with chunks of meat quickly melting. It did not smell like fresh seafood.

I didn't care. That was what I expected. I wanted to get back inside and find out why the Windwalker was distraught.

Rocklin Synk knew more about the Garrett friends and family than Garrett did. I started to give him hell for loading all the downed watchers into his Al-Khar wagons. He cut me off. "Will we be able to borrow your tracker?"

Singe was close enough to hear. "I don't have a tracker. One of my associates is a skilled tracker. If you want to avail yourself of her talent you'll have to work it out with her."

Synk did not like that at all.

Old Bones assured me that Synk was not a bad human being. My own impression was that he was about as decent as they came inside the Guard. But he was a definite product of TunFaire's human culture. He did not consider ratfolk people. There was a solid chance he didn't consider members of any of the Other Races real people.

The thinking underlying the whole Human Rights movement was unfashionable at the moment but it hadn't gone away. It could come back fast. It needed only one ugly nudge.

I added, "Though I wouldn't ordinarily presume to tell her what to do, I'd insist she got her fee up front because she's dealing with the Guard."

"Sir?" Taken totally off balance.

"Your runty boss has a habit of expecting people to help him for the sheer joy of participating in the process. It behooves those addicted to food and shelter to have the foresight to collect their pay before they do the work."

Synk honestly seemed bemused. "You don't trust the Guard?"

"When money is involved? Consult your own experience."

Seconds passed. Then, "I see. Unfortunately, I wasn't given the wherewithal to undertake any negotiations."

Singe said, "You are on your own, then, Constable." She headed for the house. Where had she found that title? Pulled it from the air, perhaps.

I shrugged. "There you have it. The track may still be there in the morning." I watched Singe close the door behind herself. I told Synk, "On an unrelated point, you won't get much joy from arresting Belinda Contague's men."

Synk engaged me in a brief semantic debate, insisting that nobody had been arrested.

"You'll have a hard time selling that to folks whose agents you're hauling off."

"I don't have to sell anything." He might have been an accountant turned loose but he did have a full ration of Civil Guard conceit. He gave me some crap about protective custody for witnesses and about making sure material witnesses got the best of health care.

"Mr. Synk, I have to hand it to you. You are a prodigy of Guard bullshit and refined Relway-speak. You'll go far. As long as you don't have direct dealings with disgruntled folk like Belinda Contague."

Synk proved he was a complete desk weenie, then, by not being concerned that he might irritate a gang princess.

Let it be, Garrett. He is a good man who believes his goodness to be a shield in itself. I understand that you think you must look out for everyone, but the crushing this man is thundering toward might be instructive to the Civil Guard as a whole.

"That lesson being?"

That righteousness is not a shield. The good die more quickly than the bad.

It's also damned subjective but I did not bring that up.

I had reached a point where my hopes and ambitions swirled exclusively round the prospect of getting back to bed.

Still, some things needed attention. I had to see how Morley had weathered the last few hours. Which proved to be, he had slumbered on through. And I wanted to hear about what had the Windwalker so glum.

I had a suspicion.

The Dead Man told me I was wrong. He did not want to fuss about it tonight. I did need to get back to bed. I had a stressful tomorrow looming.

My plan to hit the sack had to go on hold while I convinced Furious Tide of Light that Singe was doing right by putting her into the guest bedroom. Though nothing would have happened if she had been allowed to snuggle in the warm with me. I was exhausted and so not in the mood. Singe's nose told her that. But there were proprieties to be observed, as far as she was concerned.

Splitting the difference, I kissed the Windwalker on the forehead when Singe wasn't looking. A minute later I was secure beneath my own blanket. The window was shut and latched. I warmed up the snore cycle.

51

The Dead Man was a perfect prognosticator. Next day was a nightmare of visitations. General Block came and went. Belinda Contague did the same, and mother-fussed Morley till he begged her to leave. Deal Relway his own self turned up, accompanied by Rocklin Synk. I thought we'd never get shut of him, though early on, for a wonder, he granted that he must be getting the truth from me.

It was hard to keep a straight face. Relway wore a custom metal mesh coif under silver mail. His freakish ears protruded through slits provided. Weird. I'd never seen his ears before. They'd always been hidden under his hair.

The headgear was guaranteed to shield his thoughts. The Dead Man assured me that the Director had been conned. It hadn't taken him thirty seconds to break through.

Relway got no warning from me.

I wasn't sure I cared to know what was hidden inside his head.

The Windwalker stayed out of sight, upstairs. She showed no inclination to leave. Singe stoically delivered her breakfast and lunch.

Sarge turned up. I joined him in with Morley. Not much got said. Sarge was just plain misty-eyed.

While I was in there other people came by with preliminary reports. Most just shambled past and let Old Bones pluck what he needed from their heads, thus betraying no connection to us.

The Dead Man touched me. *I need you to catch Mr. Relway. He is a block east of Wizard's Reach, briefing some of his men.*

I scooted out, chock-full of message and thrilled to be running free.

I was hacking and panting before I found the Director. He wasn't wearing his magical headgear. He looked like just another red top. Five more of who got ready to thump on me. But Relway had them hold off. No need to start right this instant.

"You should get in shape, Garrett. You're way too young to be wheezing after a quarter-mile trot."

"Old Bones says to tell you that four new watchers just moved into the neighborhood and he can't read them. Yours and the Outfit's he recognizes and considers harmless. This bunch are different. They showed up right after you left. There might be more than four, too, since they're so hard to spot."

Relway's ugly little face lit up. He asked where to look. I told him. "Thank you, Garrett. I'm going to take back some of the harsher things I've said about you. Go home. Get inside. Lock your door. Don't let anyone in after sundown."

"What? Why not?"

"Because that thing might be back and maybe has a shape-shifter side to it. Which guarantees some high adventure." He turned away, handed out assignments to his escort. Those men began to hurry off.

The Director noticed me standing there with my thumb in my ear. "Why the hell are you still here, Garrett?"

I headed for the house. It was uphill all the way. Not steeply but enough to taunt my flabby muscles. The Director's men snapped up their first victim as I climbed the steps.

Shouting and threatening attended the process. The captive considered himself exempt from the attentions of the Civil Guard. Relway disagreed. An application of nightsticks ended the argument.

The Dead Man felt so smug about it that I could feel it in the street.

But once I got inside: *Double lock it, then see Dean about salt.*

That was off the wall. "All right." I headed for the kitchen, where I found a disgruntled old man making supper for twice the usual crowd, with the added burden of two meals having to be suitable for consumption by invalids. He sucked it up and didn't complain so I didn't remind him how easy he had it, overall.

I expect he liked it better when Singe was the only one he had to feed and fool.

"Salt," I said.

"Yes?"

"Do we have any? His Nibs said see you about salt. I'm seeing you. He must have let you know. Damn! That smells good."

Something in the pan had me drooling.

"I have two pounds and a pinch. I picked up some last week."

"And I have some they gave me at the place where we stayed before." I thought I knew what Old Bones wanted done. He gave me a confirmatory nudge.

52

I ate. The main course was pork chops, for him and me. Singe and Dollar Dan Justice, in with Morley for the night, got sausages and that ratfolk favorite, stewed apples. I snagged a dollop of apples for myself. Dean makes them good. For Morley and Playmate it was chicken soup.

I hoped Playmate's brother-in-law didn't destroy Play's business while he was away.

We all forgot the Windwalker. At first. Old Bones nudged me.

I hustled up and let her know it was all right to come down. The outsiders were gone and we were having supper. Downstairs, Singe let her know it was all right for her to go home. Nobody would notice her leaving. I wondered if she thought the watchers had been stricken blind.

Singe's whiskers twitched in a way that said she was irritated—probably because she didn't like something she was getting from the Dead Man.

The Windwalker stayed close, which meant she crowded into the kitchen with me and Dean. She donned her vulnerable guise and conquered Dean immediately. In a soft, breathless voice she told me, "I don't think your associate likes me."

"My associate is scared of you."

"Why?"

"She thinks she knows me better than anybody but me. She thinks I'll get infatuated, will lose my sense of proportion, will grab the short end of something, and mess up everything for all of us."

Garrett. Really.

I meant it. That would be Singe's thinking, in essence.

"She might be jealous."

"That's possible, too."

"Are you infatuated?"

"Not quite. Definitely intrigued and valiantly trying to fight it."

She smiled slightly. Maybe wistfully.

"Don't you do whatever it is you do that makes every man in sight turn into a drooling wannabe love slave."

"I'll be all business. You'll see. You won't even know I'm a girl."

Yeah. Right. And then the pigs will come home to roost.

It would be impossible for most men and some women to ignore her sex in her presence even when she didn't want to be noticed.

I thought about letting her know that the Dead Man thought well of her, decided against it. She did not need to be reminded of his existence.

Dean poured fresh tea. We sipped. I said, "Singe was right about this being a good time to slip away unnoticed."

"I don't want to."

"Fine. Then you can help with the salt."

"The salt?"

"The thing that keeps trying to get in shows some characteristics of slugs or snails. Slugs and snails don't do well when they run into salt."

Furious Tide of Light was the victim of a sheltered childhood. She had no idea.

I told her, "They melt when you put salt on them."

"Gross!" But, seconds later, her attitude brightened. "I'll help with the salt."

"Want to talk about it?"

"Talk about what?"

"Why you were so down after you followed that thing home. But now you're not."

"I don't think so."

She really believed in that metal hairnet her daughter had invented.

It does work, some.

"I'm done here. Dean, you outdid yourself."

"Not really. You've been eating inferior cooking."

Ouch! He wasn't going to turn on Tinnie, too, was he? He'd always been a booster. Though, to be perfectly accurate, the redhead was not much of a cook. With her looks that hadn't been a skill she'd needed to develop.

"Salt," I said. "Time to do it. Dean?"

Thunk! A cloth sack landed in front of me. "Save as much as you can."

"I'll use my own before I break into this. Promise."

53

The front door was easy. I opened up. The Windwalker sprinkled salt along the sill plate. I shut the door carefully. We would have to redo that one because of traffic. For now it should stay shut till Dollar Dan and the cleaning ladies traded places.

We did the back door next. That got almost no use. Likewise, the transom and one barred window that let light in during the day. That was the only window left on the ground floor. The others had gotten bricked up during the heyday of lawlessness.

Then down we went into the dank of the cellar, me with the lantern, the Windwalker lugging the salt. The steps groaned under my weight. They needed replacing. They had begun to rot. I said, "This is nasty."

"Only if you're not a spider."

She had that right. Spiderwebs and cobwebs hung everywhere. They covered the surface of the foundation stone. There was dampness on that stone, too. The air was thick. Our passage stirred dust despite the damp. The floor, nominally tamped earth, was one cup of water short of becoming pure mud.

The door to the outside was in worse shape than the steps. I said, "Be generous with that stuff down here. Yuck! This is *nasty*! I can't imagine why Singe hasn't had it cleaned out and fixed up."

Singe didn't think about those parts of the house she didn't visit, that was all. She was conscious of appearances and utility but not maintenance. She would overlook the cellar till the house fell into it.

Once we emerged from the underworld I let her know. She looked me over, sniffed, said, "Definitely. Morley is awake."

"Ten minutes. We still need to get the upstairs windows. And I need to get this gunk off me."

I returned to the kitchen for tea. The Windwalker wasn't there anymore. "Where'd she go, Dean?"

He pointed up. "She went to clean up."

"It's really nasty down there."

"I like this one, Mr. Garrett."

"What?" I wasn't paying attention because I'd noticed that salt had been laid down along the bottom of the door to the cellar.

"This woman. I like her a lot."

"You do? What about Tinnie?"

"I like Tinnie a lot, too. Tinnie is entertaining and challenging. Because she's always there, there's never been a question if she is the best woman to be there. With this one, though . . . I'm relaxed and comfortable, despite what she is. I don't worry if she'll start barking about something I have no idea . . . You do see what I mean?"

I did. Still, I was flabbergasted. A great word, that. I didn't get to use it often enough. Flabbergasted. From a root word meaning he ate too many beans.

Dean had been a booster of Tinnie Tate since the day he finally accepted the fact that he would never hook me up with one of his homely nieces.

Did I need to get nervous? In no time, with no apparent effort, Furious Tide of Light had conquered Dean and the Dead Man both. It had taken Old Bones an age to accept Tinnie. If the Windwalker seduced Singe, I was in it deep.

"Dean, she is remarkable. Like you say, easy to be around. She just naturally seems to belong. But you have to remember what she is and the people she runs with. And I don't even know her real name. She's still just the Windwalker, or Furious Tide of Light."

"That might be cumbersome, socially, if you're making introductions, especially in your circles. But it won't be a problem much longer."

"Huh?" Caution: Giant Intellect at Work.

The Windwalker's shy little girl voice piped, "My name is Strafa. Strafa Algarda." She moved very close as she came for tea of her own. She bumped me gently, at the hip. I was pretty sure she'd overheard everything.

Dean grinned almost lecherously. He'd never done that with Tinnie. He'd always been frowns and disapproval when he thought we might be playing grown-ups.

I *was* in it now, definitely and deeply, riding it without reins or a saddle, at a gallop, straight into one of those narrow places every man hates to go: a time of decision.

How could I get out of this without somebody getting mangled?

The Dead Man was amused in the extreme. He didn't have the imagination I did. He couldn't picture a future where the Tate clan hunted me down and staked me out on a termite mound. Or where one of the top dozen operators in a city renown for black-hearted and cruel sorcerers had a bone to pick with a man who done her wrong.

Do not become hysterical.

And I couldn't respond because we were still pretending that he couldn't read the Wind . . . Strafa's mind.

I wished I could get in there and look around myself. I had questions. Chuckles hadn't given me much, yet. Too, I wanted to know what he learned from that thing in the street. He should have given me that a long time ago, unless it was too scary for somebody as young as me. And, as long as I was feeling left out, how about what he had gotten out of my best pal?

On cue, sourpuss Singe stuck her head into the kitchen. "You said ten minutes an hour ago, Garrett. He's fading now."

"I've told you a million times not to exaggerate. It hasn't been anywhere near an hour."

"The point remains. You are ignoring your most important task while you indulge in flirtation."

What was this? My cheeks got hot!

I headed for the cold well, grabbed a pitcher.

Singe took it away. "I'll handle that. You go see Morley."

54

They had him propped up in a chair. He wore clean clothes. Belinda must have had those brought by. He *was* fading when I arrived, but he brightened some. "They're promising me a real bath soon."

"Be like heaven on earth."

Strafa had followed me. Morley's eyebrows rose. The hunter light sparked in his eyes. He tried on his girl-killer smile, then looked at me, curious. His face collapsed into a mild frown.

"Morley, this is Strafa. She's helping find out what happened to you. Strafa, this is Morley Dotes, purported restaurateur and genuine crime victim."

Would he recognize her?

"Pleased to meet you, ma'am." He had made that fast a read.

More politely than seemed plausible considering her feelings, Singe eased the Windwalker aside so she could deliver my pitcher. Then she herded Strafa somewhere else.

Dotes asked, "Something special there?"

"Might be."

"Uhm." He asked none of the questions my conscience primed me to expect. "Interesting."

"Frightening. I'm getting lost. This shouldn't happen to me. I'm a big boy, I'm a good boy, and I've been in the same place a long time. The place I've always ended back at since way back when we went to the Cantard to fight vampires. But now this. And I don't know her that well."

"It happens, Garrett. How well did you know Maya? Or Eleanor? Eleanor wasn't even alive. And what about Belinda?"

"Belinda was the other way around. I was mostly trying to keep from getting my throat cut."

He didn't call me on that, probably because he didn't want to talk about Belinda. "Not to worry. You being you, you'll mess it up out of some compulsion to do what you think is the right thing. You'll end up back where you started even if it isn't what you want."

Not what I needed to hear. "Let's talk about you."

"My favorite topic, but why? Hasn't the Dead Man drained me dry?"

"No. He says you've got a brain like a rock."

"What can I say? When he's right, he's right. If I had the brains of two rocks I wouldn't be in this condition."

"You starting to remember things?"

"No."

"Really?"

"Truly. It's like whole weeks have been cut out of my memory. I have a vague recollection of waking up in a bed somewhere with you and Bell hovering. Or was that . . . ? Now that's getting murky."

"That could've been four different women. Belinda had you hidden upstairs at a classy hook shop."

"Yeah? That's murk. Before that, though, it's all a dark place. Not just vague but a big black obsidian chunk of nothing. Then murk before that. I know I was walking. Not sneaking but being unobtrusive. I don't think I was following anybody. I don't know where I was coming from. Something caught me from behind."

Morley, taken by surprise? Wow.

He jumped as though pricked. His eyes lost focus. He started speaking fluent incoherent.

Old Bones was feeling benevolent. He filled my head with Morley's recollections of what had set him off.

There was a woman, vague, becoming clearer as she approached. She was tall and slim and wore black leather. She moved with natural sensual arrogance. Her hair was big and almost old lady gray. She was far from old, though. She might be just starting her twenties. Her mouth was small but her lips puffed a bit. They were an intense red.

Those lips held the only stark color in the picture.

The vision faded. Morley's mind slipped into the murk, then plunged into the obsidian oblivion.

I collected myself. "I didn't recognize her."

Old Bones fed the vision back to Morley, who said, "Me neither. And I wouldn't forget those lips."

The one task I gave Jon Salvation, because he was desperate to be included, was to recruit an artist unafraid to work with me. Once we develop portraits we may be able to make identifications.

"Portraits? Plural?"

General Block has generously agreed to lend us Jimmy Two Steps.

Singe proved she was being included by calling from her office, "Why hire an artist? Let Penny do it. She has the talent and the materials. She lives close by and she could get started right now."

She is also insanely timid around Garrett.

"I will promise her to defend whatever virtue she pretends to have left."

Oh, catty!

Singe had a problem with Penny Dreadful, too? This was news to me.

Of course, after being away so long, everything was news to me.

"Do both," I suggested. "At least once. We'll see if two different artists see the same thing. And, while we're borrowing the King's property, why not take a look at Butch and his brother?"

I tendered that request. It came too late. The younger man was released because he cooperated fully. The other received a minimal sentence to the aqueduct project.

Then, *Oho! This could be interesting. Singe, please stand by at the door.*

55

My heart jumped into my throat. There was only one person this could be. Despite all my thought, I wasn't ready.

So while I headed into panic mode, the Windwalker contributed by coming down to see what was going on.

The amusement exuded by the Dead Man was overwhelming.

Singe opened the door. Kolda came in. "Hey, Garrett, I think I found remedies for both your friends."

"Good on you, Brother Kolda. Tell me about it." My relief was so huge I was about to pee my pants.

More amusement.

Kolda produced a half dozen small bottles. "These brown ones are for your poisoned friend. The one with the green stopper will help his memory. The one with the red stopper will work on the poison. The one with the clear stopper will make him piss. A lot. He'll want a lot of water. Let him drink as much as he wants. It'll flush his body out. The blue bottles are for your sick friend. I wrote the instructions out so you don't have to remember them."

Kolda was pleased with himself. I would have to give him some strokes. He had done good.

Singe was still standing by the door. I said, "You want to take these instructions? I'll lose them just going down the hall."

"Put the paper on my desk. I'm busy." She began sliding bolts back.

I panicked all over again. And with no more need. When I shambled back from putting the medicines and instructions on Singe's desk, with the latter carefully weighted down by the former, I found Kolda pressed back against the far wall of the hall, completely rattled. DeeDee, Crush, and Miss Tea filled the hall with bounce, beauty, and chatter. DeeDee was in a blood sport mood. She had Kolda picked for the weakest game on the plain and thought he needed tormenting.

I blurted, "What are you three doing here?" Ever the boy with the golden tongue. "I'm glad I made a good impression, but . . ."

Miss Tea moved into my personal space. I cringed back into Singe's office. She chucked me under the chin. "We have the evening off. We couldn't stay away."

Crush came in close, too, but she was just looking past me.

Strafa Algarda descended the stair again, drawn by the hubbub. She began to glower. Likewise, Singe, from the doorway end of the hallway. I said, "Morley is in the room on the left, right there."

"Thank you."

Crush asked, "This is where you live? You must do pretty good."

"I was lucky on a couple of jobs. And I work with people who are the best at what they do."

Singe kept scowling. She was seriously irked about something.

Crush looked at her, Kolda now getting his breath and color back, and the Windwalker. She saw something I didn't. She said, "I see books. Can I look?"

Singe gave a grudging nod. She may have gotten advice from the Dead Man.

"Sure. Come on. They aren't mine, though, so don't touch."

Some kind of joyful reunion commenced in the other room. Morley Dotes and Miss Tea were old friends after all.

Crush asked, "Are they the witch's books?"

"The witch?"

"The woman at the end of the hall. It's obvious."

"She might resent being called a witch. She's a lot more. Height of the Hill. A Windwalker. No. The books are Singe's. The one who let you in."

"Really?" Amazed.

"Truly. She is the smartest person I know, human or rat. I couldn't survive without her." No need to mention the Dead Man.

He had to be in heaven, slithering through the secrets buried in all these fresh minds. He'd never use what he found, likely, but he would feel good knowing.

He had to be in heaven, complete with this whole mess. He was learning a lot of the secrets of this dark old city. Or so it must seem after a long dry spell.

Be careful, Garrett. That crumpet will fall in love with you for Singe's books. More amusement.

I asked Crush, "Didn't you want to see Morley?"

"Not so much. DeeDee is enough competition for Mike."

I didn't follow. I heard the front door open and close. Now what? I went to look. Crush crowded up to peek past me.

Penny Dreadful had arrived. She was loaded with artist's stuff. She froze when she saw me looking. I couldn't resist. I winked. Her gaze shifted to Crush, who wasn't much older than she. She scowled. Crush glared. Penny headed for the door to the Dead Man's room. Kolda opened it. I asked Crush, "Do you know Penny?"

"Only by type."

"Kid has lived a rough life." I sketched it.

Crush was not impressed. She had some background of her own.

"Singe, how did Penny know we needed her help?"

"I have skills, partner. I sent a message." She gave Crush a look that should have caused bone bruises.

She was not feeling charitable toward any female today.

The Dead Man finally clued me to something he should have mentioned as soon as I came into range. *It is her estrus time and today is its peak. She has taken drugs to suppress the effects. Those are not entirely efficacious where the psychological indications are concerned. I do enjoy these newcomers. I had quite forgotten how colorful some of your acquaintances can be.*

Crush said, "She was jealous when she saw me."

"What?" The Windwalker? Singe? *Penny?*

That roused the logic beast and got it shambling. It fed on things that had been happening the past few days.

Singe no longer consciously entertained the adolescent fantasies she had suffered when first we teamed up but I was top rat around here. She might have formed a deep down attachment that got the salt in the raw wound treatment when she was in heat.

Time to be careful.

She was taking some potent drugs. The rat thugs who were in and out never responded to her. Dollar Dan had been nursing a yearning for Singe since John Stretch took over as number-one rat gangster. Dan would be watching for an opportunity.

All right. Singe didn't like anyone female right now because they were competition for the boss rat's attention. Tinnie must be way up on her transitory list. But Tinnie wasn't here. Strafa Algarda was. And Crush, who was just a kid.

Crush slipped past, stepped down the hall, glanced back, gave me an unwarranted "gotcha!" look that I would have expected from DeeDee first.

That had to be for her own benefit. She thought she had proven that I could be manipulated even when I was trying to be a good guy.

Singe smoldered.

How long would this last? Would this be her worst day? I hoped.

I then realized that she had not left the door.

Oh, God and all His Saints defend me! All I needed was for the redhead to walk into this menagerie. The only female in the place Tinnie would trust might be Penny. And that would change the instant she got a look at how Penny had grown.

Someone knocked. Singe started undoing bolts.

56

Kolda sort of half whimpered. "You don't got any more need for me, Garrett, I better get on out of here." Body language screamed that he was a liar. What he really wanted was to dive into the visiting mob. Team Fire and Ice could have their way with him till the stretcher bearers carried him away. "Trudi don't like it if she has to wait up."

Who was Trudi?

Fiancée.

That old devil time playing tricks again. Did Kolda have a wife back when he was trying to poison me? I thought so but couldn't remember for sure. Well, he didn't have one now. The woman he did have scared him, though not as much as the fantasies tormenting him here.

"If you got to go, you got to go. You wouldn't want to miss supper on account of these beasts. Are you having trouble, Singe?"

"That idiot out there keeps pushing on the door. This bolt won't slide if there's pressure. I had it made that way. Ah. I've got it now." She let the door swing.

In came Jon Salvation and a companion recently escaped from a homeless shelter. The latter lugged gear similar to what Penny had dragged in. His was seedier. He was seedier, by an order of magnitude. He needed to discover soap and water. He needed to steal some clean clothes. And he maybe ought to forego the next dozen bottles of ardent spirits.

His hair was a wild, gray tangle. I shuddered to think what vile livestock he was importing into my house. He was shorter than Salvation and a whole lot dumpier. He was the epicenter of a fierce medley of smells.

Jon Salvation said, "This is the Bird, Garrett. Bird, this is the guy who needs your help." He turned. "Singe, can you show the Bird where to set up?" He nudged me a few steps toward the kitchen, whispering, "You have any hard liquor? The Bird has a problem inside his head. He needs the stuff to keep the voices quiet."

I opened my mouth with intent to remind the Remora what he was known to be full of. I received a gentle cautionary brush from the Dead Man. "Voices? Really?"

"You need to see it to believe it. This guy is a genius. When he has just the right amount of firewater in him, so the voices are softer, he paints like an angel."

I believed Salvation. I had run into something like that before.

I asked Salvation, "You have any idea what Bird's real feelings about his madness are?"

"What do you mean?"

"Does he want the voices to go away?"

"Wouldn't you?"

"I would. Yes. But would you? If that meant that you wouldn't have the magic to be a playwright anymore?"

"You're thinking that the Dead Man might be able to shut the mental doors on his demons."

"Might. Come down here one more step." I looked into the room where Morley was taking the attentions of several beautiful women as his birthright. "Crush. Got a minute?"

Young Hellbore turned away from her mother and Madam Mike. She showed me a teen's practiced expression combining boredom, embarrassment, and disgust. "What?" Her expression did not improve when she glanced at my companion.

"I told you that if I got the chance I'd introduce you to Jon Salvation. This is him." I told the Remora, "Crush likes your plays."

The kid got mad. Of course. But she didn't make a scene.

I couldn't see the big deal. This here was Pilsuds Vilchik, the Remora, a weasel who tagged along behind a friend of mine. He whined a lot, got underfoot, and had a twist in his brain that left him unable to see what Winger really was.

I considered Winger a friend but had no illusions about her character.

The idea that this noxious squirt could become a major celebrity was entirely ridiculous.

Singe came out of the Dead Man's room. The Bird delivered. He should have no problem with Old Bones. He was used to having voices inside his head. She looked at me, Salvation, Crush, leapt to some evil conclusion. Shaking her head, she told me, "I'm going to have a cup of tea before any more complications come up. Guard my office."

I didn't get that, unless she was concerned for the sanctity of her books.

Crush and Jon Salvation got along like Hellbore and Pilsuds Vilchik. He was not the giant she had sculpted in her imagination. And she was just another empty-headed kid who asked the same nimrod questions he had heard a thousand times before.

Singe came out of the kitchen carrying a tray with a teapot, sandwiches, and cups. "Join me." Inside her office, she said, "This place is turning into a zoo filled with human exotica."

"You got used to the quiet life."

"I did. And I find the habit hard to break. Eat. This is likely all we'll get for supper. Dean is exhausted. The sorceress is going to help him get upstairs."

"She's good for something, then."

"Don't do that when I'm starting to not like her a whole lot less. I'm stressed enough. And it will only get worse. We have no hard liquor."

"Old Bones ask for it?"

"He thinks he may be able to create a similar effect but wants the real thing handy."

"We could send Salvation out."

"Winger drinks, doesn't she?"

"Yes. Do I need to have Belinda get us out of your hair?"

"She couldn't get here in time."

The poor girl sounded like she was about to slide away into despair.

"You want to head upstairs yourself, Singe?"

"I'd better stay."

"I can handle this crowd."

"Maybe now. How about half an hour from now? You're too far gone. I still love you but you aren't the man you used to be."

The Windwalker joined us. Singe neither protested nor betrayed any distaste. In fact, there was a cup for Strafa on the tray she had carried in. Was peace about to break out? Or was Singe just too tired to fight?

I asked, "Everyone out there still being civilized?"

Strafa said, "A woman and two girls are fussing over your injured friend. There are three men and a girl in with your dead friend. The three of us are here. And the poisoner is missing."

Singe said, "I let Kolda out after Jon Salvation got here."

So. Crush was in with Morley and Salvation was with the Dead Man. That was a brief romance.

Poor Remora. He couldn't be what his fan wanted him to be.

57

Though there was babble from next door and some sort of foreboding from across the way, all was calm and relaxed in Singe's office. Tea got sipped. Not much got said. Strafa, Singe, and I relaxed.

After a time, Singe said, "The caretakers and night guards should be here soon. I expect John Stretch will come with them. I'm going to draw a pitcher of the dark."

The dark was the most potent beer we had. I had been unaware of its presence till now. The cold well must have been modified to handle multiple kegs.

Singe's tail vanished round the edge of the doorway. The Windwalker said, "She doesn't like me."

"No. But she's mellowing."

"Why doesn't she like me?"

"She thinks you're trying to push into our lives. She feels threatened. She's fragile." I made no mention of her season. Maybe the Dead Man could explain that later in a way that made sense to a human woman.

The Windwalker sipped tea and frowned delicately. She seemed waiflike and vulnerable. "How could I injure her?"

I gave Old Bones a few seconds to caution me before I said, "She sees all women in the mirror of Tinnie Tate." The redhead had to come up sometime.

"The abrasive woman who was there for some of the excitement at the World Theater, back when."

"That would be Tinnie."

"You're still involved."

"You know my situation perfectly well."

She smiled a wan, forlorn little smile. "I might have looked into it."

"Singe never liked Tinnie much. She feels guilty about that. She thinks she should like Tinnie because I like her. So now she feels like she needs to be a voice speaking for Tinnie because Tinnie can't speak for herself. Today she found out that both Dean and my partner across the way approve of you. So she feels more pressured."

"I see." She glowed like a kid who had just won a tough race against outstanding competition.

"I was surprised, too."

"Yes?" The glow waxed stronger. The woman was amazing. She might be who she was, one of the dozen most powerful mortals living, with potential for growth, but she was as naïve as a ten-year-old in some ways. She was starved for approval.

Strafa said, "She's right about one thing. I mean to steal you away."

She said that straightforwardly, without a hint of the fierce sensual aura she had used to taunt men, back when she was daddy's girl. She stated a fact and left it for me to digest.

"You're going too fast . . ."

Singe returned with two pitchers and four mugs. She meant to do some drinking and did not plan to do it by herself. I sniffed a pitcher. "I'm in." She had brought summer ale as well as the dark.

She told me, "You pour. I have to get the door."

My stomach plunged to the deck.

58

My panic went to waste again. Singe did not admit redheaded doom. Neither did she bring in her brother and the lady rats who nannied Morley Dotes. What she did admit was General Westman Block and two nervous villains so obviously low-life that they might as well have it tattooed on their foreheads. One was the younger of the pair who had come after me and Tinnie. The red tops had tracked him down. Reason suggested that the skinny, shaky little weasel must be Jimmy Two Steps.

Singe came back, took her seat, drank some beer. Crush came in. "Is it all right if I hang out in here till DeeDee and Mike get over that guy? I'll stay out of the way."

"Fine by me. Singe, all right if she looks at your books?"

Of course it wasn't all right. And any animus she felt toward Strafa she was willing to dump on tasty young Hellbore. But she said, "Please be gentle. And make sure your fingers are clean."

Then the General joined us. "Garrett, I hate to beg but, gods damn! I need to drink something."

Which reminded me, "Singe, how about fuel for that lunatic artist Jon Salvation brought?"

"Something will arrive soon."

How did she know that? She hadn't left the house and Kolda went before the Dead Man put in his request.

Old Bones must have sent word to someone outside. That was the only thing that made sense.

She continued, "General, would you like to try the Weider Dark Reserve? It's a limited production brew that few outside the Weider family get to taste."

"How can I resist? Count me in, Miss Pular."

Singe, Singe, you wonder child. Even the head of the whole damned tin whistle tribe considers you a real person. Which thinking I masked with a stone neutral visage.

Block was impressed despite having been around Singe since her adolescence.

It felt good, seeing my baby treated like one of the gang instead of a freak or half-wit vermin.

Big thumping at the door. I had heard the wolf cry so often that Tinnie and all the freckle speckled redheaded Tates in the world could be out there and I wouldn't raise more than a half-assed whimper.

Nor did I need to. Singe opened up for her brother, Dollar Dan, and two ratwomen. They brought distilled spirits enough to keep the Bird fueled for weeks. Singe hijacked a bottle. She poured a half mug for the General. "There's a real drink."

Crush volunteered, "I'll take some of that, please."

"No," Singe said. "You're too young for dizzy water."

Crush was startled. Then she laughed. Then, shaking her head, she went back to looking at Singe's books.

John Stretch joined us, looking Block askance. Dollar Dan and the ratwomen took up space in the hallway outside the room where Morley was holding court.

Singe told me, "I suspect that pretty young girls who ask for something that will impair their judgment seldom hear the word no."

Crush raised a hand in a gesture of agreement. She had found something to fascinate her. She handled the book reverently.

Crush fascinated Westman Block. But he would not cross that line.

Odd. Women definitely interested the General. I never heard of one getting close. No doubt there was a sad old story. There were plenty of those around.

He emptied his mug quickly and did not refuse a refill. He said, "The resurrection men are back at work." Like that dovetailed into the conversation.

Singe gave her brother her mug, filled with summer ale. He lifted that to me.

Strafa generated a squeak that drew the attention of everyone but Crush. I didn't find out why because, after another pull of the water of life, Block said, "Those men in the gray wool tights and pullovers with the wooden headgear from the incident on the north side? They were fix-ups made from pieces of dead people."

Jaws dropped. Crush let her book fall to her waist. Strafa made gurgling noises.

"Way to introduce a subject," I said. My mug was empty. I decided to give the dizzy water a try.

"Blame the drink," Block said. "I'm not supposed to let that get out."

Interesting. More Civil Guard disobedience.

Clear as iron, Block and Relway were way not happy with outside pressure. Their scorn for the rules suggested that they had gotten quiet assurances from Prince Rupert that he would notice nothing if somebody did babble too much after a mug of beer.

Somewhat nimbly, Singe moved into the hallway again, headed for the door. She needed to be nimble to get through the crowd.

I took a long sip of firewater and tried to run a census. I couldn't come up with a firm number but there had to be seventeen or eighteen warm bodies cluttering the place.

I was way out of practice for the social life. A little beer, a few sips of ardent spirits, and I was totally relaxed. I no longer had a care. Nothing troubled me. I looked at Strafa without a professional thought in my head.

She looked back. One eyebrow lifted slightly. Her small mouth betrayed a ghost of a smile of invitation, agreement, or triumph.

59

Singe said something out in the hallway. I didn't catch the words but her tone was troubled. John Stretch and I both got up and headed that way, me wondering where I had left my stick and how trouble had gotten close with the Dead Man on the job.

John Stretch put that together quicker than I did. He stopped. I bumped into him, not hard.

Singe returned to the office, headed straight for the cup she had given her brother. Had she been human she would have been pale and grim.

The reason was a step behind her. A fine looking redhead hove into view . . .

That was Kyra Tate, Tinnie's teenage niece, at first glance a dead ringer for her aunt. In the instant it took me to realize that Kyra was not my dearly beloved, the master redhead herself materialized.

Kyra was just a little older than Crush. She came with manifest teen attitude. She did not want to be here—though it soon became evident that it had been her idea to come. Behind her, Tinnie slowed down, jaw descending, as she took in the size and makeup of the crowd.

General Block lifted his mug to Tinnie. "Good evening, Miss Tate. May I say how very handsome you look tonight?"

He could get away with talking to her like she was an old lady. If I said something like that I would regret it for months.

Behind Tinnie came her uncle Oswald. Behind Uncle was cousin Artifice, who had a reputation as a brawler.

I nearly laughed, watching Tinnie's reaction to each presence. Strafa should have fallen down whimpering and crawled under something. Crush should have collapsed into a pile of ash. "Wow. And you still have to meet DeeDee and Mike. And to see how Penny has grown." Which I did not say out loud.

She wouldn't have heard me anyway. She had taken on a glazed look. In a faraway voice she announced, "I have to see the Man Across the Hall."

Said entity touched me ever so lightly, without a word, offering the gentlest of reassurances.

Tinnie had arrived primed for a knock-down, drag-out, once-and-forever showdown but had been, from the moment Singe let her in, thrown off stride. There were ratpeople everywhere. There were numerous human people, too, including the commander of the police and a highly placed sorceress off the Hill. And now she had been *summoned* to the presence of His Nibs, where she would encounter yet another crop of amazing guests.

Singe collected herself. She asked the other Tates if they would like refreshments. Uncle Oswald nodded.

Never looking up, Crush said, "I'll throw a tantrum if you let her have anything tastier than tea."

"The same rules apply," Singe said.

Kyra knew she was the subject but had no idea why. I explained. "Underage drinking. Singe doesn't approve. Singe, you better check and make sure Penny isn't sneaking anything."

"Your sense of humor never improves."

She and Old Bones both really liked that kid. I never got why. But, so what? I have foibles of my own.

I asked Kyra, "How come you're down here slumming?" She was giving Strafa a suspicious look. She remembered the Windwalker.

No need to explain Artifice and Uncle Oswald. The old man was looking out for the Tate family dignity. Artifice was there to get his butt kicked if Tinnie tried to make her points physically. Also, to make sure she got around safely.

Those streets out there were getting mean again.

Blatant amusement slithered through the ether from the Thing Across the Hall, no cause apparent.

Block recognized Oswald. They were involved in some charity together but only as distant acquaintances. They engaged in a clumsy exchange.

Strafa moved closer, as though to protect me. Kyra and Artifice overlooked that because they had become fascinated by Crush—Kyra maybe because she thought someone her own age had to be as unhappy to be here as she was. Artifice was interested for the reason any man would be. Crush just standing there begged for solicitous male attention. So toothsome was my little Hellbore.

There was, of course, no way Artifice could know that the bloom was gone from that rose and what remained was mostly thorn. Crush was not wearing work clothes.

"Kyra?"

"Sorry, Garrett." She forgot Crush. "It's kind of embarrassing."

"I don't remember you being long on shy." She could be more forceful and straightforward than her aunt. She hadn't had as much practice pretending to be socialized.

Many killers are sociopaths but only a small percentage of sociopaths are killers. Tinnie was the nonlethal sort.

So far.

60

Kyra told me, "I'm not used to having an audience."

Ha! Her problem wasn't Strafa, the General, or John Stretch. Her problem was Artifice and Uncle Oswald. "Bend down here. Whisper."

Crush murmured, "He wants to look down your blouse."

"Humorous, Hellbore, but unfair. She isn't showing a neckline."

Furious Tide of Light tried wilting Crush with her stare.

Crush went back to her book.

Singe arrived with more mugs, more beer, and muffins. That distracted the male Tates.

Kyra dropped to her knees beside me. "I'm having trouble with Kip. That's really why I talked Tinnie into coming. You know Kip. You can give me some advice."

"Amazing," I said in a conversational voice. Strafa had now posted herself behind me, leaning on the back of my chair. Singe was not pleased but her disapproval was so mild that only I got it. "There's a huge chance that I'm the last guy you should ask for relationship advice. But I'll give it a shot."

"I'm seventeen now, Garrett. Kip and I have been together ... Well, what it is? I don't want to be like you and Aunt Tinnie. Going on and on and on and never ... Oh, *I* don't blame you. What's wrong between you and Tinnie is mostly Tinnie's fault. She could've wrapped everything up years ago if she wanted. Now she might lose you."

Crush made some snide remark about here's your chance under her breath. She got the hard-eye from Strafa. Kyra ignored her. "Anyway, I decided I don't want her advice anymore. I want Kip, not the satisfaction of sitting alone in my room feeling smug about how I showed him. No games. Now and forever."

Way to go, Cyprus Prose! You got one of the hottest girls on the continent bewitched. Amazing, nerd boy. How the hell? But it looked like he was close to losing her, probably without realizing there was a problem.

"Kyra, I'm on your side. You're the best thing that ever happened to that boy. So what's the problem? Is he just being his usual dim self? Can't see what's there in front of him unless you smack him between the eyes?"

I tried mentoring the boy, back when. We had some things in common.

"It's sort of like what's going on with you and Tinnie. Only I believed him when he said a friend of his is in trouble and needs his help. My problem is, he shuts me out of that whole side of his life."

Kyra ran out of steam. She had said it all, for the moment. But Tate women seldom stay silent long. I tried to work out what she meant.

Kip did not have many friends.

Strafa still leaned on the back of my chair. Her knuckles were white. Kyra avoided looking at her even though she should have been curious.

Oh. It was the Faction again. The friend in need must be Kevans, a friend Kip had helped, despite all, back when the Windwalker and I first met.

When Kevans and Kip got their heads together technical miracles happened. They invented strange and wonderful things.

Kyra's concern fed Strafa's. Strafa was hard-pressed because she was still afraid that Kevans might be the girl in the tight black leather. Despite believing that Kevans had an alibi for . . .

She did think Kevans was capable of behavior this foul. That was the key.

Oh, my. My new ally, who might become a special new friend, could end up an enemy because the thing she feared most might turn out to be true.

Alibis can be manufactured, before and after the fact.

I had no trouble imagining Kevans dealing with resurrection men, either. I'd never gotten to know her well but I recalled a sociopathic personality. Yet that had been true of most of the Faction. And she had not been the worst.

That might be an angle worth pursuit.

So. Maybe Kevans *had* been living in that warehouse up north, making new men out of the best pieces of the old.

Where would she get money to pay the resurrection men? Kip?

I rested my right hand on Strafa's where hers lay on the back of my chair. "She can't afford it."

"What?"

"Think. Where would Kevans get enough money to set up what you saw on the north side?"

Kyra became intensely interested in my hands and dialog. No doubt Tinnie would get a detailed report.

And I, being Garrett the wonder fool, had to ease Strafa's dreads by saying, "Kevans could never look as good in black leather as . . ."

Maybe. Maybe not. When I knew her Kevans had been pretending to be a boy. If she took after her mom she could make that leather smolder. Taking a wild shot at making Strafa feel better because her kid was weirdly built was one of those special moments that make me uniquely me.

An instant after it was too late to avoid getting shoe leather caught between my teeth I had no trouble imagining a dozen voices telling me what an insensitive dumbass I was.

One was not imaginary. It came from the Thing Across the Hall and was heavy with exasperation. But that morphed into a vague apology. If I understood right he was taking out on me frustrations developed while conversing with the redhead. Tinnie had shown complete disdain for reality.

I was amazed. He had lost patience and pushed her out, a tactical error for sure. Even today's more difficult Tinnie is amenable to reason if you put in some time. You do need to be patient, to avoid preaching and rational argument. You need to be intense while you present your position. Worried or scared works best. Then you should shut up and go away. You need to have it end up looking like her agreeing with you was her idea.

Which is more work than most guys are willing to do. It's been getting a lot like involuntary overtime for me, too, lately.

Old Bones thought facts and figures should trump emotion. He was a little out of touch with the raw intensity of the living, yet could get irked by a stubborn woman. He wasn't fond of that sex to begin with. It had taken him an age to warm to Tinnie as much as he ever did. It had taken him time to get used to Singe but they were at peace now.

He'd never had a problem with Penny Dreadful, maybe because Penny came to us before puberty came to her. He had few reservations about Strafa Algarda, who was, for sure, simmering, past puberty.

His ability to be amused by my obsessions and angst remained undiminished.

I heard Tinnie talking in the hallway, presumably to Morley. She wouldn't know DeeDee or Mike. Her tone wasn't hostile.

I was able to exhaust her reserves of venom.

Too many eyes were watching. I couldn't get into a conversation. Old Bones found that amusing, too, because half the current population of the house thought he was snoozing.

I focused on Kyra, though Uncle Oswald and Artifice might be more trouble. And, while I obsessed about Tates, never-so-drunk-as-he-pretended Westman Block committed every nuance to memory. Singe and her brother exchanged significant glances. And Crush went on being every man's sweet young fantasy, pretending to be oblivious while she appreciated Singe's literary treasures.

Kyra and Strafa continued to measure one another.

I grumbled, "What can we toss into this to add a little flavor? How about some hot spice?"

Hot spice debuted, her advent entirely civil.

I wore her down.

One quick glance told me that nobody but Ma Garrett's ever-loving, blue-eyed baby boy was intimidated.

Tinnie stopped in the doorway. She eyed each individual, recognizing everyone but Crush. Crush didn't do her the honor of turning to see who had come in. Tinnie frowned when she looked at Strafa, whom she had seen briefly before.

She was impressed. In one room she had found the commander of the police forces of the greatest city in the world, the chieftain of a major underworld operation, a major player off the Hill, and me.

Clever Strafa had relaxed the intimacy of the distance between us before Tinnie arrived, though not by much.

After visiting the Dead Man and Morley, Tinnie could not
help but understand that what was going on here was not just
a conspiracy to inconvenience her.

*She is starting to get it. Take her out on the stoop and ex-
plain it.*

I hoisted myself out of my chair. Mug in hand. With murmured encouragement from the Windwalker.

*And, for the gods' sake, do not make yourself a sacrificial
victim on the altar of let us all just get along.*

What did he mean by that?

*I mean do not just give her her way because you do not like
arguing. This is important.*

There followed a psychic echo of a kitten crying, then the
crack of a whip.

Hey!

He showed me letting myself be bullied by persons of the
female persuasion, all the way back to my mother, but special-
izing in incidents that gave a certain redhead the hold she had
gained over the course of our relationship.

Well.

*You are standing there with a dumb look on your face, practi-
cally drooling, while a dozen people stare and start to wonder.*

Oh. Right.

Old Bones was staging plays inside my noggin. I wondered
if he was doing the same thing inside hers. I did hope.

I said, "Let's you and me go out on the stoop where we can
talk."

61

It was a quiet night. The sky was clear. The moon would not be up for a while. There were a trillion stars. In some parts of the sky there was more silver dust than darkness. None of the watchers in the shadows made themselves obvious. The men who had accompanied Block had gone to find a tavern. We had the night to ourselves.

Neither of us said anything till a shooting star blazed across the firmament, headed west in a hurry. Then it exploded. For an instant TunFaire was bathed in pallid light.

"This may be the most important night in our lives, Tinnie."

She responded with an inarticulate sound that seemed weighted down with sorrow. She pushed against me like she was cold. She was shivering.

I told her, "We've known each other for a long time. I can't imagine my life without you in it. But I can't go on the way we've been. I can't be what you want. Those people in there are important in my life, too."

The last light of the dying star glistened off a tear. She said nothing.

My heart sank. Old Bones had failed. She would remain stubborn till the end.

Proceed gently, Garrett. All is not lost. Even though he liked Strafa Algarda better than this woman whom he knew so much better.

Tinnie said, "Garrett, I love you. You know that. I have forever. I could say something corny like you complete me. I can't imagine myself with any other man. Whatever I said, however I behaved, whatever else happened in our lives, that's been true since I was a kid and you used to come around to see Denny. Ever since then I've tried hard to understand the Garrett who operates outside the closed field of you and me. But I can't, anymore. I *know* I shouldn't be so selfish. I *know* I'm twisting away into a darkness that some people might consider insanity. But I'm obsessed. I can't share you anymore. I *can't*. The monster inside wants to push it to the point where there is no one but you and me. No work. No distractions. Just us. I *know* that's crazy. But I can't stop it."

Now she had me scared.

What she says is true but right now she is trying to manipulate you through exaggeration. Nevertheless, that exaggeration is being built on a truth from a level so deep it has never emerged before.

"Can you help?" Tinnie was a major part of my life. I had loved her, maybe too often from a distance, almost as long as she said she had loved me. But I was not obsessed. I had been in love before. The rational side of my mind told me I would survive—if the pain insisted on coming.

The adventure called Strafa Algarda waited on the other side. I knew that. Strafa offered a chance for an adult, cooperative relationship.

I looked at Tinnie and wondered how she had gotten to this point.

She said, "The Dead Man has been inside my head, trying to show me things. He says you're part of a network of friendships and obligations. He says there is a fine woman who wants to be important to you but you still look only toward me . . ."

What game was Old Bones playing?

Tinnie surrendered to wracking sobs.

The problem here is that a part of her mind does remain fully rational. That fraction knows she is crazy. It knows that obsession drives her. But it has no control. It remains a prisoner inside the growing obsession.

"I can't believe it. How could it happen? Could Kolda come up with an herb? Can you do some kind of surgery?"

I might be able. But you will need to convince Miss Tate that she wants to have the corrective work done. And there is the further question of the strength of your own emotional commitment.

I ignored Strafa, thought a question about working Tinnie and this case in parallel.

That might be possible. Assuming she agreed.

"Curses."

I would have to search her mind memory by memory and hurt by hurt to find tipping points in need of adjustment or cauterization. Each such tipping point will have affected every other that followed. It is a three-dimensional problem. The surgery would be far more subtle than an abuse victim like Miss Algarda needs. She is content with the life she has lived. And there would be no guarantees.

Tinnie said, "You and him are talking about me, aren't you?"

"We are." I pulled her into my arms. As always, she felt exactly right, being there. Designed to fit. She cried. I cried. I told her, "We can work this out. If you let it work out. If you let Old Bones make some minor adjustments . . . I'm going to let him work on me."

That was off the top of my head and next to a bald-faced lie. Any refinements my mind needed he would have made already, without mentioning it. Maybe.

Scary thought, that.

Nobody wants to be told that they need fixing. Even when they know it themselves. Tinnie's natural first reaction was rejection. I kept on holding her tight. I said nothing. Talk would not help. What could be talked about had been talked about.

Changes in us would lead to changes in the conversation.

I thought there was a chance. I thought we could find a way.

Uncle Oswald opened the door, checking up. He had a mug in hand. The rosy glow in his cheeks said he was hard at it, enjoying my hospitality. He didn't see any guts strewn about so he grunted and shut the door.

The clinch went on. Tinnie relaxed slowly, surrendering to need. We had to go on. She had to fight the obsession that would make it impossible to do so.

I was confused, for sure. I had this, familiar and mostly comfortable though always freighted with emotion and drama. I had Strafa in the background, exercising a surprisingly powerful pull—not the way it used to be with any female between seven and seventy. That draw was there, too, absolutely. But there was more to it. An intellectual intrigue and a certainty that Strafa Algarda would involve a lot less drama.

Thou foul beast, Temptation!

I felt the amusement of the invisible observer.

It was a classic tough situation.

Tinnie had the lead by a furlong, at the moment. She was as comfortable as an old shoe once she relaxed against me. But Strafa could pull even, or push ahead, with very little effort, if Tinnie wasn't there to rattle my reason.

The invisible observer suggested, *It is time to come inside. Something is moving in the darkness. You do not want to be out there should it come this way.*

62

The Dead Man's big party rolled on. I led Tinnie into his lair. The temperature had risen there. The air had begun to smell because of the crowd. Penny and the Bird worked on their art. Jimmy Two Steps and Butch's little brother occupied a couple of folding chairs, out of the way, eyes closed, maybe unconscious. Old Bones might be picking their brains.

There is not much there to pick. In any sense.

The lighting was better than usual, on behalf of the artists. The lamps contributed to the rise in temperature.

Playmate's color had improved. It had more depth and sheen. Still, he would be a long-term project, and would demand a lot from the Dead Man at a time when all the rest of this was going on.

Old Bones was a miracle in defunct flesh but he did have limits.

When would he have time to work on Tinnie?

A complication that I am pleased you recognized before I had to bring it up myself. A scheduling problem I will be happy to leave in your keeping.

"Meaning?" I looked over Penny's shoulder. She had several sketches going, all of a very attractive girl. She was doing a sheet of full-body images in different orientations and hairdos. I could say nothing but, "Wow!"

Tinnie failed to poke me. She just looked astonished, and envious.

You are allowing imagination and expectation to carry you away. It is the daring choice of costume that makes the woman so striking. Miss Tate and her niece would appear equally impressive in that apparel.

I said nothing but thought the younger Miss Tate might have an edge on the elder.

Amusement.

"I'm not dead. I notice things."

I watched Penny work. She was talented and quick and had no trouble being close to me while she used charcoal and a variety of Amalgamated's writing sticks to shape her squad of fantasy girls.

The Bird had a color portrait going. It made an ugly, lazy-eyed son of a bitch look like he was about to bark, lean forward, and take a bite.

Tinnie seemed at a loss. I caught the edge as the Dead Man asked her to step back and stay out of the way.

I asked, "Who is this wad?"

A composite of details from many minds. I am not certain but he may be the boss of the resurrection men.

"How did we get to that?"

Mr. Bird, under my direction, is creating a portrait composed of bits taken from the minds of everyone who has come into range since I awakened. Resurrection men are part of what is going on and an angle going unexplored. They gather the bodies that get reengineered. This man could be of special interest. If we can find him.

He was right. It was an approach that had not occurred to me.

Most of our visitors never heard of him. A few have, under the singleton name Nathan. None of our friends, or anyone else, know that they have actually met him but some may have done so without realizing it.

And that, with his wondrous ability to make unlikely connections click, was why the Dead Man was so valuable. I said, "He looks a little like Barate Algarda."

It felt like the warmth went out of the room. His Nibs took a seat behind my eyes, studied the painting through my prejudices.

Not Barate Algarda. The eye. The nose. The scar. The man had a burn scar on the right side of his head, including part of his ear. *Ask the Windwalker to come in here.*

Tinnie started to follow me. She stumbled, stopped, turned, found a folding chair that she opened and carried back into the shadows.

Damn! Maybe I could get Old Bones to teach me that trick.

Strafa stared at the Bird's masterpiece. The artist himself was on break, nursing a bottle of spirits. Strafa said, "I don't know him. He does look familiar." Unaware that green eyes smoldered in the darkness behind us, she held on to my left arm with both of her hands. Those were shaky.

"I thought he looked like Barate Algarda." I could not call the man her father.

She started. She squeezed harder. "He does, a little! That's weird." She let go. She moved to view the painting from different angles.

I have what I need. You may take her back, now.

I asked Strafa, "So what do you think?"

"I think it's weird."

"Too bad. Well, that's all we needed." Crossing the hallway, I asked, "Do you know anyone who calls himself Nathan?"

"No." Two steps. "Wait! I think Dad's grandfather's name was Nathan. He died when I was four. I remember pulling myself up by the edge of his coffin so I could look." In the doorway to Singe's office, she added, "He didn't have a burn scar."

"Thanks."

Back in the Dead Man's room, I asked, "Any chance this guy could be a vampire?"

Miss Algarda was truthful. She does not know him. I doubt that he is a vampire. His face does resemble that of the man Miss Algarda saw in a coffin when she was a child, though.

Vampires did not last around TunFaire. Their suspected presence will unite classes and races like nothing else. Just a suspicion could lead to a frenzied hunt.

This situation has the potential to turn as ugly as a vampire hunt. Which argument may lie behind the Hill's go-easy attitude.

Vampire hunts always got out of hand. Innocents ended up with chopsticks through their hearts. The last full-blown vampire hunt had happened when I was nine. It had done more damage than any natural disaster since.

"Let me ask the General about that."

Ask him to come view the painting.

Block did not recognize the villain. He did concede that

dread of an outbreak of mass hysteria might be the motive behind the hands-off orders being passed around. Might be.

He was, innately, almost as suspicious as Deal Relway.

Block having returned to his firewater, the Dead Man mused,
*We need to see Barate Algarda and his daughter, here. That is a
task the Windwalker will have to undertake.*

"That might be a tough sell."

*Hardly. She will be compliant to any request so long as you
are a gentleman when you present it and you explain the reason
for it.*

I'd never had that kind of power in a relationship. It was
scary.

*Miss Algarda is ceding that power in trust. If you breach
her trust you will reap a whirlwind more cruel than you can
imagine.*

"Way to build me up, Chuckles."

It might be valuable to interview your intern, too.

"Intern?"

*The boy. Cyprus Prose. I will ask the Miss Tates to bring
him in. Making the elder Miss Tate a part of a race against
time might go a long way toward improving her attitude. The
younger Miss Tate will want to look out for her man.*

I was skeptical.

63

I had to reach an understanding with Old Bones about our priorities. Once we acknowledged the most desperate three or four things, there would be, still, time-intensive tasks like honing the ten thousand quirks that defined the mind of Tinnie Tate, all while he kept a sharp watch outside.

You understand.

I understood that everything would take precedence over reconfiguring my special redhead's mental works.

"Your judgment is better than mine. I can't take the emotion out of my choices."

The Dead Man employs profanity infrequently. In a long-winded way he informed me that I was a bone-lazy, backsliding purveyor of mushroom fertilizer determined to avoid even the appearance of contributing anything useful to the conversation.

"Damnit, Old Bones! Life shouldn't ought to be this hard."

Avoid responsibility now, if you like. Do not whine when you face the fattened consequences later.

The change was sudden. For an instant I thought the end had come. The apocalypse. The Twilight. The Rapture, sudden as a dagger in the night. Morley shrieked. Playmate screamed. Tinnie moaned and collapsed. Penny Dreadful and the Bird followed her to the floor. I blacked out for an instant.

I found myself clinging to the frame of the door to the hallway after that instant. I had to concentrate to keep my supper down.

Others had less success.

The light had gone bad. Everything had turned sepia. Those

moving did so jerkily. Bad smells developed as folks lost more
than their suppers.

Confusion reigned. Dread grew so powerful I knew it had to
be artificial. The screaming ended. The screamers had passed
out. But chatter waxed amongst the still conscious. None of it
made any sense.

No one panicked.

Odd, that.

The initial shock came when the Dead Man dropped everything to focus on one problem. Something that demanding
had to be a threat both powerful, lethal, and immediate.

And I, ever-lovin' blue-eyed boy genius that I am, I stumbled up and opened the door for a quick look outside.

Action was developing.

A dozen people in gray wool costumes, their heads inside
combination helmets and masks, were headed for the house.
Most carried torches. A few were armed. One pair lugged a
mini-battering ram that would have dented my door good. Illegally armed ratmen closed in on them from behind.

I found my head knocker and charged, partly because I suspected that a swarming attack would come from other direc-
tions, as well.

The attackers kept advancing because the Dead Man
was not strong enough to stop so many. He did slow them
till their charge looked like it was happening underwater.

His situation would improve as the number of vertical villains declined.

Fine theory, amply supported by the available evidence,
but more easily thought than executed.

The grays did not respond well to my initial efforts. My club
just bounced off. Lesson learned at the cost of getting dinged
a few times.

I shifted to kneecapping. The ratmen started hamstringing.
Their efforts were more effective.

Most of my male guests became involved. At some point
Jimmy Two Steps and Butch's brother realized they were un-
der-supervised and the door was open. They took advantage.

I pushed through the grays. They did not turn on me. They
wanted to turn the house into a bonfire.

Then I was face-to-face with a woman in skintight black
leather gifted with the most stunning shape I'd ever seen.

Penny's drawings didn't do her justice. She had a mountain of wildly curly white hair. A fierce former Marine bearing down did not rattle her. She seemed inclined to flirt.

So beautiful.

And the face of deep evil. She deserved neither quarter nor amnesty.

We had not met before but we had been at war from the moment those idiot brothers took money from Jimmy Two Steps.

She thrust what looked like a stage magician's wand my way, ever so calmly, all in a day's work, slicing sausage at the butcher shop.

Something hit her like a black lightning bolt to the right shoulder just before I knocked the wand out of her hand by running into it with my big, manly chest. She wore the most wonderful look of incredulity.

The wand delivered enough energy to make me bark and spin, flailing for airy handholds that had not yet been installed. I got one goofy, unforgettable snap view of Furious Tide of Light straddling the front peak of my house, legs dangling, kicking, a ten-year-old up to mischief. She wore a big, happy grin. She flung another dark bolt. Just a kid having fun saving her special friend from a villainess built to torment his fantasies.

That nonsense rattled around inside my gourd for the few seconds it took me to fall asleep on those comfy Macunado Street cobblestones.

I was out only briefly. Still, the excitement was over when consciousness came creeping back. Furious Tide of Light was there with me, now. My head was in her lap. That hurt like I had the mother of all hangovers. Her right hand was hot on my chest, over my heart, maybe delivering the strength I needed to push back the darkness. The agony in my head faded steadily.

Ha! Had I discovered the cure for the common hangover?

I flashed back to that incredible shape in black leather. That was one way somebody could have gotten close enough to stick Morley. That body would have distracted him. A touch of that wand would have left him unable to defend himself, though I suspected the Dead Man would have excavated the evidence if that had happened.

"That wasn't Kevans." Only a liquid weakness kept me from shoving my foot farther down my throat by offering a qualitative comparison of physiques. Kevans didn't bark but there was no way she could make leather look that good.

The time I needed to work up strength was time enough for me to see that I was about to munch a filthy shoe. "She did seem familiar, though. I must've seen her somewhere."

She had been wearing rain gear at the time, or old feed sacks. Otherwise, the moment would be seared onto the backs of my eyeballs.

"Hush, love. The danger is over. Your friends are cleaning up."

It was true. The action was done. The street was carpeted with bodies, not a one twitching. Several torches still burned on the cobblestones. I was awed because tin whistles were not shrilling. General Block was studying the scene carefully. He was both grim and puzzled.

The neighbors began to come out. I heard both negative and laudatory comments. The consensus was, this stuff didn't happen when I wasn't around.

Tin whistles did begin to arrive, from the direction of the Cardonlos house. That old biddy owed me. I was home and she was back in business.

Sleep returned. Whatever the bad girl hit me with, it drained me.

I missed my opportunity to see Tinnie spot me amongst the fallen, being tended by my sorceress friend. I missed the cleanup, too. The red tops carted off nineteen stiffs in gray wool. The lethal blonde and twenty grays got away.

Strafa should have chased them instead of fussing over me.

Tinnie did not head home in high dudgeon. She couldn't. Uncle Oswald and cousin Artifice both had been injured. Oswald could not travel except by coach. Singe sent a runner to the Tate family compound.

64

They tossed me in with Morley, to start, onto the cold, hard floor. Injured people were everywhere, especially against the walls in the hallway. Given the chance to do more than brood and fuss, Westman Block showed us why he had Prince Rupert's confidence. He sent people flying around everywhere. He roused the Guard across the city.

He came by to tell me, "They were all dead, the things in the wool tights. They were made from pieces of dead people."

That did not seem possible. Not in such numbers. Where had the bodies come from? That many people disappearing, dead or alive, should have become a major public issue.

We knew, now, beyond doubt, that there was a connection with Morley and with the break-in on Factory Slide. We knew that several people had to be involved: two women, one old, one young, and, possibly, a stuffed-bear-loving kid. Plus the resurrection men.

I wanted to ask questions but could not. Strafa was not there to ease my suffering. The hangover was back. And I felt like a bad flu had hold of me. I felt naked in a blizzard cold. I couldn't stop shaking.

Speaking of dead . . . Where was Old Bones? I got no sense of his presence at all.

That sparked a moment of panic wasted because I couldn't talk.

The chaos in the house settled out without my input. Singe and Strafa went off to stalk the blonde. The delegation from Fire and Ice headed home after taking a moment to say good-bye. Crush told me, "You have great parties. Remember me for the next one."

I couldn't say anything. I tried to wink. The effort was pathetic. I decided to send her a book.

Miss T understood. She touched my cheek. She was more of a mom to Crush than DeeDee was. DeeDee was one hundred percent self-involved. Mike thought my crowd would be better company than the folks Crush encountered in a sporting palace.

I could not disagree with that.

Jon Salvation and the Bird took off. Bird would come back. The supply of spirits was unlimited and free.

Uncle Oswald kept waiting for a coach that must have needed new wheels before it could leave the Tate compound. Kyra visited me. She didn't have much to say. After watching me shake and drool she fled to Singe's office to baby her male kin.

Dean appeared, armed with chicken soup. I could not imagine him being up so late. He considered me and Morley and found himself at a loss. His heart and mind were in the right place but he was physically unable to follow through.

I made some noise that, after years of seeing me come home tipsy, he understood. "He's asleep. It took all he had to resist long enough for the rest of you to get busy." He tried to sound positive but could not conceal the fact that he was extremely worried.

This was not a good time to lose the Dead Man.

Dean was still trying to figure out what to do when Tinnie pushed him out of her way. She brought blankets and two of the heated stones Dean used to warm his feet during winter's bitterest nights. She was calm and businesslike. She placed the rag-wrapped stones against my chest and back, then buried me in blankets. She told Dean, "I can feed them."

I tried to purr, managed to sound like I was choking on phlegm. Tinnie made sure I wasn't, then focused on Morley. Dean said, "According to Mike we lost Dotes the second the attack began."

Typical. Dean was on nickname terms with Miss T after one exposure.

He asked, "What about you, Tinnie?"

"I'm still flustered. Still not sure what's real. But I'll be all right. Worry about Penny instead."

Dean passed the soup. Tinnie settled into the seat the ratwomen used to feed Morley. She blew steam off a spoonful of broth. Dean went off to help somebody else.

"We have a world of things to talk about, Malsquando. Mostly concerning how my head has been working lately." She got Morley to take some broth; then she looked down at me. I wasn't shivering as badly. Her eyes were unreadable. "I saw things tonight that gave me a new perspective."

That did not sound good.

"I promised you and the Dead Man . . . Well, I promised. I'll stick to that. General Block explained what it's all about."

I wondered what Block was up to, stirring the pot while drunk and angry.

Tinnie got some more broth into Morley. "I see that this has to be dealt with. There are only a few people who can handle things like it. And you're one." Another spoon of soup. "I should be supporting you, not distracting you and holding you back."

That cost her. She had clamped down hard on her emotions. No doubt Strafa tending me in the street was in the front of her mind. That was a slice of reality she couldn't ignore.

I couldn't say anything. I snuggled the rocks and tried to appear grateful.

Penny came to the doorway. She looked as rocky as I felt. "I'm going to leave now, Mr. Garrett. Please send for me when he's able to go back to work."

I tried to tell her that I would.

Tinnie said, "He can't quite talk, yet. Shouldn't you just stay here? It would be safer."

Penny considered me, weighing the risk of being ravished against the certainty of safety and comfort. From behind her, Kyra said, "Stop worrying. Garrett is harmless. My aunt ought to be ashamed of the stuff she told you. It's because of her insecurities. He won't even look at *this* cross-eyed." She posed.

Oh, woe! The mighty Garrett considered harmless by the young and the beautiful?

Tinnie snapped, "That is quite enough, Kyra!" She told Penny, "She's right, though. You are safe. There's an extra bedroom upstairs. Use that. Warn Dean so neither of you get any surprises. Go on. You need to stay close to good people right now."

Good people?

What was this? That shock must have hit Tinnie hard.

Kyra said, "I'll show you."

And she knew, how? And why?

Tinnie looked like she had the same questions.

Many interesting things must have happened here in my absence.

Muted girl voices came from the kitchen. Dean definitely was exceeding the call of duty tonight. He should have been in bed hours ago.

65

The woman tried hard to drown me but I was too crafty. Whenever she shoved soup into my face I swallowed it. It was Dean Creech wonder soup. Every spoonful hit bottom, then declared itself throughout my body. Energy came back fast, along with confidence and a sense of well-being. It wasn't long before I found my voice.

"Something I've been wanting to bring up all evening, darling. I never got to it because so much was going on."

Wow. I made a miracle comeback. Almost as good as shaking that awful cold overnight. Though I hadn't, really. A host of unpleasant symptoms were back now that Old Bones was asleep.

I could not help feeling uncomfortable about how my sidekick had begun operating without consultation. Strafa had put me away drowning in my own snot. Next morning the mess was gone and almost forgotten.

Maybe Old Bones didn't think I had time to be sick.

Tinnie developed a mild glower while I rambled through distracting thoughts. "Let's have it, Malsquando! Good or bad, let's get to it."

I was nervous. When Penny and Kyra got upstairs they would see that somebody had used that bed.

The guilty flee where no man pursueth.

We could see some interesting action when Strafa returned.

"All right. Here we go. Before the good goes away and the mucus comes back. Jon Salvation has been bullying me to get you to act in his next play. He wants you bad. Did he talk to you about that?"

"He tried to talk to me about something but I didn't pay attention. And he kept hemming and hawing."

The woman can have that effect on the male of the species.

"He has a new play about fairies. He wants you to be in it."

"I'm done with that stuff." Stated entirely without conviction, damned near begging to be talked into changing her mind. "I wasn't able to be that kind of woman."

"What you weren't able to do was stop being a self-involved pain in the ass. You were Tinnie Tate to the third power."

Had to be the soup. Something in the soup was worse than alcohol for loosening the tongue.

"Garrett?"

"Let's just say you wouldn't have put up with half of what you dished out if you'd been doing Salvation's job."

Her mouth opened and closed. No words came out. She reminded me of a freshly caught trout, with distractions. Say, better, a freshly caught mermaid.

"He wants you for the lead role, darling. And he's sure this will be his biggest play yet."

Her eyes got huge. She drifted off into fantasyland, harkening to dreams she'd had before she alienated everybody.

"Really?"

"Really. I tried to talk him out of it. He insists you're perfect. I'd bet he used you when he created the character. Who you might not like much if you do get involved." Tinnie had no patience with women who had quirks like hers.

Jon Salvation had a reputation for drawing his characters from life, and writing them true.

"What?"

"What I'm saying is, we don't see ourselves the way other people see us. Not saying that what they see is any less subjective. But the way you were at the World . . ."

"Stop!"

She did not carry the argument forward.

I had unearthed ambitions my honey had kept hidden. She felt vulnerable, now. Maybe secretly ashamed.

She knew she had been a jerk back when she got kicked out of that select pool of cuties who could act without having to entertain the punters in private after the show.

She had been good but her uncles never approved.

She got all starry-eyed and lost in her imagination.

"Tinnie?"

"I'm sorry, Malsquando. This . . . It's . . . It's a lightning strike from a clear blue sky. He really said he wants me?"

"Like I told you, I think he used you to create the fairy queen. You wouldn't even have to act. You could just be you. As long as that you isn't the Tinnie that got everybody so mad . . ."

She jumped up and down like she was Kyra's age. "I know what you mean. I learned my lesson. I'm not that Tinnie anymore. Garrett, sweetheart, you know what this means?"

"It means you need to get together with the Remora and convince *him* that you aren't that Tinnie anymore."

"No, dumbhead. It means that if I don't mess this up I can tell my uncles to go to hell. They can find somebody else to keep their damned books."

Epiphany! Though she hid it well Tinnie didn't like her life much. "They'd have to *pay* somebody."

"Yeah!" She had been trying to be what they wanted her to be. I had suffered because she tried to make me into the man they thought she ought to have. "If you're running some practical joke on me, Malsquando . . ."

"He's been trying to get hold of you for days. You wouldn't let him."

"I thought . . . Never mind." She bounced up and down again. And didn't turn sour when I suggested that she move into a better light so I could more fully appreciate the view.

I was, for the moment, content. We were rolling along just the way we ought. Only one teensy gnat in the ointment.

Old Bones and I needed to have a sit-down when he woke up. He needed to make his thinking clear. He was the serpent who could slither the deepest cesspits of the human mind. He could explain why he preferred Strafa Algarda to the woman who had been closest to me for an age.

Kyra galloped in. I was sure she would want to know who had been using the guest room bed. Instead, she said, "Our coach is here."

Tinnie said, "It is way late. I need to get Uncle Oswald and Artifice home so they can be treated."

I struggled into a sitting position. "We all need sleep. Kyra, can you see if Dean needs any help? He's got to be half dead by now."

She went. Tinnie asked, "What about you?"

"I'll manage."

"You need to rest, too. But somebody has to let Singe in when she gets back."

"Dollar Dan can handle that." The ratman was in Singe's office, staying out of the way.

"That sorceress will be here, too."

"She might be," I admitted.

Tinnie took a first step in changing the rest of her life. She let that go. She didn't ask questions. She didn't try to manipulate me by telling me how much she trusted me.

Old Bones had had some impact after all.

66

I didn't know when Singe and Strafa came back. They didn't bother to wake me up. I lay back down after Dollar Dan, the Tate women, and their coachmen hauled Uncle Oswald and Artifice away. I was asleep before Dollar Dan locked up behind them.

I slept on the floor. The Windwalker used my bed. Not only did I miss out on the temptation, I knew nothing about it till late next day. By then I was in a bad temper, fighting a terrible cold or incipient flu. I was surly with everybody. Singe had to be the pleasant face of the household to the rest of the world.

I hurt all over. And Old Bones was asleep. But Playmate was awake, ambulatory, trying to help Dean. He looked a lot better, though the plan had been to keep him unconscious several days more.

He had missed his doses of the stuff that had kept Morley down.

Dotes was seated on the end of the cot. He moved gingerly when he moved at all. It hurt him to talk today.

Him being upright brightened things a lot.

He said, "I hope you feel better than you look."

"I doubt it." I climbed onto the other end of the cot, which creaked but held. I told him about my latest brush with the darkness.

Penny appeared with a stack of handkerchiefs. I suppressed the urge to grab her wrist and pull. Keeping right on, growing up.

She offered a half curtsey, fled.

Morley chuckled. "Time's been good to her. So you've made up."

"Sort of. I don't know how long it'll last without Old Bones cracking the whip."

I heard Singe talking to somebody in the next room. Then somebody left the house. Singe joined us. I said, "You look frazzled. Did you get any sleep?"

"Some. We had the usual luck." She sneezed.

"You, too?" I offered a hanky. "They lost you?"

"This is not a cold. It is a continuing reaction to something they used to stop me from following them. I did not stop to identify ingredients. I got away fast. The compound was designed to ruin my nose forever."

"You're all right?" I was concerned despite my own bad humor.

"Yes."

"Strafa?"

"She's all right, too. I owe her. She pulled me back before I got a nose full. She brought me home. She just went back out. I don't know why."

"You're suspicious?"

"Just a feeling. Probably mostly because she is so interested in you. I shouldn't distrust her for that. She is too simple to be evil."

That was an interesting notion.

Morley drank it in without comment.

I said, "I'm going to try to get up, now. I have some business that needs doing." I thought. I ought. It had been a long night.

Singe said, "I'll get a chamber pot."

I lifted my butt eight inches off the cot, could not find the strength to get any higher. Then I realized that I didn't need to go as badly as I should.

Morley grinned when he saw my frown deepen.

"Wait a minute."

Singe said, "The cleaning women took care of you, too. You hardly groaned. And you definitely needed the work."

I faced a creative linguistics challenge but was too sluggish to manage more than an apathetic, "Dirty rotten rackelfratz." I did turn red.

"It is just a job to them, Garrett. They said hardly anything. And you really needed it. You were a mess."

I used another handkerchief.

Singe added, "I will ask Dean to prepare a camphor breather." She left. I blew some more and worried about how bad the cold would get once it got down into my chest.

I was not looking forward to that.

67

Morley asked, "Do we have a plan?"

"We get us back in shape. Then we go find the people who hurt you."

"A masterpiece of strategy and tactics."

"It needs a little refinement."

"That's the usual Garrett approach. Stomp around and break things."

"It works."

"I'm not sure why. I will stipulate that you still walk among us."

Dean and Playmate turned up. Playmate carried a clever little table that folded up flat. It had the Amalgamated hallmark burned into a leg. Another Kip Prose invention, no doubt. Playmate set it up. Dean deposited a tray featuring tea, dry toast, two bowls of soup, and the thing Singe called a breather. Fresh handkerchiefs accompanied that.

Dean volunteered, "The younger Miss Tate sent us a half dozen of these tables and some more fold-up chairs."

"Thoughtful of her."

"It was, truly." He eyed me expectantly. So I thanked him for the table and tray.

He left looking sour.

Morley poured the tea. "He was hoping you would clarify the direction you're headed emotionally."

"What?"

"They're all wondering the same thing, Garrett. I can see that and I've been dead for a month."

I sipped tea, nibbled toast, downed a few spoons of soup, then suggested, "Clue me in," before I shoved my face into the inhaler device. Which did not bear an Amalgamated hallmark.

It had been created right here in this house by Dean Creech.

No doubt Kip Prose could polish it and make it a bestseller.

Morley said, "Everybody thinks Tinnie has run her course. That you've started to show some spine. Maybe because of this Strafa. They talk like she's your perfect woman."

They? "That can't be true. They can't know her well enough."

"They wouldn't talk about it in front of you. And they do know Tinnie."

"They? Who? Dean and Singe?"

"Don't get excited. People care about you. They worry. They especially worry about how your decisions might affect their lives."

Another worry I didn't need. "Let's get something straight. Do you think Strafa is better for me than Tinnie is?"

"I haven't formed an opinion. I don't know the new woman—except that she's scary and she's screaming gorgeous. Tinnie I do know."

That didn't sound like a ringing endorsement. "Meaning?"

"Tinnie has some wonderful points. But with some of us she resonates like the Remora does with you. You tolerate him because Winger is your friend. One could make a case for Tinnie being a particularly sinister proof of Dotes' First Law. Don't look at me like that."

"It could be my fault."

"That's the sinister part. She makes you think the problems are all your fault."

I muttered about us having to start recovery training, to avoid an inappropriate vent about him and Belinda. Then I wondered if I ought to poll my acquaintances for their opinions.

Of a sudden I had a distinct feeling that I liked Tinnie a lot more, and thought a lot better of her, than did most any acquaintance not named Tinnie. They tolerated her because she came with me. Odd, that. I was used to thinking that people tolerated me because I came with Tinnie.

Both views would be pure truth—depending where you are standing.

That was not the Dead Man. His Nibs continued snoozing. That was me imagining how Old Bones would respond if I asked his opinion.

I said, "Intellectually, I'm not feeling so good. I need time to get my mind right."

Morley said nothing. He had no need. His expression told the tale.

Garrett had had years to think. He had done his best to avoid that. Now he was caught in a cleft stick, with guilt twisting his arm up behind him.

Sometimes procrastination can be a blessing. And sometimes not, with personal things. Time passing lets opportunities get away and unresolved problems fester.

"Really? Isn't your actual problem that you think too much?"

"Hard to argue with that. Everyone I ever knew accused me of that."

"Let's get back to the plan."

"It's coming along. Since neither of us can go dancing with the devils right now we'll train till we are able."

"I understand the theory. But your thinking is anachronistic. It made sense back when you dealt with stuff that didn't attract attention from generals and princes."

What he meant wasn't obscure, but I didn't get it.

"You kept developing attachments, Garrett."

"I don't follow."

"In the beginning there was you, me sometimes, and a sleek new girl every couple of months. And Tinnie in and out of your life. Then you started getting entangled. There was the brewery connection. Then the Contagues." He made a gesture meant to warn me against interrupting. "You got entangled with Block and Relway and Singe. And Kip and the whole inventory of Tates."

I understood, then. As life proceeded I kept making persistent connections that created ever more complicated obligations. The hiatus under Tinnie's thumbs hadn't shaken me free. People had expectations. I had expectations of my own.

Morley said, "All those entangling people will go right on doing what they do."

I wasn't sure what he meant but he was gracious enough to go on crushing my grand strategy.

That's what it added up to. Our problems existed for other people, too. In this case, most everyone in the city.

"You put it that way, there's no point in us making plans."

"Now you've got it."

I took another shot at getting up off the cot. This time I made it upright.

A drooping Singe materialized before I took a second step. "Where are you going?"

"Upstairs. To bed."

"You just woke up."

I coughed heartily. The cold was getting there. "Ah, crap! You should get some sleep, too."

"Somebody has to run this circus. And I seem to be the only one who can stay awake."

"Unfair. You didn't get the magical smack down."

"Nor did I, eyes wide shut, charge into what a three-year-old dimwit could recognize as a deadly instrument."

"She's got you there, Garrett."

A point. When I charge around overturning and busting things sometimes it's me that gets overturned and busted.

I would have been better off hanging back, throwing rocks.

I picked up the breather. "Show me what to do."

What to do was take notes, for the Dead Man's delectation later, from people poking into things for us. Half of them I didn't know. Some I hadn't seen before. I had no idea how or when they had gotten hired. And they were, universally, boring, because they had nothing interesting to report.

After the fourth I told Singe, "This is impossible. TunFaire can't possibly be that quiet. People can't still be that ignorant. There were witnesses out there."

"Just means the powers that be kept the lid on. So far. Probably by manufacturing clever stories. Gang warfare. Ethnic strife. Something like that. There. I'm caught up."

Nothing interesting happened for the rest of the day.

68

I did get to bed before sundown, never having taken a sip of beer. Dean had gone up right after supper. Singe didn't stay up much longer than I did. We left the house to Penny and Dollar Dan.

I fell asleep snuggling with the breather and a mound of handkerchiefs. Singe had delivered a mug of fierce medicinal tea on her way to her repose. That put me under, fast.

I wakened with the sun on the rise. And I was not alone.

Strafa was spooned up against me as though she had been there every night for years. She was leaner and warmer than what I was accustomed to.

I was startled, but only for a moment. Where else could she stay? The other beds were taken.

I moved slightly. She adjusted, too. My right hand discovered something smaller and more firm than what I anticipated. I cupped it. She pushed against my hand and made a little sound of contentment. I slipped back into Nod. She was purring.

When next I wakened I was on my back. Strafa's head was on my chest, over my heart. She was against me tightly, all the way down. Her hand was on my belly, thumb resting on my navel.

It all seemed perfectly reasonable.

My heartbeat quickened.

That wakened Strafa, slightly. Her hand drifted.

I squeaked. She purred but granted a stay after brief exploration. She wrapped that arm around me, over my right shoulder, pulled herself even closer, half on top, purred some more, and went back to sleep.

Singe awakened us. She showed no attitude. "You won't have time to eat if you don't get moving." She grabbed my used handkerchiefs. "I'll get these washed. There are fresh downstairs." Her nose twitched, no doubt telling her what she wanted to know. "The Dead Man is still asleep. General Block should be here in about an hour. His message didn't say why. Otherwise, there is no news."

Strafa untangled herself from the bedding while Singe talked, exposing my nakedness. No surprise to Singe. She knows I sleep raw. But Strafa was equally bare and not the least self-conscious.

Singe's nose twitched some more. She said nothing. Her season was no longer causing completely tormenting emotions.

She collected the breather. "I'll have Dean recharge this."

"Thanks." I did not look at her. I could not stop staring at Strafa, who was digging in a trunk that hadn't been against the west wall when I went to bed.

The door shut behind Singe. Strafa looked at me, now sitting on the edge of the bed. "You're having naughty thoughts. I can tell."

Oh, yeah.

She came to me, pushed me back, straddled me, asked, "Now? Or wait till tonight?"

I was no moral hero. I was no faithful lover. Had the name Tinnie Tate come up just then my best response would have been, "Who?" I couldn't talk. My brains were scrambled. The woman had found her way deep inside my head. She had established emotional colonies. There was no way to drive her out.

I couldn't come up with an answer. So Strafa allowed herself the luxury of deciding for me.

As far as she was concerned the issue never was if but when.

69

I was still distracted when we reached the kitchen. Kind old Dean served breakfast despite the time. He was in a fine mood.

Morley shuffled in. He checked us out, smirked, but never said a word. Penny appeared as Dean set a plate in front of Morley. She sniffed as she settled into the last chair. She gave Strafa a dark look but didn't say anything, either.

Playmate stuck his head in. "Anything I can do, Dean?" While he eyeballed me and Strafa.

"You could grab a hammer, some nails, and some boards, and add on to my kitchen. Otherwise, no. We can't squeeze another body in."

It wasn't *that* crowded—though nobody would be able to move if Playmate put himself on our side of the door.

I asked, "Dean, who all is here? Besides who all I can see right now."

"Singe. Some of John Stretch's people. That creature who calls himself the Bird."

Penny said, "Bird came to paint. His Honor is napping, though. So Bird is silencing his voices instead."

That was about the longest speech she'd ever made in my presence. She sounded disconsolate. I risked panicking her. "What do you think about him, Penny? Does he really hear voices?"

She made herself reply, her voice tiny as she did so. "Yes. He hears them. And not just because he's crazy. They're real. He let me talk to them while we were working."

Kitchen business stopped. Penny shrank under the pressure of curious eyes.

"The Dead Man thinks the Bird belongs in the crazy ward at the Bledsoe."

"His Honor can't hear the voices. He only hears Bird's answers. If Bird does answer. Mostly, he just takes another drink."

"How did you talk to the voices, then?"

"Bird told me what they said. They heard me when I answered."

Dean rested a reassuring hand on Penny's shoulder. "You'll be all right."

I didn't get the girl. A couple, three years ago she had been hell on wheels, acting in her role as high priestess of a screwball country cult, hiding out from religious enemies. But she'd always been pathologically shy around me. Which, as Kyra had told her, was totally Tinnie's fault.

I asked, "You talked to them?"

"Sure."

I blew my nose. "How did that work?"

"Bird just lets the voice take over. Then I talk to the ghost. It doesn't last long. Bird only lets them talk so people will know he's telling the truth."

I made myself stay calm. I had to keep the intensity down. Penny would trample Playmate trying to get away if I tripped her panic response. "I'd sure like to see that." Penny did not volunteer to arrange it. "Who do the voices belong to?"

"Dead people. People who were murdered. Awful people, mostly."

I once spent time in a relationship with a woman who had been murdered when I was a child. I met her ghost as an adult. I had no trouble with Penny's notion. "Do tell."

"Tell what? That the ones I talked to sounded like they got what they had coming? That's what drives Bird crazy. He has these whiny haunts, who deserved what they got, insisting that he do things for them."

"I've got it." Not only did the Bird have to deal with ghosts, his spooks belonged to that select crew who think they are more special than anyone else and should get special treatment always, in the main because they survived childbirth.

In TunFaire these leeches tend to come to a bad end early, though their survivability has improved since the war's end.

Once upon a time the body politic shed its parasites in the

cauldron of the Cantard. They could be counted on to get themselves killed.

The war had had its fierce egalitarian side. There had been no buying out of it—though the clever had been able to wrangle less risky assignments. Princes and paupers, everyone took his dip in the deadly pond. Old folks were nostalgic for the days when the war kept the streets clear of loud, badly behaved, sometimes dangerous young men.

"Mr. Garrett?"

"I'm sorry. Having an old man's moment. You're used to Old Bones. Can he fix the Bird's brain so he doesn't hear those people?"

"I don't think Bird would want that. He hates the voices. But if they aren't pestering him and he doesn't drink, he can't paint." Then she asked, "How long do you think His Honor will sleep?"

"I've never figured the formula out. You'd do better to ask Singe."

"What should I do since he's not awake?"

"What would you be doing if you weren't hunkered down here?"

"Stuff. I don't know. Dean and Singe both say I shouldn't leave. Those bad people might want to get hold of someone from this house."

"Dean is a wise man. Why don't you help him? These past few days have been hard for him. And you can help Singe, if she needs it. I'm going to go bug her myself, right now."

Everyone bailed when I did. Penny stayed with Dean. I saw no enthusiasm in either of them.

Singe was writing something using an Amalgamated steel tip quill. "The Dead Man's pet girl says she talks to the ghosts that haunt the drunken artist."

"Take him along next time you dance with the dead men. Turn them around on their mistress."

"I'll run it past Old Bones when he wakes up. I have some questions for you."

"Blow your nose first. That sniffling is disgusting."

I took care of that, and coughed up some stuff besides. "Did anyone trace the giant bottles and glass vats from that warehouse?"

"Not that I know of. The Director and the Guard aren't

keeping me in the loop. I didn't think to ask last time the General was here. Speaking of whom, he's late. No one else tells me anything useful, either. Including your new wrestling partner."

"You're leaping to conclusions. What did Old Bones get out of those villains that Block loaned us?"

"He didn't say, officially. Unofficially, what I expected. Nothing that we didn't already know. They were day labor."

"Has anyone found out anything useful?"

"Not yet. You would think the resurrection men, at least, could be found. Are you bored? I'm not here to entertain you. I have work to do."

"Hokum." I suspected that she was crabby because her body was disgruntled because she had not mated successfully during her season.

"I had another question. The most important one. But I can't remember what it was. Wait! Here it is. Old Bones had me chase Relway the other day to tell him about men who were watching the house. Did Relway bother to let us know who they were?"

"Not officially."

"Unofficially?"

"General Block was informed that they belonged to the King's Household Lifeguard. The Palace Guard. He wasn't convinced. He thought they were really private police from the Hill."

Either possibility was disturbing. I didn't want to attract attention from either direction. "Not good."

"But maybe an indication that powerful people take the situation seriously."

I started to say something.

"If all you can do is chatter, take the woman back upstairs or go frighten Penny. I'm busy."

"Ah, you're no fun anymore."

"That's all your fault. Out."

70

I got the last laugh.

Someone used the knocker as I exited Singe's office. I employed the peephole, saw a fierce green eye glaring back. I opened up.

"Kyra."

"I brought some people for you to talk to. You could maybe break this one's leg for me while you're at it." She had a death grip on Kip Prose's left arm. Kip appeared to be shackled to Kevans Algarda with an invisible chain. Kevans looked like she wanted to fight but didn't know who to hit first. Kip had that numb look men get when they have hold of a Tate woman with her mind made up.

"You did indeed. And I'm most pleasantly surprised. How are you, Kip? We don't see much of you at the manufactory anymore. And yourself, Miss?"

I would not mention her mother or how Strafa worried. No point throwing naphtha on the drama. "No real need for the fancy headgear, guys. His Nibs has been out cold since the other night. But wear them if that makes you comfortable. Let's go into Singe's office."

Singe greeted my return with a bloody look. That evaporated once she saw the kids. She got up. "I'll tell Dean we have more guests. Garrett, shall I make sure you aren't disturbed by the others?"

"That would make these three more comfortable."

Kyra said, "I told them about what's going on and how your place is, like, a madhouse."

"It's getting better. We've got only six or seven extra bodies here today."

One of those, Penny, arrived with tea and a heap of the cookies that Dean always brought out when young people visit. Cookies I could never find when I wanted to nick one or three for myself. Penny offered Kip and Kevans a polite smile. She had a warmer look for Kyra. When she left, Kyra told me, "That's who you should be chasing, Garrett. She's quiet, submissive, and young enough for you to train up right."

"I'll wait a while. At least till she stops peeing herself every time I look at her."

Kip was not in a social mood. He isn't happy when life intrudes. "Kyra says there's stuff we need to talk about."

"Yeah. Kevans especially. You heard any rumors about strange stuff going on?"

Kip said, "In TunFaire? You're kidding." But he spoke without passion and nodded in concert with Kevans as he did.

"You probably heard it wrong. Except from Kyra, who was here."

Kip and Kevans both nodded. They were nervous but I sensed no guilt nor any defensive attitude.

"Bad things have been happening. People are trying to cover up. Others are putting out false reports. The whole thing could get ugly in a few days." I told them almost everything, deemphasizing the role of the Windwalker. Kevans showed no particular emotion when I mentioned her mother.

Singe returned moments after Penny left. She took notes.

Penny returned to the doorway. She wasn't sneaking so she wasn't exactly eavesdropping. "Penny, would you get your sketches and Bird's portrait? Please?"

Kip said, "That's ugly stuff, Garrett. Kyra must have sugared it."

"She's an amazing girl, Kip."

"I know. I have an awful time remembering that she isn't my imagination running wild."

Kyra was pleased. Kevans was not, though she was not strictly a romantic rival. She and Kip strove to maintain that frog's-fur rare boy-girl relationship where they were just good friends.

Kevans was, I noted belatedly, wearing girl clothes. She always dressed as a boy, before. She looked good as a girl but she didn't look nearly as good as that wicked woman in black leather.

Penny brought the sketches and painting. Singe held the latter up while Penny handled her own work.

"Anybody recognize anyone?" I asked.

Kevans countered, "Is my mother still here?"

I glanced at Kyra. Butter wouldn't melt. Then to Singe, "Miss Pular, would the Windwalker still be with us?"

Singe responded a grim rat glower. "She may be. It's hard to say for sure. She keeps flitting in and out of the upstairs windows."

I said, "Why do you ask, Kevans?"

"I wondered if she's seen these."

"I don't know. Has she, Singe?"

Singe had a grand opportunity to be lethally catty. She let it pass. "Probably not. She will not go into the Dead Man's room."

Penny agreed with Singe, though we three all knew that she had seen the artwork.

I saw Kyra doing math based on the fact that Penny Dreadful had moved into the guest room while Furious Tide of Light was staying here, too.

I concentrated on Kevans.

Kyra did not let the completed equation affect her attitude.

Singe saw what I saw. She would have smirked and sneered if nature had equipped her for it. She did observe, "Life gets more complicated every day, doesn't it?"

Kip and Kevans thought that was directed toward them. Kevans declared, "Kip and I are just friends. We challenge each other to think. There isn't anything else going on. Really."

Kyra did not appear to be reassured.

I thought the fact that Kevans needed to say anything might reveal something about what was going on inside her head.

I was fairly certain that in the past the relationship had been friendship with special benefits as two incredibly bright but socially inept kids struggled through the turbulence of puberty.

Whatever, these days Kip trudged along in his mentor's trace, essentially oblivious.

Kip's mentor took a chance and changed the subject. "Your mother is desperately frightened for you, Kevans. The Specials turned up what looks like evidence involving you in this new wickedness."

She did a wonderful job of looking unpleasantly surprised.

I told her what Singe and the Windwalker had found in Elf Town. Singe kicked in points I overlooked. I wished the Dead Man was awake to sift the secrets I was stirring off the stream-bed of Kevans' mind.

"They found your stuffed bear, and some other things." Then I went fishing. "Those hairnets don't work anymore."

Kip squeaked like I had stepped on his toes. "That can't be!"

"It can. Old Bones can adapt when he has time to think. The point I want to make is, you can't hide from His Nibs anymore."

Penny sneered. And looked me in the eye when she did.

Kip looked like he wanted to panic. Kevans was less rattled. Singe gave me an unhappy glare, thinking I had just wasted valuable household advantages.

Kevans said, "That sounds like where I hid out after we had the bug problem. I lived there almost a year."

Kip jumped in with a pretty good description of the place. Obviously he had visited. That won no points over on the redheaded girlfriend side. The redheaded girlfriend had not known.

Kyra didn't say anything but it was plain she was more comfortable with her aunt's man having female friends than she was facing that situation herself.

Kip's mouth ran. He didn't have a clue.

Kevans and Kip being friends would offer Kyra no comfort, ever.

"So you don't know these people?"

"No." Kevans sounded definite.

Kip shook his head. He was less certain. "I think I would remember her."

That got him punched from both sides.

Kyra volunteered, "I think I've seen the girl before."

"She was out front the other night."

"I know. I only got a glimpse, then. She looked like bad news."

"She was. I learned the hard way."

Kyra nodded at Penny's drawings. "I mean bad news be-cause she looks like one of those blondes who has gotten any-thing she ever wanted handed to her since she sprouted a set of knockers."

That was harsh. And a touch hypocritical. Kyra Tate had been one of those girls till she developed the mental defect that bonded her to Kip.

She said, "I might've seen this one when I was about twelve. Some older girls were teasing me about still being flat." Some pink behind the freckles on the cheeks, there. "The ringleader was sixteen or seventeen and very blessed. This looks like her. Sort of."

Sounded like a long shot. "You should go over that with the Dead Man sometime. Figure out the time and place, work outward from there."

Singe made a note.

Old Bones could sort that out in seconds.

Kyra said, "If you think it's worth it I can probably figure it out. I have a good memory for people who misuse me."

I hoped Kip heard that.

His sins, though, would be of omission, not commission. If he messed up with Kyra it would be out of blind ignorance.

I told all the youngsters, "Let's look at the man. He may be the boss of the resurrection men. Any of you know anything about him?"

No, still, though I'm sure Kevans saw the resemblance to Barate Algarda. She kept sneaking looks.

"Another hope dashed. Kevans. Kip. Please talk to me about the warehouse in Elf Town."

Kyra eyed Kip in a way that made it plain she wanted to hear more, too.

Kevans was getting tired of all this. "I hid out there for a year. I told you. I left when I stopped feeling like I had to hide."

"I'm not interested in that. But why hide there? That's a far piece for a kid off the Hill."

"I'd been there before. With my grandmother. She owned it. It was empty and starting to fall apart. I think she sold it but nobody ever used it."

I worked some calculations. Strafa had borne Kevans at a very young age. Strafa's mother had died when Strafa was a child. I had met her ghost. Kevans must have been talking about Barate Algarda's mother.

"Anything unusual happen while you were there?"

"Nothing to do with what you're fussing about."

Kip backed her up. "I used to smuggle food and stuff. It was all sad for a while."

"Singe, make a note to ask the General if his forensic sorcerers went over that warehouse. And what they found out about the glassware."

"You asked already. He told you he got warned off."

"Even so. He and Relway haven't really backed off. If they could blame the poking around on us, they'd be even happier."

"We should not be discussing that right now."

No. I should be jumping all over the youngsters. They were gaining confidence as they grew more certain that the Dead Man was sleeping.

The look I sent Singe was one of appeal. I had emptied my toolbox when it came to interrogating kids.

Singe understood.

She left her desk. She left the room. A moment later Morley appeared, assisted by Penny. He settled onto a folding chair. He stared at Kevans from the side. He is better than I am at reading females.

Dollar Dan, who must have been in the kitchen with Dean, filled up the doorway. He could be amazingly intimidating when he wanted. But he wasn't the onager Singe meant to bring to bear.

71

Furious Tide of Light arrived. She did not look like anyone's mother. She did not look like anyone's wannabe girlfriend, either. She had on the full power of what she was. I had not seen her in that mode before.

Kevans curled into herself, mentally, like an armadillo. You could almost hear bacon crackling when the Windwalker looked at Kip. Kyra gaped, astonished and thoroughly intimidated. Only Penny seemed undisturbed. She stood out of the way, watched, and learned.

The girl was getting scary. I began to picture her as a human version of Pular Singe. It was in the blood. Her father had been Chodo Contague.

She and Belinda had nothing whatsoever to do with one another.

The Windwalker, when she spoke, was gentle, with the conviction of a whip. "Are you two clear on how foul a crime has been committed? What is happening has had no equal for two hundred years."

Strafa considered the drawings and painting. "This isn't a game." She stopped. She didn't want to challenge the kids. Adolescents will push back even when they're dead wrong.

Still, she asked, "What have you been holding back?"

Headshakes I suspected of being less than completely sincere. My sense, though, was that the insincerity had to do with Kip and Kevans rather than with knowledge of horrible crimes. Their friendship might have a more experimental angle than either wanted brought out in front of her mother or his girlfriend. Both lived lonely lives. They had been friends for a long time.

Everyone caught some taste of that possibility. But that wasn't why we had gotten together. I would overrule should the discussion start to slide that way.

I exchanged glances with Singe. If ever there was a time for the Dead Man to be on the job, this was it.

Kevans continued to wilt under her mother's scowl. That the Windwalker was her mother did not matter. What did was that one of the most ferocious and talented magic users alive might be displeased by the behavior of one rogue teen.

The Windwalker demanded, "You're completely sure you don't have anything more to tell us?" I hoped she really was capable of separating Furious Tide of Light from Strafa Algarda.

She stepped in till she and Kevans were nose to nose. She whispered. The girl began to shiver. She was ready to break down but, still, did not have anything to say.

If she did know anything it was something she would not surrender willingly.

I indulged a vain hope that the Dead Man was playing possum.

The Windwalker focused on Kevans but included her audience when making it clear that TunFaire faced a test of right and wrong more terrible than any since the age of uncontrolled experimental sorcery that had produced the ratpeople, plus worse beasts that had been exterminated during the hysterical public response.

Another Time of Troubles might be coming. Ignorance and fear are with us always. Stupid is all-pervasive. TunFaire wallows in bottomless reservoirs of that. A plague of zombies could trigger something way out of proportion to the horrors we had seen.

The Windwalker changed her approach. "Kevans, come with me." She used her Windwalker voice.

They went to my old office. It was quiet over there. Morley eased himself into the more comfortable chair that Kevans had vacated. He struggled to conceal his discomfort. "I hate being like this," he said softly.

"You've been hurt before."

"Not like this. Not this stupidly. Any other time I always knew why. Singe. Anyone find out who paid that healer to drug me?"

"That would have a yes and no answer. The Dead Man saw the woman inside the healer's mind, but only vaguely." She tipped a hand toward Penny's sketches. "Probably her. Miss Contague, with an assist from Mr. Kolda and reluctant cooperation from the Children of the Light, is pursuing that." Then she volunteered, "Other acquaintances are investigating other things. The reports aren't encouraging. It's amazing that so much wickedness can leave so little evidence. These villains are heinous but careful."

I asked a question that had been nagging me. "Why?"

"Garrett?"

"Why are these people doing what they're doing? If we knew that the search range would narrow considerable."

Singe still looked puzzled.

"Come on. These villains didn't just get up some morning and decide, 'Let's have some fun. Let's cut up dead people and build some jigsaw zombies.'"

"They are not zombies, Garrett."

Literal minds! "Whatever. You know what I mean."

"Yes. And you are correct. The question of motive has not come up in so plain a form. The behavior we have seen may have little to do with that."

I said, "It has to do with covering up. A dumb effort to quash something that never got out. That's what attracted attention."

"We may never know why. I expect the Hill people to get to them first. They have the most resources."

Probably. Those people insist.

One of those people came back with her daughter. The daughter was pale. The Windwalker looked grim. "Kevans will tell Barate to come see you. She and Mr. Prose will then meet me at the warehouse in Elf Town. Question Barate, then send him to join us. No excuses. I don't expect that he will know anything so it shouldn't take long. Is there anything else you want from these two?"

"No."

Kyra certainly had something but she kept her mouth shut.

Kip would have some explaining to do later.

Singe handled the door work.

The instant that shut Morley observed, "That woman can be fierce when the mood takes her."

"She didn't think they were telling the whole truth." I turned to Kyra. "So now we need to get you home safely."

TunFaire suffered ever more virulent paroxysms of law and order but a beauty like Kyra still rated an escort, if only to keep the chatter down.

I was about to volunteer. Singe spoke up first. "Dan, please ask Toast and Packer to do the honors." She followed that with burning eye contact. There would be no adolescent bravura on her watch.

I folded.

Were Singe human she would have sneered and told me I was painfully predictable.

She could play me as easily as Tinnie could. Maybe more so because with her my ego did not feel compelled to take stands.

And Kyra never argued.

The apprentice redhead was feeling exceptionally vulnerable.

Toast and Packer turned out to be the ratmen who had come with Dollar Dan.

72

The population of the house on Macunado continued to dwindle. Dean and Penny overruled me and went out to do some desperately needed shopping. Dollar Dan tagged along. I could not refute Dean's contention that all the entertaining had seen our bones get picked. The old man kept muttering about having trouble remembering the recipe for water soup, which was what we would be eating if he didn't go.

He clinched the deal by telling me he needed to see Jerry the beer guy. We would find ourselves in a desert otherwise.

One keg was dry. The other was down to a slosh.

Singe wore the ratgirl equivalent of a troubled frown after she recorded the advance she had given Dean.

"Reality catching up?" I asked.

"Not exactly. I noticed that Amalgamated is eleven days late with the quarterly dividend. We'll need that money if we keep pouring cash into this case the way we have been."

I heard "we" a lot but chose not to quibble.

She continued, "Considering the season, the dividend ought to be strong. I will claim penalty interest."

Her shoulders hunched like she expected me to take the company line against my interest as an investor.

I disappointed her.

I didn't know what she was talking about. I left that sort of stuff to her. She understood it. She reveled in it. She wallowed in it when she could.

Playmate joined us, trying to sub for Dean. He brought tea but was too shaky to manage pouring it.

Morley told him, "Sit your ass down, man! You look like hell."

I said, "He's two hundred percent better than when he got here."

Singe fiddled with her papers, getting more restive by the moment. Finally, she snapped, "Take it across the hall, boys. Take it next door. Take it anywhere but here. I have a ton of work. I need quiet to get it done."

Morley flashed a killer grin. Playmate looked soulfully wounded. I said, "As you command, so shall it be." I collected the Bird's painting and Penny's drawings. We crossed to the Dead Man's room.

"Warmer in here," Morley opined sarcastically.

Playmate planted himself in the best chair. "The pain isn't a tenth what it was but I still don't got any energy." He had brought the tea with him. He poured while sitting.

"That will turn around," I said. "Old Bones is totally confident. Mostly, it'll just take Dean to feed you up to your fighting weight, now."

"Think he'll be out for long?" Playmate tipped a thumb at the Dead Man. "I can feel the evil starting to grow again."

"I don't know. He's unpredictable. The stuff Kolda brought isn't working?"

Playmate tapped a dusting of brown powder into his teacup. "It's working smoky-ass miracles, Garrett. But it just slows the devil down. If I take it faithfully, obeying Kolda completely, it will take me three times as long to die."

His tone was understandably strained.

Meanwhile, Morley studied the artwork like he was determined to commit every brush and pencil stroke to memory.

Playmate said, "I think I've seen that man in the painting somewhere."

I suggested, "Year and a half ago? The mess at the World Theater?"

Playmate stared some more. "I see what you mean. But that's not the same man. An older brother, maybe."

"Barate Algarda was an only child."

"I got it. Nat something. A long time ago. I was a kid. But . . ." He frowned deeply.

"What?" I asked.

Morley blurted, "You're right. He does look like that Algarda creep. But not the same. See the scar?" He pointed.

Playmate ignored him. "The man I remember looked like this over thirty years ago. Scars and all."

I enjoyed that pleasant feeling you get when you stumble onto something good, though I didn't really know if this was worth the stumble.

Playmate smacked himself upside the head. "The drug is working already. I can't hardly remember anything. I know he was a villain. Who ought to be a long time dead."

Playmate slurred. His chin dropped to his chest. Morley observed, "That is some kick-ass knockout powder."

"But of limited commercial value. Otherwise, Kolda would have a pot to pee in."

"I don't like to speak ill of your friends, Garrett, but that Kolda . . ."

Singe shoved into the room. "Don't you hear the door, Garrett?"

"No." I did so now only because she had the hallway door open. Door-answering isn't part of my special skill set, anyway. "Who is it?"

"I suppose we would know if somebody answered it."

The thumping suggested someone was getting frustrated.

Singe made an exasperated noise more appropriate to one of our recent young adult lady visitors. She stamped up the hall.

Morley said, "If she was human I'd think Aunt Flo was winding her up."

"It's about the same thing. She'll be over it soon."

He said, "I may have crossed paths with this guy myself, sometime."

73

Singe brought Barate Algarda into the Dead Man's room. He was not in a good mood but he had shown up quickly. He wasn't wearing a mesh helmet. He wasn't going to hide.

Barate Algarda was a big man, Saucerhead size, ugly, and unkempt. He looked like a down-on-his-luck thug not getting much work because of Deal Relway's impact on the shadow economy. He nurtured that image. It left people unready for the real Barate Algarda. He was as bright and quick as his female descendants. His only talent for the magical, though, was a strong natural resistance to the Dead Man's mind probes.

Algarda was darker and wider than Strafa or Kevans. Strafa took after her mother, whom I had seen in ghost form, once upon a time. Kevans had gotten a little more from the paternal side. She'd never be a beauty.

Algarda barely glanced at the Dead Man. "Well?"

Singe remained in the doorway, I suppose so she could jump in if Algarda became actively hostile. He had done so before, when he thought his daughters were threatened.

"Did Kevans explain what's been going on?"

"Honestly? Not really. I got the impression that she thought she was being hounded unfairly."

"That could be."

"She showed the same attitude when her bunch were breeding giant bugs." He added, "Gods, I'm glad they didn't do any spiders."

I shivered. Me, too. "You have to admit, Kevans has a sociopathic side."

"Runs in the family."

Indeed. "So let me sketch some situations that turn out to be tied together." I brought him up to speed.

"Bizarre. Where does my daughter fit?"

I started looking for the best words to indicate a warehouse owned by his mother.

"Not Kevans. The Windwalker."

"Oh." I gave it to him straight, leaving out the personal side.

"The Crown Prince, eh?" he interjected at one point.

"Yeah."

Morley listened quietly. Playmate joined Old Bones in dreamland, only he snored. Curious Singe looked like my sanitized tale made her want to take a nap, too.

"Glassware, eh?" Algarda mused, out of nowhere. "Unusual glassware. In a warehouse. In Elf Town."

"Where Kevans lived for a year. A place owned by your mother."

He seemed mildly surprised. "A strange woman, my mother. She kept secrets."

Why not just add another whole level of weird? Though the Dead Man would have cautioned me about jumping to conclusions based on prejudices.

I reiterated, "There was evidence that Kevans stayed there. The Specials have that. She says she was there for a year. She knew about the place because her grandmother took her there when she was twelve."

"That's how you got to my mother."

"Does the glassware mean anything special?"

"Not really."

"Morley, could you hold that lamp up so Mr. Algarda can get a look at those pictures?"

Morley turned the pictures, too. They had not been visible from where Algarda was standing. Algarda asked, "Who are these people?"

"I was hoping you could tell me."

"I can tell you who they were forty years ago. This is my great uncle Nathaniel. He died while I was in the Cantard."

"Did he have kids? Playmate remembers him as a neighborhood thug from when he was a kid. Morley remembers him vaguely, with no where, when, or why. Today he's a resurrection man called Nathan." I had to explain that because Algarda was unfamiliar with the term.

"Really? People will do anything, won't they? It took a lunatic god to create our tribe. Let me think." He put on a frown more of puzzlement than concentration. "All right. Nathaniel had one child, Jane. She would be my mother's cousin but was way younger than Mom. Younger than me, even. She was a ferociously wicked, precocious six-year-old last time I saw her. She might've looked like this at eighteen." He indicated the drawings of the woman. "She'd be in her fifties, now."

We had an old woman in the mix, though based on nothing solid I guessed she would be older than that. "Could she have produced children who looked like their ancestors?"

Algarda shrugged. "Possibly. I don't know much about those people. We never had a lot to do with them. They weren't good people." He shot me a sudden, narrow look, maybe reading something into my question. "As far as I know, their line died out during my first tour." He looked at the artwork more closely, appreciating what Penny had captured. "The man even has the scars Nathaniel had." He looked hungry when he considered Penny's drawings.

He was deeply uncomfortable when our gazes met again. "Are you some kind of diabolical facilitator?"

"Excuse me?"

"Last time the Algardas got into trouble you were digging up worms. Here you go again."

Morley interjected, "The worms were there, begging to be dug. Be grateful Garrett was manning the shovel."

Algarda was a hard guy. He tried laying a hard look on Morley. Morley took no notice. Algarda said, "You're right. There's probably some serious behind-the-scenes rumbling going on at the top of the Hill. This could even tie in to some odd questions I've been asked lately, by people I never expected to visit my new place."

He did not explain. He did say, "I'll dig into a couple of old family legends." He turned toward the doorway.

Singe did not move. She looked to me for advice. I nodded, but said, "I'm supposed to tell you to go straight to the place in Elf Town from here."

He frowned. "For who?"

"The Windwalker."

He gave me the hard-eye but then just nodded and turned

to follow Singe. She returned from the door to say, "I don't think he is happy with you."

"My heart is broken. Was his mother involved last time we had some excitement with his people? A couple of old crows got themselves dead, if I remember."

"I do not recall. I will look it up." Someone knocked. "That will be Mr. Tharpe."

"Have you started reading minds, too?"

"No. That would be crippling around you two. I saw him coming up the street when I let Mr. Algarda out." She went to open up.

Morley said, "We're inching toward something."

"Yes. And it might involve the undead or zombies after all."

74

Tharpe rolled in and crashed onto a folding chair. "Damn! This cold air feels good."

"It hot out there?"

"Working on getting there. And I need to shed about twenty-five pounds. Shit. Look at you, up on your hind legs and everything, Dotes."

I said, "Once we weaned him off the poison he came back fast. Next week he'll be able to make it to the front door with only one rest stop."

"You better watch out for the little girl, then. He'll have her giggling and squealing like a piggy in some dark corner."

Once upon a time Morley would have joined the game. Now he just scowled. "I'm a one woman man, 'Head."

Tharpe said, "Singe, honey, my dogs are worn down to the ankles. You want to take a look out front and see how big that flock of flying pigs is? Take one a them Amalgamated umber-eller thing-jobbies along in case they got the flying dyer-rear." He snickered at his own wit.

I chuckled, too.

Morley tried but only managed to look grim.

Saucerhead continued, "Ah, gotcha. A health issue, *that* woman being involved."

Maybe a real health issue. Morley looked physically uncomfortable. I asked, "You all right? You need something?"

"I've been pushing it too much. I'm starting to feel it."

"Singe, I don't think he's ready to do without his angels." I hadn't seen any ratwomen today.

"I'll make sure they're here tonight."

"Good on you."

She asked, "Why don't we ask Mr. Tharpe what he's doing here? That might prove interesting."

Saucerhead said, "Mr. Tharpe was hoping somebody would bring him a mug so he could relax while he was telling his story."

I asked, "You need musical accompaniment? I saw a mandolin somewhere the other day, when we were salting the windows. It was short two strings, though."

Singe made a growling noise.

Maybe that was enough grab-assing around. "There's a problem, 'Head. The beer barrel ran dry. Dean is out trying to find Jerry right now."

"I guess I can wait."

Singe growled even louder.

"Whatever happened to that sweet little ratgirl you brung home a few years ago, Garrett?"

Singe told him, "She spent those years around crude human men. Please do explain why you came here. Besides the obvious."

She bruised Tharpe's feelings with that, not something easy to do. He knew she was calling him a moocher. Which he was, often enough, but not the obnoxious kind you want to bang on the head with a shovel. Usually you wanted to help, gently, because Saucerhead is a good guy blessed with a plentiful supply of minor bad luck.

I told him, "You've been bubbling. You've been threatening to tell us an interesting story. So how about it?" I glanced at Singe. I had no idea what he had been asked to do.

Singe shrugged. She didn't know, either. And Saucerhead wasn't talking. He did, in fact, seem confused.

He asked, "He's really asleep? The Dead Man, I mean."

"He really is. He'd be snoring like Playmate if he was among the breathing."

"Damn! I figured he'd plunk in there and get what he wanted before it went away."

Getting exasperated, I snapped, "Just do it the old-fashioned way! I'll give him the word when he wakes up."

"Oh. Yeah. That'd work, wouldn't it? So what it is, he wanted me to prowl around the costume shops in the theater district."

TunFaire did not have a theater district as such. Theaters

were scattered across midtown, with others downtown. A few smaller venues were out in the neighborhoods. The World was four long blocks from its nearest competitor. The support shops, costume makers and set builders, were concentrated in a patch near the geographic center of the big name play-houses. And that was what Saucerhead meant.

"Costume shops," I mused.

"Yeah. Himself charging in on things from an unexpected angle. Instead of hunting a girl who wears tight black leather and spiffy wigs, find out who makes her outfits. Find out who whipped up them ugly gray wool suits and goofy helmets for the zombie brunos."

"Clever," I admitted, thinking we needed a neologism for the patchwork reanimated baddies who hung out inside the wool and weird wooden helmets.

"Definitely outside the box," Morley said. "Not an angle that would have occurred to me."

"I take it you came up with something, 'Head, on account of you've been wearing such a big shit-eating grin."

"I got to admit I never found who made the stuff for the zombies. Maybe the folks that build them have them make their own outfits. But I did find a guy that made stuff for the hot witch."

"Do tell."

"Here's the part that's got me feeling smart. This guy ain't no theater costumer. He makes custom stuff for the fetish trade."

"Really? I'm starting to think that we've been underesti-mating you, 'Head."

"People got a habit of doing that."

True enough, though usually only in regard to estimating how much abuse he can suffer and go on living.

"How come you thought of this fetish person?"

"I was passing by his place. I had this friend once, she liked to play dress up. I knew where she got her stuff. So I went in and got a little pushy, pretending like I was working for Rel-way. The tailor guy went all white and shaky and told me about this custom order for a bunch of black leather outfits that had to sync up with six different wigs. He got his gig through the wigmaker. And he got hands-on with the woman when she came for fittings."

"All right. Good story. Who was she?"

He shrugged. "I don't know. She never told him. But I guarantee you, she got to that tailor. He had stars in his eyes. His hands shook when he showed me how her body curved. And him as nancy as you can hope to find down there."

"Excellent," I said. "Just excellent. What about the wigmaker?"

"I got the name. He should be the next target."

Morley observed, "This is like taking over for the Dead Man, Garrett, us at the heart of the web while minions do the legwork."

Saucerhead frowned. He wasn't thrilled about that minions remark.

Singe said, "Mr. Tharpe, you do recall the name of that special tailor, don't you? And the wigmaker?"

Tharpe understood. Singe wasn't questioning him. She wanted to get the information committed to paper so it wouldn't get lost.

Morley said, "I meant it about just sitting around like the Dead Man."

"I know. And I'm thinking that maybe he gets frustrated, too, because he can't get out and snoop for himself."

"You? Frustrated about having to lay around and do nothing?"

"It's different when it isn't your own choice."

75

Jerry the beer guy turned up while Singe was winkling critical information out of Saucerhead. I helped bring the kegs in. Dean had gone for an extra, a standard-grade tavern beer good enough for our endless stream of guests.

Saucerhead was the first benefactor, though what he got was the last partial pitcher off the cripple in the cold well. I took half a mug. Morley got nothing but he doesn't drink. Singe got a taste off Saucerhead's pitcher.

Dean and Penny came back as Jerry and I were loading the empty kegs on his wagon. Dean had bought so much stuff he'd had to hire a cart to haul it. I did a brief apprentice stint in the porter trade.

It's good to develop new skills.

Dean's purchases didn't inspire me.

He was concerned about our finances—especially after having bought three kegs of beer and paid the deposit on the extra.

While lugging apples and potatoes, I took a look around. The complement of watchers had become disrespectfully small.

Folks thought the tale had moved on. Morley and I were not considered factors anymore. Or, maybe, the powers on the Hill had grown fangs so long and green that people formerly inclined to hang on my adventures had chosen discretion as their expression of valor.

Yeah. That felt better than thinking I wasn't worth watching anymore.

Having made sure the fresh kegs felt at home I scuttled back into the Dead Man's room. "All right, Mr. Tharpe. You've done an admirable job so far. What next?"

"I don't know." His tongue had gotten a little thick already.

He was thinking about his next pitcher. "I figure somebody else should take over. I asked so many questions people was starting to believe I was one of Relway's Runners. One of the ones so dumb he don't know how to hide it."

"They act scared?"

"Of course they did. Everybody is afraid of the Unpublished Committee, excepting you and me and maybe your napping friend across the way." He meant Morley, who had gone back to his cot while the beer barrel population was being restored to glory.

"Any threats?"

"You know anybody stupid enough to threaten Relway's thugs? Anybody still running around loose, I mean. There's probably a shitload helping drain Little Dismal Swamp."

"You're right. I don't. Anybody serious about bucking the Director better be smart enough to keep his big damned mouth shut."

Tharpe said, "So I was thinking, since I couldn't find the people who made the masks and outfits for the zombies, maybe the next step would be to look the chain back a link and find out who made that ugly cloth. And who came up with the stuff to make them stupid helmets. Did you save one of them from the other night?"

"The red tops took everything."

"That General Block, he's smarter than he lets on. I wonder if he's been thinking the way I been."

I doubted it. "Did you run into any real Runners when you were poking around?"

"No."

"You were ahead of them." I should give Block a heads-up. He could swamp that district with investigators able to scare a stone into spilling its guts.

"I'm thinking you're onto something, 'Head."

"I got one more thing. Then I'm gonna head into the kitchen and get me another pitcher. I'm gonna enjoy that. Then I'm gonna curl up in a corner and sleep for about two days."

"Sounds like a plan. What's your one more thing?"

"Get the Remora to take over where I left off. He pokes around down there, them people will lay down and spread their legs. They'll do anything for him if it might get them a shot at connecting with one of his shows."

"Saucerhead, you drink all the beer you want." I felt like the peasant boy who's just been handed the magic sword. Big things were coming.

Tharpe showed me his biggest, goofiest grin, headed for the kitchen. I went over to discuss it with Singe. She was recording Dean's purchases in her books.

76

"Saucerhead came up with an original idea." I explained.

"That is an interesting angle. Somebody has been feeding him smart pills. Let's hope Mr. Salvation feels amenable." She brushed aside my suggestion that we send for him. "He'll ignore us if we appeal to him. He needs to think things are his idea. Wrangling him takes craft."

"Did Old Bones craft him into doing something for us?"

"He did. I don't know what. Certainly something the Dead Man told him only he could manage."

I shook my head. Jon Salvation. I couldn't get used to a Remora with airs.

Focused on her books, Singe told me, "You need to put your prejudices aside when you think about that man, Garrett. He is a near complete waste of flesh in ways *you* consider important. But he *is* also the best and most powerful playwright working. And, in his mind, he is one of your inner circle."

"I got you. But do you realize how ridiculous that is to anybody who knew Pilsuds Vilchik?"

Singe asked, "Answer the door. I still have entries to make and Dean's notes look like he kept them in code."

"The door?"

"Someone is knocking."

"Damn, your ears are better than mine."

"I'm young. I'm pretty. And I'm not human."

No way could I respond to that and have anything good come of it.

She snickered as I left the room.

John Stretch and two ratwomen were on the stoop. I figured his henchrats had witnessed the beer delivery.

The so well-to-do lord of the ratfolk underworld joined me in with the Dead Man. His women joined Morley. "This cool air is wonderful."

I had worked up a sweat doing porter work so I was in complete agreement. "I'm scared to ask Singe how much we pay for the heat exchange spells but on these warm days it seems worth it."

"There must be some kind of climate change going on. Rat-people aren't usually bothered by hot weather but this much heat, this early, worries me. What will it be like when we hit the blazing heart of summer?"

"Blazing heart, eh?"

"Not original, I admit. It is from a street corner rant I heard the other day. Though he actually said, 'The blazing heat of summer.' His point was, the hottest day of summer would seem refreshingly cool once we found ourselves in hell."

"A street theater guy. You got to love them. Life would be less fun without them."

"Too true."

He had a reason for being here beyond a hope for free beer. I put on an expression of eager curiosity. I drank some beer myself.

"The reason I came by—I wanted to let you know, I just launched a special operation."

I took a long sip. "I'm all ears."

"The stink of corruption in that warehouse had to be unique. And something like it would be strong wherever the zombie makers are building their monsters now."

He looked expectant.

"I imagine so." I looked expectant right back, sure he had a point to make. "Yes?"

"Ah." Pleased with himself. "I put out word to ratfolk across the city. Sniff out places that stink of death and chemicals."

"Brilliant!" How could the people who wanted the thing left alone object? "Everybody is thinking more clever than me."

"Everybody?"

"Saucerhead Tharpe came up with the notion of looking for the people who made the costumes, then to work back from them."

"That would be interesting, too. But my method has more promise."

"You're right. Find the monster manufactory and back-tracking won't be necessary."

He wanted more pats on the back. Some parts of his life must not have been going as well as he would like.

I said, "Enjoy your beer." Which must not have been the perfect sentiment at the moment. He looked puzzled.

The day went downhill from there. The world kept intruding.

All the folks sent out by the Dead Man would come back to plague me.

77

Jon Salvation turned up first, glowing. He shook my hand. "I
don't know what you did, Garrett, but, thank you, thank you,
thank you."

"All right. Good for me. What are you talking about?"

"Tinnie. She's going to take the part. She turned up for first
readings this morning. She was an angel. *And* she nailed her
character first try. Thank you, thank you, thank you."

"Any time. But do me a favor. Tell her my dividend is late.
Way late."

"Eleven days late!" Singe said, managing a fierce growl.

"All right. I'll pass it on. To business. The Dead Man asked
me to talk to people I know about who holds the deed to the
warehouse where they were making zombies. The owner is
Constance Algarda, better known as Shadowslinger."

"Wasn't she one of the people the Bellman killed when ...?
No. I remember now. He busted her up but she lived."

"I report, sir. I don't do analysis. If she's dead she still man-
ages to be active in the real estate world. She owns other properties around town. I brought a list." He produced it. Singe
snagged it, began copying it to make sure the information got
put away safe before I could contrive to lose or destroy it.

Salvation added, "Just as a bit of practical information, I
wasn't the only one asking questions. People from the Palace,
people from the Guard, and some scary-looking people off the
Hill all poked into the same stuff before I did."

"That might not be good."

"You think?"

"There's something else you could do to help. You being
uniquely qualified." I explained the costume angle.

"I can handle that. Easy. I have a big lever. We need lots of costumes and sets for *The Faerie Queene*."

I couldn't tell the man he wasn't half the waste of human flesh that I'd always thought. But I could think it and maybe he could sense it.

Singe finished copying the list. She handed the copy to her brother. John Stretch scanned it, took a drink, bobbed his head, and left the room with Singe right behind. He was less under the weather than I thought, and more literate.

Singe returned, began making another copy. I asked, "When did he learn to read?"

"While you were away. He's slow and he has trouble with script but he understands that literacy is the most useful skill you can have in life."

"What's he going to do with that list?"

"Have his people sniff around."

"He'll need to be careful if those others are doing the same thing."

"Give the dumb rat some credit, Garrett. He heard. He'll be careful—in the unlikely event that anybody does notice ratpeople."

Ouch! She was in a mood again. But she had a point.

"I understand. Now tell me something. What are you so busy writing all the time? You can't possibly need to do that much bookkeeping."

"I keep a record of everything that happens to us."

Odd. That sounded like one of those truths that have more than one face. Like a carefully crafted answer kept on the shelf for the moment when the inevitable question arose.

Jon Salvation chuckled. He knew something.

Of course he did. The past few weeks even kids like Crush and Kyra knew more than me about almost everything.

"Jon, about the girl who was here the other night."

"Crush?"

"Yeah. She's a good kid."

Singe made a whuffing sound, maybe startled.

"I'm sure she is. And I wasn't at my best."

I showed him a raised eyebrow.

"It's so frustrating. They all have the same dumb questions. Which they can't articulate because they're starstruck. I try to remember that their questions seem unique to them. But I'm not used to all this. Sometimes I lose patience."

I gawked. I asked Singe, "What did they do with my friend the Remora?"

He laughed. "People change when the earth shifts under their feet, Garrett. I'm not Pilsuds Vilchik anymore. Nor the Remora—though that has had a hard downside for Winger. I'm all Jon Salvation, now. Which isn't always a great thing, even though Jon Salvation is living the fantasy that rocked Pilsuds Vilchik to sleep every night."

All I could say was, "Wow!" But I kept it to myself.

He said, "I'll do something to make it up to Crush."

I got all daddy.

Singe made a noise before I said anything.

My little Hellbore was a working girl with ample experience looking out for herself.

Salvation promised, "I'll be the perfect gentleman."

I must have looked skeptical.

"I am aware of her background, Garrett. Though I'd never bring it up. If she pretends to be a lady I'll pretend to be a gentleman."

Singe left her desk. "You're both sentimental, idiot romantics in a world where only pragmatists survive."

She left the room.

I said, "I just wanted something nice for Crush that she could have without having to lie down. She's a good-hearted kid. She deserves a minute when she doesn't have to be a whore."

The famous playwright gave me a goofy grin and a thumb up. "I've got it. But I'll need some help since we're going to pretend that all I know about her is that she's a cute teenager."

78

Singe deserted us to answer the door. She returned with an unlikely duo: Belinda Contague and Westman Block, both in disguise. Block was convincing as an aging hoodlum. I don't know what Belinda hoped people would see. She was dressed more conservatively than usual and wore a curly chestnut wig that changed the shape of her face. She could have passed as my sexy younger sister.

She headed for my old office.

Block appeared to have gotten an early start on White Day, the romantic holiday. Lovers give each other candy. But so do friends. I grimaced at the thought. White Day could get expensive if I fetched up friendship boxes for all the girls in my life. Ha! One for Mrs. Cardonlos! That might be fun.

I made a mental note to ask Dean to see if he could get a job lot rate on a dozen boxes.

Block was a solid one sheet to the wind and maybe closer to two. He needed Singe's assistance to get settled. "It's an ugly world out there, Garrett. An ugly world."

Jon Salvation nodded agreement.

I said, "No doubt you're right. But I'm the kind of guy who loves to hear the miserable details." I sent a questioning look Singe's way. Block had been her excuse for dragging me out so early. She shrugged.

Did Block have anything to share? Or was he just here in hopes of scoring some more free booze?

There was plenty of Bird fuel around.

Block asked, casually, "Any ardent spirits left from the other night?"

Singe produced a half gallon of the finest, smoothest sipping water-of-life ever distilled in Karenta, along with a sizable mug. She filled that for Block. For Jon Salvation and me, there were little sipping cups holding about two ounces.

What was she up to? She would have Block passed out and puking on the rug.

I did not let wondering distract me from enjoying my own drink.

This skullbust tasted like smoked medicine. But I sipped along, just to be sociable.

Block failed to expand upon his contention that the world was less than beautiful. He was too busy spooning with his ardent spirits.

Belinda joined us, evidently satisfied that Morley would live. "Give me a big-ass mug of that shit, Garrett. I'm in a mood to get wasted."

I asked, "You all right?"

"I'm better after seeing him, but, are you stupid? Of course I'm not all right. My idiot lover is still down and there isn't a godsdamned thing Belinda Contague can do to make things better."

"Actually, he was awake, aware, and functioning till a little while ago. He wore himself out. He's doing fine, Belinda. But how about you?"

She looked grim, downed water-of-life like it was small beer. "I'm so damned frustrated, I'm thinking about starting a war just to make people pay attention."

"Whoa, girl! That's not a good idea."

"Just to make them pay attention, Garrett. Just to make them pay attention."

She must have been drinking before she got here.

This side of Belinda hadn't come out for a long time.

"How did you turn up at the same time as the General? And, before you get all old-time hardcore, we have made some headway." I told her what Saucerhead and Jon Salvation had told me.

Salvation himself remained silent and motionless, hoping not to be noticed.

Block said, "There's talk that Shadowslinger doesn't own those properties despite her name being on the deeds."

Belinda slurred, "Clever, going after the costume suppliers."

She wouldn't be with us long.

Glen Cook

"I have some other odd angles going. And I've gotten possible identifications of the people whose portraits we put together."

Tipsy, bloodthirsty excitement on Belinda's part. Block was less nasty but equally thrilled.

I said, "There is a problem. The bad guys are people who should have been out of it years ago." I explained what Playmate and Barate Algarda had told me.

Block mused, "The guy's name stays the same. Hmm? Do we have ghosts, like at the World? Or a father-son-grandson thing? Or the undead? You have a theory, Garrett?"

"We haven't yet seen any of them out in the daytime."

"Vampires?"

That would have seemed silly a week ago. Now, though. "The bodies they're rebuilding could be those of their victims."

"Problem," Block said. "We got forty or fifty zombies but no missing persons. We took out nineteen but that leaves thirty to go. We for sure haven't had that many people the right age die."

Belinda was well toward becoming inarticulate but, stumbling and bumbling, she managed, "Roger keeps whining about his business getting so awful. His customers don't want to be embalmed. They just want a ride to the crematorium."

Poor Cap'n Roger.

How does a resurrection man stay in business if all the dead get burned? "What's the story in the refugee shantytowns? They wouldn't be honest with the red tops since they think you're persecuting them."

"We would know," Block said. "Deal would know. His intelligence gathering has improved since your day." He sighed. He took a long, forlorn look into his mug. I could not believe he was still speaking coherently. Belinda had started talking to herself. She could not understand a word she said. "Garrett, our problem is that we're drowning in intelligence. We have so much we can't pick out the important bits."

"What?"

"Occasionally, lately, we've found that everything we needed to know to prevent or solve a crime was in the system but the information just didn't get to the right people."

"Uhm?" I hoped he was making excuses, not fishing for suggestions.

Singe had some. She held us spellbound while she brainstormed an analytical hierarchy that would sort reports on arrival, evaluate them, then move them to people whose job it would be to determine connections or threats. Those folks would pass information to the people who would take action. The process depended on individual responsibility, with the hierarchy built so that shifting blame would be difficult. Penalties for failure by pettiness or indifference would be rough.

Block was awed. "Magnificent! Pure intellectual genius, Miss Pular! I see just one flaw."

"Sir?"

"Human nature. Even with penalties built in not everyone will strive to achieve the common goal."

Singe was deflated. "Oh. Humans. Right."

"It's still the best idea I've heard. Definitely something to build on. We'll dedicate a holding cell in your name." Which, grinning, he said to her back. She was up and moving into the hallway. "Uh . . . Did I hurt her feelings?"

79

Singe's feeling were not bruised. She had heard a knock that eluded the rest of us. She was back in a minute with Kolda, the poisoner.

Damn! Now I was doing it.

The company made Kolda nervous. He refused a seat when Singe offered it. "I can only stay a minute. I just wanted to drop off some medicines. This bottle, with the green powder in it, is for Mr. Dotes. It will help his body flush poisons. Have him use it till it's all gone, no matter how good he thinks he feels. And this bottle, with the stuff that looks like ground amber, is for the man with the cancers. Very expensive but very effective. It's exuded by an exotic tropical beetle. Give him a pinch with every meal. No more than a pinch. More could kill him. Even a pinch may leave him feeling so nauseous that he might try to talk you out of giving him any more. Make him stick it out."

"Kolda, thank you, man. You've gone beyond the call. What do I owe you?"

"This is on me, Garrett. But I figure it makes us even. I'll charge you next time."

"Something to drink?" Singe asked.

"I shouldn't. It's a bit early."

"You sure? Not even one beer?"

"Well . . . One can't hurt."

Singe headed for the kitchen.

Kolda glanced around, decided to sit after all. He leaned toward me. "There was one more thing."

"We're all friends here."

Kolda shrugged. "When I was going around the trade look-ing for something to fight tumors several chemists and apothecaries hit me up for Jane's mint seed. I don't have any. Not to wholesale. It's rare. After I'd been asked a few times I started asking back, about why."

"Uhm?"

"Jane's mint only grows in boggy places. It's not really mint but crushing the leaves produces a juice with a mint smell. It shouldn't be ingested. It used to be used to poison mice. The seeds are hard to collect. You have to catch them at exactly the right time."

"We're interested in Jane's mint seeds because?"

"Because the powdered seeds have an almost miraculous healing effect. And someone has been buying them up. The price has gone up tenfold in a month."

I exchanged looks with Block, then held up a restraining hand when he wanted to press for details. Kolda didn't notice.

Belinda didn't care. She was having trouble staying conscious.

Singe returned. Kolda accepted a mug, took a long pull, was pleasantly surprised, belched, then told me, "And that's about all I know, heading west." He drained his mug and got his feet under him again.

Singe released him into the wild, then hustled back to eavesdrop while Block and I quarreled over whether the Guard or the Outfit should make the rounds of the town's chemists. I thought Belinda's thugs would be more effective.

I wondered, "Did you get anything from the bodies you hauled away the other night?"

"They got confiscated by people who had the right warrants but not the right look."

"I smell obfuscation," Belinda said, suddenly awake. She had on a big smile. She had been faking the drunk. And she knew more than the Civil Guard thought she should.

Block said, "We did what we could in the time that we had."

"And that would be?"

"Two zombies had faces resembling those of known criminals. It wasn't for sure. The outsides of the bodies were more like leather than normal skin. The forensic sorcerers said they were dressed in whole human skins after the surgical rebuilding. The major seams were in the back. Not all of the skins fit right, which might be why they wear the woolen tights. The helmets hide the faces, which are in bad shape. The hair falls out in patches, even in the beards and eyebrows."

I hit the key point. "You recognized two of them."

"We think we did."

"And?"

"And what, Garrett?"

"Who were they? How did they die? Where? When? What were the circumstances?"

"They were housebreakers. They were sent to the work camps. Once we give them to Works they're not our problem anymore."

Things might have been starting to line up. The Dead Man's compound minds might have pushed on past what had to be obvious even to a general.

I said, "If somebody wanted a supply of corpses, she could make a deal with somebody at a work camp. Not many of those crooks finish their sentences still breathing."

"The reason they die is that they get used up. They don't get fed right, they work long hours with primitive tools, and they get no medical attention. All part of the price of being a bad guy. Works has hundreds of prisoners and has to account for them only when their sentences are up. If a prisoner dies they report it so we can tell the family that what they expected has come to pass."

I had an evil turn of mind. I imagined several ways that men more wicked than the prisoners could profit from the penal work system.

No doubt the bad guys out there had thought of them all and a dozen more.

Block said, "We're looking at it, Garrett. Supposedly in regard to complaints about prisoner abuse."

"The more I learn the more useless I feel."

I expected to hear something reassuring. Instead, he said, "That's because you haven't come to terms with having to be a desk jockey. You're sitting on your butt when you think you should be out kicking ass and taking names."

Singe made a noise suspiciously like that from someone who snorts while breaking up inside but is compelled to maintain a straight face.

Block went on, "How come you think you have to be useful? I mean, why now, suddenly, when you spent forever being an obstruction?"

I did not want to have this argument. It was the same crap I'd gotten from minions of the law since I went into business.

"I try and try but I can't figure out how me not being your brownnose butt boy qualifies as obstructionism. The gods didn't send me down here to wash your feet, kiss your ass, and whisper in your ear what a great stud you are. You know that's bullshit better than I do."

Singe and Jon Salvation popped out of their chairs, tried to calm me down. Singe made my drinking cup disappear. Block gaped like he had opened a casket full of worms.

My mouth just kept running. "I have no clue how you and that repugnant troll Relway got the idea that I'm supposed to be your tool but you need to get shut of the notion, now and forever."

I was shouting before I finished. Penny came to see what was happening. Belinda clapped and cheered. Jon Salvation told Penny, "Just a little trouble handling his drink. Ask Dean if he has anything useful in a situation like this."

The man was right. I shouldn't have had that water-of-life. It had opened a door. The frustrations were getting out.

Singe, assisted by Jon Salvation and Dollar Dan, returned me to my former place of glory beside Morley, next door. Singe and Dollar Dan sat on me. I became fixated on that rat, wondering if he hadn't moved in when I wasn't looking.

He was never underfoot. He was invisible most of the time. But he was always there when someone needed him.

I faded into a nap wondering if he was more than a ratman. He might be a living metaphor for his whole race.

80

Business rolled along while I snoozed. People came, people went. General Block, Belinda, and Saucerhead all left. Some beer and a nap were all Tharpe needed. Singe and Jon Salvation got their heads together, scheming something. Morley woke up and turned crabby because he had missed Belinda. Salvation left after his confab with Singe.

Tinnie dropped in and spent some quality time with Singe, their banter getting heated. First, Singe would not let her wake me up. She used the words "too much drama" more than once. Then the overdue dividend came up. The exchange went from heated to icy. Tinnie refused to believe that our shares had not been paid.

Singe said, "I have received no deposit receipt from our bankers. Produce evidence that payment was made."

This was when Morley entered and saw the actual exchange.

Tinnie replied, "We have not failed, ever, to meet our obligations, on time and in full. What you claim is impossible."

Singe countered, "You handle the fiscal paperwork for Amalgamated. Even when you don't authorize payments you keep records of them. So I say again, show me proof of payment. Our bankers would have given you a receipt, too. Produce it."

Morley was impressed by Tinnie's self-control. By this point most Karentines would have launched a vile rant about uppity vermin.

"Tinnie saves her bile for me."

Evidently Singe's grim, firm, confident, no-nonsense attitude got the best of the redhead. She scribbled a note, then roared out of the house.

Morley said, "I expect somebody at Amalgamated is hanging by his short hairs now. If what Singe claimed is true."

Having seen Typhoon Tinnie Tate in a category-four rage I was glad the bad weather was headed elsewhere.

I read her note.

Sorry I came when you were resting. I had a wonderful time at rehearsal. Never felt so happy. Thank you, Malsquando. Love you, and always will. X O X

It was not signed.

Had anyone read it?

Singe? Almost certainly.

Morley? No. His odd sense of honor would forbid it.

Dean might have done had he known about it and been inclined to think being aware of the contents would help him protect the household.

Penny appeared while I brooded, bringing tea. She saw the unfolded note. She reddened.

So.

Why would she be nosy?

Did she have some vague notion about getting back at Tinnie for having fed her so much slime about me?

Morley watched Penny leave. He chuckled.

"What?"

"You missed some real excitement."

"My head hurts."

"It ought to. And you did it to yourself."

Not only did my head hurt, it was still wobbly from the dizzy water. "What did I miss? Besides Tinnie?"

"Winger. She came looking for her pet playwright. He was gone by then. She was hammered. She wouldn't believe Singe. Singe and Dollar Dan got her under control. She went away, then."

"Bad shape, eh?"

"Blitzed pathetic. She's too old for melodrama."

"Aren't we all? But still it happens."

We shared a moment of silence, reflecting on the absurdities of our relationships.

Morley asked, "Is it even possible for men to get past adolescence?"

"Maybe not. I'm missing Old Bones big-time right now. He could share centuries of observation."

"Meaning?"

"Meaning he could answer your question. Me, I think we can't help but act like juvenile idiots till we can't contribute to the continuation of our tribes anymore."

"If we were well behaved and thought with our heads ..."

"We're slaves to our little best friends. But the gods had a reason for making us that way."

"A disgusting digression, Garrett. But you're probably right. And the gods made sure that girls are dim enough to believe anything we tell them until they're old. Nature wants that next generation's boots on the ground before anything else."

"Because we do think, though, we make it more of an adventure by coming up with ways to get around Nature."

Morley lost interest. He asked, "Where are we going, Garrett?"

"Nowhere. I'm going to sit here and feel sorry for myself. My head will be ready to explode in a couple more hours."

"I meant in our relationships."

What? We were men. We didn't get into stuff like that. Not seriously. Did we?

"You and Tinnie practically announced to the world that you were going to tie the knot. You moved in together. Then the invitations never came. After a while people forgot. And now you're involved with a totally delicious confection off the Hill. Who must have a love-me spell on her. Even Dean likes her better than he likes Tinnie."

"I'm not involved. Not yet."

"You're sleeping in the same bed. One of you doesn't care who knows. She moved a trunk into your room. I'm pretty sure that qualifies as involved."

"Where did you hear ... ?"

"Singe let it slip. Accidentally on purpose, I'm sure. She says the woman has no shame."

"In private. But she does have a sense of propriety. She wouldn't hurt someone deliberately."

This stuff was a lot less complicated when I was younger.

Singe came in. She gave us the fish-eye, favoring me with the magnum variety. "The ladies are here for your evening

treatment, Mr. Dotes. And you, Mr. Garrett, need to reacquaint yourself with the bathtub. A change of apparel would
not be amiss, either."

She had to be channeling my mother.

"I took a bath last week!" With a vintage eight-year-old
whine.

A bunch of stuff happened at once, starting with Dean's
announcement of a late supper as the ratwomen closed in
on Morley. Dotes got a chance to gobble a few mouths full,
then participated in the customary rituals in my former office. Singe went and worked hard in her office. I drank a mug
of beer, then took myself up to bed. I had a full belly and the
world wasn't going to let me do anything else anyway.

I just wanted to escape to dreamland before my hangover
set in.

"I'll be responsible next year, Ma."

When I woke up because I needed to commune with the
chamber pot I was no longer alone. Strafa stirred but did not
waken. When I climbed back into bed she snuggled against
me like a second skin. I found it amazing that she could get so
close and still leave me comfortable. I did not stay awake long.
I spent those moments wondering how Strafa had gotten in. I
didn't remember leaving the window open.

It was open now. The air was cool. Strafa's warmth felt
good.

81

Pular Singe was not pleased with her boss, master, partner—whatever she styled me in secret.

She blundered into my room at an inappropriate moment. She gasped something like, "Now I believe it," and went away.

Strafa didn't care. She was preoccupied.

Going downstairs told me, quickly, that the new order had become established fact. Dean greeted Strafa warmly, with perfect manners and no hint of disapproval. Singe was more formal but had put her personal feelings into a locked box. She did not dislike Strafa, she just had problems with all the changes.

It would be hard for anybody to dislike Strafa when she wasn't being Furious Tide of Light. Except for Penny Dreadful. Penny had issues of some kind.

Morley reported that. I didn't see it.

"The girl glares daggers at the woman when she thinks no one will notice."

"That makes no sense. She doesn't know Strafa. Strafa is no threat to her."

"You never know. You up for a physical workout today?"

"You aren't ready for that yet, are you?"

"I'll pace myself. It's you that needs to get busy. You're a tub of goo."

That exaggeration was unkind in the extreme but not far off the mark. I was still weak from my cold but the worst of that had passed. If I used Dean's breather occasionally, my nose stayed open and I didn't cough up chunks bigger than my fist.

Morley said, "It will be fun, getting ready for our personal war."

I doubted that the rest of the world would leave us much against which to execute even one tactical move. Scores were out there trying to make an end to the horror.

I was sure that fear of widespread panic and a breakdown of order were heavy on the minds of movers and shakers everywhere. If fear of a witch hunt did have some basis it made sense for the powerful and privileged to keep the worst quiet.

"We may be fooling ourselves, old friend."

"Doesn't matter. Whatever we do to prepare our bodies and purify our souls won't be a waste."

He was in a martial-arts-philosophy-of-life kind of mood.

I smiled and promised, "I'll do my best!"

"You prick. Now you're making fun."

"I don't like people who say things like that."

"I knew it. You have the intonation perfect. Every word from the little dying girl in the comedy *Skuffle*."

"Damn. You got me. How did you know?"

"I see everything they put on at the World. Good and bad."

"Who stuck you full of holes, then? What did you see that made somebody decide it was time you took a dirt nap?"

"All right. You got me. I suffer memory lapses. I wish I had one where that play was concerned. Alyx Weider and her pals stunk it up, trying to play kids Penny's age."

"I enjoyed it. Once I got over the old maidens factor. It was fluff."

"You're a sentimental, romantic idiot. Which, my marvelous memory reminds me, Singe was generous enough to point out not that long ago."

"My equally peerless memory allows as to how she included you in that base canard."

"Would that be a musical instrument? Might we find it in the orchestra pit? What kind of musician plays the bass canard?"

"Are you all right?"

"It must be the medication. Or I might just be relieving tension by turning it into silliness. You think we could slide out of here if we did a really quiet sneak?"

"Singe hasn't put a bell on the door yet but I don't think we'd get far. She'd be on our trail. With her nose. Then the Windwalker would swoop down and make us break out in boils, or something. If the Dead Man didn't wake up and freeze our brains in our heads."

"You're probably right."

"I am right."

"He is one hundred percent right," Strafa said from the doorway.

From behind her, Singe said, "Pular Singe agrees."

Just to be difficult, I said, "It's times like these when I miss Melondie Kadare the most."

Singe was a grown-up woman. She proved it by having to have the last word. "It is times like these that I miss the God-damn Parrot. And him we could get back. Could we not, Mr. Dotes?"

"Might be a chore. He went away with the sky elves last time they were here. You could pray that he'll be obnoxious enough for them to bring him back."

I did not comment. I wanted no crazy ideas getting stuck in anybody's head.

82

I sat down with Strafa in Singe's office, a stack of handkerchiefs close by. Singe was at her desk, hard at it pretending to be disinterested. "I'm betting you found a whole lot of nothing yesterday."

"You're psychic. I did get to spend time with my daughter and Kip. As did Barate."

That did not sound like the kids had much fun. "You didn't spank them, did you?"

"No. I was gentle as could be. Before Barate got there I hammered Kevans about them having to stop being bedroom friends. They have other commitments, now."

"I wondered if you saw that."

"I expect even Kyra saw it. I don't know if I got through. She didn't want to get it, probably because it's been them against the world for so long. And Kip may not be involved with Kyra physically, yet."

"Don't tell me. He respects her too much. And doesn't see the inconsistency."

"That would be my guess. And, then, there is you and me. Kevans threw that in my face."

"Ouch. What did Barate say?"

"He wasn't there yet. Kevans settled down fast after he showed up."

Singe wrote and pretended to be deaf. I could imagine her thoughts about our personal lives becoming ever more complicated.

I said, "We aren't in a good position to argue, 'Do as I say!'"

"True. But there is a difference."

"About the warehouse."

"Barren. Not even dust or cobwebs. People and elves around there won't talk about it. Ratpeople will. Palace Guards took everything away. Some stayed around to chase off Director Relway's Specials and General Block's forensic sorcerers. The ratpeople say there's a plan to demolish the building, now."

I muttered, "That wouldn't be legal. The Lifeguards can't tell people what to do outside the Palace."

It shouldn't be hard to trace where that much stuff went. Strafa had the answer already. The ratfolk had told her.

"It went into the Knodical underground."

"What?" The Knodical was a Royal house well separated from the Palace. Over the past few centuries its main function has been to house the Royal mistresses.

"Hired ratpeople broke stuff up into firewood, cullet, and landfill. Human bits went to a crematorium. The rest went into the Knodical."

"I see," I said. "Everything but the sense."

"It doesn't make any, does it? You don't create dozens of witnesses while trying to destroy evidence."

Not if you can't get rid of the witnesses.

"So something else was going on."

"Maybe it was about purification."

Strafa got up, stepped over, eyed my lap like she was thinking about making herself at home.

"Not in here, please," Singe said without looking up. "General Block thinks we are brushing up against a conspiracy against the Crown."

I waited expectantly. Strafa dropped her snuggle scheme and joined the wait.

"Well?"

"His goal may be to destroy wealth."

Strafa and I leaned toward her. "Whose goal?"

"Gods, think! Rupert! Suppose there is a plot against the Royals but it's well hidden. The patchwork men are part of it. Maybe they are supposed to create panic and make the people in charge look incompetent. But Rupert doesn't have to know who the bad guys are to break their toys. If they want to stay in business, they have to buy more. So they risk exposing themselves making purchases. Which will cost a lot of money."

All of which sounded weird but might make sense in a

context where the Crown came down hard and hogged everything.

Strafa said, "They don't think they can trust anyone."

"Say that's right, Singe. So what?"

"I was speculating. It won't make a lick of difference to you or me."

"You think?"

"I think. In fact, I think we should forget the whole thing. I think we should concentrate on business. Morley, I smell you. Come in."

Dotes entered, not the least chagrined.

Singe said, "The Grapevine is a class restaurant. Cherish and nurture that. Let the professionals dance with the devils and deal with the rest."

Odd stuff coming out of that girl's mouth.

Morley deadpanned, "You're right, Singe. I have The Palms to worry about, too. It made a comeback after the wine snob set moved on."

Singe's whiskers twitched. She knew Morley was messing with her.

He said, "And I had openings planned near two other theaters. One would do seafood."

I played along. "You're talking seriously upscale there, brother. Hard to keep that stuff fresh all the way up the river."

He looked past me. "I was going to ask your lady friend to come in as a partner. She could fly in shrimp and crabs, scallops, sea bass, squid, octopus, prawns, that kind of stuff, fresh every day."

Strafa chuckled. "Entrepreneurship comes to the magical realm. Let's reduce everything to the commercial and mundane."

"What about it?" Morley asked.

"It wouldn't be practical, Mr. Dotes. I can neither fly that far nor can I lift the masses that would be required."

"It was a thought. My other idea would be an ethnic foods place."

That caught Singe's interest. "That would be better. More people can afford pork buns or curries, or something they ran into once while they were doing their five, than could possibly want to put out a fortune so they can brag that they ate a squid."

"Easier to get the ingredients, too," Morley said.

"What is a squid, anyway?"

Dotes said, "That's one for you, Garrett."

I explained about squid, great and small. "Some are littler than your pinkie. Some are big enough to brawl with whales. I think the whales usually start it."

"Ratfolk aren't famous for being picky eaters, Garrett, but I would have to be damned hungry to chomp down on something like that."

"Batter it and fry it in butter, it's not so bad."

"What are we even talking about this stuff for?" Morley demanded.

"You brought it up. Going to make Strafa rich, remember?"

"I'm going crazy here. I have to get out. I need to start doing something."

"Right behind you, boss. Here's how we'll start. You go run down the hall to the kitchen, turn around and run to the front door, then charge on back in here. All without resting. I'll time you."

"Will you ladies kindly cover your ears? I'm about to say bad things about Garrett."

Singe snickered. "That means he knows he'll collapse before he completes the first lap."

Morley did not disagree. He couldn't. And he wasn't happy about it.

For the first time in the epoch that we had been friends I was in better shape than him.

Singe asked, "Are you done, now? Can I get some work done before the outside world butts in again?"

"You can," I said, more curious than ever about what was taking so much of her time and required the use of so much paper and ink.

Singe shook her head as though she despaired of seeing us survive to enjoy our tenth birthdays. She commenced to begin to ignore our very existence.

I grumbled, "Go ahead. Be that way." I thought about sampling some dizzy water, or maybe some premium beer. But what was the point if I had to go it alone? And if I was going to make myself sick all over again?

Morley asked, "What are the chances those villains will forget about us now?"

"Dumbass question, brother. How the hell would I know? Near as I can figure, they ought to have zero interest in me and only incidental interest in you. Unless you can remember why those absurd people were after you in the first place."

"Garrett, if I knew, you and Bell both would have heard a long time ago."

No doubt. No doubt.

Someone knocked.

Singe sighed, set her pen down, grumbled, "And so it begins."

83

Our visitor was General Block. He was in a good mood. He did not ask for alcohol. He reckoned black tea would be entirely adequate.

"Breakthrough?" I asked.

"We found out where the custom glassware came from. Weast Brothers, in Leifmold. Shone and Sons handled the importing using Dustin Lord Shippers. The purchasers paid cash and collected the materials from the dock using their own transport. They purchased seventy-two items that came in three shipments, the first about a month after the thing at the World Theater went quiescent."

Quiescent? Where did he ever hear a word that big?

"Is there a connection?"

"I doubt it."

Strafa said, "There weren't half that many pieces in that warehouse."

"There were twenty-six. We have friends in the crew that moved them. Only a few got broken."

"That's all interesting," I said. "But helpful how?"

"Helpful because we now know where they were manufactured. A team of Specials is headed down there already. So. What about you all? Come up with anything?"

He looked straight at Strafa. He knew she had been to the warehouse again.

She said, "We didn't find anything. Not even a speck of dust. What did your sorcerers find?"

"Some useless specks of dust. Professionals cleaned that place out."

I asked, "Any ideas about why the cover-up?"

"I know exactly why. So I'm told. I'm on my way home from the Palace. I took a serious ass-munching from Prince Rupert. He made it perfectly clear—for the benefit of witnesses who didn't think I knew they were watching. The Crown is determined to avoid a popular panic. Therefore, this business is too important to be handled by the Guard."

I snorted.

Block nodded. "Experts off the Hill say TunFaire is unstable and volatile because of high unemployment and strained racial relations resulting from the conclusion of the war with Venageta."

Singe said, "When have our lords of the Hill ever cared about that?"

Block raised a hand. "Truth has nothing to do with any of this. They did make one good point. The real hot weather will be here soon."

I could put a cot in there with the Dead Man.

"The orchestrated manipulation of a populace already hot, worried about jobs, and troubled by arcane happenings, might provoke riots and witch hunts."

"Glory Mooncalled," I said.

Block looked at me like I was nuts.

"Just speculation. There was a rumor a couple years ago that he was back, then a whole lot of nothing, like maybe somebody clamped down. This could be some kind of urban guerrilla warfare."

"You do have an imagination, Garrett. If there is any political angle, the source is more likely inside the human rights movement."

I glanced at Morley.

He shook his head. "No way. I don't know what I *was* doing when they captured me. But I wasn't on a mission from the Elven Defense League. Those people are nuts."

Block asked the question. "So you *were* taken captive, then?"

"I . . ." Morley frowned. "I guess. It stands to reason. Ugh!"

"What?"

"I had a flash vision of somewhere dark and smelly. What you would expect where you keep people locked up."

Singe was all over him immediately. "Describe the smells!"

"Back off, people! It was just a flash. There isn't anything there to get hold of yet." He met my eye, glanced eastward.

It was a shame, indeed, that the Dead Man was on hiatus.

For no reason I understood at the moment, I asked, "Where is Penny? Anybody seen her?"

No one had. A flurry of activity ended seconds later when Strafa looked into the Dead Man's room. Penny was in there with the Bird. Bird was teaching her to paint.

Back in Singe's office, I asked, "When did the Bird show up?"

No one knew. Concerned, I hustled to the kitchen to ask Dean. Dean had no idea, either, but had Playmate and Dollar Dan in there with him. Dollar Dan said, "That painter guy came the same time I did. The young girl let us in."

Interesting. "Thanks." I hustled back to the others, where I told Singe what Dollar Dan had said.

"I'll talk to Penny. She's careful about strangers but she should keep us posted about friends."

Block asked, "Anything else you people want to tell me?"

Ah, hell. He was getting that look.

I said, "Tell me what you have. I'm one hundred percent open this time so I'll give you anything you don't already have."

He did not believe me but he played along, telling me some of what the Guard had. I told him, "That's already more than we know here. What could you possibly think we're holding back?"

"You must be. You're constitutionally unable to . . ."

"Captain, stop!" Thus spake the Windwalker, Furious Tide of Light. "It would seem that you have a constitutional handicap of your own."

Captain? Block said, "Yes, ma'am." Meekly.

Singe said, "We could have something more later. You are the first of our contacts to visit us today."

I was trying to recall what I was hiding so I could keep my stories straight.

Block changed the subject. "Prince Rupert wants to see you, Garrett. He said to tell you."

"Why?"

"Going to offer you a job again. Lurking Felhske isn't as straight-arrow as he hoped."

I shrugged. "Not interested."

"You'll have to tell him yourself."

"I don't have time. I'm busy here."

"Garrett! The Crown Prince wants to talk to you."

"If it's that important he knows where to find me."

Block looked at me like he had caught me pissing on an altar.

I *was* being outrageous. But I figured Rupert was too busy to take umbrage.

Somebody knocked.

84

Somebody proved to be cousin Artifice Tate. Singe brought him into the office. He handed her a worn leather courier case. It had the Tate crest embossed on it but almost completely rubbed off. "These people can stand witness to the fact that I delivered this. Please look inside, then tell everyone what that is."

He talked bold but didn't meet any eyes.

Singe opened the foxed brown case. She removed papers. She read. She said, "This is the Amalgamated corporate response to our contention that we did not receive our quarterly dividends. These are deposit receipts, all legally executed. And, note, dated today. There is a letter of apology from a Nestor Tate admitting no malice, stating that because of outside distractions the chief accountant overlooked a number of dividend payments. Possibly, further, due to misbehavior by a family member who should not have had access to the financial offices."

So. It was my fault because Tinnie had stuff besides business on her mind. But if it couldn't be pinned on me, then a straw man did something bad. "They're going to put it onto Rose."

Artifice said, "Maybe. If it is her fault."

I glanced at Morley. Once upon a time he and Tinnie's troubled cousin Rose had had a fiery thing.

He said, "First Law."

"And some luck."

Singe said, "Thank you, Artifice. Inform your uncles that we are impressed with the quickness and graciousness of their response. Would you care for refreshments before you go back into the heat?" She was busy writing again.

"No, thank you. But I'd like something written to acknowledge the fact that I did make it here and you got what I was supposed to deliver."

I was going to like this Tate. He had attitude. Very subtle attitude.

"Already done," Singe said. "General, will you and the Windwalker add your chops? To make this exchange completely legal?"

Those two did as requested while I boggled. My little girl knew exactly what to do and was so businesslike nobody thought to demur.

She was getting scarier by the hour.

Block had on a half sneer that told me he saw me slipping to errand boy status around here.

Artifice did some shallow bows and headed for the front door armed with his ragged case and notarized receipt. Clever Garrett volunteered to let him out, fooling nobody. Including Artifice, who told me, as I opened the door, "I'm sorry. I don't have anything for you from Tinnie. She suddenly don't have time for anything. She does play stuff all morning, then works the books at night." He sucked in a bushel of air, released it in a long, sad sigh. "Man, I think she gave up. She moved her stuff back to the compound when the ratgirl wouldn't let her see you. Marmie said she heard her crying last night."

He reached out, rested a hand on my left shoulder. "I don't know what I ought to be feeling, man. She's hurting. But I think you done your part. She dug the hole. I'm supposed to be on her side 'cause she's family, but . . . What I'm trying to tell you is, whatever, the family won't be as unhappy with you as you probably think. We're gonna be all right with you. Unless you do something dumb now."

I wondered if I would ever actually see Tinnie again.

"Thank you." Which surprised him.

Would we become enemies? He was trying to say no. And I couldn't see it happening. Business trumps with the Tates. These days their principal business is manufacturing the wonders that spring from Kip's mind. And bad man Garrett has an undue influence over the genius boy.

Glower and grumble some might but they would not munch any feeding hand.

It might be gods help us all, though, if Kip ever ran dry.

All assuming everything went on the way it appeared to be headed now.

Is fear of your girl's family a good enough reason to keep a relationship going?

85

I stayed on the porch waiting for Sarge and Puddle. Let's hope those two never get into a last-man-standing ugly contest. The refs would call a draw after the twenty-seventh round.

"Hey, gents. What's up?"

"We just swung by to see how Morley was doing," Puddle said. Clearly nervous.

"The Dead Man is snoozing."

"You always say that."

"And it's usually true. Even if it isn't right now, you want to see Morley, you got to come inside. Plus, it's too late. You're already inside his range."

Up the steps they came.

Clever me, I scooted in, got Morley out of Singe's office and shut that door before his boys noticed General Block. No need having them wonder why the head tin whistle spent so much time at my house, close to their boss. I took them into the Dead Man's room.

Puddle told me, "I don't like it in here wit' dat t'ing. It's creepy. But da cool air is nice."

"I'm not real fond of being in here, either. But you're right about the air. Penny, my love, can you take a second to show these gentlemen the pictures you and Bird made?"

The girl had sass enough to mutter, "I know a gentleman when I see one. There aren't any in this room."

Sarge said, "Hey, she's cute. I like dat. You wanna sell her?"

Penny stood up to it. Having Old Bones right there fired up her confidence. She said, "We don't 'make' 'pictures.'" Last word gotten, she did do as I asked.

I leaned close to Sarge, murmured, "Little known fact.

I need to keep it in mind myself. The kid is Belinda's half-sister."

"Ouch!"

Not that Belinda ever showed the least indication of caring.

The boys ignored the painting of the man entirely. Had a renowned shy girl not been holding the drawings of the woman in leather I'm sure they would have paid the model some crudely enthusiastic compliments.

Morley asked, "You guys know either of these people?"

Heads shook. Sarge stated the obvious. "I wouldn't mind getting to know *her*. 'Specially if she's got a t'ing for old guys wit' big bellies an' not much hair."

"Get in line."

"Dat figures."

Morley added, "The man is the important one. I've seen him somewhere but I can't remember where or when. He's the boss of a gang of resurrection men. His name is Nat, Nate, Nathan, something like that."

The henchmen shook their heads. Puddle said, "We wouldn't never have nothing ta do wit' dat kinda creep."

I believed him. The street climbed right up and proclaimed itself loudly in his speech. Along with abiding repugnance.

Good to know that Morley surrounded himself with associates who had moral limits.

My interest satisfied, I left Morley with his crew and went back to Singe's office. "We need to keep the door shut for a few minutes."

I stepped back out and went to the front door, where Jon Salvation was tap-tap-tapping.

86

"I won't come in, Garrett. I don't have time. These are notes I made during my rounds of the costume shops. They should be useful."

"Thanks. How is Tinnie doing?"

"So far, marvelously. But we aren't that far along. She'll have plenty of chances to be herself before we take the show live. I'm having Alyx Weider be her understudy. The competition should keep her focused."

"If you stick with Alyx."

"I know what I want to do for the girl. Crush."

"I'm listening." I used every second to look around. I was sure we were being watched but I didn't see anyone.

Morley, Sarge, and Puddle came out of the house, breaking my concentration.

Salvation asked, "Why are you sniffing like that?"

"Still fighting the cold." I lied. I knew a man who could be invisible when he was watching. He gave himself away sometimes because he never developed a sufficiently intimate relationship with soap and water.

I smelled nothing unusual.

Salvation, jostled by Sarge and Puddle, scowled as he said, "I'll have the actors sign a copy of the play and send her that. One of the rehearsal copies. Through you, so she doesn't take it the wrong way. I'll tuck in a pass to the premiere, in my box."

"That's overkill, Jon. She'll be absolutely sure you're out to get into her pants."

"Think so?"

"I think so. Crush may not have a lot of years on her but the ones she has have been rough enough to turn her completely cynical."

"That's too bad. She seems like a bright kid."

"She is. She thinks she's a complete realist, too. I know how you feel. I feel that way. She shouldn't waste herself the way she is. But I don't think she'd reach out to grab a helping hand to be rescued."

Salvation nodded. "She wouldn't because she would expect to be pulled into something worse."

"Exactly. But keep those options open. If I see her again I'll find out what she thinks. Subtly."

Morley had been waving to his troops and eavesdropping. He said, "You be subtle with a woman, Garrett? I find that hard to picture."

"You're probably right."

"Go for underkill, Salvation. Have Garrett pass the word she can come by and watch a rehearsal sometime, if she wants. Open-end offer. No big deal if she does or doesn't. Just an option. You're not buying anything that way."

Salvation and I gaped.

Morley said, "The way it sounds, you're interested in making an act of friendship. You don't buy friendship. Close your mouth, Garrett. A pigeon will fly in there and lay eggs."

He went back inside, leaving the door ajar.

I said, "That made sense, Jon."

"It did."

I thanked him for the notes. I followed Morley, pausing just long enough to add, "Tell your security crew to let Crush in if she shows up." Wondering if Mike would give a star that much freedom of motion.

"Yeah. It's Stage Two. Six in the morning till three. Then we clear out so they can set up for the early performance of *King Kristine*. We're almost always gone by one, though. Everyone has other things to do." He sneered.

King Kristine was not one of his. It was the story of a prince who was born a girl but her father hid the fact. A romantic comedy aimed at a female audience. As a newly crowned king, Kristine would fall for Waldon of the kingdom next door, just when her advisers wanted a war.

There have been numerous variations on the theme since plays got popular. It might turn out that Waldon was a girl, too. Or the princess the king was supposed to marry would be a pretty boy in drag. Along the way there would be lots of misunderstandings and mischief by friends.

Romantic comedies don't have legs but they sell well for a short while. They make nice fillers between the big dramas that draw the repeat customers.

The Faerie Queene would replace *King Kristine* about as soon as Jon Salvation had it ready to present.

I shut the door, went to Singe's office. On time. Dean and Playmate were delivering tea and sandwiches. The new drug had Playmate looking much better. He wore a smile that took no strain to produce.

I ate with one hand, read Jon Salvation's notes with the other, then passed them on to Singe. She kept a straight face, too.

"That something I should know about?" Block asked.

"It's mostly a lot of frustration. Plus instructions about what he wants Singe to put into a letter that he wants to go to a woman without her realizing that the letter came from him."

"He's going to do romantic comedy now?" Block gave me the fish-eye. He was ready to get all moody because I was lying. But I was only massaging the truth.

I said, "Here's a suggestion. Check around your shop. See if somebody has been buying a lot of costumes."

"We have been. We intend to put some patrolmen into uniform next quarter."

"That's a relief, then. I guess."

"You thought it was us behind all this?"

No. But I did want a brief distraction and Jon Salvation's notes did mention the Guard hiring costumers to produce uniforms for the troops and shiny outfits for their commanders.

I yakked. Singe worked some sleight of hand. Several sheets of notes disappeared. "Stop being a knee-jerk obstructionist and pass the notes to the General." She handed them to me, I handed them to Block. She said, "General, please pass those to the Windwalker once you read them."

So the notes made the rounds. And Block grumbled, "You *were* holding out. This tracking the costumes . . ."

Singe said, "You were informed, General. Your ability to comprehend what you were hearing may have been compro-

mised by your determination to lay waste to our reserve of
ardent spirits."

She made me chuckle. And it might even have been true.
I couldn't remember.

Block grumbled, "So I'm a little behind." He got up, did
some mild twists to loosen up. "I'll catch up."

Singe gestured. I led the General to the door, asking, "How
come you're always out by yourself? You ought to be tripping
over escorts."

"When I go out alone I go where I want and see what I
want."

"Damn. I didn't think of it that way. Well, go spank some
bad guys."

I shut the door and scooted back to Singe's office. "Morley.
Did you get a chance . . . ? No wonder he hasn't said anything
for a while."

He was sound asleep.

"All right, Singe. Let's do it. Strafa, we held back a couple
of things. I wanted you to see them first."

The notes Block had not seen named people who had ordered stuff that may have become part of the midnight road
show.

A woman calling herself Constance Algarda had taken delivery of seven hundred yards of coarse gray wool fabric and
a score of well-seasoned bracer logs twelve feet long. Bracer
is a lightweight tropical wood prized for its workability. A
younger woman calling herself Kevans Algarda had ordered
two pairs of high-top black-leather fuck-me boots from a cobbler associated with the tailor who specialized in fetish wear.
Said cobbler believed the same woman patronized a nearby
wigmaker. The cobbler had waxed poetic about the Algarda
woman's structure.

A man who claimed to be Barate Algarda paid for the
goods in each case. In neither case had a delivery been made.
These people transported their own goods.

Jon Salvation had worked wonders just by being Jon Salvation.

Strafa said, "This is impossible."

"I agree."

"As do I," Singe said. "That is why I hid the notes. As Garrett requested."

I told Strafa, "This part has to be on you. And you need to move fast. Block and Relway will be all over this. It puts them ahead of the busybodies from the Palace and the Hill." Only Saucerhead had gone round the theater support shops before Salvation.

"I'll start with Barate. I don't know where he'd get the money, but if he *is* the one . . ." She whisked out, turned left toward the kitchen and stair instead of toward the front door.

I looked at Singe. She said, "I don't believe it is those three. Well, maybe the old woman . . . We need to be careful."

"You think Shadowslinger would frame her own flesh and blood?"

"Most of those Hill monsters would. My concern is us getting tangled up in guilt by association."

"Oh." Maybe I picked the exact wrong time to get involved with a Windwalker.

Singe said, "It's too bad she is the only one who can go out. Someone ought to take the artwork to show the cobbler, wigmaker, and fetish tailor."

Scarier and scarier. "You should have thought of that before she left."

"I will talk to her when she gets back."

87

Playmate leaned in the doorway. "Dean says come and get it. You lot first."

Singe and I were up and going immediately. She said, "You'll have to wake him up."

Morley had not responded to the mention of food, though he had been making up for lost time lately.

"I'll do it when we get back."

We left Playmate setting up folding tables.

Dean had reorganized. The kitchen table was set up so customers could come in, grab a plate and tools, circle the table taking food from platters and bowls, then snag a ready-filled mug of beer or tea and be gone. Playmate held the door due to our lack of extra hands.

Singe again suggested that I waken Morley. "We should start getting him onto a normal schedule."

I set my mountain of fried chicken down to cool. I went after my best pal.

"Don't make a passion play out of it, Garrett. You can see he isn't going to wake up. Go ahead and eat."

Playmate arrived with a pitcher as I chomped on my first drumstick. Then he crossed the hall to collect the crowd over there. Dollar Dan, licking grease off his whiskers, passed the doorway, headed up front.

Penny and the Bird sounded excited about supper. I expected that Bird didn't eat well normally.

Dollar Dan reappeared with John Stretch. "Just in time for supper," Singe said, her tone critical.

"Not this time, sister. I had a nice cheese pie before I came over. I can afford to feed myself, you know."

Singe had taken mostly vegetables. She attacked a baked yam, no apology to her brother or the yam.

"Got news?" I asked with my mouth full.

"Bad news that is good. We have located three places that smell of death and chemicals. Two are much like the warehouse in Elf Town, particularly in the way they fit into their locales." He gave rough addresses.

I said, "Neither one is in a human neighborhood."

"Exactly. Though with so many dwarves gone back to the mountains their neighborhood is mostly human now. But all foreigners who don't speak a word of Karentine."

"Wonderful. Wonderful. What about the third place?"

"That one is different. Death and chemicals smells are there, too, but not as strong. The stench of human madness and terror overrides all that."

"Where is that one?"

"In the Landing. Another abandoned warehouse. My people could not get close. There were guards out."

I said, "We're getting somewhere, Singe!"

Playmate showed up with another pitcher and a mug for John Stretch. He left again but was gone for less than a minute. He brought his own supper in and joined us.

"Too busy in the kitchen. I'm not barging in on secret stuff, am I?"

"Not hardly. You're part of the game. How are you feeling?"

"Better than I have in years. That Kolda is high up on my good guys list."

"Let him know when you see him. He doesn't get many strokes."

Singe and John Stretch kept quiet. They were among the folks who had reservations about Kolda.

John Stretch asked, "What should we do with this information?"

Considering the constraints on me, and Morley's condition, the logical course was to pass it onto the Civil Guard. But they were operating under restraints of their own and might get warned off before they could do any good.

"Did your people notice anyone else poking around?"

"No. Why?"

"I have trouble believing that we can find out stuff before the people who are supposed to be doing the digging."

Singe, thumbing through papers in search of something, said, "Do not overlook the fact that we have not been trying to make something go away by sweeping it under the rug."

"They are not looking very hard," John Stretch opined.

Morley made a noise like he was choking on phlegm. He got over it before Playmate reached him. He opened his eyes for a moment but was not awake or seeing.

"Here it is," Singe said.

"What's that?"

"The list of properties registered to Constance Algarda. There are no matches with the properties Humility has located."

"Be interesting to find out who does own them."

"We have no one we can send to find out."

"I could go. Dollar Dan and his crew can manage here."

Singe reflected. "You may be past caring but . . . how would that play with Tinnie? You leaving the house for a title search but not for her?"

"I'll do what I always do. Apologize later."

"It's too late to do it today. I'll put it on the list."

Now I had a young-adult ratgirl telling me what to do.

When God scribbled my fate on my forehead, He included a glyph saying I had to be a toy of the yin half of the universe.

Morley mumbled something.

Playmate popped up. "I'll get him some dinner."

I went over, lifted Morley's chin.

"I'm fine, Garrett. I was just asleep. Now I'm awake."

"And cranky."

"And eager to break some bones. I had a dream."

I held back on the wisecrack. This might be important.

"It's trying to get away, now. But the guy in the picture the nut job painted. He was in it. He had me chained up in a bad place. Hypnotizing me. I wasn't the only one there. There were lots of others. But their situation was different." He raised a hand because he saw me getting ready to ask questions. "That's all I have."

"It might be from when you were a prisoner."

"I must have escaped. Maybe I got stabbed when they caught me."

"That makes sense." I recalled that Belinda still hadn't found that witness again. "Hey, Belinda has one of those wooden masks and some scraps of gray cloth she found where she thinks you were attacked."

Morley and Singe both said, "What?"

"When we talked about what happened to you, first or second time, she told me she visited the place where you were attacked. A witness took her. She found the mask when she was looking around."

"So?" Singe asked.

"So we have some evidence that nobody knows about. The other stuff got confiscated."

Morley said, "That's interesting, but does it matter? With what John Stretch found, this shouldn't go on much longer."

Good point. Maybe I just wanted to feel clever. Maybe I just felt a need to do something.

Were we getting close?

We didn't know who the real villains were. We didn't know what they were up to. The Director's theoretical conspiracy to overthrow the monarchy seemed weak. A lot of people thought it was political, though. Maybe because politicians thought everything was.

We didn't know why Morley was full of holes but I thought I could guess.

He had seen something he shouldn't have. For that he had been snatched and locked up, probably with other prisoners. Somebody had tried to hypnotize him. Being Morley, he had found a way to escape. His captors had resented that. They had chased him. He had headed for Elf Town thinking he could shed them there. Outsiders threatening someone with elf blood wouldn't last long in that quarter.

He had never gotten there. Maybe forewarned folks from that ugly warehouse had intercepted him.

Those people and the gray things had left him for dead. His body had no value because it wasn't human. Later, they had heard that he had survived. Belinda and I had led them to Fire and Ice. They had tried to get him there. Failing that, they had bribed Brother Hoto. Hoto would have brought out the news that Morley hadn't yet said anything.

Eventually they undertook the raid on my place. That did not go well.

Now they were hunkered down. False trails had been laid and red herrings dragged.

The more I reflected the less likely it seemed that the mess was political.

What else it could be I had no idea.

"Garrett? Are you still with us?" Morley demanded.

"I know you aren't used to witnessing it, but I was thinking. Somewhere inside your noggin, though you don't know what yet, is a nugget of info that can ruin the lives of the folks involved in the resurrection scheme."

"They think so. But what? I still have only a general impression of the place where they penned me up."

Singe pounced. "Penned?"

"That's probably not exact. It was more like a filthy cellar. It stank because it was so crowded . . ."

"You weren't alone."

"I told you that."

"Did anyone else escape when you did?"

"I don't know."

Singe said, "If they did and talked, word would have gotten around."

I said, "How about this? Maybe our villains aren't waiting for people to die to use them."

Morley reminded me, "That many people disappearing would cause a big uproar."

"No. We figured that out. Block was going to look into it."

"The operation in Little Dismal Swamp," Singe said. "The convicts. As good as dead when they're sentenced. Nobody expects them to survive. If you were in charge you could sell them and put them on the books as having died in the swamp."

I said, "They don't have to produce the bodies." Then, "Some whats and hows might be falling into place. It would be nice to stumble over an occasional why."

Singe said, "Just be patient. It will all bubble to the surface—unless the cover-up crowd shoves Block and Relway into their own cells."

Morley growled. He thought he was more ready than he was. Now was when he would be most dangerous to himself.

Singe said, "Think before you do anything, boys." She pushed her chair back, rose, left the room.

88

Singe called, "Garrett, you better come see this."

I went. She was at the peephole, looking out.

I took her place.

The view wasn't great but it was broad enough to be disturbing. "Let's go upstairs and get a better look."

I was huffing and puffing by the time I reached the window that was Strafa's preferred entrance. Singe leaned past to look out. "Your loose lips did it this time."

A big coach and a covered wagon had parked across the street. Teamsters were unhitching the horses. Men in strange uniforms meant to stick around for a while.

There were twelve of those.

Another big wagon and a more modest coach arrived with another dozen men. Teamsters got the team for the wagon out of harness.

An officer stepped down from the smaller coach. He surveyed the street, then my place, nodded, unfolded and consulted a large sheet of paper. He barked. A guy who looked like a career sergeant major joined him after bellowing at four men putting up an awning beside the big coach. That had a chimney. Smoke began to drift out.

The sergeant major stood beside the officer. He poked the map with a beefy forefinger. The officer nodded. Moments later ten armed men had been distributed around my house. The rest went on making the big coach and two wagons into a home away from home.

"What the hell are they up to?" I muttered.

"They want to isolate us."

"But those are Palace Guards. Probably most of them. Why are they here?"

"Gee, Garrett, what did I just say?"

"Really. This is ridiculous. Prince Rupert wouldn't go all hard-ass because I didn't come running like Good Dog Nagel."

"You think? You want to consider the time factor? Somebody else sent them. Say, like, I don't know. The guy they actually work for?"

"The King? Well, he is the one they're supposed to protect. But why me? He can't have any reason to come after me. He's never heard of me."

Singe asked, "Are you sure? He wants the man-building mess left alone and his cronies on the Hill agree. Where do all the noseys get together? Here."

"This makes sense if Rupert is under pressure."

"Dinklebrain. Forget Rupert!"

"All right." Prince Rupert didn't have that small a mind, anyway. Narrow, certainly, but not petty.

And this was beyond his budget.

"First thing we need to do is find out what's what."

She demanded, "Do you have shit in your ears?"

"What?"

"I just told you. It's a blockade, blockhead. Nobody will come in. Nobody will go out. People could get arrested for the crime of knowing you. Eventually, we will get hungry."

"You'd better wake the Dead Man up."

"I'm considering options already."

I said, "Oh, crap!"

Belinda's big black coach had turned onto Macunado off Wizard's Reach. It was accompanied by the usual footmen and outriders.

Singe said, "This could prove illuminating."

"Or disastrous if she's been drinking."

Belinda had not been drinking. She remained respectful and courteous in her exchange with the officer, who did not recognize her. I could see she was in a seething rage. "We're good for now, but let's hope she doesn't drink anything stronger than small beer before she calms down. The Crown's armed gang is bigger than hers."

Singe grunted. She said nothing till Belinda's coach was out of sight. "Miss Contague is astute but dangerous. She will make this personal between herself and the Palace Guard. And they are not a gang bigger than hers."

I said "Crap!" again. The Palace Guards would not number fifty men if they had every slot filled. Twelve would be assigned to the Crown Prince, the rest to the King. Meaning most of the King's share were outside now.

Belinda might think she could handle them if she got some firewater in her.

I asked Singe, "Do some of those guys look like they might not be real soldiers?" Some uniforms did not fit right. Some faces were not as cleanly shaven as they ought to be.

"You are correct. Nice catch. If the Windwalker were here, I suspect she might recognize men from the private patrol on the Hill."

If that was true Belinda could get herself into even deeper poo.

Those people might declare war if she yanked their beards. But that prospect wouldn't give her a moment's pause even sober. She lived her life on a bull's-eye.

"This could get ugly."

"Yes. I am going down to see Dean. We will take inventory. Then we can plan for the siege."

"I wish I had a crossbow. I could pick those guys off."

"Are you serious?"

Not really.

"Because it would be just as easy for them to sneak around back and set the house on fire."

"I *was* joking, Singe."

"Be a little less deadpan, then." She stomped out.

Bright as she was, she had trouble grasping the full range of human humor.

Of course, she wasn't the only one who didn't get me.

I moved my little nightstand over so I could settle my butt while I watched the King's men work.

89

Those guys weren't even real soldiers, let alone Marines, but, despite themselves, they even kept a miserable, drunken, fighting-mad Winger from getting to my front door, without getting physical.

Those guys might be candy-asses in a fight but as public-relations operators, they were smooth.

That left me feeling optimistic.

Somebody would come along and ruin their day.

Strafa appeared outside. This time, for whatever reason, she sat astride a great, honking broomstick. She wore dark clothes that did not flatter, but she had disdained the traditional pointy hat.

I opened the window wide.

Down she swooped, face aflame with adolescent mischief. She spun, plunged, tugged the sergeant major's mustache, then sideslipped and swiped the commander's fancy hat.

Hands grabbed at her. She shot straight up. The hat drifted down, carried by the breeze. Strafa followed but leveled off at the height of my window. She stretched herself out on her broomstick, shot forward into my room.

There was almost no clearance but she came through unscathed. "That was fun." She laughed. It was the first time I heard her let it all go. She was totally happy. She was totally at peace. She rolled off her broom, bounced into my arms. "Did you see the looks on their faces?"

For one instant I saw the face of a redheaded woman. I felt pain, guilt, then a sourceless admonition to do the right thing.

Strafa's simple joy over having thumbed her nose at gloomy

functionaries changed things more in a moment than had the physical connection earlier.

I was lost. I was hooked.

I was miserably guilty. I did love Tinnie Tate, but I had been ambushed by something hugely more potent. Something that Strafa had sensed and been frightened by way back when our paths first crossed. She had teased me then, but that was all she had risked.

Strafa shared some psychology with DeeDee: neither looked or acted her age. Both were more simple and innocent than seemed plausible. Each had a daughter more touched by and in tune with the real world.

Crush, though, was better equipped to survive there than Kevans was. Kevans lacked sufficient cynicism.

"Damn, darling, that was as good as you making me groan! Why are those buttheads out there, anyway?"

"Your guess would be better than mine. You know the people who tell them what to do."

"Kiss me."

I did so, to the best of my ability, with considerable enthusiasm.

"Wow! That was all right. I forgot the world completely." She went to the window. "You have to wonder who was thinking what, sending them out to harass subjects in the city. You bad man. Keep your hands to yourself. I'm trying to think."

She had more to say, mostly playful, but I didn't pay attention. One final shard of rationality was trying to figure out what had happened to us and why it had happened so fast.

Then I recalled any number of friends, across the ages, telling me I think too much.

This time Strafa was the responsible one. "Down, boy! I'm as eager as you are, but we have bigger issues to deal with."

Strafa saw things through different eyes. Olive, at the moment.

She leaned out the window. She waved. She blew kisses. I caught the back draft as she stoked up the girl power. Any man down there who wasn't moon-eyed and holding his hat in front of his fly was in serious violation of the most draconian prohibition of most of the thousand and one religions plaguing ... er, gracing our great city.

I looked over her shoulder. It was amazing what she could do to men.

"You are a wicked woman."

"I could be. But I'm too lazy." She retreated just far enough to become invisible to the soldiers.

"You could be queen of the world by now."

She said, "We're going to do some things now, beloved."

"Yes?"

"I'm going to go see those men. I'm going to cloud their minds. You get yourself and your friend ready to move somewhere else."

"Where?"

"Your province. Mine is to fix it so those men besiege an empty castle."

"You lost me. But I'm so infatuated, I trust you completely."

She looked startled. "Pular Singe told me I should wear old, high-top boots if I really want to spend my life close to you. Maybe she wasn't just jealous and teasing."

"Strafa, whatever it was, I take it back. I don't want to be the guy to you that I seem to be to everybody else. I just want to be your guy, no games. No ifs, ands, or bullshit."

90

Strafa rode her broomstick out the window.

I hustled downstairs. A grim Singe told me, "We won't last long if they try to starve us out."

"We won't be here. Strafa will fly us out, me first, then Morley, then you, and Dean."

The more I reflected, though, the less likely it seemed that those men could sustain a long siege. What they were doing was illegal.

Legality aside, those clowns might leave once they saw us fly away.

Which made me wonder how serious they were. If they broke out the longbows and started sniping . . .

That would make me unhappy.

Singe said, "I know your mind doesn't work that way, but why not just flit over to the Al-Khar and let them know what is going on?"

"Clearing them off could get ugly."

"I'm just a simpleminded ratgirl. I cannot grasp the political ramifications. But I cannot believe that anyone would start a civil war just to keep embarrassing sorcery hidden."

I had begun to wonder how committed Block and Relway were to the rule of law. Would they go to war on its behalf? Against the Crown?

I hoped they never found themselves forced to decide.

"I'll be upstairs. Have Morley get up there as soon as he can."

Morley clumped into my bedroom. He looked grim. "Garrett, I'm not quite ready to go on the warpath. Just getting up here kicked my butt." He joined me at the window. "What's up?"

"She's putting the girl magic on those guys."

"The what?"

"I call it girl magic. Remember when she came into the World the first time, back in the day? She's doing that, only at full power."

Thank the gods she turned it off before she came back. She told me, "I'm ready. But where should we go?"

"Let's catch Belinda. She doesn't have a huge head start." I leaned out the window, lifted a leg to start working my way through. There was no way Strafa and I would fit at the same time. That big-ass broomstick took up too much territory.

The roof of the stoop was four feet down. I hoped it was in good repair. The pitch was steep enough that loose slates might go slip-sliding away, taking my favorite former Marine along.

I completed my part without disaster, though that might yet come. The Palace Guards had their brains scrambled but they noticed me anyway. Some still had a vague notion that they might ought to commence to begin to fix to get ready to keep people from getting away.

They knew I was a runner when Strafa darted out and had me drag my dead ass onto the broomstick behind her.

She began to climb, not nearly as fast as I liked. Several of those guys were immune to girl magic. Sling bullets burred around us.

The sergeant major roared like a bear who'd broken a tooth while gnoshing on somebody's skull. I made out no distinct words but in all the history of the universe sergeants major never have been required to be coherent to be understood. This one did not want to have to answer questions about why a Windwalker, from the rarified air on the Hill, had been struck out of the sky by men in full uniform, fully armed, operating illegally miles from the venue they were supposed to protect. Only in the King's own presence were they allowed to take their show on the road.

That gave me a killer idea. I'd have to try it out on Jon Salvation.

Disguised thugs from the Hill helped the sergeant major make his point. Masquerading, they would not enjoy the legal umbrella protecting the real Guards. Guardsmen had to take orders. Their superiors had to worry about legalities.

Strafa said, "Hang on tight."

"You're preaching to the choir, sweetness. Go high." I had flown before, during other adventures. I never liked it. "Head north along Wizard's Reach."

Belinda could follow that only so far, though. The street dropped down, crossed Deer Creek, climbed again but dead-ended at Handycot Way, which marked the southern boundary of Woodland Park, from which every scrap of wood had been stolen.

Strafa said, "It would be a huge help if . . . That looks like her over there, almost to Grand."

Who else would be out with so large a convoy?

Strafa's eyes were better than mine in these circumstances. She had been flying since she was little. I bet they worked her half to death doing recon in the Cantard.

Say that for her class. They *all* did their time in the war zone, boys, girls, and everything in between. Most did multiple tours. Strafa's father had.

We tilted downward and streaked toward the coach. I shut my eyes. The roar of air passing made it hard to talk.

Strafa ended up floating alongside the coach. That caused enough excitement for Belinda to look see what was happening. I told Strafa, "Keep an eye on the guy beside the driver." Joel looked like he was tempted to do something that I would regret.

91

"You won't like this but I don't care," Belinda told me. "Go back to Fire and Ice. Mike will cover you. You." She spoke to Strafa. I hoped she remembered who Strafa was. "Once Garrett shows you where to take him I would be most appreciative if you would move the others to the same place, Morley first."

I said, "Dean won't leave and Singe will want to stay to wrangle the Dead Man."

Belinda shrugged. "You can't force people. You and Morley are the souls that matter to me. Hole up there and wait. I may be a while." She told Strafa. "I'll be ever so grateful if you'll let me know when my boys are safe."

"Certainly."

Strafa felt no further need to converse, nor did Belinda. I did but everyone ignored me. Nobody disagrees that I overthink and overquestion—then, after the fuss, go hey-diddle-diddle straight up the middle.

Strafa did say, "Let's go, darling." Belinda's crowd surged into a big U-turn. My old pal Joel shot me one last poisonous look.

Strafa went up only a little above the rooftops this time. Curious bats swooshed around us. A huge, elderly owl flapped alongside for a while, hoping we would startle up something tasty.

We followed Grand all the way. We were spotted several times. There would be talk tomorrow but no popular excitement. Dozens of sorcerers, great and small, infest TunFaire.

I asked Strafa to set down in the street beneath the window of the room where Morley and I had stayed. I meant to go in the back way. But that window was wide open and no light burned behind it.

Someone had undone my masterful carpentry.

"Pop up there and see if anyone is in that room."

"All right." Up she went, then inside. She came back out and down. "There is no one there. The furnishings have been changed."

"Good enough. Pop me in, then go get Morley. Please?" In case she thought I was getting presumptuous and bossy.

"Just this once. Get on."

I straddled the broom. Up we went. Strafa hovered while I tumbled through the window. When I got up to say something she was gone.

My night vision was not acute. I felt my way through the unfamiliar layout, found the door, listened, heard nothing. I opened up a cautious crack.

Two small sconces with their wicks turned down illuminated the empty hallway. Enough light got in to show me the new layout. I spotted a lamp.

I lit that off the nearest sconce, got back inside the room, shut the door.

The furniture was all new. Paint had been applied to the woodwork, especially the windowsill. The door now had a bolt on the inside. I threw it, began a detailed inspection. I was still at that when Strafa brought Morley. He clambered through the window. She darted away.

Morley plopped into the only available chair. "What the hell are you doing? Why didn't you just walk in through the front door?"

"Being sneaky seemed like a good idea at the time. But you're right. Using the door would mean fewer misunderstandings when they find us squatting up here."

"You think? I'll go find Mike in a minute. Maybe I can talk fast enough to save you some broken bones."

"I'll be counting on you, buddy."

"Sure. Meanwhile, you want to explain why we're even here?"

"Belinda's idea. Because the house is under siege, the Dead Man is sleeping, and there was only food enough for a few days."

"Somebody panicked."

"They did?" I had been thinking exactly that since I stopped moving.

"I didn't think about it, either, till I was on my way. But, really, your house was not under attack and that crew was there illegally. How long are they likely to stay?"

"If the King stays stubborn about the law being whatever he says it is . . ."

"I bet the point of the exercise was to get the reaction they got. They wanted us to run."

"You'd better see Mike. If that was the point . . ." I recalled seeing a barn cat pick off mice startled into flight by another cat.

"On my way." He got up and went. "Sit tight. Whatever happens, sit tight."

"Will do."

I worried, though. He was bone pale. He wouldn't last much longer.

Strafa came back. She gave me no chance to say anything this time, either.

She dropped Penny and skedaddled.

92

Miss Tea preceded Morley into the room. DeeDee followed. Mike scowled at me, at Penny, then said, "You can't bring your own beer to the theater, and you can't bring your own playmate to Fire and Ice."

Penny turned a ferocious red. She made a pitifully small squeaky noise. I thought she would melt down to a puddle of goo.

I said, "That was cruel and uncalled for, Miss Tea." I whispered, "And she's the Capa's little sister."

"You're right. I shouldn't take it out on the kid. You're a plenty big target yourself."

"Morley already told you this is the Capa's idea."

"I can't take my anger out on her. What were you thinking, climbing in the damned window? Which I ought to charge you for getting fixed."

"I wasn't thinking. I admit that."

"You could have ended up with more holes in you than this other idiot had. Then what would I do?"

I shrugged. "Pay a specialist to get rid of the bloodstains?"

"It would've put the kibosh on our future together, that's for sure."

I said, "Huh?"

Penny squeaked in dismay.

Morley made a snorting sound. He collapsed into the only chair. He would have giggled if he was a girl.

DeeDee took up the slack. She thought that was hilarious.

And here came Crush, uninvited. Her excuse was a tray with tea, six cups, and a pound of frou-frou cookies so thin you could read through them. She was taken aback by Penny's presence, too. "I don't have any appointments for a while."

Mike grumbled, "So you thought you would be nosy."

"Yeah. I did think I'd stick my honker in."

A hint of a smile flickered on Mike's lips. There was a streak of affection for Crush hidden inside Miss Teagarden.

I said, "I'm glad you did, kid. I have a message for you." I glanced at Morley. He had no advice to offer. His eyes were shut. A fussing DeeDee was in the way.

Mike eyed me suspiciously. Crush looked at me askance.

"It's nothing huge. I introduced Crush to Jon Salvation at my house, the other day. He was having a bad one. She asked questions he was tired of hearing. He was rude to her. He felt bad about it later. I told him I'd apologize."

"That was after he found out what I do, right?"

"He has no idea what you do. He wouldn't believe me if I told him. You aren't anything like what he would expect . . . No. You're not what . . . Mike, can you save my dumb ass here?"

"Suppose she was a shop girl? Men. Just say what you have to say."

I knew that. But it's hard to remember, sometimes.

Mike added, "You don't need to walk on eggshells. We know what we do."

"All right. Jon felt bad about being a jerk. He knows Crush is a big fan because we both told him. So he said, if you're around the World sometime, when they're in rehearsal, you can come in and watch them work on his next play. Which means you get to see it before anybody and you get to see how a play gets put together. And, I figure, you'd get the answers to your questions."

"That's it? That's all?" Mike demanded.

"That's all. Her virtue would be safe."

"Smart ass. I should ought not to believe you just because it's you."

What was that? "You don't know me that well."

"I probably know enough. Out of curiosity I had a long talk with the Capa one night. She does know you that well."

Crush demanded, "Is that for real?"

"Which? What Mike is on about or the invitation?"

"The invitation. Mike flirting is too cerebral to be interesting."

"Yes, then. Jon Salvation is a good guy. He's desperate to have people like him. Most theater people are. So, if you have the time, and you want, go by there."

Crush looked to Mike, perhaps asking permission.

Mike said, "DeeDee, you should be getting ready for your next appointment." Once DeeDee went away, Mike told Crush, "That might be good for you." To me, tapping herself on the left breast, "Heart of gold." Then to Crush, "You don't go giving it away just because this scribbler is famous."

Crush was horrified. "I would never . . ."

Through all this Penny's eyes just kept getting bigger.

Mike's heart of gold ran maybe eight carat.

She said, "Crush, go back down to the parlor. You don't need to take any random clients. Just sing a few songs."

With Crush gone, she said, "She has a marvelous voice. She might not be in the life if she had found that out first."

"Probably not as much money in singing."

"Not with her looks. So. What's the plan?"

"Belinda said come here, hunker down, and sit tight. That sounded like a good idea at the time but once we got here we decided it was stupid. We should have stayed where we were."

Mike had a black look for me but the one she laid on Morley was special. Crisp chips of seared Dotes should have flaked off him. Penny's presence saved us some ugly language.

She said, "I don't know what I did to bring this stuff down on myself."

"We can leave."

"Of course you can. Any time you want. With wonder boy asleep and the Capa likely to turn up any second to ask if I'm bending over and taking it like a good girl."

"Are you really that bitter?"

"Only on days of the week ending in 'day.' I have a nice business here. We like each other, mostly. We look out for each other. I do everything by the numbers. I pay off the right people without complaining. So is it really too much to ask to be left alone in return?"

"Probably not. So why not just go back to work and forget us?"

"Best idea I've ever heard from you." She stamped out.

Penny said, "She isn't very nice, is she?"

"Don't let her fool you. That was all show." I had seen a mischievous twinkle in her eye.

"So what now?"

"We wait. That's mostly what I do. Sit. Watch. Wait. If you're tired you can have the bed. I'll get a folding chair out of the corner."

"I couldn't do that."

"Why not?"

"People use it for . . . Well, you know."

I knew, but I was a jaded old cynic. "A bed is a bed, girl, with some more comfortable than others. When you're tired whatever else happened doesn't matter. Though you might be smart to see how big the bugs are before you take the plunge."

"Mr. Garrett! Do you have to be a jerk all the time?"

"You bring out the worst in me. Do you want the bed or not? Because if you're going to be all bluestocking, I'll snag it for myself. I'm not the gentleman you think I am."

"I believe that would make you exactly the man I think you are, sir. I will sit out the night on a folding chair, thank you."

"Suit yourself. Turn the lamp down when you're ready. And don't lock the door. People will come to see us at some point."

Yes. I was that way with the kid. She wanted to be part of the household on Macunado Street, I would treat her like family.

I climbed into the bed.

It was a far better bed than the one it had replaced. It was miles better than the cot.

It was a comfortably cool night so I just stretched out on the covers. Despite the excitement, the strange bed, and the fact that I had had nothing to drink, I fell asleep immediately. Despite the fact that even after she turned the lamp down I could see a sour-faced teenager scowling my way if I cracked an eyelid.

93

"So what is this?"

Was that Belinda?

"Do you believe this?"

The question died in a great, roaring snore from Morley Dotes.

I was on my back, the right side of me pressed against the wall. I did not feel inclined to be awake and sociable so I pretended I was asleep.

Strafa said, "I thought yours would give in to temptation first."

"Obviously you thought wrong."

I detected some amusement in both voices.

I rolled toward them, away from the wall.

All right.

I got it.

I wasn't alone.

Penny had her back to me. She was balanced precariously on the edge but she was in the same bed. And the old women were having fun with that.

That folding chair must have gotten awful hard.

When I rolled she moved too, both of us into the slight depression in the middle.

Belinda and Strafa each said something that did not flatter me.

But for Penny I would have said something juvenile to irritate them.

Then Strafa won me back. "We'd better get Penny up first. Carefully. Otherwise, she'll die of embarrassment."

"Really? She's snuggled up to him in the same bed."

"Please. Be empathetic for one minute of your life."

Wow. That was my girl telling Belinda Contague to develop a human side. A-maz-ing!

Belinda bowed to Strafa's demands because Strafa was the Windwalker, Furious Tide of Light, who could turn her into a pond's worth of frogs.

I went on pretending to be a sleeping frog in need of the kiss of a princess. I did nothing while Strafa extricated a muzzy Penny from a situation likely to cause a panic attack.

DeeDee and Mike turned up before the ladies started on Morley and me. They brought a meal suitable for the empress of the Combine and her dearest henchfolk. DeeDee fussed over Morley till Mike, high on surviving the night, herded her out.

Miss Tea had little to say, otherwise. She stood by looking grim. She was extremely unhappy.

Strafa read her perfectly. "We'll clear out shortly, ma'am."

Belinda nodded. "As soon as Mr. Dotes is fed and ready to travel."

Strafa said, "We blundered. We misread a situation completely, then panicked."

"Misread, huh?" I said. "Like how?" Her angle might have been different.

"The Palace Guards were all for show. Prince Rupert wanted somebody to see that he could come down hard on busybodies."

"Rupert didn't send them. The King did."

"Whatever, Rupert is at the house now." Strafa's laughter was pure music. "Wait till you see his headgear. He is *determined* not to have his mind read." She described a monster rat's nest of silver mesh and tangle. "We never told him that the Dead Man is asleep."

"We?" Had there been a party while I was away?

"Easy, boy."

Belinda said, "You'll have to get used to him getting his exercise by jumping to conclusions."

Strafa said, "If we hurry, lover, I can get you there before Rupert's men finish cleaning up."

"That doesn't sound good. What happened? What did you do?"

"Well . . . After I moved Penny and Playmate, Bell and I

started picking off Palace Guards. You were right. Some were patrolmen from the Hill."

"Picking off? What does that mean?"

I was a little loud. Mike had to pop out to the hallway to reassure her security goons.

Belinda said, "Is it too much to ask that you just relax and listen, Garrett? What possible use is there to you bellowing and stomping like a bull in rut?"

"It helps me pretend that I have some kind of control over my own life."

Miss Contague let loose a championship sigh. She looked at Strafa. "And you really want to partner up with this dope?"

"He'll be all right. You'll see. He just needs a chance to relax. He's been away for a long time." She gave me a big happy puppy dog look.

How the hell can you go on being grumpy when a beautiful woman looks at you like you're the culmination of the man-creation process and she just adores you? How, when you look back at her, get caught up in a little heavy breathing, and she gets just a hint of virginal blush to her cheeks?

Belinda muttered, "I think I'm going to puke. So. Let's move out. Let's go storm the ramparts of reality."

Strafa said, "Garrett and I will go ahead so he can see the Crown Prince. Please bring the young miss with you and Mr. Dotes." She turned to Mike. "And thank you so much for your hospitality, Miss Teagarden."

Belinda agreed. "Yeah. Twice, now. You've won a special place in my heart, Mike. You want some special considerations, ask. Just don't be unreasonable."

Miss Tea inclined her head in a ghost of a bow. "A bit more flexibility in the way we are permitted to operate wouldn't be amiss."

The upcoming negotiation should be fascinating.

I got no chance to find out. Strafa dragged me to the window. I whined, "Why can't we go out the front door like regular people?"

"Because we're special people and the regular people need to be reminded."

I glanced at Penny as I clambered out, twisting, turning, picking up scratches and scrapes. The girl seemed forlorn but she had not melted down in shame.

94

Westman Block and a clutch of red tops infested my stoop and the street in front of my house. Strafa, a broom, and I slid down through the morning air. They spotted us as Strafa eased up to my window. Block had a lot to say down there but I couldn't hear him over Strafa's grumbling. I gave him a big grin and a bold thumbs up.

Strafa was exasperated. "It's shut again."

"What is?"

"The window. Somebody keeps shutting it while I'm gone." She made gestures and muttered sourly.

I could guess who had done the shutting. I wasn't sure why.

Did Singe want to sabotage the new order?

The window slid upward. It made no sound.

"You'd make a great second-story man, woman."

"Sweetheart, please climb through. Same as when we left."

I dismounted without losing my composure or footing. I focused on the window. I have trouble with heights when I'm just standing around, looking down, from a place whence I could actually fall if I did something stupid. The fear is more manageable when I'm doing something implausible, like riding a broomstick with a witch.

I got inside without discovering a need to change my underwear.

Strafa darted in before I finished celebrating. The tip of her broom handle bonked me in the back of the head.

We treated ourselves to a few seconds of kissy-face huggy-bear; then the grown-up half of the crowd said, "You'd better go downstairs and see if Prince Rupert is still here."

"That bed sure looks inviting. And I mean for sleeping."

"Downstairs. Go. Barate used to say, 'We can sleep as much as we want after we're dead.'"

"Yeah. He missed his calling as a top kick in the corps."

Always literal minded, Strafa said, "He was a counterespionage specialist in Full Harbor. He did two tours, one before I was born and another after my mother died."

No comment. One more hug. One more kiss, me having trouble believing this was happening. Then downstairs we went.

We found the Crown Prince asleep in Singe's office. Singe was not there. She was in bed. So was Dean. The number-two man in Karenta was being entertained by Dollar Dan Justice to the extent that the ratman was in the same room. He was asleep, too.

I wakened both gently, Dollar Dan first. He muttered something about making tea and shuffled out.

Rupert wakened with an exaggerated start, obviously unsure where he was or why he was there. I found keeping a straight face to be a huge effort.

He had the most ridiculous, wonderful confection on his head, a massive ball of silver thread, wire, ribbon, and nonsense. It dropped down to his shoulders in back, his neck on the sides, and even covered most of his face.

"Did something tickle your funny bone, Mr. Garrett?"

He had the voice of a lord, I'll grant that. It was a rich deep voice made for command.

"Your chapeau took me by surprise."

"Now you're going to tell me I wasted my time."

"You did, Your Grace. Himself is asleep." I should make some cheat cards. I don't spend enough time around royalty to know the proper forms of address. Rupert didn't puff up and turn red so Your Grace was good enough for now.

"So I understand. It probably doesn't matter, anyway. I came here to keep my brother from making a big mistake, trying to use the Palace Guard that way."

I shrugged. "I don't know what his thoughts were, either."

"I sent word that I wanted to talk to you."

"I've been busy." I thought I had my mouth under control. Strafa, though, shuffled uncomfortably. "But here I am. Let's do it quick. I still have things that need doing."

I should not have added that. *His* time was precious. Mine was the worthless property of a trivial subject.

He did glance at Strafa, plainly wondering if she was what was distracting me from becoming an instrument of his will. "All right, then. I've already missed a night of sleep because of my brother. A while with you won't make any difference."

"What do you want from me, then?"

"Two things: this business of the thread men, then a renewal of my offer of employment. Tribune Felhske isn't working out."

"He's a better investigator than I am. And he wants the job."

"He is better than you only in a limited sense. What you lack in specific skills and ambition you make up in honesty."

"Felhske is a crook?"

"He takes excessive advantage of his position. He isn't yet aware that I know about his bad behavior."

"I'm disappointed. I recommended him. But I'm still not interested. I like my life the way it is."

"Talk it over with Strafa. She ought to have some say."

"I'll do that. Though . . . Never mind. There was another matter?"

"The important thing. I want you, Strafa, and all of your friends, to back off and stay backed off of the thread men thing. And I do mean it."

"Why?"

"Because I told you to." He frowned, puzzled by the fact that I would even ask.

"Ain't gonna happen."

"Excuse me?" He lurched forward in his chair, as though his ears must have betrayed him because of the distance between us.

"You've been telling lots of people to back off. You won't say why. Has even one of them listened? I don't think so. Some maybe try to be less obvious but they're keeping on keeping on. I'll keep on myself till I get my hands on whoever tried to kill my friend."

Strafa made a hissing sound, trying to caution me.

Rupert reddened till I feared he might have a stroke. He was not accustomed to hearing straight talk.

I said, "It isn't about you. Or your brother, which is where this must be coming from. None of the people working on rooting out the thread men . . . Why did you call them that?"

"Because they're sewn together."

"Oh. Clever. They aren't so much of a problem. It's the people doing the sewing that we want."

"It is necessary that those people be left to their peers."

"The villains who run the Hill? I saw their thugs out there masquerading as Palace Guards. Makes you wonder who's in charge."

Prince Rupert's eyes bugged. He opened his mouth but nothing came out.

Strafa asked, "You didn't know? You didn't see them?"

I said, "They blend in like gorillas in skirts."

"That isn't possible."

"Talk to your commander. Talk to your top kick. They had to know."

The Prince got a grip. "Be that as it may, I have my orders. I will execute them."

"Even if they're illegal? You're the great champion of the rule of law."

"The Crown is the law, Mr. Garrett."

"I don't think so."

Strafa said, "Garrett!"

"Even an ignorant peasant like me knows divine right don't click anymore. If your brother starts thinking he can make up laws as he goes along he won't get to make very many. Add up how many kings we've had in our lifetimes. You might have to take off a shoe to count them all."

Strafa said, "Garrett, that's enough."

Prince Rupert was furious. I, being tired and twisted, was reverting to contrary Garrett. I saw me doing it but could not engage the governor on my jaw.

Singe arrived with the tea that Dollar Dan had gone to get. There were some yesterday biscuits and hard-boiled eggs. "Please pardon Mr. Garrett, Your Grace. He suffers from a congenital defect that makes him say stupid things when he is awake." She deposited the tray on a folding table beside Prince Rupert, then faced me. "You. Come with me." Over her shoulder, "If you will excuse us for a moment, Your Grace?"

We crossed the hallway to the Dead Man's room. I spotted the Bird snoring on the floor in a corner. I had thought he had left a long time ago.

"What the hell is the matter with you? That's the gods-

damned Crown Prince of Karenta in there. You're acting like
he is . . . Like he is another Bird." She waved a paw. "Don't
you have the sense the gods gave a drunken goose? Are you
bucking for a career in swamp drainage?"

"If I could get a word . . ."

"You don't need to get a word in. It will be some godsdamned absurd excuse. I have heard you state that excuses are
like assholes. Everyone has one, and they all stink."

"I . . ."

"Grow up, Garrett."

"But . . ."

"Ten years ago . . . *Five* years ago you could indulge in all
this obnoxious, stupid shit you wanted. It did not matter. No
one but you got pounded over the head. You do not have that
luxury anymore. Making yourself feel big by being a dick toward people in authority is no longer an option."

Wow! Singe was well and thoroughly pissed off. And she
was just getting warmed up.

"Go back in there. Go on being a jerk. But before you start,
tell me what will come of it after you get your moment of
strutting around congratulating yourself on how you showed
somebody?"

"All right, Singe. I get it. I'll jump in there and kiss his ass
and lick his boots and beg him to use a little lard when he
bends me over."

She slapped me.

That stunned me silent.

Her arms were not long enough to let her get a good windup
but the impact stung plenty anyway.

My little girl was *seriously* upset. I might want to invest a
few seconds in trying to work out why.

I had told Prince Rupert that things were not all about him.
I suppose Singe wanted me to recognize that they were not all
about me, either.

That unhappy man across the hall had the power to make
me and everyone I ever met extremely unhappy. And he was
just one breath away from having the power to make that un-
happiness eternal.

Rupert might be a fool but he was not just some passing
moron that I could sneer at and disdain to his face.

"I get what you want me to see, Singe." But I couldn't surrender completely. "I'll go kiss the idiot and make it better."

The way Singe moved then, I feared she might be looking for a club big enough to pound me into a shape she found acceptable.

95

"I want to apologize for my antagonistic attitude, Your Grace. I have been under a great deal of stress. I shall do my best to defer to your wisdom henceforth—except in the matter of going to work for you, which you should not view as any reflection upon yourself."

Singe showed me her teeth. That was not good enough, apparently.

Other than being renown for having promulgated his First Law, Morley might be most famous for having observed that the world would be a better place if we just had sense enough to kill the right people.

I don't disagree—so long as I get to make the list.

Prince Rupert was determined to become a featured name.

He said, "I expect some social gaps are too broad to bridge even with the best intentions."

I started to open my mouth. Singe lifted a knickknack off her desk and wound up.

I said, "That's true. Before you leave, couldn't you indulge us with just a hint as to why General Block and Director Relway can't pursue the mission . . ."

"Stop. There are times . . . There are special circumstances . . ."

Perhaps. But he, Block, and Relway had been savagely diligent about crushing that justification. Till now. "If you want to change the rules suddenly you need to support it with something more than, 'Because I said so.' Because that is total bullshit. Which you have said a hundred times yourself."

"My brother needs it. He'll die otherwise. I don't want to be King."

What the hell was that?

Singe had that bookend thing in hand again.

Rupert sputtered some, then said, "Even more, I don't want my brother Eugene or nephew Kansa to be king. Either would be a disaster. As has been this visit. I must go."

I escorted him to the door. Before I could shut it behind him, he told me, "Stay away from this, Garrett." His tone said he didn't hold out much hope that he would get his way.

I told Singe and Strafa, "There's a political angle after all."

Strafa said, "It's one that turned up, for Rupert, only in the last few days."

"I'll buy that. We have a little night left. I'm going to go catch a nap. Singe. No luck with the Dead Man?"

"Not yet. That last incident really wasted him."

No shit.

96

I did not fall asleep right away, though not because Strafa crawled in and snuggled up. She went away instantly.

She had worked hard.

My mind had snagged on the possibility that the King was involved in the bad stuff to the point of trying to protect the evildoers.

Though there was no testimony yet I was sure the bad guys were buying prisoners from the Little Dismal operation and using them to build their thread men. Why, though, was beyond my imagination. The thread men were not aggressive unless driven. They were less dangerous than the zombies they resembled.

I reviewed each attack, over and over. I came up with nothing new, except that the lines of flight from Fire and Ice not only headed toward the Hill, they passed Knodical, supposedly currently untenanted.

That deserved investigation. The plunder from the Elf Town warehouse had gone there.

Were the Hill folk treading carefully because the King was entangled in something dark?

Waking was brisk but intense. Strafa Algarda turned loving into a religious experience. She whispered, "I can't wait till we can take our time."

"Me, neither." I became part of a strange and wonderful beast when I failed to show character enough to say no.

"So get yourself up, love. We have work to do."

"For example?"

"Today we are going to confound the Crown Prince and all the instruments of the night."

I glanced out the window. It was raining.

"Let's go, sourpuss!" She giggled. "Put on a smile. It will make itself at home. It's going to be a wonderful day."

I didn't want to be that guy who spins around and looks to the past as soon as the future hits. But I wasn't sure I could survive a diet of cheerful, happy, and positive—all before noon—for the rest of my life. And I knew, with no need for an outside consultant, that I'd signed on for the duration.

Strafa was perfect. She was everything a guy wove in his fantasies. Her sole flaw was that she lacked a sense of despair. She couldn't work up a good gloom to save her own delectable patootie.

I nearly laughed. And then found out that I could be wrong.

As we dressed, I said, "We never got a chance to talk about what you found out when you visited Barate. And the kids."

"Nothing useful. Their names may have been used but they weren't the ones wearing them."

The cheer had gone right out of her.

"Barate said he was going to check out some family legends."

"He did. Though they were more like rumors to the effect that some of the old people weren't actually inside their coffins when they went into the ground. The only way to be sure would be to dig them up."

"I don't think it will come to that." I moved behind her and pulled her back against my chest. "What's wrong?"

No artifice. "I saw my grandmother, too."

"Shadowslinger?"

"Yes. She wishes us well. You and me, together."

That came out of nowhere. "She knows?"

"Everyone seems to. I'm not sure how." She pressed back and crossed my arms in front of her.

"Is that a problem?"

She found some slight bounce. "It's a weight off, actually. I was worried about how to break the news."

"Then what's the problem?"

"My grandmother has been under a lot of pressure to use her influence to get me to back away from all this."

"That's it? You have to stop? You can. It's all right. But I won't."

"Neither will I. And nor will my grandmother."

"Then what . . . ?"

"My grandmother Constance felt obligated to relay the anxious desires of her class. She decided she was on our side only after I described Bird and Penny's artwork. She may come by for a closer look. She wouldn't explain but its obviously old family history. Probably to do with what Barate had in mind."

She seemed small in my arms right then, like a frightened little girl.

She said, "What we're doing may change the city as much as the end of the war did."

"How so?"

"I don't know. I'm not one of the insiders caught up in a froth of anxiety. But I feel the shift lurking out there, waiting to pounce. Why don't we forget all that stuff I said we need to do and go back to bed. Right now I'd be much happier if the world was just you and me."

"It's a temptation. But you know Singe will walk in just when . . ."

Singe arrived early, as usual without knocking. "Good. I don't have to throw cold water on you."

And so the workday began.

97

Dean was in a glowing good mood when we got downstairs. I grumbled, "Can't you see that it's raining?"

"Isn't it marvelous? We really need it." He went on to tell me how fresh the air would smell later.

Didn't he realize that the humidity would be torture?

Strafa poured mugs of something that wasn't tea. It smelled monstrously good. I said, "Definitely tasty but I wouldn't go out of my way."

Dean said, "I tried to follow instructions but I think I missed."

Strafa said, "It's a novelty. Dean's hard black tea is fine, robust daily fare."

Dean and I looked at her askance, having trouble remembering that there was no need to read between her lines.

Singe came to the kitchen doorway. Strafa asked, "Did you see anything?"

"Rain. There isn't a soul out there. It's like they got washed away with the offal."

Being a trained detective—albeit home-schooled—I detected something odd. "What's going on?"

Strafa said, "There were Palace Guards going and Civil Guards arriving when we went to bed. General Block wanted in. We ignored him."

Singe said, "I didn't see anyone through the peephole so I went out to check." She was damp. Soon she would develop a pong. "They're gone. Every last man. There aren't any watchers. A ratwoman told me they all got excited and charged off somewhere just when it was getting light."

That wasn't right. Block's mob wouldn't suddenly change

their minds. Odd connections clicked. "What did we do when we bailed out of here last night?"

Strafa laughed. "We wasted time that we could have used getting to know each other. And made ourselves look like fraidy cats."

"And we told anyone who cared to think about it that the Dead Man really is asleep."

Singe gasped. "If he was awake we would not have run."

"Exactly. Where are Morley and Belinda? Why aren't they back yet?"

Strafa muttered something like, "Uh-oh." She reached across and squeezed my hand. "I'll go look."

Singe warned, "You'll get soaked."

"I'll go naked, then."

We all stared.

"Come on, people. I can joke, too. There must be rain gear around here somewhere. Darling, you check the salt. In case we outwitted ourselves." She clumped away fast. Dean went and dug out his rain gear for her.

Singe said, "We may have pulled a major stupid, right?"

"I don't know how much 'we' there is for anybody besides me and Strafa. I do think we got snookered." Dean came back. "Did you buy more salt, Dean?"

Wasted breath. He had his nose in a cupboard already. Out came a ten pound bag of pickling salt. He wasted no breath admonishing me to be frugal.

Singe got stuck with helping me. The cellar got her talking to herself. She told me, "As soon as it is safe I am having this cared for."

"Can we afford it?"

"The annual gift to Tholozan House arrives next week. I have not tapped that fund since I took over your finances."

I didn't know what she meant. "What's Tholozan House?"

"That is where I invest the gifts you get from your lapsed vampire girlfriend."

"Oh."

Kayean Kronk. The first woman I had ever loved and gotten close enough to touch. Morley and I had rescued her from vampires in the Cantard while the war was still raging. For the Tates. Two of who, Tinnie and Rose, had tagged along. Yesterday and tomorrow, when Kayean had been lost and Tinnie started looking like more than my pal Denny's incredibly hot but unattainable cousin.

"You still here, Garrett?"

"I haven't thought about Kayean in ages."

"She thinks of you. She still sends the gifts she promised."

She had inherited a fabulous fortune because of me. Her first gift had helped me buy my house and rehabilitate it around the Dead Man.

Singe asked, "Can you see who is at the door?"

I went despite not having heard a thing.

Kyra Tate. She came in looking like the proverbial drowned rat. "My umbrella blew away." Singe arrived with a huge towel. I wondered when we had acquired that. Kyra said, "I don't know why I'm out in this weather, anyway. Except that we love you."

"Let's get you back to the kitchen where we can get you warmed up." Ever clever Singe was headed that way already. By the time Kyra and I arrived she had hot tea poured and Dean had brought the cookies out of hiding. I planted the girl, then asked, "So why are you out in this?"

"All the usual, plus I remembered where I saw the woman before."

"Who?"

"The one in Penny's sketches. I said I thought I saw her before. I did. But only once. It was at a party on the Hill. I was eleven. Our family got invited because they were part of some conglomerate including the people giving the party. The group had just gotten a huge army contract. Everybody was going to get a lot richer. The girl's name was Jane something. She was only sixteen but she was already somebody's mistress. She was so awful that the girls running with her were embarrassed. I never saw her again. I never heard anything about her again. Probably because Hill don't socialize with people who actually do creative stuff."

I smiled, did not comment other than to ask, "How can any of that help us now?"

"Other than to tell you Jane Whatsit is unpleasant? Not much. Except that I've gotten myself some pretty nice boobs since then." She was too wet and had too limited an audience to flaunt the niceties. "And she hasn't changed at all."

I glanced at Singe. "Six years? In the dark we might not be able to see much difference."

"Yeah. Well. Too. I saw Kip and Kevans yesterday. We talked a lot. Us girls ganged up on him. I think we got it worked out. Kevans tried hard to make Kip understand that she doesn't need him protecting her all the time, anymore. That she's fine with the life she's living."

"I'm thrilled to hear that. I hope you are, too."

"I am, Mr. Garrett. Since he doesn't have to worry about Kevans he can focus all that devotion on me."

Yeah. A familiar echo there. "He will if he's got any sense at all."

"I don't know where you and my aunt are anymore."

"Neither do I."

"Kevans' mom knows, though, don't she?"

"She's never confused."

Kyra shut her eyes. "Can't believe I'm going to say this. You're really a good man. You do good for everybody you can. So I think you should be with Kevans' mom."

"Kyra?"

"I know. I sound like a traitor. But Tinnie is never going to be anybody but who she is. Only getting more so, according to my uncles, who figure she'll be hell on wheels in ten more years."

"Thank you, Kyra." I didn't want to talk about it anymore. I didn't want to think about it.

Kyra said, "They grew up with her mother. They knew her grandmother."

Kyra was dried out, warm again, full of tea, and Singe said the rain had stopped. Singe found Dollar Dan napping on Morley's cot. She wakened him and bullied him into walking Kyra home. After taking time to let Kyra know that young girls should not be roaming the city alone, however unappealing they made themselves appear.

"That was wicked," I said after Singe closed the door.

"She is concerned about her looks. It will have a positive impact."

"Now that she's not here to hear me say so, I'm seriously worried, Singe."

"As am I. Strafa has been out there far too long."

Strafa. So. The final heart had surrendered.

I suggested, "You go nag Old Bones. I'll sit here and worry enough for both of us."

98

Strafa returned, dripping. The rain had started up again. She asked Singe, "Why is he so glum?"

"He is remembering the sad times before he found you. How bad is it?" She produced a twin to the towel she had used to dry Kyra.

A glance at Strafa told me she had bad news.

"There was an attack on that place we went last night. They burned it to the ground."

"Oh, shit. Crush! DeeDee. Mike."

"It started just after Belinda left. She heard the racket and went back. There was a huge fight."

It must not have gone well. "Penny?"

"I don't know. They were just starting to pick up the pieces. The fire wasn't out yet. They were concentrating on that. The Guard turned up in time to get into the fight. The woman in black leather was there. She did some sorcery. Her thread men got wiped out. I counted eighteen. The woman and the cart took off. There was a running fight with Specials armed with military weapons. They stopped the cart by killing the goats. The woman got away. So did the thing that was in the cart. Nobody would swear it, but the talk was, a giant squid thing crawled out and turned into a naked man that ran off with the woman. She was wounded. Singe, could you track her?"

"In this weather? Not likely."

I asked, "How about Belinda? How about Morley?"

"I don't know. They wouldn't let me get close. It looked like most of Belinda's escort went down. Their mounts, too. The coach is on its side in the street, the team dead in the traces.

On the upside, it didn't look like the people from the house suffered much."

"What should we do?" I asked the air.

The air did not reply.

"Singe, we have *got* to get him awake."

"I have a job to do, as Strafa just said."

"And, as you pointed out, it's raining."

"I am going to give it a try. The squid man should have a serious reek."

Getting feisty, my little girl. Her charming adolescent deference and diffidence were fading.

"If you're sure that's what you need to do, go for it." I asked Strafa, "Are you going to take her?" Hoping the prospect would turn Singe's bones to jelly. If a shape-changing guy who turned into a giant squid didn't do the trick.

"I have to go back anyway, to see about our friends."

They were my friends so they were her friends. "I guess you do. Bless you, Strafa Algarda."

"Garrett?"

"Just a sentimental moment. You are too perfect. Too precious. It's frightening."

And she didn't get embarrassed by mushy stuff. She just laughed like wind chimes. Her eyes turned a violet shade that made me want to kiss each lid about a thousand times.

"The next few years could get really saccharine around here," Singe grumbled. "Are we going to go, Strafa? Or would you rather stand around with a goofy expression, twisting Garrett till he looks like he's mentally challenged?"

"That one for sure. But I was raised up to honor my civic responsibilities first."

"Yes. Yes," I said. "What will all this do to the political situation? They got everything calmed down once. Prince Rupert thought the cover-up would stick. But another attack could rip the head off a butt of chaos."

Strafa kissed me. She made it clear that she meant it when she said she would rather stay and make me crazy. Then she headed out, with Singe right behind.

I asked the air, "Did the evil genius behind everything deliberately create a new crisis?"

Dean showed up. "Do you think it's too risky for me to go out?"

"Yes, I do. There are people out there who want to commit murder for no obvious reason. Is there something we need desperately? Have Dollar Dan make the run when he gets back. Or go wake Bird up and promise him a bottle."

"We face no critical shortages. I wanted a couple pounds of beef to slice for a dish I want to try. And I was hoping to swing by to see how Playmate is managing."

"He took his medicine with him?"

"He did."

"Strafa can check on him later."

"That is best, I expect." A pause. "I'm having trouble adjusting to the excitement being back."

"I'm sorry."

He chuckled. "I wasn't fishing for an apology." He made a search-and-capture sweep of Singe's space, collecting rogue cups, trays, pots, and flatware. "It should all turn tediously domestic once this insanity gets sorted out."

"Really?"

"The only challenge I foresee is you deciding if you'll go live in the Windwalker's mansion or if she'll move in here. I'm thinking this place will get cramped with a gaggle of little Garretts underfoot."

"Gleep!" Or, maybe better said, "Gleep?"

"I'll give odds. You'll be a daddy inside a year. And you will awe and amaze us all by turning out to be a good one."

I couldn't answer that. I didn't have the words. "Gleep?" That stuff didn't sound absurd when he said it.

The redhead, with her usual steadfast self-assertion, entered my mind. Hands on hips. Head cocked to her right. Chin lowered. "Well?"

The question never came up. Not even as speculation, excepting in the lateral sense of prevention. We'd never discussed our attitudes toward children let alone thought about making our own. Which surprised me, in retrospect.

I muttered, "God, strike me down now. I can't possibly be old enough to be a parent."

Dean broke out in the biggest shit-eating grin I ever saw on his ugly old clock.

"You prick."

His grin got bigger. "We should move to her place. There'll be room for your own kids and strays like Penny, too."

"Penny isn't my stray."

We exchanged troubled looks. Hanging around our house might have gotten that girl into the worst trouble of a short, troubled life. And we might have gotten Crush, DeeDee, Mike, and the gang at Fire and Ice into the worst trouble of their troubled lives, too.

I said, "Well, for now let's just be gay bachelors—the way we were before the females began to accumulate and complicate."

"Yeah," Dean said, with a marked absence of enthusiasm. He headed for the door. A moment later I heard Dollar Dan ask why he looked so glum.

Rain was falling again. I got a strong whiff of Dollar Dan as he followed Dean to the kitchen.

99

I went out onto the stoop. I'm not sure why. Maybe some vague notion about seeing for myself if all the watchers had been chased off by the rain. Or maybe I just wanted to enjoy the sound of rain on the stoop roof.

It was an odd rainfall, not heavy but steady, with big drops.

The street was empty. No people. No animals. The Palace Guard vehicles were gone. The air was cold and it was clean. For a moment all was right with my world.

Dean came out. "Can you come back in? We have a problem."

I gripped the cold, wet, recently painted balustrade. I did not want to leave contentment to deal with whatever had him upset.

My imagination was capable of encompassing only one terrible possibility. The Dead Man had given up the ghost, for real and forever. Henceforth my life would revolve around removing a quarter ton of moldering corpse.

Dean did head for the Dead Man's room. "Here," he said, indicating the Bird with the toe of his right shoe.

"I know. I thought he went home, too."

"That's the problem."

"Huh?"

"He's dead. He'll start smelling pretty soon, no matter how cold we make it."

I knelt for a closer look. A voice not Bird's told me, "Get your boot out of my back, asshole, unless you don't want to keep them ugly teeth."

I touched Bird's neck. No pulse. "Penny was right."

"Apparently. But how can they use him after he's one of them?"

"I don't know." I was upright again and oozing toward the door. "But this strikes me as a sound reason for procrastination. Suppose we just let dead Birds lie till Strafa gets back? She'll know what to do. Or she can tell us who does."

Dead Bird said something obnoxious. How? Voices came out of his mouth, not like the Dead Man talking inside my head.

Dean said, "Perhaps I was hasty when I pronounced him dead. Look. He's breathing, now."

He was, but only to collect wind to mutter and snarl in several voices, squabbling over how best to use the artist's corpse.

I said, "Just to make sure we don't get any unhappy surprises, how about we tie him up?"

"Clothesline is on the way." Dean headed for the kitchen.

The quarreling voices stilled. Bird's body began to shake. Then one voice shrieked, "Oh, shit! What's that?"

Another squealed in pure terror.

100

So there I was. My witchy girlfriend was gone. My sidekick was sound asleep. My trusty ratgirl assistant was far away. And something I was not going to like was about to happen.

A solid boom came from up front. Somebody my size and about as bright had just charged into the door at full gallop.

I went to take a look.

Dean yelled, "Garrett!" as I bent to the peephole. His holler preceded an inhuman shriek so violent the house shuddered on its foundations. Something crashed in Singe's office.

I finished my peek, sprinted for the kitchen.

Stuff had fallen in there, too, but I didn't take inventory. Dean and Dollar Dan were staring out the back window, into the barren space that had been an herb garden back when Dean was young enough to wrangle one.

"You have got to be shitting me," I said, in deadpan awe, without inflexion.

The world's biggest and probably only land-going kraken was out there thrashing megatentacles and making hideous messes while casting a mad yellow eye at the snacks behind the glass.

Several tentacles had been truncated recently. They oozed ichor, or whatever you call implausible monster blood. The beast's body quivered like an epileptic dog suffering a grand seizure. "The salt. It works. Dean. Salt. Get ready. Use it if that thing gets any part of itself inside."

I had seen that old man stressed a hundred times. I had seen him hopping mad and slow-burn, sullenly angry. I had seen him everything but outright panicky. I did not see him panic now. Nor did Dollar Dan, though ratfolk are notoriously flighty when straits get tight.

Dean retrieved the remaining pickling salt. He collected two small pots and started sharing it out.

I asked, "What did Singe do with the family arsenal when you started having youngsters underfoot?" There was a closet upstairs that once boasted an enviable collection of illegal weaponry. At latest check it contained two backup head knockers, a rusty throwing knife, two worn-out brooms, and several saps that were actually memorabilia. They had been used on me before I took them away.

"Singe didn't. I did. Penny is fascinated by things that are sharp and pointy. The dangerous stuff is in the black wooden case under my bed."

He wanted to say more but time was tight. There had been three more huge blows against the front door, of a magnitude that promised to break through eventually.

Then would come the fire.

Getting the case out from under Dean's bed required maneuvering. It was six feet long. It was two and a half feet wide. It was eight inches tall. It was freaking heavy. I grumbled, "What the hell is this, old man? You been holding out on me?"

He had, indeed. All my illegal weaponry was in the box but that was a minority of the tools of death stashed there. Where in the hell had Dean gotten light infantry pila? There were four of those. There were three classical javelins, two halberd heads, a variety of swords (some of them mine), two finely crafted longbows with bundled arrows beside and strings presumably handy. There were spearheads and lots of knives.

I wanted to stand there marveling and wondering whence it all had come but they hadn't given up on the door and I didn't hear any tin whistles.

There were three crossbows to choose from. I assembled a standard Marine Corps heavy piece in seconds. I hadn't lost the knack. I grabbed a twelve-pack magazine of iron-tipped bolts, added a selection of other deadly tools, then got my beautiful young behind to my bedroom window—just in time to greet a slow-moving thread man who had climbed up with the intention of chucking firebombs inside. Somebody down below tossed one up, not quite high enough. The villain missed it. Down it went. I heard it break, then heard a *whoosh!* as the fuel ignited.

A roil of fire and smoke headed skyward.

I used an old time pileum to evict the thread man from my roof. He staggered into the arms of demon gravity while trying to pull the business end of the spear out of his cold chest.

I stopped watching. I was looking down the length of my crossbow at the woman who had been created to glamorize black leather. Tonight she wore a pink wig in what they call a pageboy cut. Her eyes were enormous. Gods, she looked good!

But I was in the soldier zone. It didn't matter how good she looked. I squeezed the trigger just the way they taught me. The bolt flew true but the woman moved in that exact instant when it became too late to shift my aim.

The bolt missed her heart. It went in where her left arm joined her shoulder. The impact spun her. She grabbed at that bit of bolt still protruding. Her feet tangled. She fell, making an inarticulate yelp of surprise.

People do not get shot in the TunFaire shaped by today's Civil Guard. Especially not villains.

By the time she managed to look up at me, from her knees, while still falling, I had the crossbow spanned and another bolt laid in. I might be out of practice on the mental stuff but operating one of these things had become a part of me. I'd still be able to span, load, and shoot on my deathbed.

The woman was trying to get up when my second bolt arrived. It ripped into the left cheek of what had to be the sweetest female behind ever minted.

She squealed like the proverbial stuck pig. She tried to run. Her left leg didn't want to engage in that enterprise. She shrieked something high-pitched, incoherent, and desperate.

A thunderous thud marked another attempt to break my front door. Obviously, I had been smart to get the work done on that, back when.

The incredible vision in black had not come just with thread men and a monster. Her shrieking summoned a goat cart. I thought she had lost that at Fire and Ice. Only later did it occur to me that the baddies could have more than one.

The goats trotted up. I loosed my worst shot yet. It missed the women entirely, grazed one of the critters. Both animals said something foul in goat and took off.

Leather, ever so tasty woman lunged, snagged the back of the cart, hung on and let herself be dragged out of the kill zone.

The thread men and thing out back were on their own.

Wishful thinking had me hearing whistles that weren't really there.

I backed off the window, grabbed up instruments of mayhem, scuttled back to Dean's room. I broke the crossbow down, put everything back in the case and pushed the case back under Dean's bed. Then I headed downstairs.

The monster had broken in through the back window. Dollar Dan had two tentacles nailed to the windowsill with kitchen knives. Dean was delivering salt to any other part that came in range.

I said, "Excellent. You've got it under control. Just don't go out there after it. I'm going to see what they've done to the door." I grabbed a long, two-tine fork Dean used when turning a roast. At the same time I saw something I had not noticed before.

Our kraken had no suckers on its tentacles. One side looked just like the other. I don't think I ever saw a squid or octopus that didn't have suckers. Some had suckers with teeth.

I found the front door frame almost free of its anchor bolts. Despite its massive design the door itself showed cracks. Splinters littered the hallway.

The peephole still worked.

I saw bits of fire burning. I saw two thread men, one down and the other ambling in a small circle, constantly turning left. Easing my head to the right I spied one more just standing in one place.

I tried the bolts and locks. Every one worked, though the one Singe had complained about before had to be forced. The bottom of the door hit the floor when it was halfway open. It would go no farther. But that was room enough for me to get out, heavily armed with a custom club and a cook's fork.

I didn't want to be seen with anything more useful at a time when some of my betters would appreciate excuses to lock me up.

I saw nine thread men: three down, four standing still, one smoldering, and one circling to his left. Then a tenth fell out of the sky, firebomb in hand. Fire oozed out from under him.

I was about to go galloping back inside when I spotted the goat cart just standing in the street up near the Cardonlos place. A dark lump lay ten yards closer to me. It moved.

Oh, yes! Time for that sweet thing and me to get friendly. I ducked back into Singe's office and conscripted a small lantern to share patrol duty.

The door would not shut all the way again.

The woman had trouble making headway with her left arm and left leg damaged but she was stubborn. She almost caught up with her cart before I caught her.

I found the pink wig about two thirds of the way there.

"You dropped something, precious. Here. Let me give you a hand." Odd. She no longer made that outfit look as good as she had just minutes ago.

She turned to see who was talking.

"Goo!" That face was a good forty hard years old. "This a magic wig?" I tossed the wig into the back of the cart.

A big uproar broke out behind my house. A cloud of brown dust rolled up, illuminated by the burning thread man.

Several thread men got motivated and started our way.

A big scream came from behind my house. It was a lost soul kind of yowl.

The woman gasped, "This can't be happening!"

She was determined to get up without help. Her now drooping posterior betrayed her. Down she went, leading with her chin.

The thread men did the same.

The woman now looked a hard rode fifty.

"The more you move around the more the barbs on those bolts will chew you up inside."

"Can't let go now." She started to get up again.

I tucked my tools into my belt, set my lantern down, stepped over to the cart, yanked the canvas cover off. That released a pocket of stench so pungent it almost laid me out. Even so, I hoisted the woman up there and stretched her out on her right side. "Hang in there. Neither bolt cut a big vein. I'll get them out before they do lethal damage." Where the hell were the tin whistles? I got busy eliminating evidence that might suggest the use of illegal weapons in a civil confrontation. "Grit those teeth, girl. This will hurt like hell."

I started with the bolt in back. Its head was peeking out already. I could just push it through. "Thanks for coming by. You helped me figure it all out."

Shouting erupted down the street. A ratman wanted my attention. Other ratmen were with him, making sure the thread men would not get up again. The work apparently required the use of hatchets.

The ratman screamed at me. It couldn't make out what it said.

I slipped the bloody bolt inside my shirt. "One down. Now for the one that's really going to hurt." She had been a trooper during the first removal. She had an old truce with pain.

Several ratmen were yelling now. Two were headed my way. I turned to see what their big-ass problem was.

Something hit me with all the enthusiasm of a haymaker delivered by a truly pissed-off war god.

101

There were faces all round me, looking down, when badly blurred vision began to return. I tried to say, "Hey! You guys are all right."

Unless I was hallucinating, the circle included Morley, Belinda, Penny, John Stretch and Dollar Dan, Dean, and Strafa shouting down a long tunnel about how leaving me unsupervised was worse than leaving a three-year-old home alone.

Penny was crying. I heard General Block and several others yammering farther away.

Singe hove into view armed with a pitcher and mugs. She said something about how it was too damned expensive to have me live at home anymore. Mr. Mulclar was already at work repairing the door.

I'm not sure how my head was working. I wondered how long I had been out but what came out was, "The Bird?"

"It has been handled," Morley told me. "You have been unconscious for sixteen hours." Which meant it was the middle of the night, now. Why were all these people here in the middle of the night?

While I was thinking that Crush and Mike poked their clocks in to check the status of my breathing. I heard DeeDee giggle somewhere, apparently at a joke Saucerhead told Playmate.

Dean reported, "The monster did it. It shape-shifted into the man Bird painted, only in awful shape. Big chunks were missing. He looked like he'd been rotting. But he was in good enough shape to go pound you. He took off with the woman and the cart."

Singe said, "I tracked them to the Knodical. The woman

who hit Fire and Ice went there, too. They wouldn't take these two in. They headed up the hill from the Knodical. I lost them. They poisoned the trail again."

Strafa said, "I checked my house. They didn't go there."

"Don't matter where they run," I tried to say. "I know what they're doing. I think I know where they're doing it."

So there I was, with people crowding in, eager to hear the big revelation.

I went back to sleep amidst a great fuss about concussions.

I wakened to a remixed set of faces. This set included Deal Relway and Westman Block. The latter was in no mood for foreplay. "We've been fired."

I made noises.

"Can they do that? They can. For cause. Strictly speaking, for actually doing the kind of corrupt stuff they're insisting that we do. In a broader sense, they have to make it stick. Right now it doesn't look like they have the horses."

I made more noises while wondering why they were here instead of out doing something useful.

"The public temper is fragile right now. People are nervous and upset. Two attacks in one night by monsters and zombies is a little excessive. Dismissing the Civil Guard officer corps for trying to deal with it may be too much. We have every man out trying to keep the head on the barrel."

"How come you're here?"

"Because the King's men don't dare come after us here. Word is out that the Dead Man is awake and extremely unhappy."

He was not. I got no sense of Himself at all.

"Last resort, we will let out the truth about the thread men."

Several people helped me up, including Morley. "Trying to play Little Dead Man, eh? Going to sleep right after dropping a big hint that you had it all worked out."

They moved me to Singe's office, installed me in the best chair. I could not help seeing the empty doorway during the journey. I whined.

Singe told me, "Mr. Mulclar will have it fixed by this time tomorrow."

Mulclar had been maintaining the door for several years.

"What happened to the F and I girls?"

"Gone to watch a Jon Salvation play rehearse. Then they'll head for Strafa's. She's going put them up for a couple nights."

I glanced at Strafa. She nodded. "You'd better get over there and lock up your valuables. How about the Bird?"

Block said, "In a cell at the Al-Khar and still bitching. Forensics is trying to figure out how."

"Thought you were fired."

Relway said, "Only in theory. The King and Crown Prince are isolated in Knodical. The Specials have kept them from communicating with the cavalry barracks."

Some bright monarch, having attained the throne with the assistance of the city garrison, had bought insurance against a repetition by moving all the barracks outside the city wall. Now the troops were in no position to put down a mutiny by the tin whistles.

"That's a big risk."

Block said, "We know. We took it because the Windwalker told us you figured the mess out and can tell us what we need to do to restore order."

Strafa made kissy lips from across the room.

Now I had to deliver.

"I still don't know how Morley fits. Maybe the gods just wanted to get our attention. He'll remember eventually."

"Time is wasting," Block said. "Don't go wallowing in it the way your sidekick does."

"What's been happening is, villains from an old branch of the Algarda family tree, armed with the family talent for sorcery, found a way to stay young and beautiful—and to make dramatic physical improvements."

I had them. Everybody wants to be beautiful forever.

"I don't know how they do it. Your forensic sorcerers can figure that out. But it has to be the cruelest sorcery ever. They started out using dead people. Resurrection men have been around for ages, keeping a low profile, stealing corpses to sell to sorcerers for their research. The bodies could be patched together to use as . . . We don't know what they used them for, back when. Maybe illegal stuff that a live villain couldn't survive. We may turn up answers to a lot of old questions before we're done."

"What changed?" Relway asked.

"Several things. The most important was, the cost of staying young kept going up. The longer they lived, the harder it got to stay beautiful. Gilded latten."

"What does that mean?" Relway demanded.

"Remember Belle Chimes? The Bellman? No? Doesn't matter. He apprenticed in a jewelry shop. He told me about an alloy called latten. It has four or five metals in it. There is no fixed formula. The main ingredient is zinc. The point is, latten makes a perfect base for cheap jewelry, candlesticks, and whatnot, that look like something rich. The gold in one sovereign can coat more than a hundred pieces of latten jewelry—every one as pretty as a piece crafted from solid noble metal."

"Gilded latten?"

"In this case, gilded latten bones."

Block and Relway both scowled at me.

I said, "Their real troubles started when they took on clients outside the family."

They rewarded me with a nice little stir.

I thought I understood the Dead Man a little better.

"Demand for bodies outstripped supply even after they made a deal with the Works Department for its dead."

"You think they started buying them still on the hoof?"

"I do. Live bodies should have a lot more of whatever it was they were taking." I looked to Strafa. She offered an uncertain nod. It was not her area of expertise. "They probably only took the dying to start. But they got hungry. And maybe greedy."

Strafa said, "Note that the undead have always favored live victims."

The Director made a weird noise. "We can invoke the Undead Protection Acts! The King himself can't overrule those because the King could be a vampire covering his own ass." The ugly little man stamped around chuckling and rubbing his hands together.

Block said, "You're scaring the mundanes, Deal."

"Maybe. Maybe. But that has got to be our angle. Once we proclaim the invocation on the steps of the Chancellery, everything stops till the King proves he's not undead."

I said, "I think that might be something like what's really true."

"He's a vampire?" Relway asked.

"No. He's a horndog fool who charged in with eyes wide shut. Anybody who's seen the women in black has to know they can get anything they want from most any man alive. One broke the heart of a nancy tailor when she was getting fitted."

"You saying there's more than one?"

"Has to be. One was wounded at Fire and Ice. She couldn't possibly have healed up in time to come at us here." But if she had quick access to the life-magic she used to stay young . . .

Singe reminded me, "That one is holed up in the Knodical with Prince Rupert and the King."

Morley asked, "You think they were taking turns being the old woman and the young woman?"

"Something like that." I hadn't thought it out that far.

"Where does the King fit?"

"I think he saw and decided he wanted. They might have set him up. They could do themselves a lot of good if they controlled the head of state."

Morley didn't say anything but I could practically hear him wondering how he had gotten involved.

I said, "The Little Dismal notion came up before. You said you'd look at it. What happened?"

Block said, "Arrests have been made. More will follow after the bean counters go through the records. Specials have taken charge. The wicked won't tap that pool again."

"Excellent. Then all we have to do is to go down to their place of business and root them out."

"Their place of business?"

"That abandoned warehouse on the Landing."

"Which abandoned warehouse?"

"The one I sent John Stretch to tell you about the other day."

Relway growled, "You sent a ratman with a message?"

Said ratman was in the room and he was not happy. "The message was delivered to the Al-Khar, at the door. The duty constable assured me that it would be passed along. She and the guards there would not let me deliver the message in person."

Block told a scowling Relway, "We just found our volunteers for the Bustee patrols."

Relway said, "It's time to go into action."

Before anyone could suggest a better or more cautious course those two were clambering past the crippled front door.

I was aggravated. There were matters in need of discussion and resolution.

Even my new sweetie took off, claiming a need for face time with colleagues on the Hill.

That angle of our thing scared the crap out of me. I could relate to Furious Tide of Light, no problem. But hobnob with her class? I didn't think I had it in me.

102

The ladies from Fire and Ice stopped by. Jon Salvation floated in their wake. Crush bubbled. "It was so exciting, Mr. Garrett!" Mike sneered over her shoulder, silently pointing a fat red arrow at that "Mister."

Salvation declared, "This child can sing!" Both a statement and an expression of wonder.

I said, "You should write a play with lots of singing."

"And dancing," DeeDee said. "I'm a good dancer, Jon."

Salvation shuddered. He looked like he might melt.

Mike continued to be amused. DeeDee's dancing probably involved a progressive movement toward her birthday suit.

I told Salvation, "I had an idea the other day you might think about. Suppose you send your understudies out to put your plays on in other towns and cities? You could keep them going for years."

He stared at me for a while, then said, "I think Tinnie is going to work out. She's really dedicated. It's like she's trying to lose herself in something." He glanced at Strafa, just downstairs after returning from the Hill. She shook her head at me.

She looked the girls over, never down her nose, which left me that much bigger a fan. She had no problem being around the kinds of people who can be found around me. I had to make an effort to get along with the kinds of people to be found around her.

This was going to be an unusual relationship.

Strafa asked Mike, "You ready to go to my house?"

Mike nodded. "Mr. Salvation. Are you sure it's all right for us to take the coach?"

"No problem. I'm used to walking. And I need to talk to Garrett."

Yet another of Mike's secretive smiles.

She figured Salvation was taken with one of her charges.

She asked Strafa, "Can we stop along the way? None of us have anything but what we left the house wearing."

"Of course."

DeeDee and Crush were not in their work clothes but DeeDee's taste tended toward flashy trash.

"Before we go," Mike said. And dragged me back to the kitchen. Dean and Dollar Dan scrunched up and let us in, Dean automatically beginning to rattle teacups. He had gotten the window fixed already.

Mike pressed up against me tight. I said, "I'm flattered but . . ."

"You ought to be. That Salvation."

"What about him?"

"Is he really as naïve as he seems?"

"Oh, yeah. More so. He's good at faking being cool."

"So he doesn't know about us?"

I understood. "Actually, he does. He thinks it's all kind of romantic."

She shook her head. She sneered a little. Part of me was proving not to be loyal to any one woman. "You're alive after all." She relented, stepped back. I was not as flustered as she had hoped. She asked, "What's his interest? Guys his age, it's usually Crush. But he treats her like he doesn't know she's a girl."

"He knows. I guarantee. But he doesn't want her to think that's what's on his mind. If he's interested in anybody that way, I figure it's you." Which I said for the hell of it.

"Which is why his drool is all over DeeDee's shoulders, I suppose."

"He's shy. He doesn't know how to interact with a refined lady."

"Wiseass."

"He's good people, Mike. Don't mess him up."

"We never mess first. It's one of my rules." She turned to the door but had a wicked thought. "But I'll let me break it just this once."

She stepped back against me, wiggled a little. "You and the

Windwalker split up, stop by." Chuckling, she winked at Dean, pushed off, and left the kitchen.

Dean said, "You don't want her, I'll take her."

"You old villain." I took half a minute to catch my breath and let the swelling subside, then headed up the hall to make my farewells.

103

Morley told me, "I have to be in on this. I won't contribute, but . . . It will be historic."

This was next day. Mr. Mulclar had finished fixing the door but it remained open in honor of the man's special faculty. He has a digestive disorder. It doesn't improve if he eats gravel. His leave-behind here suggested a diet exclusively of fermented beans and thousand-day eggs.

Over the past twenty-plus hours the principals dealt with personal issues, political issues, squabbled over turf, and behaved like a pack of four-year-olds. The Director and General Block got heads together with some senior military people and talked them into staying out of the way unless there were disorders the Civil Guard could not manage.

The people inside the Knodical remained stubborn. Strafa's peers on the Hill made excuses for doing nothing, though they did agree to deal with any villains who came their way.

I was convinced that a witch hunt was a sure thing, but the peace held.

Block and Relway had every man helping keep the lid on.

Belinda was in the woodwork somewhere, licking her wounds, sulking, scheming bloody retribution—and helping keep the peace.

She had all her troops called up, too.

The battle at Fire and Ice had gone her way. Some good guys had survived. Everyone from the sporting house escaped. Belinda owed her own continued existence to the superhuman efforts of Joel, who had proven his love.

Joel was alive but not expected to stay that way.

I suffered mild episodes of grogginess and was unsure of

the boundary between reality and fantasy. Still, I boarded a coach hired by the Guard and rode it down to the Landing. The Landing is called that because some old-time explorer first set foot in the city there. The city already existed, but was savage, pagan, and uncivilized. Its people neither spoke the explorer's language nor worshipped his god.

The neighborhood swarmed with Civil Guards and Outfit soldiers.

I told Singe, "I don't think this is the smart thing to do."

"Then call it off."

"You're kidding. You think I'm in charge? Besides, it's too late."

"You could stop this cold by presenting a reasoned argument for holding off till better evidence is collected."

Me deliver a solid argument for restraint? Hopeless. Besides, a lot of people wanted to make something happen. It didn't have to be a good something so long as some fur flew.

Singe stayed close, on my left. So did Strafa, to my right. She snuggled up close enough to make me regret having left the house. Then she gave herself some space and became the Windwalker, Furious Tide of Light. The change was impressive.

General Block, Director Relway, and Belinda Contague all were in sight. Morley was close by, surrounded by his old crew. John Stretch had brought a dozen of his hardest men, three of who screened Singe and me. The rest were out sniffing, which was unnecessary. The air was still and heavy. I could smell it myself.

The Windwalker drifted upward. Singe and I caught up with General Block. He said, "The guards have done a runner."

"Think the villains have cleared out, too?"

Morley squeaked something from a few yards away. "What's up?" I asked Sarge.

"He's remembering something."

"The smell," Dotes said. "And that place straight ahead. Made with the odd color bricks. That was the place."

The bricks in question were gray. Most bricks used in Tun-Faire are some shade of red.

The scouts agreed. The gray brick building was the place. The smell increased as we got closer. There was a taint of death in it overridden by the stenches of urine and feces.

The Guards, Outfit thugs, and the rest collapsed inward till we established a cordon round three and a half sides. The rest of one side faced the river and consisted of a pair of concrete-walled, silted channels where once upon a time army barges had been loaded from the warehouse. Someone had begun making an effort to clear the silt.

I said, "That's what you do with your thread men when you aren't using them to set fire to people's houses."

"There," Morley said, indicating a small, broken, wooden door that opened on the divider between channels. A wooden ladder in a dangerous state of disrepair clung to the side of the warehouse nearby, leading to the roof. "That's where I got out."

Singe asked, "You climbed that ladder?"

"I did. All the way. In the rain. I stayed on the roof for a day and a half. I should have stayed longer. They heard me coming back down because I said something too loud when I slipped. I got a head start but it didn't do me any good."

Directing Guards by gesture, General Block asked, "And how did you get in there in the first place?"

Relway announced, "We're set at all the entrances. Say when."

"When."

Morley said, "I don't remember that part yet."

I asked, "How are you doing now? You able to keep going?"

"I'll have Puddle piggyback me when I can't manage anymore."

Puddle expressed his opinion about that rather pithily.

Civil Guards broke down doors. Outfit bone breakers rushed inside. Somebody yelled something about idiots not forgetting the godsdamned colored lanterns so friends wouldn't bust the skulls of friends in the dark.

I looked up.

Strafa was way up there, watching the whole neighborhood. Her clothes faded into the background overcast. She was hard to spot.

Singe gagged.

"What?"

"They opened something in there. I have to move back. It's too much." She headed toward the coaches. Most of the ratmen were doing the same. John Stretch went a few seconds after Singe. "It's too foul."

Too foul for a rat?

I smelled it. It was everything that had been there before, but a hundred times worse.

Guards stumbled out of the nearest doorway, desperate for clean air. One headed toward Block. He had thrown up on himself.

Block asked, "Is it really that bad?"

"Worse than you can imagine, sir. Way worse." He threw up again.

I said, "I suggest we don't send anybody in that we don't have to."

Morley, using a stick for a cane, asked, "Remember the smell when we raided that vampire nest?"

"Yeah. This may be worse."

Ten minutes later a pair of red tops emerged with a limp figure between them. The man screamed when they brought him into the light.

"More stuff like that nest," Morley said.

There wasn't much light for those of us used to the surface world. The overcast was growing heavier. It would rain again soon.

The Windwalker plunged like a striking hawk. A bolt of actinic light preceded her.

104

I started to yell at Block. That wasn't necessary. He grabbed able bodies and headed out. I told Morley, "I'll be right back."

"Take your time. I'll be here."

Strike point for the Windwalker's bolt was two blocks away. I was winded when I joined the circle. The Windwalker remained upright, right foot planted on the throat of the woman in black. The latter wore a silver wig and was at her absolute peak of perfection, fully recovered from my brutality. She was singed and had a bad case of the shakes.

The Windwalker growled, "Can't any of you stop staring at her tits long enough to do something useful?"

I have mentioned how good the woman looked going away. With her top torn open the full frontal view was even more striking.

I rolled her over. That helped. The red tops bound her hands behind her and hobbled her. Relway took her wig. That helped some more.

The Windwalker said, "Stuff her into a gunnysack if that's what it takes." She stepped close to me, shut down the Windwalker some and hit me with a minor dose of her own magic. "You did good. I'm proud of you. You might find a little something special in your bed tonight."

A big racket broke out back whence we had come. The Windwalker reestablished herself. She floated upward. "Yeah! I am so ready for this." She shot that direction, did a loop and plunged. I charged after her, huffing and puffing. She swooped and darted like a smaller bird harassing a raider raven.

Something below her screamed and screamed.

Morley's mention of the vampire nest reminded me that I had heard that kind of scream before. It was rooted in the agony of knowing that immortality had been betrayed.

Tentacles whipped at the Windwalker. She dodged them easily.

Coming into the last hundred fifty feet of my run I saw that the monster had only two tentacles free to fend off an aerial attacker. The rest all had hold of people, the most notable of who was Morley. Several men threw things ineffectively. Nobody had come prepared to deal with this. But it could not flee while in squid form.

I was fifty feet away, lungs afire, wishing I'd had the stones to bring something lethal to the fight. The Windwalker made a quick run.

She pelted the beast with precisely delivered handfuls of rock salt.

It stopped trying to fight. It began to shudder, to shake. It turned loose of Morley and the others. I got in close, grabbed Sarge's arms, and started dragging. Other guys got hold of other victims, some of who had gotten thoroughly squeezed.

The Windwalker dropped down beside me. She turned into Strafa Algarda again. She was not breathing as hard as I was. "I ran out of salt!" She was exasperated.

"But you had enough."

She slipped her right hand into my left hand and pulled me forward.

The monster ripped through one final, violent, screaming convulsion, followed by a bizarre, noisy death rattle. It relaxed into the Nathan of the Bird's portrait, only looking as he might have at twenty, improved by a vast suite of cosmetic enhancements.

This was the male equivalent of the sweet thing in black leather—except for proportional wounds where its alternate form had been showered with salt.

Block caught up. He clamped his right hand on my left shoulder, facing me, while he fought for wind. "We got 'em. Finally."

"Not all of them. Not yet."

Morley stumbled over and hung on to Block. He could not take his eyes off our prisoner. "I remember most of it." He pointed at Nathan, who was getting the hog-tie treatment despite his poor health. "Him. He was the one who locked me up down there. I think because I saw them bringing prisoners off a barge over there." At which point he became completely confused.

I asked the question that was troubling him. "What were you doing here in the middle of the night?"

"I don't remember." But he did before he finished saying that. And it was something he dared not discuss with Westman Block close by.

This near the river, after dark, meant smuggling. In Morley's case, undoubtedly to avoid import duties. He donned a broad, weak grin.

Block said, "We won this round." His men had Nathan cocooned in rope in case he decided to come back to life. "But we still have work to do."

105

They picked me to step up to the Knodical door and ask for Prince Rupert. Strafa went along. The door opened. We went inside.

Other than the servants who admitted us there were no visible staff. The place was halfway a ruin. Maintenance had been neglected for years.

I went in all worked up to protect my best girl. A few minutes later I was thinking more rationally. I understood who would be protecting whom.

The servants led us to Prince Rupert. He was the absolute antithesis of happy. My message was brief. "The people outside want you to see something before this situation gets any uglier."

He had no choice. We had seen the inside of the Knodical. We would take that information back with us. And go we would because the Windwalker would make it happen.

"What?"

"You need to see it with a virgin mind."

Strafa said, "You have no choice, Rupert. See what you must see. Then we'll put this trial to bed."

He asked, "Is it still raining?"

Prince Rupert shared our coach. We reached the Landing. General Block had the army setting up a field hospital. Morley, Belinda, and Deal Relway were still on site and getting underfoot. The ratpeople were all gone. Nobody offered the Crown Prince a welcoming smile.

Rupert was fresh out of smiles himself. Life was a nightmare that was sure to get worse.

The rain picked up.

As we approached it three valiant red tops emerged from the nearest door with a liberated prisoner. The man was just barely alive. One of the Guards said, "This is the last live one, General. There's still a dozen corpses."

"Leave them. Your Highness, do you smell that?"

"I do." Making no pretence to misunderstand.

"It's worse inside. I won't force you to experience it. I don't want to give you any more reason to hate me. This was their headquarters. This was where they made themselves young. One level down is another laboratory like the one on the edge of Elf Town, a tailor shop, and a woodshop. Below that are the cellars where they kept their human resources."

Relway joined us. "I told Berry to break through the back wall so we can flood the cellars."

"That should help. Windwalker, Mr. Garrett, His Highness grasps the true enormity of the situation. You may return him to the Knodical."

I wasn't part of the in-group here. I was day labor. "Yes, sir."

Block and Relway eyed me with immense suspicion.

Block said, "Day after tomorrow we'll open this to the public."

Rupert said, "You don't want to do that."

"You're right. I don't. But I will. I remind you, it was Crown Prince Rupert who proclaimed a new Civil Guard and an era when no one would be above the law."

Rupert had nothing more to say. We returned him to the Knodical, at which point we had to give up the coach. The Windwalker flew us back to my house. In a downpour.

Though it was not yet late everyone but Penny had gone to bed. Penny helped slap together a half-assed supper. There were loose ends to the day but I didn't care. All I wanted was a full belly and a warm bed.

Strafa was more exhausted than I was. She had put in a heavy, hard day. I carried her upstairs. We collapsed on top of the covers in our wet clothes. Singe and Dean would raise hell in the morning.

106

I woke a couple of times, used the pot, shed some of the miserable wet clothing, went back to sleep. Hunger brought me out after fourteen hours.

Strafa remained dead to the world. She hadn't moved since I laid her down.

The night did tell me one more thing about her. She snored like a longshoreman when she was exhausted.

Dean fed me an indifferent meal. He was distracted. He foresaw a crowd gathering. I told him, "If you don't open the door you won't have to entertain them."

"No doubt true. However, I lack your facility for pragmatic rudeness." Muttering, he headed out to answer a knock.

He was back in a minute with Playmate. I said, "That wasn't so bad. Put him to work. How goes, Play?"

"Screaming fine. But I do need to find Kolda. I'm almost out of medicine."

"We'll hunt him down as soon as . . ." Done eating, I was moving into the hallway. Penny was at the peephole. She looked rather nice.

I am still alive. I do notice things.

Penny opened up. John Stretch and Dollar Dan trundled in. Singe was right behind. She had the boys doing porter work. She had looted a stationery shop.

"What the hell?"

"I was out of paper and low on ink. What did the Dead Man say?"

"How much paper do you . . . ? He didn't say anything. He tends not to talk in his sleep."

"He woke up hours ago, Garrett. Definitely dragging, for him, though. What did you do?" Suddenly suspicious.

"I didn't do anything. I just got up. Why do you need so much paper?"

"I'm recording the family history."

Garrett. Please join me.

He was back. That was the difference I'd felt. The place just fits different when he's awake. Though Singe had it right. This was just barely.

I stepped into his room. A handful of candles burned there. The cold was a shock. The light was for Penny. She had a painting going.

Saucerhead had arrived at some point. He sprawled in a corner, snoring.

I told Penny, "That's really good. You even got Sarge's wart."

The kid flinched but beamed. She was doing a collage of faces, working from memory. I had no trouble recognizing anyone.

You managed without me.

I sensed both pride and disappointment. "I worried every minute of it, too."

A virtual sneer. *So I see. Nor have you fully worked out your woman issues yet.*

"That's a little harder. I want to do the right thing."

Really? Or might it be that you do not want people seeing you as the bad guy when the crying starts?

"There is that."

It is safe for Mr. Dotes to go when he wishes. The threat no longer exists. The Royals gave up the last villain. Fear of the mob moved them. The King, when glimpsed by General Block, appeared to be a scant sixteen. The antiaging process must be highly unpredictable. Though he has been aging since before you and Mr. Dotes became involved, he remains a decade younger than was his target.

It is probable, by the way, that Mr. Dotes was taken originally not because he saw prisoners being shifted but because he might have seen the King's coach. I found a glimpse, never noticed or recognized, in a backwater of what he has been able to recall of that night.

"Dramatic age shifts? Could that explain the child's room

in the Elf Town warehouse? Did one of the female villains get pushed back all the way to childhood?"

A plausible theory. I expect that the wild unpredictability began when they started using live bodies. The dead would be at a near ground state and much alike but the living would sprawl across a vast range.

That sounded good but didn't make much sense. I stopped listening. Nor did I harken to Dean and Singe squabbling about the work involved in throwing a victory party. Strafa had come into the Dead Man's room. She had cleaned up and dressed herself fit to kill. She didn't have to turn on the girl power.

So. I believe that issue has been worked out, too.

Maybe. A choice had been made. Questions remained. And I still had to summon the guts to face Tinnie and tell her there was nothing more she could do. I had to say good-bye.

I didn't want to see that being brave, sad, resigned look. But I couldn't disrespect her and what we had been to one another by just turning my back.

I wished there was a way we could stay friends. But that wouldn't work any better for us than it had for Kevans, Kip, and Kyra.

Old Bones settled back virtually and included the entire household in the warm glow of his approval.

He had gotten his boy all growed up.

Even Penny gave up a grudging smile.

About the Author

Glen Cook was born in 1944 in New York City. He has served in the United States Navy, and lived in Columbus, Indiana; Rocklin, California; and Columbia, Missouri, where he went to the state university. He attended the Clarion Writers Workshop in 1970, where he met his wife, Carol. "Unlike most writers, I have not had strange jobs like chicken plucking and swamping out health bars. Only full-time employer I've ever had is General Motors." He is now retired from GM. He's "still a stamp collector and book collector, but mostly, these days, I hang around the house and write." He has three sons—an Army officer, an architect, and a music major.

In addition to the Garrett, P.I., series, he is also the author of the popular Black Company series.

SWEET SILVER BLUES

Book 1 in the Garrett, P.I. Series

by Glen Cook

It should have been a simple job.

But for Garrett, a human detective in a
fantastical world, tracking down the
woman to whom his dead pal Danny
left a fortune in silver is no slight task.
Even with the aid of Morley, the toughest
half-elf around, Garrett isn't sure he'll
make it through this case in a land where magic
can be murder, the dead still talk,
and vampires are always hungry for
human blood.

Available wherever books are sold or at
penguin.com

R0033

ROC

THE
DRESDEN FILES
The #1 *New York Times* bestselling series
by Jim Butcher

"Think *Buffy the Vampire Slayer* starring Philip Marlowe." —*Entertainment Weekly*

Available wherever books are sold or at penguin.com

R0037

P.O. 0003457718